The leaden messengers of death whistled past Betty. They sped before her and behind her, scattering pebbles in her path, striking up the dust, and ploughing little furrows in the ground. . . . Betty had passed the top of the knoll now and she was going down the gentle slope like the wind. . . . The yelling and screeching had become deafening. The reports of the rifles blended in a roar. A hot, stinging pain shot through Betty's arm, but she heeded it not. The bullets were raining about her. They sang over her head; hissed close to her ears, and cut the grass in front of her; they pattered like hail on the stockade fence, but still untouched, unharmed, the slender brown figure sped toward the gate.

Betty Zane

Zane Grey

GROSSET & DUNLAP

A NATIONAL GENERAL COMPANY

Publishers, New York

TEMPO BOOKS IS REGISTERED IN THE U.S. PATENT OFFICE
ALL RIGHTS RESERVED
PUBLISHED SIMULTANEOUSLY IN CANADA

ISBN: 0-448-05389-6
TEMPO BOOKS EDITION 1971

FIRST PRINTING, SEPTEMBER 1971

PRINTED IN THE UNITED STATES OF AMERICA

Prologue

On June 16, 1716, Alexander Spotswood, Governor of the Colony of Virginia, and a gallant soldier who had served under Marlborough in the English wars, rode, at the head of a dauntless band of cavaliers, down the quiet street of quaint old Williamsburg.

The adventurous spirits of this party of men urged them toward the land of the setting sun, that unknown west far beyond the blue crested mountains rising so grandly before them.

Months afterward they stood on the western range of the Great North mountains towering above the picturesque Shenandoah Valley, and from the summit of one of the loftiest peaks, where, until then, the foot of a white man had never trod, they viewed the vast expanse of plain and forest with glistening eyes. Returning to Williamsburg they told of the wonderful richness of the newly discovered country and thus opened the way for the venturesome pioneer who was destined to overcome all difficulties and make a home in the western world.

But fifty years and more passed before a white man penetrated far beyond the purple spires of those majestic mountains.

One bright morning in June, 1769, the figure of a stalwart, broad shouldered man could have been seen standing on the wild and rugged promontory which rears its rocky bluff high above the Ohio river, at a point near the mouth of Wheeling Creek. He was alone save for the companionship of a deerhound that crouched at his feet. As he leaned on a long rifle, contemplating the glorious scene that stretched before him, a smile flashed across his bronzed cheek, and his heart bounded as he forecast the future of that spot. In the river below him lay an island so round and green that it resembled a huge lily pad floating placidly on the water. The fresh green foliage of the trees sparkled with glittering dewdrops. Back of him rose the high ridges, and, in front, as far as eye could reach, extended an unbroken forest.

Beneath him to the left and across a deep ravine he saw a wide level clearing. The few scattered and blackened tree stumps showed the ravages made by a forest fire in the years gone by. The field was now overgrown with hazel and laurel bushes, and intermingling with them were the trailing arbutus, the honeysuckle, and the wild rose. A fragrant perfume was wafted upward to him. A rushing creek bordered one edge of the clearing. After a long quiet reach of water, which could be seen winding back in the hills, the stream tumbled madly over a rocky ledge, and white with foam, it hurried onward as if impatient of long restraint, and lost its individuality in the broad Ohio.

This solitary hunter was Colonel Ebenezer Zane. He was one of those daring men, who, as the tide of emigration started westward, had left his friends and family and had struck out alone into the wilderness. Departing from his home in Eastern Virginia he had plunged into the woods, and after many days of hunting and exploring, he reached the then far western Ohio valley.

The scene so impressed Colonel Zane that he concluded to found a settlement here. Taking "tomahawk possession" of the locality (which consisted of blazing a few trees with his tomahawk), he built himself a rude shack and remained that summer on the Ohio.

In the autumn he set out for Berkeley County, Virginia, to tell his people of the magnificent country he had discovered. The following spring he persuaded a number of settlers, of a like spirit with himself, to accompany him to the wilderness. Believing it unsafe to take their families with them at once, they left them at Red Stone on the Monongahela river, while the men, including Colonel Zane, his brothers Silas, Andrew, Jonathan and Isaac, the Wetzels, McCollochs, Bennets, Metzars and others, pushed on ahead.

The country through which they passed was one tangled, almost impenetrable forest; the axe of the pioneer had never sounded in this region, where every rod of the way might harbor some unknown danger.

These reckless bordermen knew not the meaning of fear; to all, daring adventure was welcome, and the screech of a redskin and the ping of a bullet were familiar sounds; to the Wetzels, McCollochs and Jonathan Zane the hunting of Indians was the most thrilling passion of their lives; indeed, the Wetzels, particularly, knew no other occupation. They had attained a wonderful skill with the rifle; long practice had rendered their senses as acute as those of the fox. Skilled in every variety of woodcraft, with lynx eyes ever on the alert for detecting a trail, or the curling smoke of some camp fire, or the minutest sign of an enemy, these men stole onward through the forest with the cautious but dogged and persistent determination that was characteristic of the settler.

They at length climbed the commanding bluff overlooking the majestic river, and as they gazed out on the undulating and uninterrupted area of green, their hearts beat high with hope.

The keen axe, wielded by strong arms, soon opened the clearing and reared stout log cabins on the river bluff. Then Ebenezer Zane and his followers moved their families and soon the settlement began to grow and flourish. As the little village commenced to prosper the redmen became troublesome. Settlers were shot while plowing the fields or gathering the harvests. Bands of hostile Indians prowled around and made it dangerous for anyone to leave the clearing. Frequently the first person to appear in the early morning would be shot at by an Indian concealed in the woods.

General George Rogers Clark, commandant of the Western Military Department, arrived at the village in 1774. As an attack from the savages was apprehended during the year the settlers determined to erect a fort as a defense for the infant settlement. It was planned by General Clark and built by the people themselves. At first they called it Fort Fincastle, in honor of Lord Dunmore, who, at the time of its erection, was Governor of the Colony of Virginia. In 1776 its name was changed to Fort Henry, in honor of Patrick Henry.

For many years it remained the most famous fort on the frontier, having withstood numberless Indian attacks and two memorable sieges, one in 1777, which year is called the year of the "Bloody Sevens," and again in 1782. In this last siege the British Rangers under Hamilton took part with the Indians, making the attack practically the last battle of the Revolution.

Chapter 1

THE ZANE family was a remarkable one in early days, and most of its members are historical characters.

The first Zane of whom any trace can be found was a Dane of aristocratic lineage, who was exiled from his country and came to America with William Penn. He was prominent for several years in the new settlement founded by Penn, and Zane street, Philadelphia, bears his name. Being a proud and arrogant man, he soon became obnoxious to his Quaker brethren. He therefore cut loose from them and emigrated to Virginia, settling on the Potomac river, in what was then known as Berkeley county. There his five sons, and one daughter, the heroine of this story, were born.

Ebenezer Zane, the eldest, was born October 7, 1747, and grew to manhood in the Potomac valley. There he married Elizabeth McColloch, a sister of the famous McColloch brothers so well known in frontier history.

Ebenezer was fortunate in having such a wife and no pioneer could have been better blessed. She was not only a handsome woman, but one of remarkable force of character as well as kindness of heart. She was particularly noted for a rare skill in the treatment of illness, and her deftness in handling the surgeon's knife and extracting a poisoned bullet or arrow from a wound had restored to health many a settler when all had despaired.

1

The Zane brothers were best known on the border for their athletic prowess, and for their knowledge of Indian warfare and cunning. They were all powerful men, exceedingly active and as fleet as deer. In appearance they were singularly pleasing and bore a marked resemblance to one another, all having smooth faces, clear cut, regular features, dark eyes and long black hair.

When they were as yet boys they had been captured by Indians, soon after their arrival on the Virginia border, and had been taken far into the interior, and held as captives for two years. Ebenezer, Silas, and Jonathan Zane were then taken to Detroit and ransomed. While attempting to swim the Scioto river in an effort to escape, Andrew Zane had been shot and killed by his pursuers.

But the bonds that held Isaac Zane, the remaining and youngest brother, were stronger than those of interest or revenge such as had caused the captivity of his brothers. He was loved by an Indian princess, the daughter of Tarhe, the chief of the puissant Huron race. Isaac had escaped on various occasions, but had always been retaken, and at the time of the opening of our story nothing had been heard of him for several years, and it was believed he had been killed.

At the period of the settling of the little colony in the wilderness, Elizabeth Zane, the only sister, was living with an aunt in Philadelphia, where she was being educated.

Colonel Zane's house, a two story structure built of rough hewn logs, was the most comfortable one in the settlement, and occupied a prominent site on the hillside about one hundred yards from the fort. It was constructed of heavy timber and presented rather a forbidding appearance with its square corners, its ominous looking portholes, and strongly barred doors and windows. There were three rooms on the ground floor, a kitchen, a magazine room for military supplies, and a large room for general use. The several sleeping rooms were on the second floor, which was reached by a steep stairway.

The interior of a pioneer's rude dwelling did not reveal, as a rule, more than bare walls, a bed or two, a table and a few chairs—in fact, no more than the necessities of life. But Colonel Zane's house proved an exception to this. Most interesting was the large room. The chinks between the logs had been plastered up with clay and then the walls covered with white birch bark; trophies of the chase, Indian bows and arrows, pipes and tomahawks hung upon them; the wide spreading antlers of a noble buck adorned the space above the mantel piece; buffalo robes covered the couches; bearskin rugs lay scattered about on the hardwood floor. The wall on the western side had been built over a huge stone, into which had been cut an open fireplace.

This blackened recess, which had seen two houses burned over it, when full of blazing logs had cheered many noted men with its warmth. Lord Dunmore, General Clark, Simon Kenton, and Daniel Boone had sat beside that fire. There Cornplanter, the Seneca chief, had made his famous deal with Colonel Zane, trading the island in the river opposite the settlement for a barrel of whiskey. Logan, the Mingo chief and friend of the whites, had smoked many pipes of peace there with Colonel Zane. At a later period, when King Louis Phillippe, who had been exiled from France by Napoleon, had come to America, during the course of his melancholy wanderings he had stopped at Fort Henry a few days. His stay there was marked by a fierce blizzard and the royal guest passed most of his time at Colonel Zane's fireside. Musing by those roaring logs perhaps he saw the radiant star of the Man of Destiny rise to its magnificent zenith.

One cold, raw night in early spring the Colonel had

just returned from one of his hunting trips and the tramping of horses mingled with the rough voices of the negro slaves sounded without. When Colonel Zane entered the house he was greeted affectionately by his wife and sister. The latter, at the death of her aunt in Philadelphia, had come west to live wth her brother, and had been there since late in the preceding autumn. It was a welcome sight for the eyes of a tired and weary hunter. The tender kiss of his comely wife, the cries of the delighted children, and the crackling of the fire warmed his heart and made him feel how good it was to be home again after a three days' march in the woods. Placing his rifle in a corner and throwing aside his wet hunting coat, he turned and stood with his back to the bright blaze. Still young and vigorous, Colonel Zane was a handsome man. Tall, though not heavy, his frame denoted great strength and endurance. His face was smooth; his heavy eyebrows met in a straight line; his eyes were dark and now beamed with a kindly light; his jaw was square and massive; his mouth resolute; in fact, his whole face was strikingly expressive of courage and geniality. A great wolf dog had followed him in and, tired from travel, had stretched himself out before the fireplace, laying his noble head on the paws he had extended toward the warm blaze.

"Well! Well! I am nearly starved and mighty glad to get back," said the Colonel, with a smile of satisfaction at the steaming dishes a negro servant was bringing from the kitchen.

"We are glad you have returned," answered his wife, whose glowing face testified to the pleasure she felt. "Supper is ready—Annie, bring in some cream—yes, indeed, I am happy that you are home. I never have a moment's peace when you are away, especially when you are accompanied by Lewis Wetzel."

"Our hunt was a failure," said the Colonel, after he had helped himself to a plate full of roast wild turkey.

"The bears have just come out of their winter's sleep and are unusually wary at this time. We saw many signs of their work, tearing rotten logs to pieces in search of grubs and bees' nests. Wetzel killed a deer and we baited a likely place where we had discovered many bear tracks. We stayed up all night in a drizzling rain, hoping to get a shot. I am tired out. So is Tige. Wetzel did not mind the weather or the ill luck, and when we ran across some Indian sign he went off on one of his lonely tramps, leaving me to come home alone."

"He is such a reckless man," remarked Mrs. Zane.

"Wetzel is reckless, or rather, daring. His incomparable nerve carries him safely through many dangers, where an ordinary man would have no show whatever. Well, Betty, how are you?"

"Quite well," said the slender, dark-eyed girl who had just taken the seat opposite the Colonel.

"Bessie, has my sister indulged in any shocking escapade in my absence? I think that last trick of hers, when she gave a bucket of hard cider to that poor tame bear, should last her a spell."

"No, for a wonder Elizabeth has been very good. However, I do not attribute it to any unusual change of temperament; simply the cold, wet weather. I anticipate a catastrophe very shortly if she is kept indoors much longer."

"I have not had much opportunity to be anything but well behaved. If it rains a few days more I shall become desperate. I want to ride my pony, roam the woods, paddle my canoe, and enjoy myself," said Elizabeth.

"Well! Well! Betts, I knew it would be dull for you, but you must not get discouraged. You know you got here late last fall, and have not had any pleasant weather yet. It is perfectly delightful in May and June. I can take you to fields of wild white honeysuckle and

May flowers and wild roses. I know you love the woods, so be patient a little longer."

· Elizabeth had been spoiled by her brothers—what girl would not have been by five great big worshippers? —and any trivial thing gone wrong with her was a serious matter to them. They were proud of her, and of her beauty and accomplishments were never tired of talking. She had the dark hair and eyes so characteristic of the Zanes; the same oval face and fine features; and added to this was a certain softness of contour and a sweetness of expression which made her face bewitching. But, in spite of that demure and innocent face, she possessed a decided will of her own, and one very apt to be asserted; she was mischievous; inclined to coquettishness, and more terrible than all she had a fiery temper which could be aroused with the most surprising ease.

Colonel Zane was wont to say that his sister's accomplishments were innumerable. After only a few months on the border she could prepare the flax and weave a linsey dresscloth with admirable skill. Sometimes to humor Betty, the Colonel's wife would allow her to get the dinner, and she would do it in a manner that pleased her brothers, and called forth golden praises from the cook, old Sam's wife, who had been with the family twenty years. Betty sang in the little church on Sundays; she organized and taught a Sunday school class; she often beat Colonel Zane and Major McColloch at their favorite game of checkers, which they had played together since they were knee high; in fact, Betty did nearly everything well, from baking pies to painting the birch bark walls of her room. But these things were insignificant in Colonel Zane's eyes. If the Colonel were ever guilty of bragging it was about his sister's ability in those acquirements demanding a true eye, a fleet foot, a strong arm and a daring spirit. He had told all the people in the settlement, to many of

whom Betty was unknown, that she could ride like an Indian and shoot with undoubted skill; that she had a generous share of the Zanes' fleetness of foot, and that she would send a canoe over as bad a place as she could find. The boasts of the Colonel remained as yet unproven, but, be that as it may, Betty had, notwithstanding her many faults, endeared herself to all. She made sunshine and happiness everywhere; the old people loved her; the children adored her, and the broad shouldered, heavy footed young settlers were shy and silent, yet blissfully happy in her presence.

"Betty, will you fill my pipe?" asked the Colonel, when he had finished his supper and had pulled his big chair nearer the fire. His oldest child, Noah, a sturdy lad of six, climbed upon his knee and plied him with questions.

"Did you see any bars and bufflers?" he asked, his eyes large and round.

"No, my lad, not one."

"How long will it be until I am big enough to go?"

"Not for a very long time, Noah."

"But I am not afraid of Betty's bar. He growls at me when I throw sticks at him, and snaps his teeth. Can I go with you next time?"

"My brother came over from Short Creek today. He has been to Fort Pitt," interposed Mrs. Zane. As she was speaking a tap sounded on the door, which, being opened by Betty, disclosed Captain Boggs, his daughter Lydia, and Major Samuel McColloch, the brother of Mrs. Zane.

"Ah, Colonel! I expected to find you at home tonight. The weather has been miserable for hunting and it is not getting any better. The wind is blowing from the northwest and a storm is coming," said Captain Boggs, a fine, soldierly looking man.

"Hello, Captain! How are you? Sam, I have not had

the pleasure of seeing you for a long time," replied Colonel Zane, as he shook hands with his guests.

Major McColloch was the eldest of the brothers of that name. As an Indian killer he ranked next to the intrepid Wetzel; but while Wetzel preferred to take his chances alone and track the Indians through the untrodden wilds, McColloch was a leader of expeditions against the savages. A giant in stature, massive in build, bronzed and bearded, he looked the typical frontiersman. His blue eyes were like those of his sister and his voice had the same pleasant ring.

"Major McColloch, do you remember me?" asked Betty.

"Indeed I do," he answered, with a smile. "You were a little girl, running wild, on the Potomac when I last saw you!"

"Do you remember when you used to lift me on your horse and give me lessons in riding?"

"I remember better than you. How you used to stick on the back of that horse was a mystery to me."

"Well, I shall be ready soon to go on with those lessons in riding. I have heard of your wonderful leap over the hill and I should like to have you tell me all about it. Of all the stories I have heard since I arrived at Fort Henry, the one of your ride and leap for life is the most wonderful."

"Yes, Sam, she will bother you to death about that ride, and will try to give you lessons in leaping down precipices. I should not be at all surprised to find her trying to duplicate your feat. You know the Indian pony I got from that fur trader last summer. Well, he is as wild as a deer and she has been riding him without his being broken," said Colonel Zane.

"Some other time I shall tell you about my jump over the hill. Just now I have important matters to discuss," answered the Major to Betty.

It was evident that something unusual had occurred,

for after chatting a few moments the three men withdrew into the magazine room and conversed in low, earnest tones.

Lydia Boggs was eighteen, fair haired and blue eyed. Like Betty she had received a good education, and, in that respect, was superior to the border girls, who seldom knew more than to keep house and to make linen. At the outbreak of the Indian wars General Clark had stationed Captain Boggs at Fort Henry and Lydia had lived there with him two years. After Betty's arrival, which she hailed with delight, the girls had become fast friends.

Lydia slipped her arm affectionately around Betty's neck and said, "Why did you not come over to the Fort today?"

"It has been such an ugly day, so disagreeable altogether, that I have remained indoors."

"You missed something," said Lydia, knowingly.

"What do you mean? What did I miss?"

"Oh, perhaps, after all, it will not interest you."

"How provoking! Of course it will. Anything or anybody would interest me tonight. Do tell me, please."

"It isn't much. Only a young soldier came over with Major McColloch."

"A soldier? From Fort Pitt? Do I know him? I have met most of the officers."

"No, you have never seen him. He is a stranger to all of us."

"There does not seem to be so much in your news," said Betty, in a disappointed tone. "To be sure, strangers are a rarity in our little village, but judging from the strangers who have visited us in the past, I imagine this one cannot be much different."

"Wait until you see him," said Lydia, with a serious little nod of her head.

"Come, tell me all about him," said Betty, now much interested.

"Major McColloch brought him in to see papa, and he was introduced to me. He is a southerner and from one of those old families. I could tell by his cool, easy, almost reckless air. He is handsome, tall and fair, and his face is frank and open. He has such beautiful manners. He bowed low to me and really I felt so embarrassed that I hardly spoke. You know I am used to these big hunters seizing your hand and giving it a squeeze which makes you want to scream. Well, this young man is different. He is a cavalier. All the girls are in love with him already. So will you be."

"I? Indeed not. But how refreshing. You must have been strongly impressed to see and remember all you have told me."

"Betty Zane, I remember so well because he is just the man you described one day when we were building castles and telling each other what kind of a hero we wanted."

"Girls, do not talk such nonsense," interrupted the Colonel's wife, who was perturbed by the colloquy in the other room. She had seen those ominous signs before. "Can you find nothing better to talk about?"

Meanwhile Colonel Zane and his companions were earnestly discussing certain information which had arrived that day. A friendly Indian runner had brought news to Short Creek, a settlement on the river between Fort Henry and Fort Pitt, of an intended raid by the Indians all along the Ohio valley. Major McColloch, who had been warned by Wetzel of the fever of unrest among the Indians—a fever which broke out every spring—had gone to Fort Pitt with the hope of bringing back reinforcements, but, excepting the young soldier, who had volunteered to return with him, no help could he enlist, so he journeyed back post-haste to Fort Henry.

The information he brought disturbed Captain Boggs, who commanded the garrison, as a number of men were away on a logging expedition up the river, and were not expected to raft down to the Fort for two weeks.

Jonathan Zane, who had been sent for, joined the trio at this moment, and was acquainted with the particulars. The Zane brothers were always consulted where any question concerning Indian craft and cunning was to be decided. Colonel Zane had a strong friendly influence with certain tribes, and his advice was invaluable. Jonathan Zane hated the sight of an Indian and except for his knowledge as a scout, or Indian tracker or fighter, he was of little use in a council. Colonel Zane informed the men of the fact that Wetzel and he had discovered Indian tracks within ten miles of the Fort, and he dwelt particularly on the disappearance of Wetzel.

"Now, you can depend on what I say. There are Wyandots in force on the war path. Wetzel told me to dig for the Fort and he left me in a hurry. We were near that cranberry bog over at the foot of Bald mountain. I do not believe we shall be attacked. In my opinion the Indians would come up from the west and keep to the high ridges along Yellow creek. They always come that way. But, of course, it is best to know surely, and I daresay Lew will come in tonight or tomorrow with the facts. In the meantime put out some scouts back in the woods and let Jonathan and the Major watch the river."

"I hope Wetzel will come in," said the Major. "We can trust him to know more about the Indians than any one. It was a week before you and he went hunting that I saw him. I went to Fort Pitt and tried to bring over some men, but the garrison is short and they need men as much as we do. A young soldier named Clarke volunteered to come and I brought him along with me. He has not seen any Indian fighting, but he is a likely looking chap, and I guess will do. Captain Boggs will give him a place in the block house if you say so."

"By all means. We shall be glad to have him," said Colonel Zane.

"It would not be so serious if I had not sent the men up the river," said Captain Boggs, in anxious tones. "Do you think it possible they might have fallen in with the Indians?"

"It is possible, of course, but not probable," answered Colonel Zane. "The Indians are all across the Ohio. Wetzel is over there and he will get here long before they do."

"I hope it may be as you say. I have much confidence in your judgment," returned Captain Boggs. "I shall put out scouts and take all the precaution possible. We must return now. Come, Lydia."

"Whew! What an awful night this is going to be," said Colonel Zane, when he had closed the door after his guests' departure. "I should not care to sleep out tonight."

"Eb, what will Lew Wetzel do on a night like this?" asked Betty, curiously.

"Oh, Lew will be as snug as a rabbit in his burrow," said Colonel Zane, laughing. "In a few moments he can build a birch bark shack, start a fire inside and go to sleep comfortably."

"Ebenezer, what is all this confab about? What did my brother tell you?" asked Mrs. Zane, anxiously.

"We are in for more trouble from the Wyandots and Shawnees. But, Bessie, I don't believe it will come soon. We are too well protected here for anything but a protracted siege."

Colonel Zane's light and rather evasive answer did not deceive his wife. She knew her brother and her husband would not wear anxious faces for nothing. Her usually bright face clouded with a look of distress. She had seen enough of Indian warfare to make her shudder with horror at the mere thought. Betty seemed unconcerned. She sat down beside the dog and patted him on the head.

"Tige, Indians! Indians!" she said.

The dog growled and showed his teeth. It was only necessary to mention Indians to arouse his ire.

"The dog has been uneasy of late," continued Colonel Zane. "He found the Indian tracks before Wetzel did. You know how Tige hates Indians. Ever since he came home with Isaac four years ago he has been of great service to the scouts, as he possesses so much intelligence and sagacity. Tige followed Isaac home the last time he escaped from the Wyandots. When Isaac was in captivity he nursed and cared for the dog after he had been brutally beaten by the redskins. Have you ever heard that long mournful howl Tige gives out sometimes in the dead of night?"

"Yes I have, and it makes me cover up my head," said Betty.

"Well, it is Tige mourning for Isaac," said Colonel Zane.

"Poor Isaac," murmured Betty.

"Do you remember him? It has been nine years since you saw him," said Mrs. Zane.

"Remember Isaac? Indeed I do. I shall never forget him. I wonder if he is still living?"

"Probably not. It is now four years since he was recaptured. I think it would have been impossible to keep him that length of time, unless, of course, he has married that Indian girl. The simplicity of the Indian nature is remarkable. He could easily have deceived them and made them believe he was content in captivity. Probably, in attempting to escape again, he has been killed, as was poor Andrew."

Brother and sister gazed with dark, sad eyes into the

fire, now burned down to a glowing bed of coals. The silence remained unbroken save for the moan of the rising wind outside, the rattle of hail, and the patter of rain drops on the roof.

Chapter 2

FORT HENRY stood on a bluff overlooking the river and commanded a fine view of the surrounding country. In shape it was a parallelogram, being about three hundred and fifty-six feet in length, and one hundred and fifty in width. Surrounded by a stockade fence twelve feet high, with a yard wide walk running around the inside, and with bastions at each corner large enough to contain six defenders, the fort presented an almost impregnable defense. The blockhouse was two stories in height, the second story projecting out several feet over the first. The thick white oak walls bristled with portholes. Besides the blockhouse, there were a number of cabins located within the stockade. Wells had been sunk inside the inclosure, so that if the spring happened to go dry, an abundance of good water could be had at all times.

In all the histories of frontier life mention is made of the forts and the protection they offered in time of savage warfare. These forts were used as homes for the settlers, who often lived for weeks inside the walls.

Forts constructed entirely of wood without the aid of nail or spike (for the good reason that these things could not be had) may seem insignificant in these days of great naval and military garrisons. However, they answered the purpose at that time and served to protect many an infant settlement from the savage attacks of Indian tribes. During a siege of Fort Henry, which had

15

occurred about a year previous, the settlers would have lost scarcely a man had they kept to the fort. But Captain Ogle, at that time in charge of the garrison, had led a company out in search of the Indians. Nearly all of his men were killed, several only making their way to the fort.

On the day following Major McColloch's arrival at Fort Henry, the settlers had been called in from their spring plowing and other labors, and were now busily engaged in moving their stock and the things they wished to save from the destructive torch of the redskin. The women had their hands full with the children, the cleaning of rifles and moulding of bullets, and the thousand and one things the sterner tasks of their husbands had left them. Major McColloch, Jonathan and Silas Zane, early in the day, had taken different directions along the river to keep a sharp lookout for signs of the enemy. Colonel Zane intended to stay in his own house and defend it, so he had not moved anything to the fort excepting his horses and cattle. Old Sam, the negro, was hauling loads of hay inside the stockade. Captain Boggs had detailed several scouts to watch the roads and one of these was the young man, Clarke, who had accompanied the Major from Fort Pitt.

The appearance of Alfred Clarke, despite the fact that he wore the regulation hunting garb, indicated a young man to whom the hard work and privation of the settler were unaccustomed things. So thought the pioneers who noticed his graceful walk, his fair skin and smooth hands. Yet those who carefully studied his clearcut features were favorably impressed; the women, by the direct, honest gaze of his blue eyes and the absence of ungentle lines in his face; the men, by the good nature, and that indefinable something by which a man marks another as true steel.

He brought nothing with him from Fort Pitt except

his horse, a black-coated, fine limbed thoroughbred, which he frankly confessed was all he could call his own. When asking Colonel Zane to give him a position in the garrison he said he was a Virginian and had been educated in Philadalphia; that after his father died his mother married again, and this, together with a natural love of adventure, had induced him to run away and seek his fortune with the hardy pioneer and the cunning savage of the border. Beyond a few months' service under General Clark he knew nothing of frontier life; but he was tired of idleness; he was strong and not afraid of work, and he could learn. Colonel Zane, who prided himself on his judgment of character, took a liking to the young man at once, and giving him a rifle and accoutrements, told him the border needed young men of pluck and fire, and that if he brought a strong hand and a willing heart he could surely find fortune. Possibly if Alfred Clarke could have been told of the fate in store for him he might have mounted his black steed and have placed miles between him and the frontier village; but, as there were none to tell, he went cheerfully out to meet that fate.

On this bright spring morning he patrolled the road leading along the edge of the clearing, which was distant a quarter of a mile from the fort. He kept a keen eye on the opposite side of the river, as he had been directed. From the upper end of the island, almost straight across from where he stood, the river took a broad turn, which could not be observed from the fort windows. The river was high from the recent rains and brush heaps and logs and *debris* of all descriptions were floating down with the swift current. Rabbits and other small animals, which had probably been surrounded on some island and compelled to take to the brush or drown, crouched on floating logs and piles of driftwood. Happening to glance down the road, Clarke saw a horse galloping in his direction. At first he thought it was a messenger for himself, but as it neared him he saw that the horse was an Indian pony and the rider a young girl, whose long, black hair was flying in the wind.

"Hello! I wonder what the deuce this is? Looks like an Indian girl," said Clarke to himself. "She rides well, whoever she may be."

He stepped behind a clump of laurel bushes near the roadside and waited. Rapidly the horse and rider approached him. When they were but a few paces distant he sprang out and, as the pony shied and reared at sight of him, he clutched the bridle and pulled the pony's head down. Looking up he encountered the astonished and bewildered gaze from a pair of the prettiest dark eyes it had ever been his fortune, or misfortune, to look into.

Betty, for it was she, looked at the young man in amazement, while Alfred was even more surprised and disconcerted. For a moment they looked at each other in silence. But Betty, who was scarcely ever at a loss for words, presently found her voice.

"Well, sir! What does this mean?" she asked indignantly.

"It means that you must turn around and go back to the fort," answered Alfred, also recovering himself.

Now Betty's favorite ride happened to be along this road. It lay along the top of the bluff a mile or more and afforded a fine unobstructed view of the river. Betty had either not heard of the Captain's order, that no one was to leave the fort, or she had disregarded it altogether; probably the latter, as she generally did what suited her fancy.

"Release my pony's head!" she cried, her face flushing, as she gave a jerk to the reins. "How dare you? What right have you to detain me?"

The expression Betty saw on Clarke's face was not new to her, for she remembered having seen it on the faces of young gentlemen whom she had met at her aunt's house in Philadelphia. It was the slight, provoking smile of the man familiar with the various moods of young women, the expression of an amused contempt for their imperiousness. But it was not that which angered Betty. It was the coolness with which he still held her pony regardless of her commands.

"Pray do not get excited," he said. "I am sorry I cannot allow such a pretty little girl to have her own way. I shall hold your pony until you say you will go back to the fort."

"Sir!" exclaimed Betty, blushing a bright red. "You—you are impertinent!"

"Not at all," answered Alfred, with a pleasant laugh. "I am sure I do not intend to be. Captain Boggs did not acquaint me with full particulars or I might have declined my present occupation; not, however, that it is not agreeable just at this moment. He should have mentioned the danger of my being run down by Indian ponies and imperious young ladies."

"Will you let go of that bridle, or shall I get off and walk back for assistance?" said Betty, getting angrier every moment.

"Go back to the fort at once," ordered Alfred, authoritatively. "Captain Boggs' orders are that no one shall be allowed to leave the clearing."

"Oh! Why did you not say so? I thought you were Simon Girty, or a highwayman. Was it necessary to keep me here all this time to expalin that you were on duty?"

"You know sometimes it is difficult to explain," said Alfred, "besides, the situation had its charm. No, I am not a robber, and I don't believe you thought so. I have only thwarted a young lady's whim, which I am aware is a great crime. I am very sorry. Goodbye."

Betty gave him a withering glance from her black eyes, wheeled her pony and galloped away. A mellow laugh was borne to her ears before she got out of hearing, and again the red blood mantled her cheeks.

"Heavens. What a little beauty," said Alfred to himself, as he watched the graceful rider disappear. "What spirit! Now, I wonder who she can be. She had on moccasins and buckskin gloves and her hair tumbled like a tomboy's, but she is no backwoods girl, I'll bet on that. I'm afraid I was a little rude, but after taking such a stand I could not weaken, especially before such a haughty and disdainful little vixen. It was too great a temptation. What eyes she had! Contrary to what I expected, this little frontier settlement bids fair to become interesting."

The afternoon wore slowly away, and until late in the day nothing further happened to disturb Alfred's meditations, which consisted chiefly of different mental views and pictures of red lips and black eyes. Just as he decided to return to the fort for his supper he heard the barking of a dog that he had seen running along the road some moments before. The sound came from some distance down the river bank and nearer the fort. Walking a few paces up the bluff Alfred caught sight of a large black dog running along the edge of the water. He would run into the water a few paces and then come out and dash along the shore. He barked furiously all the while. Alfred concluded he must have been excited by a fox or perhaps a wolf; so he climbed down the steep bank and spoke to the dog. Thereupon the dog barked louder and more fiercely than ever, ran to the water, looked out into the river and then up at the man with almost human intelligence.

Alfred understood. He glanced out over the muddy water, at first making out nothing but driftwood. Then suddenly he saw a log with an object clinging to it which he took to be a man, and an Indian at that. Alfred raised his rifle to his shoulder and was in the act of pressing the trigger when he thought he heard a faint halloo. Looking closer, he found he was not covering the smooth polished head adorned with the small tuft of hair, peculiar to a redskin on the warpath, but a head from which streamed long black hair.

Alfred lowered his rifle and studied intently the log with its human burden. Drifting with the current it gradually approached the bank, and as it came nearer he saw that it bore a white man, who was holding to the log with one hand and with the other was making feeble strokes. He concluded the man was either wounded or nearly drowned, for his movements were becoming slower and weaker every moment. His white face lay against the log and barely above water. Alfred shouted encouraging words to him.

At the bend of the river a little rocky point jutted out a few yards into the water. As the current carried the log toward this point, Alfred, after divesting himself of some of his clothing, plunged in and pulled it to the shore. The pallid face of the man clinging to the log showed that he was nearly exhausted, and that he had been rescued in the nick of time. When Alfred reached shoal water he slipped his arm around the man, who was unable to stand, and carried him ashore.

The rescued man wore a buckskin hunting shirt and leggins and moccasins of the same material, all very much the worse for wear. The leggins were torn into tatters and the moccasins worn through. His face was pinched with suffering and one arm was bleeding from a gunshot wound near the shoulder.

"Can you not speak? Who are you?" asked Clarke, supporting the limp figure.

The man made several efforts to answer, and finally said something that to Alfred sounded like "Zane" then he fell to the ground unconscious.

All this time the dog had acted in a most peculiar manner, and if Alfred had not been so intent on the man he would have noticed the animal's odd maneu-

vers. He ran to and fro on the sandy beach; he
scratched up the sand and pebbles, sending them flying
in the air; he made short, furious dashes; he jumped,
whirled, and, at last, crawled close to the motionless
figure and licked its hand.

Clarke realized that he would not be able to carry
the inanimate figure, so he hurriedly put on his clothes
and set out on a run for Colonel Zane's house. The first
person whom he saw was the old negro slave, who was
brushing one of the Colonel's horses.

Sam was deliberate and took his time about everything. He slowly looked up and surveyed Clarke with
his rolling eyes. He did not recognize in him any one he
had ever seen before, and being of a sullen and taciturn
nature, especially with strangers, he seemed in no hurry
to give the desired information as to Colonel Zane's
whereabouts.

"Don't stare at me that way, you damn nigger," said
Clarke, who was used to being obeyed by negroes.
"Quick, you idiot. Where is the Colonel?"

At that moment Colonel Zane came out of the barn
and started to speak, when Clarke interrupted him.

"Colonel, I have just pulled a man out of the river
who says his name is Zane, or if he did not mean that,
he knows you, for he surely said 'Zane.' "

"What!" ejaculated the Colonel, letting his pipe fall
from his mouth.

Clarke related the circumstances in a few hurried
words. Calling Sam they ran quickly down to the river,
where they found the prostrate figure as Clarke had left
it, the dog still crouched close by.

"My God! It is Isaac!" exclaimed Colonel Zane,
when he saw the white face. "Poor boy, he looks as if
he were dead. Are you sure he spoke? Of course he
must have spoken for you could not have known. Yes,
his heart is still beating."

Colonel Zane raised his head from the unconscious

man's breast, where he had laid it to listen for the beating heart.

"Clarke, God bless you for saving him," said he fervently. "It shall never be forgotten. He is alive, and, I believe, only exhausted, for that wound amounts to little. Let us hurry."

"I did not save him. It was the dog," Alfred made haste to answer.

They carried the dripping form to the house, where the door was opened by Mrs. Zane.

"Oh, dear, another poor man," she said, pityingly. Then, as she saw his face, "Great Heavens, it is Isaac! Oh! don't say he is dead!"

"Yes, it is Isaac, and he is worth any number of dead men yet," said Colonel Zane, as they laid the insensible man on the couch. "Bessie, there is work here for you. He has been shot."

"Is there any other wound beside this one in his arm?" asked Mrs. Zane, examining it.

"I do not think so, and that injury is not serious. It is loss of blood, exposure and starvation. Clarke, will you please run over to Captain Boggs and tell Betty to hurry home? Sam, you get a blanket and warm it by the fire. That's right, Bessie, bring the whiskey," and Colonel Zane went on giving orders.

Alfred did not know in the least who Betty was, but, as he thought that unimportant, he started off on a run for the fort. He had a vague idea that Betty was the servant, possibly Sam's wife, or some one of the Colonel's several slaves.

Let us return to Betty. As she wheeled her pony and rode away from the scene of her adventure on the river bluff, her state of mind can be more readily imagined than described. Betty hated opposition of any kind, whether justifiable or not; she wanted her own way, and when prevented from doing as she pleased she invariably got angry. To be ordered and compelled to give up her ride, and that by a stranger, was intolerable. To make it all the worse this stranger had been decidedly flippant. He had familiarly spoken to her as "a pretty little girl." Not only that, which was a great offense, but he had stared at her, and she had a confused recollection of a gaze in which admiration had been ill disguised. Of course, it was that soldier Lydia had been telling her about. Strangers were of so rare an occurrence in the little village that it was not probable there could be more than one.

Approaching the house she met her brother who told her she had better go indoors and let Sam put up the pony. Accordingly, Betty called the negro, and then went into the house. Bessie had gone to the fort with the children. Betty found no one to talk to, so she tried to read. Finding she could not become interested she threw the book aside and took up her embroidery. This also turned out a useless effort; she got the linen hopelessly twisted and tangled, and presently she tossed this upon the table. Throwing her shawl over her shoulders, for it was now late in the afternoon and growing chilly, she walked downstairs and out into the yard. She strolled aimlessly to and fro awhile, and then went over to the fort and into Captain Bogg's house, which adjoined the blockhouse. Here she found Lydia preparing flax.

"I saw you racing by on your pony. Goodness, how you can ride! I should be afraid of breaking my neck," exclaimed Lydia, as Betty entered.

"My ride was spoiled," said Betty, petulantly.

"Spoiled? By what—whom?"

"By a man, of course," retorted Betty, whose temper still was high. "It is always a man that spoils everything."

"Why, Betty, what in the world do you mean? I never heard you talk that way," said Lydia, opening her blue eyes in astonishment.

"Well, Lyde, I'll tell you. I was riding down the river road and just as I came to the end of the clearing a man jumped out from behind some bushes and grasped Madcap's bridle. Imagine! For a moment I was frightened out of my wits. I instantly thought of the Girtys, who, I have heard, have evinced a fondness for kidnapping little girls. Then the fellow said he was on guard and ordered me, actually commanded me to go home."

"Oh, is that all?" said Lydia, laughing.

"No, that is not all. He—he said I was a pretty little girl and that he was sorry I could not have my own way; that his present occupation was pleasant, and that the situation had its charm. The very idea. He was most impertinent," and Betty's telltale cheeks reddened again at the recollection.

"Betty, I do not think your experience was so dreadful, certainly nothing to put you out as it has," said Lydia, laughing merrily. "Be serious. You know we are out in the backwoods now and must not expect so much of the men. These rough border men know little of refinement like that with which you have been familiar. Some of them are quiet and never speak unless addressed; their simplicity is remarkable; Lew Wetzel and your brother Jonathan, when they are not fighting Indians, are examples. On the other hand, some of them are boisterous and if they get anything to drink they will make trouble for you. Why, I went to a party one night after I had been here only a few weeks and they played a game in which every man in the place kissed me."

"Gracious! Please tell me when any such games are likely to be proposed and I'll stay home," said Betty.

"I have learned to get along very well by simply making the best of it," continued Lydia. "And to tell the truth, I have learned to respect these rugged fellows. They are uncouth; they have no manners, but their hearts are honest and true, and that is of much greater importance in frontiersmen than the little attentions and courtesies upon which women are apt to lay too much stress."

"I think you speak sensibly and I shall try and be more reasonable hereafter. But, to return to the man who spoiled my ride. He, at least, is no frontiersman, notwithstanding his gun and his buckskin suit. He is an educated man. His manner and accent showed that. Then he looked at me so differently. I know it was that soldier from Fort Pitt."

"Mr. Clarke? Why, of course!" exclaimed Lydia, clapping her hands in glee. "How stupid of me!"

"You seem to be amused," said Betty, frowning.

"Oh, Betty, it is such a good joke."

"Is it? I fail to see it."

"But I can. I am very much amused. You see, I heard Mr. Clarke say, after papa told him there were lots of pretty girls here, that he usually succeeded in finding those things out and without any assistance. And the very first day he has met you and made you angry. It is delightful."

"Lyde, I never knew you could be so horrid."

"It is evident that Mr. Clarke is not only discerning, but not backward in expressing his thoughts. Betty, I see a romance."

"Don't be ridiculous," retorted Betty, with an angry blush. "Of course, he had a right to stop me, and perhaps he did me a good turn by keeping me inside the clearing, though I cannot imagine why he hid behind the bushes. But he might have been polite. He made me angry. He was so cool and—and——"

"I see," interrupted Lydia, teasingly. "He failed to recognize your importance."

"Nonsense, Lydia. I hope you do not think I am a silly little fool. It is only that I have not been accustomed to that kind of treatment, and I will not have it."

Lydia was rather pleased that some one had appeared on the scene who did not at once bow down before Betty, and therefore she took the young man's side of the argument.

"Do not be hard on poor Mr. Clarke. Maybe he mistook you for an Indian girl. He is handsome. I am sure you saw that."

"Oh, I don't remember how he looked," said Betty. She did remember, but would not admit it.

The conversation drifted into other channels after this, and soon twilight came stealing down on them. As Betty rose to go there came a hurried tap on the door.

"I wonder who would knock like that," said Lydia, rising. "Betty, wait a moment while I open the door."

On doing this she discovered Carke standing on the step with his cap in his hand.

"Why, Mr. Clarke! Will you come in?" exclaimed Lydia.

"Thank you, only for a moment," said Alfred. "I cannot stay. I came to find Betty. Is she here?"

He had not observed Betty, who had stepped back into the shadow of the darkening room. At his question Lydia became so embarrassed she did not know what to say or do, and stood looking helplessly at him.

But Betty was equal to the occasion. At the mention of her first name in such a familiar manner by this stranger, who had already grievously offended her once before that day, Betty stood perfectly still a moment, speechless with surprise, then she stepped quickly out of the shadow.

Clarke turned as he heard her step and looked straight into a pair of dark, scornful eyes and a face pale with anger.

"If it be necessary that you use my name, and I do not see how that can be possible, will you please have courtesy enough to say Miss Zane?" she cried haughtily.

Lydia recovered her composure sufficiently to falter out:

"Betty, allow me to introduce—"

"Do not trouble yourself, Lydia. I have met this person once before today, and I do not care for an introduction."

When Alfred found himself gazing into the face that had haunted him all the afternoon, he forgot for the moment all about his errand. He was finally brought to a realization of the true state of affairs by Lydia's words.

"Mr. Clarke, you are all wet. What has happened?" she exclaimed, noticing the water dripping from his garments.

Suddenly a light broke in on Alfred. So the girl he had accosted on the road and "Betty" were one and the same person. His face flushed. He felt that his rudeness on that occasion may have merited censure, but that it had not justified the humiliation she had put upon him.

These two persons, so strangely brought together, and on whom Fate had made her inscrutable designs, looked steadily into each other's eyes. What mysterious force thrilled through Alfred Clarke and made Betty Zane tremble?

"Miss Boggs, I am twice unfortunate," said Alfred, turning to Lydia, and there was an earnest ring in his deep voice. "This time I am indeed blameless. I have just left Colonel Zane's house, where there has been an accident, and I was dispatched to find 'Betty,' being entirely ignorant as to who she might be. Colonel Zane did not stop to explain. Miss Zane is needed at the house, that is all."

And without so much as a glance at Betty he bowed low to Lydia and then strode out of the open door.

"What did he say?" asked Betty, in a small trembling voice, all her anger and resentment vanished.

"There has been an accident. He did not say what or to whom. You must hurry home. Oh, Betty, I hope no one has been hurt! And you were very unkind to Mr. Clarke. I am sure he is a gentleman, and you might have waited a moment to learn what he meant."

Betty did not answer, but flew out of the door and down the path to the gate of the fort. She was almost breathless when she reached Colonel Zane's house, and hesitated on the step before entering. Summoning her courage she pushed open the door. The first thing that struck her after the bright light was the pungent odor of strong liniment. She saw several women neighbors whispering together. Major McColloch and Jonathan Zane were standing by a couch over which Mrs. Zane was bending. Colonel Zane sat at the foot of the couch. Betty saw this in the first rapid glance, and then, as the Colonel's wife moved aside, she saw a prostrate figure, a white face and dark eyes that smiled at her.

"Betty," came in a low voice from those pale lips.

Her heart leaped and then seemed to cease beating. Many long years had passed since she had heard that voice, but it had never been forgotten. It was the best beloved voice of her childhood, and with it came the sweet memories of her brother and playmate. With a cry of joy she fell on her knees beside him and threw her arms around his neck.

"Oh, Isaac, brother, brother!" she cried, as she kissed him again and again. "Can it really be you? Oh. it is too good to be true! Thank God! I have prayed and prayed that you would be restored to us."

Then she began to cry and laugh at the same time in that strange way in which a woman relieves a heart too full of joy.

"Yes, Betty. It is all that is left of me," he said,

running his hand caressingly over the dark head that
lay on his breast.

"Betty, you must not excite him," said Colonel Zane.

"So you have not forgotten me?" whispered Isaac.

"No, indeed, Isaac. I have never forgotten," answered Betty, softly. "Only last night I spoke of you
and wondered if you were living. And now you are
here. Oh, I am so happy!" The quivering lips and the
dark eyes bright with tears spoke eloquently of her joy.

"Major, will you tell Captain Boggs to come over
after supper? Isaac will be able to talk a little by then,
and he has some news of the Indians," said Colonel
Zane.

"And ask the young man who saved my life to come
that I may thank him," said Isaac.

"Saved your life?" exclaimed Betty, turning to her
brother, in surprise, while a dark red flush spread over
her face. A humiliating thought had flashed into her
mind.

"Saved his life, of course," said Colonel Zane, answering for Isaac. "Young Clarke pulled him out of the
river. Didn't he tell you?"

"No," said Betty, rather faintly.

"Well, he is a modest young fellow. He saved Isaac's
life, there is no doubt of that. You will hear all about it
after supper. Don't make Isaac talk any more at
present."

Betty hid her face on Isaac's shoulder and remained
quiet a few moments; then, rising, she kissed his cheek
and went quietly to her room. Once there she threw
herself on the bed and tried to think. The events of the
day, coming after a long string of monotonous, wearying days, had been confusing; they had succeeded one
another in such rapid order as to leave no time for
reflection. The meeting by the river with the rude but
interesting stranger; the shock to her dignity; Lydia's
kindly advice; the stranger again, this time emerging

from the dark depths of disgrace into the luminous light as the hero of her brother's rescue—all these thoughts jumbled in her mind making it difficult for her to think clearly. But after a time one thing forced itself upon her. She could not help being conscious that she had wronged some one to whom she would be forever indebted. Nothing could alter that. She was under an eternal obligation to the man who had saved the life she loved best on earth. She had unjustly scorned and insulted the man to whom she owed the life of her brother.

Betty was passionate and quicktempered, but she was generous and tenderhearted as well, and when she realized how unkind and cruel she had been she felt very miserable. Her position admitted of no retreat. No matter how much pride rebelled; no matter how much she disliked to retract anything she had said, she knew no other course lay open to her. She would have to apologize to Mr. Clarke. How could she? What would she say? She remembered how cold and stern his face had been as he turned from her to Lydia. Perplexed and unhappy, Betty did what any girl in her position would have done: she resorted to the consoling and unfailing privilege of her sex—a good cry.

When she became composed again she got up and bathed her hot cheeks, brushed her hair, and changed her gown for a becoming one of white. She tied a red ribbon about her throat and put a rosette in her hair. She had forgotten all about the Indians. By the time Mrs. Zane called her for supper she had her mind made up to ask Mr. Clarke's pardon, tell him she was sorry, and that she hoped they might be friends.

Isaac Zane's fame had spread from the Potomac to Detroit and Louisville. Many an anxious mother on the border used the story of his captivity as a means to frighten truant youngsters who had evinced a love for running wild in the woods. The evening of Isaac's return every one in the settlement called to welcome home the wanderer. In spite of the troubled times and the dark cloud hanging over them they made the occasion one of rejoicing.

Old John Bennet, the biggest and merriest man in the colony, came in and roared his appreciation of Isaac's return. He was a huge man, and when he stalked into the room he made the floor shake with his heavy tread. His honest face expressed his pleasure as he stood over Isaac and nearly crushed his hand.

"Glad to see you, Isaac. Always knew you would come back. Always said so. There are not enough damn redskins on the river to keep you prisoner."

"I think they managed to keep him long enough," remarked Silas Zane.

"Well, here comes the hero," said Colonel Zane, as Clarke entered, accompanied by Captain Boggs, Major McColloch and Jonathan. "Any sign of Wetzel or the Indians?"

Jonathan had not yet seen his brother, and he went over and seized Isaac's hand and wrung it without speaking.

"There are no Indians on this side of the river," said Major McColloch, in answer to the Colonel's question.

"Mr. Clarke, you do not seem impressed with your importance," said Colonel Zane. "My sister said you did not tell her what part you took in Isaac's rescue."

"I hardly deserve all the credit," answered Alfred. "Your big black dog merits a great deal of it."

"Well, I consider your first day at the fort a very satisfactory one, and an augury of that fortune you came west to find."

"How are you?" said Alfred, going up to the couch where Isaac lay.

"I am doing well, thanks to you," said Isaac, warmly shaking Alfred's hand.

"It is good to see you pulling all right," answered

Alfred. "I tell you, I feared you were in a bad way when I got you out of the water."

Isaac reclined on the couch with his head and shoulders propped up by pillows. He was the handsomest of the brothers. His face would have been but for the marks of privation, singularly like Betty's; the same low, level brows and dark eyes; the same mouth, though the lips were stronger and without the soft curves which made his sister's mouth so sweet.

Betty appeared at the door, and seeing the room filled with men she hesitated a moment before coming forward. In her white dress she made such a dainty picture that she seemed out of place among those surroundings. Alfred Clarke, for one, thought such a charming vision was wasted on the rough settlers, every one of whom wore a faded and dirty buckskin suit and a belt containing a knife and a tomahawk. Colonel Zane stepped up to Betty and placing his arm around her turned toward Clarke with pride in his eyes.

"Betty, I want to make you acquainted with the hero of the hour, Mr. Alfred Clarke. This is my sister."

Betty bowed to Alfred, but lowered her eyes instantly on encountering the young man's gaze.

"I have had the pleasure of meeting Miss Zane twice today," said Alfred.

"Twice?" asked Colonel Zane, turning to Betty. She did not answer, but disengaged herself from his arm and sat down by Isaac.

"It was on the river road that I first met Miss Zane, although I did not know her then," answered Alfred. "I had some difficulty in stopping her pony from going to Fort Pitt, or some other place down the river."

"Ha! Ha! Well, I know she rides that pony pretty hard," said Colonel Zane, with a hearty laugh. "I'll tell you, Clarke, we have some riders here in the settlement. Have you heard of Major McColloch's leap over the hill?"

"I have heard it mentioned, and I would like to hear the story," responded Alfred. "I am fond of horses, and think I can ride a little myself. I am afraid I shall be compelled to change my mind."

"That is a fine animal you rode from Fort Pitt," remarked the Major. "I would like to own him."

"Come, draw your chairs up and we'll listen to Isaac's story," said Colonel Zane.

"I have not much of a story to tell," said Isaac, in a voice still weak and low. "I have some bad news, I am sorry to say, but I shall leave that for the last. This year, if it had been completed, would have made my tenth year as a captive of the Wyandots. This last period of captivity, which has been nearly four years, I have not been ill-treated and have enjoyed more comfort than any of you can imagine. Probably you are all familiar with the reason for my long captivity. Because of the interest of Myeerah, the Indian Princess, they have importuned me for years to be adopted into the tribe, marry the White Crane, as they call Myeerah, and become a Wyandot chief. To this I would never consent, though I have been careful not to provoke the Indians. I was allowed the freedom of the camp, but have always been closely watched. I should still be with the Indians had I not suspected that Hamilton, the British Governor, had formed a plan with the Hurons, Shawnees, Delawares, and other tribes, to strike a terrible blow at the whites along the river. For months I have watched the Indians preparing for an expedition, the extent of which they had never before undertaken. I finally learned from Myeerah that my suspicions were well founded. A favorable chance to escape presented and I took it and got away. I outran all the braves, even Arrowswift, the Wyandot runner, who shot me through the arm. I have had a hard time of it these last three or four days, living on herbs and roots, and when I reached the river I was ready to drop. I pushed a log into the water and started to drift over. When the old dog saw me I knew I was safe if I could hold on. Once, when the young man pointed his gun at me, I thought it was all over. I could not shout very loud."

"Were you going to shoot?" asked Colonel Zane of Clarke.

"I took him for an Indian, but fortunately I discovered my mistake in time," answered Alfred.

"Are the Indians on the way here?" asked Jonathan.

"That I cannot say. At present the Wyandots are at home. But I know that the British and the Indians will make a combined attack on the settlements. It may be a month, or a year, but it is coming."

"And Hamilton, the hair buyer, the scalp buyer, is behind the plan," said Colonel Zane, in disgust.

"The Indians have their wrongs. I sympathize with them in many ways. We have robbed them, broken faith with them, and have not lived up to the treaties. Pipe and Wingenund are particularly bitter toward the whites. I understand Cornplanter is also. He would give anything for Jonathan's scalp, and I believe any of the tribes would give a hundred of their best warriors for 'Black Wind,' as they call Lew Wetzel."

"Have you ever seen Red Fox?" asked Jonathan, who was sitting near the fire and as usual saying but little. He was the wildest and most untamable of all the Zanes. Most of the time he spent in the woods, not so much to fight Indians, as Wetzel did, but for pure love of outdoor life. At home he was thoughtful and silent.

"Yes, I have seen him," answered Isaac. "He is a Shawnee chief and one of the fiercest warriors in that tribe of fighters. He was at Indian-head, which is the name of one of the Wyandot villages, when I visited there last, and he had two hundred of his best braves with him."

"He is a bad Indian. Wetzel and I know him. He

swore he would hang our scalps up in his wigwam," said Jonathan.

"What has he in particular against you?" asked Colonel Zane. "Of course, Wetzel is the enemy of all Indians."

"Several years ago Wetzel and I were on a hunt down the river at the place called Girty's Point, where we fell in with the tracks of five Shawnees. I was for coming home, but Wetzel would not hear of it. We trailed the Indians and, coming up on them after dark, we tomahawked them. One of them got away crippled, but we could not follow him because we discovered that they had a white girl as captive, and one of the red devils, thinking we were a rescuing party, had tomahawked her. She was not quite dead. We did all we could to save her life. She died and we buried her on the spot. They were Red Fox's braves and were on their way to his camp with the prisoner. A year or so afterwards I learned from a friendly Indian that the Shawnee chief had sworn to kill us. No doubt he will be a leader in the coming attack."

"We are living in the midst of terrible times," remarked Colonel Zane. "Indeed, these are the times that try men's souls, but I firmly believe the day is not far distant when the redmen will be driven far over the border."

"Is the Indian Princess pretty?" asked Betty of Isaac.

"Indeed she is, Betty, almost as beautiful as you are," said Isaac. "She is tall and very fair for an Indian. But I have something to tell about her more interesting than that. Since I have been with the Wyandots this last time I have discovered a little of the jealously guarded secret of Myeerah's mother. When Tarhe and his band of Hurons lived in Canada their home was in the Muskoka Lakes region on the Moon river. The old warriors tell wonderful stories of the beauty of that country. Tarhe took captive some French travellers, among them a woman named La Durante. She had a beautiful little girl. The prisoners, except this little girl, were released. When she grew up Tarhe married her. Myeerah is her child. Once Tarhe took his wife to Detroit and she was seen there by an old Frenchman who went crazy over her and said she was his child. Tarhe never went to the white settlements again. So you see, Myeerah is from a great French family on her mother's side, as this old Frenchman was probably Chevalier La Durante, and Myeerah's grandfather."

"I would love to see her, and yet I hate her. What an odd name she has," said Betty.

"It is the Indian name for the white crane, a rare and beautiful bird. I never saw one. The name has been celebrated among the Hurons as long as any one of them can remember. The Indians call her the White Crane, or Walk-in-the-Water, because of her love for wading in the stream."

"I think we have made Isaac talk enough for one night," said Colonel Zane. "He is tired out. Major, tell Isaac and Betty, and Mr. Clarke, too, of your jump over the cliff."

"I have heard of that leap from the Indians," said Isaac.

"Major, from what hill did you jump your horse?" asked Alfred.

"You know the bare rocky bluff that stands out prominently on the hill across the creek. From that spot Colonel Zane first saw the valley, and from there I leaped my horse. I can never convince myself that it really happened. Often I look off that cliff in doubt. But the Indians and Colonel Zane, Jonathan, Wetzel and others say they actually saw the deed done, so I must accept it," said Major McColloch.

"It seems incredible!" said Alfred. "I cannot understand how a man or horse could go over that precipice and live."

"That is what we all say," responded the Colonel. "I suppose I shall have to tell the story. We have fighters and makers of history here, but few talkers."

"I am anxious to hear it," answered Clarke, "and I am curious to see this man Wetzel, whose fame has reached as far as my home, way down in Virginia."

"You will have your wish gratified soon, I have no doubt," resumed the Colonel. "Well, now for the story of McColloch's mad ride for life and his wonderful leap down Wheeling hill. A year ago, when the fort was besieged by Indians, the Major got through the lines and made off for Short Creek. He returned next morning with forty mounted men. They marched boldly up to the gate, and all succeeded in getting inside save the gallant Major, who had waited to be the last man to go in. Finding it impossible to make the short distance without going under the fire of the Indians, who had rushed up to prevent the relief party from entering the fort, he wheeled his big stallion, and, followed by the yelling band of savages, he took the road leading around back of the fort to the top of the bluff. The road lay along the edge of the cliff and I saw the Major turn and wave his rifle at us, evidently with the desire of assuring us that he was safe. Suddenly, on the very summit of the hill, he reined in his horse as if undecided. I knew in an instant what had happened. The Major had run right into the returning party of Indians, which had been sent out to intercept our reinforcements. In a moment more we heard the exultant yells of the savages, and saw them gliding from tree to tree, slowly lengthening out their line and surrounding the unfortunate Major. They did not fire a shot. We in the fort were stupefied with horror, and stood helplessly with our useless guns, watching and waiting for the seemingly inevitable doom of our comrade. Not so with the Major! Knowing that he was a marked man by the Indians and feeling that any death was preferable to the gauntlet, the knife, the state and torch of the merciless savage, he had grasped at a desperate chance. He saw his enemies stealthily darting from rock to tree, and tree to bush, creeping through the brush, and slipping closer and closer every moment. On three sides were his hated foes and on the remaining side—the abyss. Without a moment's hesitation the intrepid Major spurred his horse at the precipice. Never shall I forget that thrilling moment. The three hundred savages were silent as they realized the Major's intention. Those in the fort watched with staring eyes. A few bounds and the noble steed reared high on his hind legs. Outlined by the clear blue sky the magnificent animal stood for one brief instant, his black mane flying in the wind, his head thrown up and his front hoofs pawing the air like Marcus Curtius' mailed steed of old, and then down with a crash, a cloud of dust, and the crackling of pine limbs. A long yell went up from the Indians below, while those above ran to the edge of the cliff. With cries of wonder and baffled vengeance they gesticulated toward the dark ravine into which horse and rider had plunged rather than wait to meet a more cruel death. The precipice at this point is over three hundred feet in height, and in places is almost perpendicular. We believed the Major to be lying crushed and mangled on the rocks. Imagine our frenzy of joy when we saw the daring soldier and his horse dash out of the bushes that skirt the base of the cliff, cross the creek, and come galloping to the fort in safety."

"It was wonderful! Wonderful!" exclaimed Isaac, his eyes glistening. "No wonder the Indians call you the 'Flying chief.'"

"Had the Major not jumped into the clump of pine trees which grow thickly some thirty feet below the summit he would not now be alive," said Colonel Zane. "I am certain of that. Nevertheless that does not detract from the courage of his deed. He had no time to pick out the best place to jump. He simply took his one chance, and came out all right. That leap will live in the minds of men as long as yonder bluff stands a monument to McColloch's ride for life."

Alfred had listened with intense interest to the Colonel's recital. When it ended, although his pulses quickened and his soul expanded with awe and reverence for the hero of that ride, he sat silent. Alfred honored courage in a man more than any other quality. He marvelled at the simplicity of these bordermen who, he thought, took the most wonderful adventures and daring escapes as a matter of course, a compulsory part of their daily lives. He had already, in one day, had more excitement than had ever befallen him; and was beginning to believe his thirst for a free life of stirring action would be quenched long before he had learned to become useful in his new sphere. During the remaining half hour of his call on his lately acquired friends, he took little part in the conversation, but sat quietly watching the changeful expressions on Betty's face, and listening to Colonel Zane's jokes. When he rose to go he bade his host good-night, and expressed a wish that Isaac, who had fallen asleep, might have a speedy recovery. He turned toward the door to find that Betty had intercepted him.

"Mr. Clarke," she said, extending a little hand that trembled slightly. "I wish to say—that—I want to say that my feelings have changed. I am sorry for what I said over at Lydia's. I spoke hastily and rudely. You have saved my brother's life. I will be forever grateful to you. It is useless to try to thank you. I—I hope we may be friends."

Alfred found it desperately hard to resist that low voice, and those dark eyes which were raised shyly, yet bravely, to his. But he had been deeply hurt. He pretended not to see the friendly hand held out to him, and his voice was cold when he answered her.

"I am glad to have been of some service," he said, "but I think you overrate my action. Your brother would not have drowned, I am sure. You owe me nothing. Good-night."

Betty stood still one moment staring at the door through which he had gone before she realized that her overtures of friendship had been politely, but coldly, ignored. She had actually been snubbed. The impossible had happened to Elizabeth Zane. Her first sensation after she recovered from her momentary bewilderment was one of amusement, and she laughed in a constrained manner; but, presently, two bright red spots appeared in her cheeks, and she looked quickly around to see if any of the others had noticed the incident. None of them had been paying any attention to her and she breathed a sigh of relief. It was bad enough to be snubbed without having others see it. That would have been too humiliating. Her eyes flashed fire as she remembered the disdain in Clarke's face, and that she had not been clever enough to see it in time.

"Tige, come here!" called Colonel Zane. "What ails the dog?"

The dog had jumped to his feet and ran to the door, where he sniffed at the crack over the threshold. His aspect was fierce and threatening. He uttered low growls and then two short barks. Those in the room heard a soft moccasined footfall outside. The next instant the door opened wide and a tall figure stood disclosed.

"Wetzel!" exclaimed Colonel Zane. A hush fell on the little company after that exclamation, and all eyes were fastened on the new comer.

Well did the stranger merit close attention. He stalked into the room, leaned his long rifle against the mantelpiece and spread out his hands to the fire. He was clad from head to foot in fringed and beaded buckskin, which showed evidence of a long and arduous tramp. It was torn and wet and covered with mud. He was a magnificently made man, six feet in height, and stood straight as an arrow. His wide shoulders, and his muscular, though not heavy, limbs denoted a wonderful strength and activity. His long hair, black as a raven's wing, hung far down his shoulders. Presently he turned and the light shone on a remarkable face. So calm and cold and stern it was that it seemed chiselled out of marble. The most striking features were its unusual pallor, and the eyes, which were cold black, and piercing as the dagger's point.

"If you have any bad news out with it," cried Colonel Zane, impatiently.

"No need fer alarm," said Wetzel. He smiled slightly as he saw Betty's apprehensive face. "Don't look scared, Betty. The redskins are miles away and goin' fer the Kanawha settlement."

Chapter 3

MANY WEEKS of quiet followed the events of the last chapter. The settlers planted their corn, harvested their wheat and labored in the fields during the whole of one spring and summer without hearing the dreaded war cry of the Indians. Colonel Zane, who had been a disbursing officer in the army of Lord Dunmore, where he had attained the rank of Colonel, visited Fort Pitt during the summer in the hope of increasing the number of soldiers in his garrison. His effort proved fruitless. He returned to Fort Henry by way of the river with several pioneers, who with their families were bound for Fort Henry. One of these pioneers was a minister who worked in the fields every week day and on Sunday preached the Gospel to those who gathered in the meeting house.

Alfred Clarke had taken up his permanent abode at the fort, where he had been installed as one of the regular garrison. His duties, as well as those of the nine other members of the garrison, were light. For two hours out of the twenty-four he was on guard. Thus he had ample time to acquaint himself with the settlers and their families.

Alfred and Isaac had now become firm friends. They spent many hours fishing in the river, and roaming the woods in the vicinity, as Colonel Zane would not allow Isaac to stray far from the fort. Alfred became a regular visitor at Colonel Zane's house. He saw Betty every day, but as yet, nothing had mended the breach between them. They were civil to each other when chance threw them together, but Betty usually left the room on some pretext soon after he entered. Alfred regretted his hasty exhibition of resentment and would have been glad to establish friendly relations with her. But she would not give him an opportunity. She avoided him on all possible occasions. Though Alfred was fast succumbing to the charm of Betty's beautiful face, though his desire to be near her had grown well nigh resistless, his pride had not yet broked down. Many of the summer evenings found him on the Colonel's doorstep, smoking a pipe, or playing with the children. He was that rare and best company—a good listener. Although he laughed at Colonel Zane's stories, and never tired of hearing of Isaac's experiences among the Indians, it is probable he would not have partaken of the Colonel's hospitality nearly so often had it not been that he usually saw Betty, and if he got only a glimpse of her he went away satisfied. On Sundays he attended the services at the little church, and listened to Betty's sweet voice as she led the singing.

There were a number of girls at the fort near Betty's age. With all of these Alfred was popular. He appeared so entirely different from the usual young man on the frontier that he was more than welcome everywhere. Girls in the backwoods are much the same as girls in thickly populated and civilized districts. They liked his manly ways; his frank and pleasant manners; and when to these virtues he added a certain deferential regard, a courtliness to which they were unaccustomed, they were all the better pleased. He paid the young women little attentions, such as calling on them, taking them to parties and out driving, but there was not one of them who could think that she, in particular, interested him.

The girls noticed, however, that he never approached Betty after service, or on any occasion, and while it caused some wonder and gossip among them, for Betty enjoyed the distinction of being the belle of the border, they were secretly pleased. Little hints and knowing smiles, with which girls are so skillful, made known to Betty all of this, and, although she was apparently indifferent, it hurt her sensitive feelings. It had the effect of making her believe she hated the cause of it more than ever.

What would have happened had things gone on in this way, I am not prepared to say; probably had not a meddling Fate decided to take a hand in the game, Betty would have continued to think she hated Alfred, and I would never have had occasion to write his story; but Fate did interfere, and, one day in the early fall, brought about an incident which changed the whole world for the two young people.

It was the afternoon of an Indian summer day—in that most beautiful time of all the year—and Betty, accompanied by her dog, had wandered up the hillside into the woods. From the hilltop the broad river could be seen winding away in the distance, and a soft, bluish, smoky haze hung over the water. The forest seemed to be on fire. The yellow leaves of the poplars, the brown of the white and black oaks, the red and purple of the maples, and the green of the pines and hemlocks flamed in a glorious blaze of color. A stillness, which was only broken now and then by the twittering of birds uttering the plaintive notes peculiar to them in the autumn as they band together before their pilgrimage to the far south, pervaded the forest.

Betty loved the woods, and she knew all the trees. She could tell their names by the bark or the shape of the leaves. The giant black oak, with its smooth shiny bark and sturdy limbs, the chestnut with its rugged, seamed sides and bristling burrs, the hickory with its lofty height and curled shelling bark, were all well known and well loved by Betty. Many times had she wondered at the trembling, quivering leaves of the aspen, and the foliage of the silver-leaf as it glinted in the sun. Today, especially, as she walked through the woods, did their beauty appeal to her. In the little sunny patches of clearing which were scattered here and there in the grove, great clusters of goldenrod grew profusely. The golden heads swayed gracefully on the long stems. Betty gathered a few sprigs and added to them a bunch of warmly tinted maple leaves.

The chestnut burrs were opening. As Betty mounted a little rocky eminence and reached out for a limb of a chestnut tree, she lost her footing and fell. Her right foot had twisted under her as she went down, and when a sharp pain shot through it she was unable to repress a cry. She got up, tenderly placed the foot on the ground and tried her weight on it, which caused acute pain. She unlaced and removed her moccasin to find that her ankle had commenced to swell. Assured that she had sprained it, and aware of the serious consequences of an injury of that nature, she felt greatly distressed. Another effort to place her foot on the ground and bear her weight on it caused such severe pain that she was compelled to give up the attempt. Sinking down by the trunk of the tree and leaning her head against it she tried to think of a way out of her difficulty.

The fort, which she could plainly see, seemed a long distance off, although it was only a little way down the grassy slope. She looked and looked, but not a person was to be seen. She called to Tige. She remembered that he had been chasing a squirrel a short while ago, but now there was no sign of him. He did not come at her call. How annoying! If Tige were only there she could have sent him for help. She shouted several times, but the distance was too great for her voice to carry to the fort. The mocking echo of her call came back from the bluff that rose to her left. Betty now began to be alarmed in earnest, and the tears started to roll down her cheeks. The throbbing pain in her ankle, the dread of having to remain out in that lonesome forest after dark, and the fear that she might not be found for hours, caused Betty's usually brave spirit to falter; she was weeping unreservedly.

In reality she had been there only a few minutes—although they seemed hours to her—when she heard the light tread of moccasined feet on the moss behind her. Starting up with a cry of joy she turned and looked up into the astonished face of Alfred Clarke.

Returning from a hunt back in the woods he had walked up to her before being aware of her presence. In a single glance he saw the wildflowers scattered beside her, the little moccasin turned inside out, the woebegone, tearstained face, and he knew Betty had come to grief.

Confused and vexed, Betty sank back at the foot of the tree. It is probable she would have encountered Girty or a member of his band of redmen, rather than have this young man find her in this predicament. It provoked her to think that of all the people at the fort it should be the only one she could not welcome who should find her in such a sad plight.

"Why, Miss Zane!" he exclaimed, after a moment of hesitation. "What in the world has happened? Have you been hurt ? May I help you?"

"It is nothing," said Betty, bravely, as she gathered up her flowers and the moccasin and rose slowly to her feet. "Thank you, but you need not wait."

The cold words nettled Alfred and he was in the act of turning away from her when he caught, for the fleetest part of a second, the full gaze of her eyes. He stopped short. A closer scrutiny of her face convinced him that she was suffering and endeavoring with all her strength to conceal it.

"But I will wait. I think you have hurt yourself. Lean upon my arm," he said, quietly.

"Please let me help you," he continued, going nearer to her.

But Betty refused his assistance. She would not even allow him to take the goldenrod from her arms. After a few hesitating steps she paused and lifted her foot from the ground.

"Here, you must not try to walk a step farther," he said, resolutely, noting how white she had suddenly become. "You have sprained your ankle and are needlessly torturing yourself. Please let me carry you?"

"Oh, no, no, no!" cried Betty, in evident distress. "I will manage. It is not so—very—far."

She resumed the slow and painful walking, but she had taken only a few steps when she stopped again and this time a low moan issued from her lips. She swayed slightly backward and if Alfred had not dropped his rifle and caught her she would have fallen.

"Will you—please—go—for some one?" she whispered faintly, at the same time pushing him away.

"How absurd!" burst out Alfred, indignantly. "Am I, then, so distasteful to you that you would rather wait here and suffer a half hour longer while I go for assistance? It is only common courtesy on my part. I do not want to carry you. I think you would be quite heavy."

He said this in a hard, bitter tone, deeply hurt that she would not accept even a little kindness from him. He looked away from her and waited. Presently a soft, half-smothered sob came from Betty and it expressed such utter wretchedness that his heart melted. After all she was only a child. He turned to see the tears running down her cheeks, and with a suppressed imprecation upon the wilfulness of young women in general, and this one in particular, he stepped forward and before she could offer any resistance, he had taken her up in his arms, goldenrod and all, and had started off at a rapid walk toward the fort.

Betty cried out in angry surprise, struggled violently

for a moment, and then, as suddenly, lay quietly in his arms. His anger changed to self-reproach as he realized what a light burden she made. He looked down at the dark head lying on his shoulder. Her face was hidden by the dusky rippling hair, which tumbled over his breast, brushed against his cheek, and blew across his lips. The touch of those fragrant tresses was a soft caress. Almost unconsciously he pressed her closer to his heart. And as a sweet mad longing grew upon him he was blind to all save that he held her in his arms, that uncertainty was gone forever, and that he loved her. With these thought running riot in his brain he carried her down the hill to Colonel Zane's house.

The negro, Sam, who came out of the kitchen, dropped the bucket he had in his hand and ran into the house when he saw them. When Alfred reached the gate Colonel Zane and Isaac were hurrying out to meet him.

"For Heaven's sake! What has happened? Is she badly hurt? I have always looked for this," said the Colonel, excitedly.

"You need not look so alarmed," answered Alfred. "She has only sprained her ankle, and trying to walk afterward hurt her so badly that she became faint and I had to carry her."

"Dear me, is that all?" said Mrs. Zane, who had also come out. "We were terribly frightened. Sam came running into the house with some kind of a wild story. Said he knew you would be the death of Betty."

"How ridiculous! Colonel Zane, that servant of yours never fails to say something against me," said Alfred, as he carried Betty into the house.

"He doesn't like you. But you need not mind Sam. He is getting old and we humor him, perhaps too much. We are certainly indebted to you," returned the Colonel.

Betty was laid on the couch and consigned to the

skillful hands of Mrs. Zane, who pronounced the injury
a bad spain.

"Well, Betty, this will keep you quiet for a few
days," said she, with a touch of humor, as she gently
felt the swollen ankle.

"Alfred, you have been our good angel so often that
I don't see how we shall ever reward you," said Isaac to
Alfred.

"Oh, that time will come. Don't worry about that,"
said Alfred, jestingly, and then, turning to the others he
continued, earnestly. "I will apologize for the manner
in which I disregarded Miss Zane's wish not to help
her. I am sure I could do no less. I believe my rudeness
has spared her considerable suffering."

"What did he mean, Betts?" asked Isaac, going back
to his sister after he had closed the door. "Didn't you
want him to help you?"

Betty did not answer. She sat on the couch while
Mrs. Zane held the little bare foot and slowly poured
the hot water over the swollen and discolored ankle.
Betty's lips were pale. She winced every time Mrs. Zane
touched her foot, but as yet she had not uttered even a
sigh.

"Betty, does it hurt much?" asked Isaac.

"Hurt? Do you think I am made of wood? Of course
it hurts," retorted Betty. "That water is so hot. Bessie,
will not cold water do as well?"

"I am sorry. I won't tease any more," said Isaac,
taking his sister's hand. "I'll tell you what, Betty, we
owe Alfred Clarke a great deal, you and I. I am going
to tell you something so you will know how much more
you owe him. Do you remember last month when that
red heifer of yours got away. Well, Clarke chased her
all day and finally caught her in the woods. He asked
me to say I had caught her. Somehow or other he seems
to be afraid of you. I wish you and he would be good
friends. He is a mighty fine fellow."

In spite of the pain Betty was suffering a bright blush suffused her face at the words of her brother, who, blind as brothers are in regard to their own sisters, went on praising his friend.

Betty was confined to the house a week or more and during this enforced idleness she had ample time for reflection and opportunity to inquire into the perplexed state of her mind.

The small room, which Betty called her own, faced the river and fort. Most of the day she lay by the window trying to read her favorite books, but often she gazed out on the quiet scene, the rolling river, and the everchanging trees and the pastures in which the red and white cows grazed peacefully; or she would watch with idle, dreamy eyes the flight of the crows over the hills, and the graceful motion of the hawk as he sailed around and around in the azure sky, looking like a white sail far out on a summer sea.

But Betty's mind was at variance with this peaceful scene. The consciousness of a change, which she could not readily define, in her feelings toward Alfred Clarke, vexed and irritated her. Why did she think of him so often? True, he had saved her brother's life. Still she was compelled to admit to herself that this was not the reason. Try as she would, she could not banish the thought of him. Over and over again, a thousand times, came the recollection of that moment when he had taken her up in his arms as though she were a child. Some vague feeling stirred in her heart as she remembered the strong yet gentle clasp of his arms.

Several times from her window she had seen him coming across the square between the fort and her brother's house, and womanlike, unseen herself, she had watched him. How erect was his carriage. How pleasant his deep voice sounded as she heard him talking to her brother. Day by day, as her ankle grew stronger and she knew she could not remain much long-

er in her room, she dreaded more and more the
thought of meeting him. She could not understand herself; she had strange dreams; she cried seemingly without the slightest cause, and she was restless and unhappy. Finally she grew angry and scolded herself. She
said she was silly and sentimental. This had the effect
of making her bolder, but it did not quiet her unrest.
Betty did not know that the little blind God, who steals
unawares on his victim, had marked her for his own,
and that all this sweet perplexity was the unconscious
awakening of the heart.

One afternoon, near the end of Betty's siege indoors,
two of her friends, Lydia Boggs and Alice Reynolds,
called to see her.

Alice had bright blue eyes, and her nut brown hair
hung in rebellious curls around her demure and pretty
face. An adorable dimple lay hidden in her rosy cheek
and flashed into light with her smiles.

"Betty, you are a lazy thing!" exclaimed Lydia. "Lying here all day long doing nothing but gaze out of the
window."

"Girls, I am glad you came over," said Betty. "I am
blue. Perhaps you will cheer me up."

"Betty needs some one of the sterner sex to cheer
her," said Alice, mischievously, her eyes twinkling.
"Don't you think so, Lydia?"

"Of course," answered Lydia. "When I get blue
——"

"Please spare me," interrupted Betty, holding up her
hands in protest. "I have not a single doubt that your
masculine remedies are sufficient for all your ills. Girls
who have lost their interest in the old pleasures, who
spend their spare time in making linen and quilts, and
who have sunk their very personalities in a great big
tyrant of a man, are not liable to get blue. They are
afraid he may see a tear or a frown. But, thank goodness, I have not yet reached that stage."

"Oh, Betty Zane! Just you wait! Wait!" exclaimed Lydia, shaking her finger at Betty. "Your turn is coming. When it does do not expect any mercy from us, for you shall never get it."

"Unfortunately, you and Alice have monopolized the fort," said Betty, with a laugh.

"Nonsense. There are plenty of young men all eager for your favor, you little coquette," answered Lydia. "Harry Martin, Will Metzer, Captain Swearengen, of Short Creek, and others too numerous to count. Look at Lew Wetzel and Billy Bennet."

"Lew cares for nothing except hunting Indians and Billy is only a boy," said Betty.

"Well, have it your own way," said Lydia. "Only this, I know Billy adores you, for he told me so, and a better lad never lived."

"Lyde, you forget to include one other among those prostrate before Betty's charms," said Alice.

"Oh, yes, you mean Mr. Clarke. To be sure, I had forgotten him," answered Lydia. "How odd that he should be the one to find you the day you hurt your foot. Was it an accident?"

"Of course. I slipped off the bank," said Betty.

"No, no. I don't mean that. Was his finding you an accident?"

"Do you imagine I waylaid Mr. Clarke, and then sprained my ankle on purpose?" said Betty, who began to look dangerous.

"Certainly not that; only it seems so odd that he should be the one to rescue all the damsels in distress. Day before yesterday he stopped a runaway horse, and saved Nell Metzer, who was in the wagon, a severe shaking up, if not something more serious. She is desperately in love with him. She told me. Mr. Clarke ——"

"I really do not care to hear about it," interrupted Betty.

"But, Betty, tell us. Wasn't it dreadful, his carrying you?" asked Alice, with a sly glance at Betty. "You know you are so— so prudish, one may say. Did he take you in his arms? It must have been very embarrassing for you, considering your dislike of Mr. Clarke, and he so much in love with———"

"You hateful girls," cried Betty, throwing a pillow at Alice, who just managed to dodge it. "I wish you would go home."

"Never mind, Betty. We will not tease anymore," said Lydia, putting her arm around Betty. "Come, Alice, we will tell Betty you have named the day for your wedding. See! She is all eyes now."

* * * * * * * * *

The young people of the frontier settlements were usually married before they were twenty. This was owing to the fact that there was little distinction of rank and family pride. The object of the pioneers in moving West was, of course, to better their condition; but, the realization of their dependence on one another, the common cause of their labors, and the terrible dangers to which they were continually exposed, brought them together as one large family.

Therefore, early love affairs were encouraged, not frowned upon as they are today—and they usually resulted in early marriages.

However, do not let it be imagined that the path of the youthful swain was strewn with flowers. Courting or "sparking" his sweetheart had a painful as well as a joyous side. Many and varied were the tricks played on the fortunate lover by the gallants who had vied with him for the favor of the maid. Brave, indeed, he who won her. If he marched up to her home in the early evening he was made the object of innumerable jests, even the young lady's family indulging in and enjoying the banter. Later, when he came out of the door, it was more than likely that, if it were winter, he would be met by a volley of water soaked snowballs, or big buckets of icewater, or a mountain of snow shoved off the roof by some trickster, who had waited patiently for such an opportunity. On summer nights his horse would be stolen, led far into the woods and tied, or the wheels of his wagon would be taken off and hidden, leaving him to walk home. Usually the successful lover, and especially if he lived at a distance, would make his way only once a week and then late at night to the home of his betrothed. Silently, like a thief in the dark, he would crawl through the grass and shrubs until beneath her window. At a low signal, prearranged between them, she would slip to the door and let him in without disturbing her parents. Fearing to make a light, and perhaps welcoming that excuse to enjoy the darkness beloved by sweethearts, they would sit quietly, whispering low, until the brightening in the east betokened the break of day, and then he was off, happy and light-hearted, to his labors.

A wedding was looked forward to with much pleasure by old and young. Practically, it meant the only gathering of the settlers which was not accompanied by the work of reaping the harvest, building a cabin, planning an expedition to relieve some distant settlement, or a defense for themselves. For all, it meant a rollicking good time; to the old people a feast, and the looking on at the merriment of their children—to the young folk, a pleasing break in the monotony of their busy lives, a day given up to fun and gossip, a day of romance, a wedding, and best of all, a dance. Therefore, Alice Reynold's wedding proved a great event to the inhabitants of Fort Henry.

The day dawned bright and clear. The sun, rising like a ball of red gold, cast its yellow beams over the bare, brown hills, shining on the cabin roofs white with frost, and making the delicate weblike coat of ice on the river sparkle as if it had been sprinkled with powdered diamonds. William Martin, the groom, and his attendants, met at an appointed time to celebrate an old time-honored custom which always took place before the party started for the house of the bride. This performance was called "the race for the bottle."

A number of young men, selected by the groom, were asked to take part in this race, which was to be run over as rough and dangerous a track as could be found. The worse the road, the more ditches, bogs, trees, stumps, brush, in fact, the more obstacles of every kind, the better, as all these afforded opportunity for daring and expert horsemanship. The English fox race, now famous on three continents, while it involves risk and is sometimes dangerous, cannot, in the sense of hazard to life and limb, be compared to this race for the bottle.

On this day the run was not less exciting than usual. The horses were placed as nearly abreast as possible and the starter gave an Indian yell. Then followed the cracking of whips, the furious pounding of heavy hoofs, the commands of the contestants, and the yells of the onlookers. Away they went at a mad pace down the road. The course extended a mile straight away down the creek bottom. The first hundred yards the horses were bunched. At the ditch beyond the creek bridge a beautiful, clean limbed animal darted from among the furiously galloping horses and sailed over the deep furrow like a bird. All recognized the rider as Alfred Clarke on his black thoroughbred. Close behind was George Martin mounted on a large roan of powerful frame and long stride. Through the willows they dashed, over logs and brush heaps, up the little ridges of rising ground, and down the shallow gullies, unheeding the stinging branches and the splashing water. Half the distance covered and Alfred turned, to find the roan close behind. On a level road he would have laughed at the attempt of that horse to keep up with his racer, but he was beginning to fear that the strong limbed stallion deserved his reputation. Directly before them rose a pile of logs and matted brush, placed there by the dare devil settlers who had mapped out the route. It was too high for any horse to be put at. With pale cheek and clinched teeth Alfred touched the spurs to Roger and then threw himself forward. The gallant beast responded nobly. Up, up, up he rose, clearing all but the topmost branches. Alfred turned again and saw the giant roan make the leap without touching a twig. The next instant Roger went splash into a swamp. He sank to his knees in the soft black soil. He could move but one foot at a time, and Alfred saw at a glance he had won the race. The great weight of the roan handicapped him here. When Alfred reached the other side of the bog, where the bottle was swinging from a branch of a tree, his rival's horse was floundering hopelessly in the middle of the treacherous mire. The remaining three horsemen, who had come up by this time, seeing that it would be useless to attempt further efforts, had drawn up on the bank. With friendly shouts to Clarke, they acknowledged themselves beaten. There were no judges required for this race, because the man who reached the bottle first won it.

The five men returned to the starting point, where the victor was greeted by loud whoops. The groom got the first drink from the bottle, then came the attendants, and others in order, after which the bottle was put away to be kept as memento of the occasion.

The party now repaired to the village and marched to the home of the bride. The hour for the observance of the marriage rites was just before the midday meal. When the groom reached the bride's home he found her in readiness. Sweet and pretty Alice looked in her gray linsey gown, perfectly plain and simple though it was, without an ornament or a ribbon. Proud indeed looked her lover as he took her hand and led her up to the waiting minister. When the whisperings had ceased the minister asked who gave this woman to be married. Alice's father answered.

"Will you take this woman to be your wedded wife, to love, cherish and protect her all the days of her life?" asked the minister.

"I will," answered a deep bass voice.

"Will you take this man to be your wedded husband, to love, honor and obey him all the days of your life?"

"I will " said Alice, in a low tone.

"I pronounce you man and wife. Those whom God has joined together let no man put asunder."

There was a brief prayer and the ceremony ended. Then followed the congratulations of relatives and friends. The felicitations were apt to be trying to the nerves of even the best tempered groom. The hand shakes, the heavy slaps on the back, and the pommeling he received at the hands of his intimate friends were as nothing compared to the anguish of mind he endured while they were kissing his wife. The young bucks would not have considered it a real wedding had they been prevented from kissing the bride, and for that matter, every girl within reach. So fast as the burly young settlers could push themselves through the densely packed rooms they kissed the bride, and then the first girl they came to.

Betty and Lydia had been Alice's maids of honor. This being Betty's first experience at a frontier wedding, it developed that she was much in need of Lydia's advice, which she had previously disdained. She had rested secure in her dignity. Poor Betty! The first man to kiss Alice was George Martin, a big, strong fellow who gathered his brother's bride into his arms and gave her a bearish hug and a resounding kiss. Releasing her he turned toward Lydia and Betty. Lydia eluded him, but one of his great hands clasped around Betty's wrist.

She tried to look haughty, but with everyone laughing, and the young man's face expressive of honest fun and happiness she found it impossible. She stood still and only turned her face a little to one side while George kissed her. The young men now made a rush for her. With blushing cheeks Betty, unable to stand her ground any longer, ran to her brother, the Colonel. He pushed her away with a laugh. She turned to Major McColloch, who held out his arms to her. With an exclamation she wrenched herself free from a young man, who had caught her hand, and flew to the Major. But alas for Betty! The Major was not proof against the temptation and he kissed her himself.

"Traitor!" cried Betty, breaking away from him.

Poor Betty was in despair. She had just made up her mind to submit when she caught sight of Wetzel's familiar figure. She ran to him and the hunter put one of his long arms around her.

"I reckon I kin take care of you, Betty," he said, a smile playing over his usually stern face. "See, here, you young bucks. Betty don't want to be kissed, and if you keep on pesterin' her I'll have to scalp a few of you."

The merriment grew as the day progressed. During the wedding feast great hilarity prevailed. It eliminated in the dance which followed the dinner. The long room of the block-house had been decorated with evergreens, autumn leaves and goldenrod, which were scattered profusely about, hiding the blackened walls and bare rafters. Numerous blazing pine knots, fastened on sticks which were stuck into the walls, lighted up a scene, which for color and animation could not have been surpassed.

Colonel Zane's old slave, Sam, who furnished the music, sat on a raised platform at the upper end of the hall, and the way he sawed away on his fiddle, accompanying the movements of his arm with a swaying of his body and a stamping of his heavy foot, showed he had a hearty appreciation of his own value.

Prominent among the men and women standing and sitting near the platform could be distinguished the tall forms of Jonathan Zane, Major McColloch and Wetzel, all, as usual, dressed in their hunting costumes and carrying long rifles. The other men had made more or less effort to improve their appearance. Bright homespun shirts and scarfs had replaced the everyday buckskin garments. Major McColloch was talking to Colonel Zane. The genial faces of both reflected the pleasure they felt in the enjoyment of the younger people. Jonathan Zane stood near the door. Moody and silent he watched the dance. Wetzel leaned against the wall. The black barrel of his rifle lay in the hollow of his arm. The hunter was gravely contemplating the members of the bridal party who were dancing in front of him. When the dance ended Lydia and Betty stopped before Wetzel and Betty said: "Lew, aren't you going to ask us to dance?"

The hunter looked down into the happy, gleaming faces, and smiling in his half sad way, answered: "Every man to his gifts."

"But you can dance. I want you to put aside your gun long enough to dance with me. If I waited for you to ask me, I fear I should have to wait a long time. Come, Lew, here I am asking you, and I know the other men are dying to dance with me," said Betty, coaxingly, in a roguish voice.

Wetzel never refused a request of Betty's, and so, laying aside his weapons, he danced with her, to the wonder and admiration of all. Colonel Zane clapped his hands, and everyone stared in amazement at the unprecedented sight. Wetzel danced not ungracefully. He was wonderfully light on his feet. His striking figure, the long black hair, and the fancifully embroidered costume he wore contrasted strangely with Betty's slender, graceful form and pretty gray dress.

"Well, well, Lewis, I would not have believed anything but the evidence of my own eyes," said Colonel Zane, with a laugh, as Betty and Wetzel approached him.

"If all the men could dance as well as Lew, the girls would be thankful, I can assure you," said Betty.

"Betty, I declare you grow prettier every day," said old John Bennet, who was standing with the Colonel and the Major. "If I were only a young man once more I should try my chances with you, and I wouldn't give up very easily."

"I do not know, Uncle John, but I am inclined to think that if you were a young man and should come a-wooing you would not get a rebuff from me," answered Betty, smiling on the old man, of whom she was very fond.

"Miss Zane, will you dance with me?"

The voice sounded close by Betty's side. She recognized it, and an unaccountable sensation of shyness suddenly came over her. She had firmly made up her mind, should Mr. Clarke ask her to dance, that she would tell him she was tired, or engaged for that number—anything so that she could avoid dancing with him. But, now that the moment had come she either forgot her resolution or lacked the courage to keep it, for as the music commenced, she turned and without saying a word or looking at him, she placed her hand on his arm. He whirled her away. She gave a start of surprise and delight at the familiar step and then gave herself up to the charm of the dance. Supported by his strong arm she floated around the room in a sort of dream. Dancing as they did was new to the young people at the Fort—it was a style then in vogue in the east—and everyone looked on with great interest and curiosity. But all too soon the dance ended and before

Betty had recovered her composure she found that her partner had led her to a secluded seat in the lower end of the hall. The bench was partly obscured from the dancers by masses of autumn leaves.

"That was a very pleasant dance," said Alfred. "Miss Boggs told me you danced the round dance."

"I was much surprised and pleased," said Betty, who had indeed enjoyed it.

"It has been a delightful day," went on Alfred, seeing that Betty was still confused. "I almost killed myself in that race for the bottle this morning. I never saw such logs and brush heaps and ditches in my life. I am sure that if the fever of recklessness which seemed in the air had not suddenly seized me I would never have put my horse at such leaps."

"I heard my brother say your horse was one of the best he had ever seen, and that you rode superbly," murmured Betty.

"Well, to be honest, I would not care to take that ride again. It certainly was not fair to the horse."

"How do you like the fort by this time?"

"Miss Zane, I am learning to love this free, wild life. I really think I was made for the frontier. The odd customs and manners which seemed strange at first have become very acceptable to me now. I find everyone so honest and simple and brave. Here one must work to live, which is right. Do you know, I never worked in my life until I came to Fort Henry. My life was all uselessness, idleness."

"I can hardly believe that," answered Betty. "You have learned to dance and ride and——"

"What?" asked Alfred, as Betty hesitated.

"Never mind. It was an accomplishment with which the girls credited you," said Betty, with a little laugh.

"I suppose I did not deserve it. I heard I had a singular aptitude for discovering young ladies in distress."

"Have you become well acquainted with the boys?" asked Betty, hastening to change the subject.

"Oh, yes, particularly with your Indianized brother, Isaac. He is the finest fellow, as well as the most interesting, I ever knew. I like Colonel Zane immensely too. The dark, quiet fellow, Jack, or John, they call him, is not like your other brothers. The hunter, Wetzel, inspires me with awe. Everyone has been most kind to me and I have almost forgotten that I was a wanderer."

"I am glad to hear that," said Betty.

"Miss Zane," continued Alfred, "doubtless you have heard that I came West because I was compelled to leave my home. Please do not believe everything you hear of me. Some day I may tell you my story if you care to hear it. Suffice it to say now that I left my home of my own free will and I could go back tomorrow."

"I did not mean to imply—" began Betty, coloring.

"Of course not. But tell me about yourself. Is it not rather dull and lonesome here for you?"

"It was last winter. But I have been contented and happy this summer. Of course, it is not Philadelphia life, and I miss the excitement and gayety of my uncle's house. I knew my place was with my brothers. My aunt pleaded with me to live with her and not go to the wilderness. I had everything I wanted there— luxury, society, parties, balls, dances, friends, all that the heart of a girl could desire, but I preferred to come to this little frontier settlement. Strange choice for a girl, was it not?"

"Unusual, yes," answered Alfred, gravely. "And I cannot but wonder what motives actuated our coming to Fort Henry. I came to seek my fortune. You came to bring sunshine into the home of your brother, and left your fortune behind you. Well, your motive has the element of nobility. Mine has nothing but that of recklessness. I would like to read the future."

"I do not think it is right to have such a wish. With the veil rolled away could you work as hard, accomplish as much? I do not want to know the future. Perhaps some of it will be unhappy. I have made my choice and will cheerfully abide by it. I rather envy your being a man. You have the world to conquer. A woman—what can she do? She can knead the dough, ply the distaff, and sit by the lattice and watch and wait."

"Let us postpone such melancholy thoughts until some future day. I have not as yet said anything that I intended. I wish to tell you how sorry I am that I acted in such a rude way the night your brother came home. I do not know what made me do so, but I know I have regretted it ever since. Will you forgive me and may we not be friends?"

"I—I do not know," said Betty, surprised and vaguely troubled by the earnest light in his eyes.

"But why? Surely you will make some little allowance for a naturally quick temper, and you know you did not—that you were——"

"Yes, I remember I was hasty and unkind. But I made amends, or at least, I tried to do so."

"Try to overlook my stupidity. I will not give up until you forgive me. Consider how much you can avoid by being generous."

"Very well, then, I will forgive you," said Betty, who had arrived at the conclusion that this young man was one of determination.

"Thank you. I promise you shall never regret it. And the sprained ankle? It must be well, as I noticed you danced beautifully."

"I am compelled to believe what the girls say—that you are inclined to the language of compliment. My ankle is nearly well, thank you. It hurts a little now and then."

"Speaking of your accident reminds me of the day it

happened," said Alfred, watching her closely. He desired to tease her a little, but he was not sure of his ground. "I had been all day in the woods with nothing but my thoughts—mostly unhappy ones—for company. When I met you I pretended to be surprised. As a matter of fact I was not, for I had followed your dog. He took a liking to me and I was extremely pleased, I assure you. Well, I saw your face a moment before you knew I was near you. When you heard my footsteps you turned with a relieved and joyous cry. When you saw whom it was your glad expression changed, and if I had been a hostile Wyandot you could not have looked more unfriendly. Such a woeful, tear-stained face I never saw."

"Mr. Clarke, please do not speak any more of that," said Betty, with dignity. "I desire that you forget it."

"I will forget all except that it was I who had the happiness of finding you and of helping you. I cannot forget that. I am sure we should never have been friends but for that accident."

"There is Isaac. He is looking for me," answered Betty, rising.

"Wait a moment longer—please. He will find you," said Alfred, detaining her. "Since you have been so kind I have grown bolder. May I come over to see you tomorrow?"

He looked straight down into the dark eyes which wavered and fell before he had completed his question.

"There is Isaac. He cannot see me here. I must go."

"But not before telling me. What is the good of your forgiving me if I may not see you. Please say yes."

"You may come," answered Betty, half amused and half provoked at his persistence. "I should think you would know that such permission invariably goes with a young woman's forgiveness."

"Hello, here you are. What a time I have had in finding you," said Isaac, coming up with flushed face and eyes bright with excitement. "Alfred, what do you mean by hiding the belle of the dance away like this? I want to dance with you, Betts. I am having a fine time. I have not danced anything but Indian dances for ages. Sorry to take her away, Alfred. I can see she doesn't want to go. Ha! Ha!" and with a mischievous look at both of them he led Betty away.

Alfred kept his seat awhile lost in thought. Suddenly he remembered that it would look strange if he did not make himself agreeable, so he got up and found a partner. He danced with Alice, Lydia, and the other young ladies. After an hour he slipped away to his room. He wished to be alone. He wanted to think; to decide whether it would be best for him to stay at the fort, or ride away in the darkness and never return. With the friendly touch of Betty's hand the madness with which he had been battling for weeks rushed over him stronger than ever. The thrill of that soft little palm remained with him, and he pressed the hand it had touched to his lips.

For a long hour he sat by his window. He could dimly see the broad winding river, with its curtain of pale gray mist, and beyond, the dark outline of the forest. A cool breeze from the water fanned his heated brow, and the quiet and solitude soothed him.

Chapter 4

"GOOD MORNING, Harry. Where are you going so early?" called Betty from the doorway.

A lad was passing down the path in front of Colonel Zane's house as Betty hailed him. He carried a rifle almost as long as himself.

"Mornin', Betty. I am goin' 'cross the crick fer that turkey I hear bogglin'," he answered, stopping at the gate and smiling brightly at Betty.

"Hello, Harry Bennet. Going after that turkey? I have heard him several mornings and he must be a big, healthy gobbler," said Colonel Zane, stepping to the door. "You are going to have company. Here comes Wetzel."

"Good morning, Lew. Are you too off on a turkey hunt?" said Betty.

"Listen," said the hunter, as he stopped and leaned against the gate. They listened. All was quiet save for the tinkle of a cow-bell in the pasture adjoining the Colonel's barn. Presently the silence was broken by a long, shrill, peculiar cry.

"Chug-a-lug, chug-a-lug, chug-a-lug-chug."

"Well, it's a turkey, all right, and I'll bet a big gobbler," remarked Colonel Zane, as the cry ceased.

"Has Jonathan heard it?" asked Wetzel.

"Not that I know of. Why do you ask?" said the Colonel in a low tone. "Look here, Lew, is that not a genuine call?"

"Goodbye, Harry, be sure and bring me a turkey," called Betty, as she disappeared.

"I calkilate it's a red turkey," answered the hunter, and motioning the lad to stay behind, he shouldered his rifle and passed swiftly down the path.

Of all the Wetzel family—a family noted from one end of the frontier to the other—Lewis was the most famous. The early history of West Virginia and Ohio is replete with the daring deeds of this wilderness roamer, this lone hunter and insatiable Nemesis, justly called the greatest Indian slayer known to men.

When Lewis was about twenty years old, and his brothers John and Martin little older, they left their Virginia home for a protracted hunt. On their return they found the smoking ruins of the home, the mangled remains of father and mother, the naked and violated bodies of their sisters, and the scalped and bleeding corpse of a baby brother.

Lewis Wetzel swore sleepless and eternal vengeance on the whole Indian race. Terribly did he carry out that resolution. From that time forward he lived most of the time in the woods, and an Indian who crossed his trail was a doomed man. The various Indian tribes gave him different names. The Shawnees called him "Long Knife;" the Hurons, "Destroyer;" the Delawares, "Death Wind," and any one of these names would chill the heart of the stoutest warrior.

To most of the famed pioneer hunters of the border, Indian fighting was only a side issue—generally a necessary one—but with Wetzel it was the business of his life. He lived solely to kill Indians. He plunged recklessly into the strife, and was never content unless roaming the wilderness solitudes, trailing the savages to their very homes and ambushing the village bridlepath like a panther waiting for his prey. Often in the gray of the morning the Indians, sleeping around their camp fire, were awakened by a horrible, screeching yell. They started up in terror only to fall victims to the tomahawk of their merciless foe, or to hear a rifle shot and get a glimpse of a form with flying black hair disappearing with wonderful quickness in the forest. Wetzel always left death behind him, and he was gone before his demoniac yell ceased to echo throughout the woods. Although often pursued, he invariably eluded the Indians, for he was the fleetest runner on the border.

For many years he was considered the right hand of the defense of the fort. The Indians held him in superstitious dread, and the fact that he was known to be in the settlement had averted more than one attack by the Indians.

Many regarded Wetzel as a savage, a man who was mad for the blood of the red men, and without one redeeming quality. But this was an unjust opinion. When that restless fever for revenge left him—it was not always with him—he was quiet and peaceable. But Wetzel, although known to everyone, cared for few. He spent little time in the settlements and rarely spoke except when addressed.

Nature had singularly fitted him for his pre-eminent position among scouts and hunters. He was tall and broad across the shoulders; his strength, agility and endurance were marvelous; he had an eagle eye, the sagacity of the blood hound, and that intuitive knowledge which plays such an important part in a hunter's life. He knew not fear. He was daring where daring was the wiser part. Crafty, tireless and implacable, Wetzel was incomparable in his vocation.

His long raven-black hair, of which he was vain, when combed out reached to within a foot of the ground. He had a rare scalp, one for which the Indians would have bartered anything.

A favorite Indian decoy, and the most fatal one, was the imitation of the call of the wild turkey. It had often happened that men from the settlements who had gone out for a turkey which had been gobbling, had not returned.

For several mornings Wetzel had heard a turkey call, and becoming suspicious of it, had determined to satisfy himself. On the east side of the creek hill there was a cavern some fifty or sixty yards above the water. The entrance to this cavern was concealed by vines and foliage. Wetzel knew of it, and, crossing the stream some distance above, he made a wide circuit and came up back of the cave. Here he concealed himself in a clump of bushes and waited. He had not been there long when directly below him sounded the cry, "Chug-a-lug, Chug-a-lug, Chug-a-lug." At the same time the polished head and brawny shoulders of an Indian warrior rose out of the cavern. Peering cautiously around, the savage again gave the peculiar cry, and then sank back out of sight. Wetzel screened himself safely in his position and watched the savage repeat the action at least ten times before he made up his mind that the Indian was alone in the cave. When he had satisfied himself of this he took a quick aim at the twisted tuft of hair and fired. Without waiting to see the result of his shot—so well did he trust his unerring aim—he climbed down the steep bank and brushing aside the vines entered the cave. A stalwart Indian lay in the entrance with his face pressed down on the vines. He still clutched in his sinewy fingers the buckhorn mouthpiece with which he had made the calls that had resulted in his death.

"Huron," muttered the hunter to himself as he ran the keen edge of his knife around the twisted tuft of hair and tore off the scalp-lock.

The cave showed evidence of having been inhabited for some time. There was a cunningly contrived fireplace made of stones, against which pieces of birch bark were placed in such a position that not a ray of light could get out of the cavern. The bed of black coals between the stones still smoked; a quantity of parched corn lay on a little rocky shelf which jutted out from the wall; a piece of jerked meat and a buckskin pouch hung from a peg.

Suddenly Wetzel dropped on his knees and began examining the footprints in the sandy floor of the cavern. He measured the length and width of the dead warrior's foot. He closely scrutinized every moccasin print. He crawled to the opening of the cavern and carefully surveyed the moss.

Then he rose to his feet. A remarkable transformation had come over him during the last few moments. His face had changed; the calm expression was replaced by one sullen and fierce; his lips were set in a thin, cruel line, and a strange light glittered in his eyes.

He slowly pursued a course leading gradually down to the creek. At intervals he would stop and listen. The strange voices of the woods were not mysteries to him. They were more familiar to him than the voices of men.

He recalled that, while on his circuit over the ridge to get behind the cavern, he had heard the report of a rifle far off in the direction of the chestnut grove, but, as that was a favorite place of the settlers for shooting squirrels, he had not thought anything of it at the time. Now it had a peculiar significance. He turned abruptly from the trail he had been following and plunged down the steep hill. Crossing the creek he took to the cover of the willows, which grew profusely along the banks, and striking a sort of bridle path he started on a run. He ran easily, as though accustomed to that mode of travel, and his long strides covered a couple of miles in short order. Coming to the rugged bluff, which marked the end of the ridge, he stopped and walked slowly along the edge of the water. He struck the trail of the Indians where it crossed the creek, just where he expected. There were several moccasin tracks in the wet

sand and, in some of the depressions made by the
heels the rounded edges of the imprints were still
smooth and intact. The little pools of muddy water,
which still lay in these hollows, were other indications
to his keen eyes that the Indians had passed this point
early that morning.

The trail led up the hill and far into the woods.
Never in doubt the hunter kept on his course; like a
shadow he passed from tree to tree and from bush to
bush; silently, cautiously, but rapidly he followed the
tracks of the Indians. When he had penetrated the dark
backwoods of the Black Forest, tangled underbrush,
windfalls and gullies crossed his path and rendered fast
trailing impossible. Before these almost impassable bar-
riers he stopped and peered on all sides, studying the
lay of the land, the deadfalls, the gorges, and all the
time keeping in mind the probable route of the redskins. Then he turned aside to avoid the roughest
travelling. Sometimes these detours were only a few
hundred feet long; often they were miles; but nearly
always he struck the trail again. This almost superhuman knowledge of the Indian's ways of traversing the
forest, which probably no man could have possessed
without giving his life to the hunting of Indians, was
the one feature of Wetzel's woodcraft which placed him
so far above other hunters, and made him so dreaded
by the savages.

Descending a knoll he entered a glade where the
trees grew farther apart and the underbrush was only
knee high. The black soil showed that the tract of land
had been burned over. On the banks of a babbling
brook which wound its way through this open space,
the hunter found tracks which brought an exclamation
from him. Clearly defined in the soft earth was the
impress of a white man's moccasin. The foot prints of
an Indian toe inward. Those of a white man are just the
opposite. A little farther on Wetzel came to a slight

crushing of the moss, where he concluded some heavy body had fallen. As he had seen the tracks of a buck and doe all the way down the brook he thought it probable one of them had been shot by the white hunter. He found a pool of blood surrounded by moccasin prints; and from that spot the trail led straight toward the west, showing that for some reason the Indians had changed their direction.

This new move puzzled the hunter, and he leaned against the trunk of a tree, while he revolved in his mind the reasons for this abrupt departure— for such he believed it. The trail he had followed for miles was the devious trail of hunting Indians, stealing slowly and stealthily along watching for their prey, whether it be man or beast. The trail toward the west was straight as the crow flies; the moccasin prints that indented the soil were wide apart, and to an inexperienced eye looked like the track of one Indian. To Wetzel this indicated that the Indians had all stepped in the tracks of a leader.

As was usually his way, Wetzel decided quickly. He had calculated that there were eight Indians in all, not counting the chief whom he had shot. This party of Indians had either killed or captured the white man who had been hunting. Wetzel believed that a part of the Indians would push on with all possible speed, leaving some of their number to ambush the trail or double back on it to see if they were pursued.

An hour of patient waiting, in which he never moved from his position, proved the wisdom of his judgment. Suddenly, away at the other end of the grove, he caught a flash of brown, of a living, moving something, like the flitting of a bird behind a tree. Was it a bird or a squirrel? Then again he saw it, almost lost in the shade of the forest. Several minutes passed, in which Wetzel never moved and hardly breathed. The shadow had disappeared behind a tree. He fixed his keen eyes on that tree and presently a dark object glided from it and darted stealthily forward to another tree. One, two, three dark forms followed the first one. They were Indian warriors, and they moved so quickly that only the eyes of a woodsman like Wetzel could have discerned their movements at that distance.

Probably most hunters would have taken to their heels while there was yet time. The thought did not occur to Wetzel. He slowly raised the hammer of his rifle. As the Indians came into plain view he saw they did not suspect his presence, but were returning on the trail in their customary cautious manner.

When the first warrior reached a big oak tree some two hundred yards distant, the long, black barrel of the hunter's rifle began slowly, almost imperceptibly, to rise, and as it reached a level the savage stepped forward from the tree. With the sharp report of the weapon he staggered and fell.

Wetzel sprang up and knowing that his only escape was in rapid flight, with his well known yell, he bounded off at the top of his speed. The remaining Indians discharged their guns at the fleeing, dodging figure, but without effect. So rapidly did he dart in and out among the trees that an effectual aim was impossible. Then, with loud yells, the Indians, drawing their tomahawks, started in pursuit, expecting soon to overtake their victim.

In the early years of his Indian hunting, Wetzel had perfected himself in a practice which had saved his life many times, and had added much to his fame. He could reload his rifle while running at topmost speed. His extraordinary fleetness enabled him to keep ahead of his pursuers until his rifle was reloaded. This trick he now employed. Keeping up his uneven pace until his gun was ready, he turned quickly and shot the nearest Indian dead in his tracks. The next Indian had by this time nearly come up with him and close enough to throw his tomahawk, which whizzed dangerously near Wetzel's head. But he leaped forward again and soon his rifle was reloaded. Every time he looked around the Indians treed, afraid to face his unerring weapon. After running a mile or more in this manner, he reached an open space in the woods where he wheeled suddenly on his pursuers. The foremost Indian jumped behind a tree, but, as it did not entirely screen his body, he, too, fell a victim to the hunter's aim. The Indian must have been desperately wounded, for his companion now abandoned the chase and went to his assistance. Together they disappeared in the forest.

Wetzel, seeing that he was no longer pursued, slackened his pace and proceeded thoughtfully toward the settlement.

* * * * * * * * *

That same day, several hours after Wetzel's departure in quest of the turkey, Alfred Clarke strolled over from the fort and found Colonel Zane in the yard. The Colonel was industriously stirring the contents of a huge copper kettle which swung over a brisk wood fire. The honeyed fragrance of apple-butter mingled with the pungent odor of burning hickory.

"Morning, Alfred, you see they have me at it," was the Colonel's salute.

"So I observe," answered Alfred, as he seated himself on the wood-pile. "What is it you are churning so vigorously?"

"Apple-butter, my boy, apple-butter. I don't allow even Bessie to help when I am making apple-butter."

"Colonel Zane, I have come over to ask a favor. Ever since you notified us that you intended sending an expedition up the river I have been worried about my horse Roger. He is too light for a pack horse, and I cannot take two horses."

"I'll let you have the bay. He is big and strong

enough. That black horse of yours is a beauty. You leave Roger with me and if you never come back I'll be in a fine horse. Ha! Ha! But, seriously, Clarke, this proposed trip is a hazardous undertaking, and if you would rather stay——"

"You misunderstand me," quickly replied Alfred, who had flushed. "I do not care about myself. I'll go and take my medicine. But I do mind about my horse."

"That's right. Always think of your horses. I'll have Sam take the best care of Roger."

"What is the nature of this excursion, and how long shall we be gone?"

"Jonathan will guide the party. He says it will take six weeks if you have pleasant weather. You are to go by way of Short Creek, where you will help put up a blockhouse. Then you go to Fort Pitt. There you will embark on a raft with the supplies I need and make the return journey by water. You will probably smell gunpowder before you get back."

"What shall we do with the horses?"

"Bring them along with you on the raft, of course."

"That is a new way to travel with horses," said Alfred, looking dubiously at the swift river. "Will there be any way to get news from Fort Henry while we are away?"

"Yes, there will be several runners."

"Mr. Clarke, I am going to feed my pets. Would you like to see them?" asked a voice which brought Alfred to his feet. He turned and saw Betty. Her dog followed her, carrying a basket.

"I shall be delighted," answered Alfred. "Have you more pets than Tige and Madcap?"

"Oh, yes, indeed. I have a bear, six squirrels, one of them white, and some pigeons."

Betty led the way to an enclosure adjoining Colonel Zane's barn. It was about twenty feet square, made of pine saplings which had been split and driven firmly into the ground. As Betty took down a bar and opened the small gate a number of white pigeons fluttered down from the roof of the barn, several of them alighting on her shoulders. A half-grown black bear came out of a kennel and shuffled toward her. He was unmistakably glad to see her, but he avoided going near Tige, and looked doubtfully at the young man. But after Alfred had stroked his head and had spoken to him he seemed disposed to be friendly, for he sniffed around Alfred's knees and then stood up and put his paws against the young man's shoulders.

"Here, Cæsar, get down," said Betty. "He always wants to wrestle, especially with anyone of whom he is not suspicious. He is very tame and will do almost anything. Indeed, you would marvel at his intelligence. He never forgets an injury. If anyone plays a trick on him you may be sure that person will not get a second opportunity. The night we caught him Tige chased him up a tree and Jonathan climbed the tree and lassoed him. Ever since he has evinced a hatred of Jonathan, and if I should leave Tige alone with him there would be a terrible fight. But for that I could allow Cæsar to run free about the yard."

"He looks bright and sagacious," remarked Alfred.

"He is, but sometimes he gets into mischief. I nearly died laughing one day. Bessie, my brother's wife, you know, had the big kettle on the fire, just as you saw it a moment ago, only this time she was boiling down maple syrup. Tige was out with some of the men and I let Cæsar loose awhile. If there is anything he loves it is maple sugar, so when he smelled the syrup he pulled down the kettle and the hot syrup went all over his nose. Oh, his howls were dreadful to hear. The funniest part about it was he seemed to think it was intentional, for he remained sulky and cross with me for two weeks."

"I can understand your love for animals," said Alfred. "I think there are many interesting things about wild creatures. There are comparatively few animals down in Virginia where I used to live, and my opportunities to study them have been limited."

"Here are my squirrels," said Betty, unfastening the door of a cage. A number of squirrels ran out. Several jumped to the ground. One perched on top of the box. Another sprang on Betty's shoulder. "I fasten them up every night, for I'm afraid the weasels and foxes will get them. The white squirrel is the only albino we have seen around here. It took Jonathan weeks to trap him, but once captured he soon grew tame. Is he not pretty?"

"He certainly is. I never saw one before; in fact, I did not know such a beautiful little animal existed," answered Alfred, looking in admiration at the graceful creature, as he leaped from the shelf to Betty's arm and ate from her hand, his great, bushy white tail arching over his back and his small pink eyes shining.

"There! Listen," said Betty. "Look at the fox squirrel, the big brownish red one. I call him the Captain, because he always wants to boss the others. I had another fox squirrel, older than this fellow, and he ran things to suit himself, until one day the grays united their forces and routed him. I think they would have killed him had I not freed him. Well, this one is commencing the same way. Do you hear that odd clicking noise? That comes from the Captain's teeth, and he is angry and jealous because I show so much attention to this one. He always does that, and he would fight too if I were not careful. It is a singular fact, though, that the white squirrel has not even a little pugnacity. He either cannot fight, or he is too well behaved. Here, Mr. Clarke, show Snowball this nut, and then hide it in your pocket, and see him find it."

Alfred did as he was told, except that while he

pretended to put the nut in his pocket he really kept it concealed in his hand.

The pet squirrel leaped lightly on Alfred's shoulder, ran over his breast, peeped in all his pockets, and even pushed his cap to one side of his head. Then he ran down Alfred's arm, sniffed in his coat sleeve, and finally wedged a cold little nose between his closed fingers.

"There, he has found it, even though you did not play fair," said Betty, laughing gaily.

Alfred never forgot the picture Betty made standing there with the red cap on her dusky hair, and the loving smile upon her face as she talked to her pets. A white fan-tail pigeon had alighted on her shoulder and was picking daintily at the piece of cracker she held between her lips. The squirrels were all sitting up, each with a nut in his little paws, and each with an alert and cunning look in the corner of his eye, to prevent, no doubt, being surprised out of a portion of his nut. Cæsar was lying on all fours, growling and tearing at his breakfast, while the dog looked on with a superior air, as if he knew they would not have had any breakfast but for him.

"Are you fond of canoeing and fishing?" asked Betty, as they returned to the house.

"Indeed I am. Isaac has taken me out on the river often. Canoeing may be pleasant for a girl, but I never knew one who cared for fishing."

"Now you behold one. I love dear old Izaak Walton. Of course, you have read his books?"

"I am ashamed to say I have not."

"And you say you are a fisherman? Well, you have a great pleasure in store, as well as an opportunity to learn something of the 'contemplative man's recreation.' I shall lend you the books."

"I have not seen a book since I came to Fort Henry."

"I have a fine little library, and you are welcome to

any of my books. But to return to fishing. I love it, and yet I nearly always allow the fish to go free. Sometimes I bring home a pretty sunfish, place him in a tub of water, watch him and try to tame him. But I must admit failure. It is the association which makes fishing so delightful. The canoe gliding down a swift stream, the open air, the blue sky, the birds and trees and flowers—these are what I love. Come and see my canoe."

Thus Betty rattled on as she led the way through the sitting-room and kitchen to Colonel Zane's magazine and store-house which opened into the kitchen. This little low-roofed hut contained a variety of things. Boxes, barrels and farming implements filled one corner; packs of dried skins were piled against the wall; some otter and fox pelts were stretched on the wall, and a number of powder kegs lined a shelf. A slender canoe swung from ropes thrown over the rafters. Alfred slipped it out of the loops and carried it outside.

The canoe was a superb specimen of Indian handiwork. It had a length of fourteen feet and was made of birch bark, stretched over a light framework of basswood. The bow curved gracefully upward, ending in a carved image representing a warrior's head. The sides were beautifully ornamented and decorated in fanciful Indian designs.

"My brother's Indian guide, Tomepomehala, a Shawnee chief, made it for me. You see this design on the bow. The arrow and the arm mean in Indian language, 'The race is to the swift and the strong.' The canoe is very light. See, I can easily carry it," said Betty, lifting it from the grass.

She ran into the house and presently came out with two rods, a book and a basket.

"These are Jack's rods. He cut them out of the heart of ten-year-old basswood trees, so he says. We must be careful of them."

Alfred examined the rods with the eye of a connoisseur and pronounced them perfect.

"These rods have been made by a lover of the art. Anyone with half an eye could see that. What shall we use for bait?" he said.

"Sam got me some this morning."

"Did you expect to go?" asked Alfred, looking up in surprise.

"Yes, I intended going, and as you said you were coming over, I meant to ask you to accompany me."

"That was kind of you."

"Where are you young people going?" called Colonel Zane, stopping in his task.

"We are going down to the sycamore," answered Betty.

"Very well. But be certain and stay on this side of the creek and do not go out on the river," said the Colonel.

"Why, Eb, what do you mean? One might think Mr. Clarke and I were children," exclaimed Betty.

"You certainly aren't much more. But that is not my reason. Never mind the reason. Do as I say or do not go," said Colonel Zane.

"All right, brother. I shall not forget," said Betty, soberly, looking at the Colonel. He had not spoken in his usual teasing way, and she was at a loss to understand him. "Come, Mr. Clarke, you carry the canoe and follow me down this path and look sharp for roots and stones or you may trip."

"Where is Isaac?" asked Alfred, as he lightly swung the canoe over his shoulder.

"He took his rifle and went up to the chestnut grove an hour or more ago."

A few minutes' walk down the willow skirted path and they reached the creek. Here it was a narrow stream, hardly fifty feet wide, shallow, and full of stones over which the clear born water rushed noisily.

"Is it not rather risky going down there?" asked Alfred, as he noticed the swift current and numerous boulders poking treacherous heads just above the water.

"Of course. That is the great pleasure in canoeing," said Betty, calmly. "If you would rather walk——"

"No, I'll go if I drown. I was thinking of you."

"It is safe enough if you can handle a paddle," said Betty, with a smile at his hesitation. "And, of course, if your partner in the canoe sits trim."

"Perhaps you had better allow me to use the paddle. Where did you learn to steer a canoe?"

"I believe you are actually afraid. Why, I was born on the Potomac, and have used a paddle since I was old enough to lift one. Come, place the canoe in here and we will keep to the near shore until we reach the bend. There is a little fall just below this and I love to shoot it."

He steadied the canoe with one hand while he held out the other to help her, but she stepped nimbly aboard without his assistance.

"Wait a moment while I catch some crickets and grasshoppers."

"Gracious! What a fisherman. Don't you know we have had frost?"

"That's so," said Alfred, abashed by her simple remark.

"But you might find some crickets under those logs," said Betty. She laughed merrily at the awkward spectacle made by Alfred crawling over the ground, improvising a sort of trap out of his hat, and pouncing down on a poor little insect.

"Now, get in carefully, and give the canoe a push. There, we are off," she said, taking up the paddle.

The little bark glided slowly down stream, at first hugging the bank as though reluctant to trust itself to the deeper water, and then gathering headway as a few gentle strokes of the paddle swerved it into the current. Betty knelt on one knee and skillfully plied the paddle, using the Indian stroke in which the paddle was not removed from the water.

"This is great!" exclaimed Alfred, as he leaned back in the bow facing her. "There is nothing more to be desired. This beautiful clear stream, the air so fresh, the gold lined banks, the autumn leaves, a guide who——"

"Look," said Betty. "There is the fall over which we must pass."

He looked ahead and saw that they were swiftly approaching two huge stones that reared themselves high out of the water. They were only a few yards apart and surrounded by smaller rocks, about which the water rushed white with foam.

"Please do not move!" cried Betty, her eyes shining bright with excitement.

Indeed, the situation was too novel for Alfred to do anything but feel a keen enjoyment. He had made up his mind that he was sure to get a ducking, but, as he watched Betty's easy, yet vigorous sweeps with the paddle, and her smiling, yet resolute lips, he felt reassured. He could see that the fall was not a great one, only a few feet, but one of those glancing sheets of water like a mill race, and he well knew that if they struck a stone disaster would be theirs. Twenty feet above the white-capped wave which marked the fall, Betty gave a strong forward pull on the paddle, a deep stroke which momentarily retarded their progress even in that swift current, and then, a short backward stroke, far under the stern of the canoe, and the little vessel turned straight, almost in the middle of the course between the two rocks. As she raised her paddle into the canoe and smiled at the fascinated young man, the bow dipped, and with that peculiar downward movement, that swift, exhilarating rush so dearly loved by canoeists, they shot down the smooth incline of water, were lost for a moment in a white cloud of mist, and in another they floated into a placid pool.

"Was not that delightful?" she asked, with just a little conscious pride glowing in her dark eyes.

"Miss Zane, it was more than that. I apologize for my suspicions. You have admirable skill. I only wish that on my voyage down the River of Life I could have such a sure eye and hand to guide me through the dangerous reefs and rapids."

"You are poetical," said Betty, who laughed, and at the same time blushed slightly. "But you are right about the guide. Jonathan says 'always get a good guide,' and as guiding is his work he ought to know. But this has nothing in common with fishing, and here is my favorite place under the old sycamore."

With a long sweep of the paddle she ran the canoe alongside a stone beneath a great tree which spread its long branches over the creek and shaded the pool. It was a grand old tree and must have guarded that sylvan spot for centuries. The gnarled and knotted trunk was scarred and seamed with the ravages of time. The upper part was dead. Long limbs extended skyward, gaunt and bare, like the masts of a storm-beaten vessel. The lower branches were white and shining, relieved here and there by brown patches of bark which curled up like old parchment as they shelled away from the inner bark. The ground beneath the tree was carpeted with a velvety moss with little plots of grass and clusters of maiden-hair fern growing on it. From under an overhanging rock on the bank a spring of crystal water bubbled forth.

Alfred rigged up the rods, and baiting a hook directed Betty to throw her line well out into the current and let it float down into the eddy. She complied, and hardly had the line reached the circle of the eddy, where bits of white foam floated round and round, when there was a slight splash, a scream from Betty and she was standing up in the canoe holding tightly to her rod.

"Be careful!" exclaimed Alfred. "Sit down. You will have the canoe upset in a moment. Hold your rod steady and keep the line taut. That's right. Now lead him round toward me. There," and grasping the line he lifted a fine rock bass over the side of the canoe.

"Oh! I always get so intensely excited," breathlessly cried Betty. "I can't help it. Jonathan always declares he will never take me fishing again. Let me see the fish. It's a goggle-eye. Isn't he pretty? Look how funny he bats his eyes," and she laughed gleefully as she gingerly picked up the fish by the tail and dropped him into the water. "Now, Mr. Goggle-eye, if you are wise, in future you will beware of tempting looking bugs."

For an hour they had splendid sport. The pool teemed with sunfish. The bait would scarcely touch the water when the little orange colored fellows would rush for it. Now and then a black bass darted wickedly through the school of sunfish and stole the morsel from them. Or a sharp-nosed fiery-eyed pickerel—vulture of the water—rising to the surface, and, supreme in his indifference to man or fish, would swim lazily round until he had discovered the cause of all this commotion among the smaller fishes, and then, opening wide his jaws would take the bait with one voracious snap.

Presently something took hold of Betty's line and moved out toward the middle of the pool. She struck and the next instant her rod was bent double and the tip under water.

"Pull your rod up!" shouted Alfred. "Here, hand it to me."

But it was too late. A surge right and left, a vicious tug and Betty's line floated on the surface of the water.

"Now, isn't that too bad? He has broken my line. Goodness, I never before felt such a strong fish. What shall I do?"

"You should be thankful you were not pulled in. I have been in a state of fear ever since we commenced fishing. You move round in this canoe as though it were a raft. Let me paddle out to that little ripple and try once there; then we will stop. I know you are tired."

Near the center of the pool a half submerged rock checked the current and caused a little ripple of the water. Several times Alfred had seen the dark shadow of a large fish followed by a swirl of the water, and the frantic leaping of little bright-sided minnows in all directions. As his hook, baited with a lively shiner, floated over the spot, a long, yellow object shot from out that shaded lair. There was a splash, not unlike that made by the sharp edge of a paddle impelled by a short, powerful stroke, the minnow disappeared, and the broad tail of the fish flapped on the water. The instant Alfred struck, the water boiled and the big fish leaped clear into the air, shaking himself convulsively to get rid of the hook. He made mad rushes up and down the pool, under the canoe, into the swift current and against the rocks, but all to no avail. Steadily Alfred increased the strain on the line and gradually it began to tell, for the plunges of the fish became shorter and less frequent. Once again, in a last magnificent effort, he leaped straight into the air, and failing to get loose, gave up the struggle and was drawn gasping and exhausted to the side of the canoe.

"Are you afraid to touch him?" asked Alfred.

"Indeed I am not," answered Betty.

"Then run your hand gently down the line, slip your fingers in under his gills and lift him over the side carefully."

"Five pounds," exclaimed Alfred, when the fish lay at his feet. "This is the largest black bass I ever caught. It is a pity to take such a beautiful fish out of his element."

"Let him go, then. May I?" said Betty.

"No, you have allowed them all to go, even the pickerel, which I think ought to be killed. We will keep this fellow alive, and place him in that nice clear pool over in the fort yard."

"I like to watch you play a fish," said Betty. "Jonathan always hauls them right out. You are so skillful. You let this fish run so far and then you checked him. Then you gave him a line to go the other way, and no doubt he felt free once more when you stopped him again."

"You are expressing a sentiment which has been, is, and always will be particularly pleasing to the fair sex, I believe," observed Alfred, smiling rather grimly as he wound up his line.

"Would you mind being explicit?" she questioned.

Alfred had laughed and was about to answer when the whip-like crack of a rifle came from the hillside. The echoes of the shot reverberated from hill to hill and were finally lost far down the valley.

"What can that be?" exclaimed Alfred anxiously, recalling Colonel Zane's odd manner when they were about to leave the house.

"I am not sure, but I think that is my turkey, unless Lew Wetzel happened to miss his aim," said Betty, laughing. "And that is such an unprecedented thing that it can hardly be considered. Turkeys are scarce this season. Jonathan says the foxes and wolves ate up the broods. Lew heard this turkey calling and he made little Harry Bennet, who had started out with his gun, stay at home and went after Mr. Gobbler himself."

"Is that all? Well, that is nothing to get alarmed about, is it? I actually had a feeling of fear, or a presentiment, we might say."

They beached the canoe and spread out the lunch in the shade near the spring. Alfred threw himself at length upon the grass and Betty sat leaning against the tree. She took a biscuit in one hand, a pickle in the other, and began to chat volubly to Alfred of her school life, and of Philadelphia, and the friends she had made there. At length, remarking his abstraction, she said: "You are not listening to me."

"I beg your pardon. My thoughts did wander. I was thinking of my mother. Something about you reminds me of her. I do not know what, unless it is that little mannerism you have of pursing up your lips when you hesitate or stop to think."

"Tell me of her," said Betty, seeing his softened mood.

"My mother was very beautiful, and as good as she was lovely. I never had a care until my father died. Then she married again, and as I did not get on with my step-father I ran away from home. I have not been in Virginia for four years."

"Do you get homesick?"

"Indeed I do. While at Fort Pitt I used to have spells of the blues which lasted for days. For a time I felt more contented here. But I fear the old fever of restlessness will come over me again. I can speak freely to you because I know you will understand, and I feel sure of your sympathy. My father wanted me to be a minister. He sent me to the theological seminary at Princeton, where for two years I tried to study. Then my father died. I went home and looked after things until my mother married again. That changed everything for me. I ran away and have since been a wanderer. I feel that I am not lazy, that I am not afraid of work, but four years have drifted by and I have nothing to show for it. I am discouraged. Perhaps that is wrong, but tell me how I can help it. I have not the stoicism of the hunter, Wetzel, nor have I the philosophy of your brother. I could not be content to sit on my doorstep and smoke my pipe and watch the wheat and corn grow. And then, this life of the borderman, environed as it is by untold dangers, leads me, fascinates me, and yet appalls me with the fear that here I shall fall a victim to an Indian's bullet or spear, and find a nameless grave."

A long silence ensued. Alfred had spoken quietly, but with an undercurrent of bitterness that saddened Betty. For the first time she saw a shadow of pain in his eyes. She looked away down the valley, not seeing the brown and gold hills boldly defined against the blue sky, nor the beauty of the river as the setting sun cast a ruddy glow on the water. Her companion's words had touched an unknown chord in her heart. When finally she turned to answer him a beautiful light shone in her eyes, a light that shines not on land or sea—the light of woman's hope.

"Mr. Clarke," she said, and her voice was soft and low, "I am only a girl, but I can understand. You are unhappy. Try to rise above it. Who knows what will befall this little settlement? It may be swept away by the savages, and it may grow to be a mighty city. It must take that chance. So must you, so must we all take chances. You are here. Find your work and do it cheerfully, honestly, and let the future take care of itself. And let me say—do not be offended—beware of idleness and drink. They are as great a danger—nay, greater than the Indians."

"Miss Zane, if you were to ask me not to drink I would never touch a drop again," said Alfred earnestly.

"I did not ask that," answered Betty, flushing slightly. "But I shall remember it as a promise and some day I may ask it of you."

He looked wonderingly at the girl beside him. He had spent most of his life among educated and cultured people. He had passed several years in the backwoods. But with all his experience with people he had to confess that this young woman was a revelation to him. She could ride like an Indian and shoot like a hunter.

He had heard that she could run almost as swiftly as her brothers. Evidently she feared nothing, for he had just seen an example of her courage in a deed that had tried even his own nerve, and, withal, she was a bright, happy girl, earnest and true, possessing all the softer graces of his sisters, and that exquisite touch of feminine delicacy and refinement which appeals more to men than any other virtue.

"Have you not met Mr. Miller before he came here from Fort Pitt?" asked Betty.

"Why do you ask?"

"I think he mentioned something of the kind."

"What else did he say?"

"Why—Mr. Clarke, I hardly remember."

"I see," said Alfred, his face darkening. "He has talked about me. I do not care what he said. I knew him at Fort Pitt, and we had trouble there. I venture to say he has told no one about it. He certainly would not shine in the story. But I am not a tattler."

"It is not very difficult to see that you do not like him. Jonathan does not, either. He says Mr. Miller was friendly with McKee, and the notorious Simon Girty, the soldiers who deserted from Fort Pitt and went to the Indians. The girls like him, however."

"Usually if a man is good looking and pleasant that is enough for the girls. I noticed that he paid you a great deal of attention at the dance. He danced three times with you."

"Did he? How observing you are," said Betty, giving him a little sidelong glance. "Well, he is very agreeable, and he dances better than many of the young men."

"I wonder if Wetzel got the turkey. I have heard no more shots," said Alfred, showing plainly that he wished to change the subject.

"Oh, look there! Quick!" exclaimed Betty, pointing toward the hillside.

He looked in the direction indicated and saw a doe

and a spotted fawn wading into the shallow water. The mother stood motionless a moment, with head erect and long ears extended. Then she dropped her graceful head and drank thirstily of the cool water. The fawn splashed playfully round while its mother was drinking. It would dash a few paces into the stream and then look back to see if its mother approved. Evidently she did not, for she would stop her drinking and call the fawn back to her side with a soft, crooning noise. Suddenly she raised her head, the long ears shot up, and she seemed to sniff the air. She waded through the deeper water to get round a rocky bluff which ran out into the creek. Then she turned and called the little one. The fawn waded until the water reached its knees, then stopped and uttered piteous little bleats. Encouraged by the soft crooning it plunged into the deep water and with great splashing and floundering managed to swim the short distance. Its slender legs shook as it staggered up the bank. Exhausted or frightened, it shrank close to its mother. Together they disappeared in the willows which fringed the side of the hill.

"Was not that little fellow cute? I have had several fawns, but have never had the heart to keep them," said Betty. Then, as Alfred made no motion to speak, she continued:

"You do not seem very talkative."

"I have nothing to say. You will think me dull. The fact is when I feel deepest I am least able to express myself."

"I will read to you," said Betty, taking up the book. He lay back against the grassy bank and gazed dreamily at the many hued trees on the little hillside; at the bare rugged sides of McColloch's Rock which frowned down upon them. A silver-breasted eagle sailed slowly round and round in the blue sky, far above the bluff. Alfred wondered what mysterious power sustained that solitary bird as he floated high in the air without perceptible movement of his broad wings. He envied the king of birds his reign over that illimitable space, his far-reaching vision, and his freedom. Round and round the eagle soared, higher and higher, with each perfect circle, and at last, for an instant poising as lightly as if he were about to perch on his lonely crag, he arched his wings and swooped down through the air with the swiftness of a falling arrow.

Betty's low voice, the water rushing so musically over the falls, the great yellow leaves falling into the pool, the gentle breeze stirring the clusters of golden-rod—all came softly to Alfred as he lay there with half closed eyes.

The time slipped swiftly by as only such time can.

"I fear the melancholy spirit of the day has prevailed upon you," said Betty, half wistfully. "You did not know I had stopped reading, and I do not believe you heard my favorite poem. I have tried to give you a pleasant afternoon and have failed."

"No, no," said Alfred, looking at her with a blue flame in his eyes. "The afternoon has been perfect. I have forgotten my role, and have allowed you to see my real self, something I have tried to hide from all."

"And are you always sad when you are sincere?"

"Not always. But I am often sad. Is it any wonder? Is not all nature sad? Listen! There is the song of the oriole. Breaking in on the stillness it is mournful. The breeze is sad, the brook is sad, this dying Indian summer day is sad. Life itself is sad."

"Oh, no. Life is beautiful."

"You are a child," said he, with a thrill in his deep voice. "I hope you may always be as you are today, in heart, at least."

"It grows late. See, the shadows are falling. We must go."

"You know I am going away tomorrow. I don't want to go. Perhaps that is why I have been such poor company today. I have a presentiment of evil. I am afraid I may never come back."

"I am sorry you must go."

"Do you really mean that?" asked Alfred, earnestly, bending toward her. "You know it is a very dangerous undertaking. Would you care if I never returned?"

She looked up and their eyes met. She had raised her head haughtily, as if questioning his right to speak to her in that manner, but as she saw the unspoken appeal in his eyes her own wavered and fell while a warm color crept into her cheek.

"Yes, I would be sorry," she said, gravely. Then, after a moment: "You must portage the canoe round the falls, and from there we can paddle back to the path."

The return trip made, they approached the house. As they turned the corner they saw Colonel Zane standing at the door talking to Wetzel. They saw that the Colonel looked pale and distressed, and the face of the hunter was dark and gloomy.

"Lew, did you get my turkey?" said Betty, after a moment of hesitation. A nameless fear filled her breast.

For answer Wetzel threw back the flaps of his coat and there at his belt hung a small tuft of black hair. Betty knew at once it was the scalp-lock of an Indian. Her face turned white and she placed a hand on the hunter's arm.

"What do you mean? That is an Indian's scalp. Lew, you look so strange. Tell me, is it because we went off in the canoe and have been in danger?"

"Betty, Isaac has been captured again," said the Colonel.

"Oh, no, no, no," cried Betty in agonized tones, and wringing her hands. Then, excitedly, "Something can be done. You must pursue them. Oh, Lew, Mr. Clarke, cannot you rescue him? They have not had time to go far."

"Isaac went to the chestnut grove this morning. If he

had stayed there he would not have been captured. But he went far into the Black Forest. The turkey call we heard across the creek was made by a Wyandot concealed in the cave. Lewis tells me that a number of Indians have camped there for days. He shot the one who was calling and followed the others until he found where they had taken Isaac's trail."

Betty turned to the younger man with tearful eyes, and with beseeching voice implored them to save her brother.

"I am ready to follow you," said Clarke to Wetzel.

The hunter shook his head, but did not answer.

"It is that hateful White Crane," passionately burst out Betty, as the Colonel's wife led her weeping into the house.

"Did you get more than one shot at them?" asked Clarke.

The hunter nodded, and the slight, inscrutable smile flitted across his stern features. He never spoke of his deeds. For this reason many of the thrilling adventures which he must have had will forever remain unrevealed. That evening there was sadness at Colonel Zane's supper table. They felt the absence of the Colonel's usual spirits, his teasing of Betty, and his cheerful conversation. He had nothing to say. Betty sat at the table a little while, and then got up and left the room saying she could not eat. Jonathan, on hearing of his brother's recapture, did not speak, but retired in gloomy silence. Silas was the only one of the family who was not utterly depressed. He said it could have been a great deal worse; that they must make the best of it, and that the sooner Isaac married his Indian Princess the better for his scalp and for the happiness of all concerned.

"I remember Myeerah very well," he said. "It was eight years ago, and she was only a child. Even then she was very proud and willful, and the loveliest girl I ever laid eyes on."

Alfred Clarke stayed late at Colonel Zane's that night. Before going away for so many weeks he wished to have a few more moments alone with Betty. But a favorable opportunity did not present itself during the evening, so when he had bade them all goodbye and goodnight, except Betty, who opened the door for him, he said softly to her:

"It is bright moonlight outside. Come, please, and walk to the gate with me."

A full moon shone serenely down on hill and dale, flooding the valley with its pure white light, and bathing the pastures in its glory; at the foot of the bluff the waves of the river gleamed like myriads of stars all twinkling and dancing on a bed of snowy clouds. Thus illumined the river wound down the valley, its brilliance growing fainter and fainter until at last, resembling the shimmering of a silver thread which joined the earth to heaven, it disappeared in the horizon.

"I must say goodbye," said Alfred, as they reached the gate.

"Friends must part. I am sorry you must go, Mr. Clarke, and I trust you may return safe. It seems only yesterday that you saved my brother's life, and I was so grateful and happy. Now he is gone."

"You should not think about it so much nor brood over it," answered the young man. "Grieving will not bring him back nor do you any good. It is not nearly so bad as if he had been captured by some other tribe. Wetzel assures us that Isaac was taken alive. Please do not grieve."

"I have cried until I cannot cry any more. I am so unhappy. We were children together, and I have always loved him better than any one since my mother died. To have him back again and then to lose him! Oh! I cannot bear it."

She covered her face with her hands and a low sob escaped her.

"Don't, don't grieve," he said in an unsteady voice, as he took the little hands in his and pulled them away from her face.

Betty trembled. Something in his voice, a tone she had never heard before startled her. She looked up at him half unconscious that he still held her hands in his. Never had she appeared so lovely.

"You cannot understand my feelings."

"I loved my mother."

"But you have not lost her. That makes all the difference."

"I want to comfort you and I am powerless. I am unable to say what—I——"

He stopped short. As he stood gazing down into her sweet face, burning, passionate words came to his lips; but he was dumb; he could not speak. All day long he had been living in a dream. Now he realized that but a moment remained for him to be near the girl he loved so well. He was leaving her, perhaps never to see her again, or to return to find her another's. A fierce pain tore his heart.

"You—you are holding my hands," faltered Betty, in a doubtful, troubled voice. She looked up into his face and saw that it was pale with suppressed emotion.

Alfred was mad indeed. He forgot everything. In that moment the world held nothing for him save that fair face. Her eyes, uplifted to his in the moonlight, beamed with a soft radiance. They were honest eyes, just now filled with innocent sadness and regret, but they drew him with irresistible power. Without realizing in the least what he was doing he yielded to the impulse. Bending his head he kissed the tremulous lips.

"Oh," whispered Betty, standing still as a statue and looking at him with wonderful eyes. Then, as reason returned, a hot flush dyed her face, and wrenching her hands free she struck him across the cheek.

"For God's sake, Betty, I did not mean to do that! Wait. I have something to tell you. For pity's sake, let me explain," he cried, as the full enormity of his offense dawned upon him.

Betty was deaf to the imploring voice, for she ran into the house and slammed the door.

He called to her, but received no answer. He knocked on the door, but it remained closed. He stood still awhile, trying to collect his thoughts, and to find a way to undo the mischief he had wrought. When the real significance of his act came to him he groaned in spirit. What a fool he had been! Only a few short hours and he must start on a perilous journey, leaving the girl he loved in ignorance of his real intentions. Who was to tell her that he loved her? Who was to tell her that it was because his whole heart and soul had gone to her that he had kissed her?

With bowed head he slowly walked away toward the fort, totally oblivious of the fact that a young girl, with hands pressed tightly over her breast to try to still a madly beating heart, watched him from her window until he disappeared into the shadow of the blockhouse.

Alfred paced up and down his room the four remaining hours of that eventful day. When the light was breaking in at the east and dawn near at hand he heard the rough voices of men and the tramping of iron-shod hoofs. The hour of his departure was at hand.

He sat down at his table and by the aid of the dim light from a pine knot he wrote a hurried letter to Betty. A little hope revived in his heart as he thought that perhaps all might yet be well. Surely some one would be up to whom he could intrust the letter, and if no one he would run over and slip it under the door of Colonel Zane's house.

In the gray of the early morning Alfred rode out with the daring band of heavily armed men, all grim and stern, each silent with the thought of the man who knows he may never return. Soon the settlement was left far behind.

Chapter 5

DURING THE last few days, in which the frost had cracked open the hickory nuts, and in which the squirrels had been busily collecting and storing away their supply of nuts for winter use, it had been Isaac's wont to shoulder his rifle, walk up the hill, and spend the morning in the grove.

On this crisp autumn morning he had started off as usual, and had been called back by Col. Zane, who advised him not to wander far from the settlement. This admonition, kind and brotherly though it was, annoyed Isaac. Like all the Zanes he had born in him an intense love for the solitude of the wilderness. There were times when nothing could satisfy him but the calm of the deep woods.

One of these mods possessed him now. Courageous to a fault and daring where daring was not always the wiser part, Isaac lacked the practical sense of the Colonel and the cool judgment of Jonathan. Impatient of restraint, independent in spirit, and it must be admitted, in his persistence in doing as he liked instead of what he ought to do, he resembled Betty more than he did his brothers.

Feeling secure in his ability to take care of himself, for he knew he was an experienced hunter and woodsman, he resolved to take a long tramp in the forest. This resolution was strengthened by the fact that he did not believe what the Colonel and Jonathan had told him—that it was not improbable some of the Wyandot braves were lurking in the vicinity, bent on killing or recapturing him. At any rate he did not fear it.

Once in the shade of the great trees the fever of discontent left him, and, forgetting all except the happiness of being surrounded by the silent oaks, he penetrated deeper and deeper into the forest. The brushing of a branch against a tree, the thud of a falling nut, the dart of a squirrel, and the sight of a bushy tail disappearing round a limb—all these things which indicated that the little gray fellows were working in the treetops, and which would usually have brought Isaac to a standstill, now did not seem to interest him. At times he stooped to examine the tender shoots growing at the foot of a sassafras tree. Then, again, he closely examined marks he found in the soft banks of the streams.

He went on and on. Two hours of this still-hunting found him on the bank of a shallow gully through which a brook went rippling and babbling over the mossy green stones. The forest was dense here; rugged oaks and tall poplars grew high over the tops of the first growth of white oaks and beeches; the wild grapevines which coiled round the trees like gigantic serpents, spread out in the upper branches and obscured the sun; witch-hopples and laurel bushes grew thickly; monarchs of the forest, felled by some bygone storm, lay rotting on the ground; and in places the wind-falls were so thick and high as to be impenetrable.

Isaac hesitated. He realized that he had plunged far into the Black Forest. Here it was gloomy; a dreamy quiet prevailed, that deep calm of the wilderness, unbroken save for the distant note of the hermit-thrush, the strange bird whose lonely cry, given at long intervals, pierced the stillness. Although Isaac had never seen one of these birds, he was familiar with that cry which was never heard except in the deepest woods, far from the haunts of man.

A black squirrel ran down a tree and seeing the hunter scampered away in alarm. Isaac knew the habits of the black squirrel, that it was a denizen of the wildest woods and frequented only places remote from civilization. The song of the hermit and the sight of the black squirrel caused Isaac to stop and reflect, with the result that he concluded he had gone much farther from the fort than he had intended. He turned to retrace his steps when a faint sound from down the ravine came to his sharp ears.

There was no instinct to warn him that a hideously painted face was raised a moment over the clump of laurel bushes to his left, and that a pair of keen eyes watched every move he made.

Unconscious of impending evil Isaac stopped and looked around him. Suddenly above the musical babble of the brook and the rustle of the leaves by the breeze came a repetition of the sound. He crouched close by the trunk of a tree and strained his ears. All was quiet for some moments. Then he heard the patter, patter of little hoofs coming down the stream. Nearer and nearer they came. Sometimes they were almost inaudible and again he heard them clearly and distinctly. Then there came a splashing and the faint hollow sound caused by hard hoofs striking the stones in shallow water. Finally the sounds ceased.

Cautiously peering from behind the tree Isaac saw a doe standing on the bank fifty yards down the brook. Trembling she had stopped as if in doubt or uncertainty. Her ears pointed straight upward, and she lifted one front foot from the ground like a thoroughbred pointer. Isaac knew a doe always led the way through the woods and if there were other deer they would come up unless warned by the doe. Presently the willows parted and a magnificent buck with wide spreading antlers stepped out and stood motionless on the bank. Although they were down the wind Isaac knew the deer suspected some hidden danger. They looked steadily at the clump of laurels at Isaac's left, a circumstance he remarked at the time, but did not understand the real significance of until long afterward.

Following the ringing report of Isaac's rifle the buck sprang almost across the stream, leaped convulsively up the bank, reached the top, and then his strength failing, slid down into the stream, where, in his dying struggles, his hoofs beat the water into white foam. The doe had disappeared like a brown flash.

Isaac, congratulating himself on such a fortunate shot—for rarely indeed does a deer fall dead in his tracks even when shot through the heart—rose from his crouching position and commenced to reload his rifle. With great care he poured the powder into the palm of his hand, measuring the quantity with his eye—for it was an evidence of a hunter's skill to be able to get the proper quantity for the ball. Then he put the charge into the barrel. Placing a little greased linsey rag, about half an inch square, over the muzzle, he laid a small lead bullet on it, and with the ramrod began to push the ball into the barrel.

A slight rustle behind him, which sounded to him like the gliding of a rattlesnake over the leaves, caused him to start and turn round. But he was too late. A crushing blow on the head from a club in the hand of a brawny Indian laid him senseless on the ground.

When Isaac regained his senses he felt a throbbing pain in his head, and when he opened his eyes he was so dizzy that he was unable to discern objects clearly. After a few moments his sight returned. When he had struggled to a sitting posture he discovered that his hands were bound with buckskin thongs. By his side he saw two long poles of basswood, with some strips of green bark and pieces of grapevine laced across and tied fast to the poles. Evidently this had served as a litter on which he had been carried. From his wet clothes and the position of the sun, now low in the west, he concluded he had been brought across the river and was now miles from the fort. In front of him he saw three Indians sitting before a fire. One of them was cutting thin slices from a haunch of deer meat, another was drinking from a gourd, and the third was roasting a piece of venison which he held on a sharpened stick. Isaac knew at once the Indians were Wyandots, and he saw they were in full war paint. They were not young braves, but middle aged warriors. One of them Isaac recognized as Crow, a chief of one of the Wyandot tribes, and a warrior renowned for his daring and for his ability to make his way in a straight line through the wilderness. Crow was a short, heavy Indian and his frame denoted great strength. He had a broad forehead, high cheek bones, prominent nose, and his face would have been handsome and intelligent but for the scar which ran across his cheek, giving him a sinister look.

"Hugh!" said Crow, as he looked up and saw Isaac staring at him. The other Indians immediately gave vent to a like exclamation.

"Crow, you have caught me again," said Isaac, in the Wyandot tongue, which he spoke fluently.

"The white chief is sure of eye and swift of foot, but he cannot escape the Huron. Crow has been five times on his trail since the moon was bright. The white chief's eyes were shut and his ears were deaf," answered the Indian loftily.

"How long have you been near the fort?"

"Two moons have the warriors of Myeerah hunted the pale face."

"Have you any more Indians with you?"

The chief nodded and said a party of nine Wyandots had been in the vicinity of Wheeling for a month. He named some of the warriors.

Isaac was surprised to learn of the renowned chiefs

who had been sent to recapture him. Not to mention Crow, the Delaware chiefs Son-of-Wingenund and Wapatomeka were among the most cunning and sagacious Indians of the west. Isaac reflected that his year's absence from Myeerah had not caused her to forget him.

Crow untied Isaac's hands and gave him water and venison. Then he picked up his rifle and with a word to the Indians he stepped into the underbrush that skirted the little dale, and was lost to view.

Isaac's head ached and throbbed so that after he had satisfied his thirst and hunger he was glad to close his eyes and lean back against the tree. Engrossed in thoughts of the home he might never see again, he had lain there an hour without moving, when he was aroused from his meditations by low guttural exclamations from the Indians. Opening his eyes he saw Crow and another Indian enter the glade, leading and half supporting a third savage.

They helped this Indian to the log, where he sat down slowly and wearily, holding one hand over his breast. He was a magnificent specimen of Indian manhood, almost a giant in stature, with broad shoulders in proportion to his height. His head-dress and the gold rings which encircled his bare muscular arms indicated that he was a chief high in power. The seven eagle plumes in his scalp-lock represented seven warriors that he had killed in battle. Little sticks of wood plaited in his coal black hair and painted different colors showed to an Indian eye how many times this chief had been wounded by bullet, knife, or tomahawk.

His face was calm. If he suffered he allowed no sign of it to escape him. He gazed thoughtfully into the fire, slowly the while untying the belt which contained his knife and tomahawk. The weapons were raised and held before him, one in each hand, and then waved on high. The action was repeated three times. Then slowly and reluctantly the Indian lowered them as if he knew their work on earth was done.

It was growing dark and the bright blaze from the camp fire lighted up the glade, thus enabling Isaac to see the drooping figure on the log, and in the background Crow, holding a whispered consultation with the other Indians. Isaac heard enough of the colloquy to guess the facts. The chief had been desperately wounded; the palefaces were on their trail, and a march must be commenced at once.

Isaac knew the wounded chief. He was the Delaware Son-of-Wingenund. He married a Wyandot squaw, had spent much of his time in the Wyandot village and on warring expeditions which the two friendly nations made on other tribes. Isaac had hunted with him, slept under the same blanket with him, and had grown to like him.

As Isaac moved slightly in his position the chief saw him. He straightened up, threw back the hunting shirt and pointed to a small hole in his broad breast. A slender stream of blood issued from the wound and flowed down his chest.

"Wind-of-Death is a great white chief. His gun is always loaded," he said calmly, and a look of pride gleamed across his dark face, as though he gloried in the wound made by such a warrior.

"Deathwind" was one of the many names given to Wetzel by the savages, and a thrill of hope shot through Isaac's heart when he saw the Indians feared Wetzel was on their track. This hope was short lived, however, for when he considered the probabilities of the thing he knew that pursuit would only result in his death before the settlers could come up with the Indians, and he concluded that Wetzel, familiar with every trick of the redmen would be the first to think of the hopelessness of rescuing him and so would not attempt it.

The four Indians now returned to the fire and stood

beside the chief. It was evident to them that his end
was imminent. He sang in a low, not unmusical tone
the death-chant of the Hurons. His companions silently
bowed their heads. When he had finished singing he
slowly rose to his great height, showing a commanding
figure. Slowly his features lost their stern pride, his face
softened, and his dark eyes, gazing straight into the
gloom of the forest, bespoke a superhuman vision.

"Wingenund has been a great chief. He has crossed
his last trail. The deeds of Wingenund will be told in
the wigwams of the Lenape," said the chief in a loud
voice, and then sank back into the arms of his comrades. They laid him gently down.

A convulsive shudder shook the stricken warrior's
frame. Then, starting up he straightened out his long
arm and clutched wildly at the air with his sinewy
fingers as if to grasp and hold the life that was escaping
him.

Isaac could see the fixed, sombre light in the eyes,
and the pallor of death stealing over the face of the
chief. He turned his eyes away from the sad spectacle,
and when he looked again the majestic figure lay still.

The moon sailed out from behind a cloud and shed
its mellow light down on the little glade. It showed the
four Indians digging a grave beneath the oak tree. No
word was spoken. They worked with their tomahawks
on the soft duff and soon their task was completed. A
bed of moss and ferns lined the last resting place of the
chief. His weapons were placed beside him, to go with
him to the Happy Hunting Ground, the eternal home
of the redmen, where the redmen believe the sun will
always shine, and where they will be free from their
cruel white foes.

When the grave had been filled and the log rolled on
it the Indians stood by it a moment, each speaking a
few words in a low tone, while the night wind moaned
the dead chief's requiem through the tree tops.

Accustomed as Isaac was to the bloody conflicts common to the Indians, and to the tragedy that surrounded the life of a borderman, the ghastly sight had unnerved him. The last glimpse of that stern, dark face, of that powerful form, as the moon brightened up the spot in seeming pity, he felt he could never forget. His thoughts were interrupted by the harsh voice of Crow bidding him get up. He was told that the slightest inclination on his part to lag behind on the march before them, or in any way to make their trail plainer, would be the signal for his death. With that Crow cut the thongs which bound Isaac's legs and placing him between two of the Indians, led the way into the forest.

Moving like spectres in the moonlight they marched on and on for hours. Crow was well named. He led them up the stony ridges where their footsteps left no mark, and where even a dog could not find their trail; down into the valleys and into the shallow streams where the running water would soon wash away all trace of their tracks; then out on the open plain, where the soft, springy grass retained little impress of their moccasins.

Single file they marched in the leader's tracks as he led them onward through the dark forests, out under the shining moon, never slacking his rapid pace, ever in a straight line, and yet avoiding the roughest going with that unerring instinct which was this Indian's gift. Toward dawn the moon went down, leaving them in darkness, but this made no difference, for, guided by the stars, Crow kept straight on his course. Not till break of day did he come to a halt.

Then, on the banks of a narrow stream, the Indians kindled a fire and broiled some of the venison. Crow told Isaac he could rest, so he made haste to avail himself of the permission, and almost instantly was wrapped in the deep slumber of exhaustion. Three of the Indians followed suit, and Crow stood guard. Sleepless, tireless, he paced to and fro on the bank, his keen eyes vigilant for signs of pursuers.

The sun was high when the party resumed their flight toward the west. Crow plunged into the brook and waded several miles before he took to the woods on the other shore. Isaac suffered severely from the sharp and slippery stones, which in no wise bothered the Indians. His feet were cut and bruised; still he struggled on without complaining. They rested part of the night, and the next day the Indians, now deeming themselves practically safe from pursuit, did not exercise unusual care to conceal their trail.

That evening about dusk they came to a rapidly flowing stream which ran northwest. Crow and one of the other Indians parted the willows on the bank at this point and dragged forth a long birch-bark canoe which they ran into the stream. Isaac recognized the spot. It was near the head of Mad River, the river which ran through the Wyandot settlements.

Two of the Indians took the bow, the third Indian and Isaac sat in the middle, back to back, and Crow knelt in the stern. Once launched on that wild ride Isaac forgot his weariness and his bruises. The night was beautiful; he loved the water, and was not lacking in sentiment. He gave himself up to the charm of the silver moonlight, of the changing scenery, and the musical gurgle of the water. Had it not been for the cruel face of Crow, he could have imagined himself on one of those enchanted canoes in fairyland, of which he had read when a boy. Ever varying pictures presented themselves as the canoe, impelled by vigorous arms, flew over the shining bosom of the stream. Here, in a sharp bend, was a narrow place where the trees on each bank interlaced their branches and hid the moon, making a dark and dim retreat. Then came a short series of ripples, with merry, bouncing waves and foamy currents; below lay a long, smooth reach of water, deep and placid, mirroring the moon and the countless stars. Noiseless as a shadow the canoe glided down this stretch, the paddle dipping regularly, flashing brightly, and scattering diamond drops in the clear moonlight.

Another turn in the stream and a sound like the roar of an approaching storm as it is borne on a rising wind, broke the silence. It was the roar of rapids or falls. The stream narrowed; the water ran swifter; rocky ledges rose on both sides, gradually getting higher and higher. Crow rose to his feet and looked ahead. Then he dropped to his knees and turned the head of the canoe into the middle of the stream. The roar became deafening. Looking forward Isaac saw that they were entering a dark gorge. In another moment the canoe pitched over a fall and shot between two high, rocky bluffs. These walls ran up almost perpendicularly two hundred feet; the space between was scarcely twenty feet wide, and the water fairly screamed as it rushed madly through its narrow passage. In the center it was like a glancing sheet of glass, weird and dark, and was bordered on the sides by white, seething foam-capped waves which tore and dashed and leaped at their stony confines.

Though the danger was great, though Death lurked in those jagged stones and in those black walls Isaac felt no fear; he knew the strength of that arm, now rigid and again moving with lightning swiftness; he knew the power of the eye which guided them.

Once more out under the starry sky; rifts, shallows, narrows, and lake-like basins were passed swiftly. At length as the sky was becoming gray in the east, they passed into the shadow of what was called the Standing Stone. This was a peculiarly shaped stone-faced bluff, standing high over the river, and taking its name from Tarhe, or Standing Stone, chief of all the Hurons.

At the first sight of that well known landmark, which stood by the Wyandot village, there mingled with

Isaac's despondency and resentment some other feeling
that was akin to pleasure; with a quickening of the
pulse came a confusion of expectancy and bitter memories as he thought of the dark eyed maiden from
whom he had fled a year ago.

"Co-wee-Co-wee," called out one of the Indians in
the bow of the canoe. The signal was heard, for immediately an answering shout came from the shore.

When a few moments later the canoe grated softly
upon a pebbly beach, Isaac saw, indistinctly in the
morning mist, the faint outlines of tepees and wigwams,
and he knew he was once more in the encampment of
the Wyandots.

    *   *   *   *   *   *   *   *   *

Late in the afternoon of that day Isaac was awakened from his heavy slumber and told that the chief
had summoned him. He got up from the buffalo robes
upon which he had flung himself that · morning,
stretched his aching limbs, and walked to the door of
the lodge.

The view before him was so familiar that it seemed
as if he had suddenly come home after being absent a
long time. The last rays of the setting sun shone ruddy
and bright over the top of the Standing Stone; they
touched the scores of lodges and wigwams which dotted
the little valley; they crimsoned the swift, narrow river,
rushing noisily over its rocky bed. The banks of the
stream were lined with rows of canoes; here and there a
bridge made of a single tree spanned the stream. From
the campfires long, thin columns of blue smoke curled
lazily upward; giant maple trees, in their garb of purple
and gold, rose high above the wigwams, adding a further beauty to this peaceful scene.

As Isaac was led down a lane between two long lines
of tepees the watching Indians did not make the
demonstration that usually marked the capture of

a paleface. Some of the old squaws looked up from their work round the campfires and steaming kettles and grinned as the prisoner passed. The braves who were sitting upon their blankets and smoking their long pipes, or lounging before the warm blaze, maintained a stolid indifference; the dusky maidens smiled shyly, and the little Indian boys, with whom Isaac had always been a great favorite, manifested their joy by yelling and running after him. One youngster grasped Isaac round the leg and held on until he was pulled away.

In the center of the village were several lodges connected with one another and larger and more imposing than the surrounding tepees. These were the wigwams of the chief, and thither Isaac was conducted. The guards led him to a large and circular apartment and left him there alone. This room was the council-room. It contained nothing but a low seat and a knotted war-club.

Isaac heard the rattle of beads and bear claws, and as he turned a tall and majestic Indian entered the room. It was Tarhe, the chief of all the Wyandots. Though Tarhe was over seventy, he walked erect; his calm face, dark as a bronze mask, showed no trace of his advanced age. Every line and feature of his face had race in it; the high forehead, the square, protruding jaw, the stern mouth, the falcon eyes—all denoted the pride and unbending will of the last of the Tarhes.

"The White Eagle is again in the power of Tarhe," said the chief in his native tongue. "Though he had the swiftness of the bounding deer or the flight of the eagle it would avail him not. The wild geese as they fly northward are not swifter than the warriors of Tarhe. Swifter than all is the vengeance of the Huron. The young paleface has cost the lives of some great warriors. What has he to say?"

"It was not my fault," answered Isaac quickly. "I was struck down from behind and had no chance to use a weapon. I have never raised my hand against a Wyandot. Crow will tell you that. If my people and friends kill your braves I am not to blame. Yet I have had good cause to shed Huron blood. Your warriors have taken me from my home and have wounded me many times."

"The White Chief speaks well. Tarhe believes his words," answered Tarhe in his sonorous voice. "The Lenapee seek the death of the pale face. Wingenund grieves for his son. He is Tarhe's friend. Tarhe is old and wise and he is king here. He can save the White Chief from Wingenund and Corn-planter. Listen. Tarhe is old and he has no son. He will make you a great chief and give you lands and braves and honors. He shall not ask you to raise your hand against your people, but help to bring peace. Tarhe does not love this war. He wants only justice. He wants only to keep his lands, his horses, and his people. The White Chief is known to be brave; his step is light, his eye is keen, and his bullet is true. For many long moons Tarhe's daughter has been like the singing bird without its mate. She sings no more. She shall be the White Chief's wife. She has the blood of her mother and not that of the last of the Tarhes. Thus the mistakes of Tarhe's youth come to disappoint his old age. He is the friend of the young paleface. Tarhe has said. Now go and make your peace with Myeerah."

The chief motioned toward the back of the lodge. Isaac stepped forward and went through another large room, evidently the chief's, as it was fitted up with a wild and barbaric splendor. Isaac hesitated before a bearskin curtain at the farther end of the chief's lodge. He had been there many times before, but never with such conflicting emotions. What was it that made his heart beat faster? With a quick movement he lifted the curtain and passed under it.

The room which he entered was circular in shape

and furnished with all the bright colors and luxuriance known to the Indian. Buffalo robes covered the smooth, hard-packed clay floor; animals, allegorical pictures, and fanciful Indian designs had been painted on the wall; bows and arrows, shields, strings of bright-colored beads and Indian scarfs hung round the room. The wall was made of dried deerskins sewed together and fastened over long poles which were planted in the ground and bent until the ends met overhead. An oval-shaped opening let in the light. Through a narrow aperture, which served as a door leading to a smaller apartment, could be seen a low couch covered with red blankets, and a glimpse of many hued garments hanging on the wall.

As Isaac entered the room a slender maiden ran impulsively to him and throwing her arms round his neck hid her face on his breast. A few broken, incoherent words escaped her lips. Isaac disengaged himself from the clinging arms and put her from him. The face raised to his was strikingly beautiful. Oval in shape, it was as white as his own, with a broad, low brow and regular features. The eyes were large and dark and they dilated and quickened with a thousand shadows of thought.

"Myeerah, I am taken again. This time there has been blood shed. The Delaware chief was killed, and I do not know how many more Indians. The chiefs are all for putting me to death. I am in great danger. Why could you not leave me in peace?"

At his first words the maiden sighed and turned sorrowfully and proudly away from the angry face of the young man. A short silence ensued.

"Then you are not glad to see Myeerah?" she said, in English. Her voice was music. It rang low, sweet, clear-toned as a bell.

"What has that to do with it? Under some circumstances I would be glad to see you. But to be dragged back here and perhaps murdered—no, I don't welcome it. Look at this mark where Crow hit me," said Isaac, passionately, bowing his head to enable her to see the bruise where the club had struck him.

"I am sorry," said Myeerah, gently.

"I know that I am in great danger from the Delawares."

"The daughter of Tarhe has saved your life before and will save it again."

"They may kill me in spite of you."

"They will not dare. Do not forget that I saved you from the Shawnees. What did my father say to you?"

"He assured me that he was my friend and that he would protect me from Wingenund. But I must marry you and become one of the tribe. I cannot do that. And that is why I am sure they will kill me."

"You are angry now. I will tell you. Myeerah tried hard to win your love, and when you ran away from her she was proud for a long time. But there was no singing of birds, no music of the waters, no beauty in anything after you left her. Life became unbearable without you. Then Myeerah remembered that she was a daughter of kings. She summoned the bravest and greatest warriors of two tribes and said to them, 'Go and bring to me the paleface, White Eagle. Bring him to me alive or dead. If alive, Myeerah will smile once more upon her warrior. If dead, she will look once upon his face and die.' Ever since Myeerah was old enough to remember she has thought of you. Would you wish her to be inconstant, like the moon?"

"It is not that I wish you to be. It is that I cannot live always without seeing my people. I told you that a year ago."

"You told me other things in that past time before you ran away. They were tender words that were sweet to the ear of the Indian maiden. Have you forgotten them?"

"I have not forgotten them. I am not without feeling. You do not understand. Since I have been home this last time I have realized more than ever that I could not live away from my home."

"Is there any maiden in your old home whom you have learned to love more than Myeerah?"

He did not reply, but looked gloomily out of the opening in the wall. Myeerah had placed her hand upon his arm, and as he did not answer the hand tightened its grasp.

"She shall never have you."

The low tones vibrated with intense feeling, with a deathless resolve. Isaac laughed bitterly and looked up at her. Myeerah's face was pale and her eyes burned like fire.

"I should not be surprised if you gave me up to the Delawares," said Isaac, coldly. "I am prepared for it, and I would not care very much. I have despaired of your ever becoming civilized enough to understand the misery of my sister and family. Why not let the Indians kill me?"

He knew how to wound her. A quick, shuddering cry broke from her lips. She stood before him with bowed head and wept. When she spoke again her voice was broken and pleading.

"You are cruel and unjust. Though Myeerah has Indian blood she is a white woman. She can feel as your people do. In your anger and bitterness you forget that Myeerah saved you from the knife of the Shawnees. You forget her tenderness; you forget that she nursed you when you were wounded. Myeerah has a heart to break. Has she not suffered? Is she not laughed at, scorned, called a 'paleface' by the other tribes? She thanks the Great Spirit for the Indian blood that keeps her true. The white man changes his loves and his wives. That is not an Indian gift."

"No, Myeerah, I did not say so. There is no other

woman. It is that I am wretched and sick at heart. Do you not see that this will end in a tragedy some day? Can you not realize that we would be happier if you would let me go? If you love me you would not want to see me dead. If I do not marry you they will kill me; if I try to escape again they will kill me. Let me go free."

"I cannot! I cannot!" she cried. "You have taught me many of the ways of your people, but you cannot change my nature."

"Why cannot you free me?"

"I love you, and I will not live without you."

"Then come and go to my home and live there with me," said Isaac, taking the weeping maiden in his arms. "I know that my people will welcome you."

"Myeerah would be pitied and scorned," she said, sadly, shaking her head.

Isaac tried hard to steel his heart against her, but he was only mortal and he failed. The charm of her presence influenced him; her love wrung tenderness from him. Those dark eyes, so proud to all others, but which gazed wistfully and yearningly into his, stirred his heart to its depths. He kissed the tear-wet cheeks and smiled upon her.

"Well, since I am a prisoner once more, I must make the best of it. Do not look so sad. We shall talk of this another day. Come, let us go and find my little friend, Captain Jack. He remembered me, for he ran out and grasped my knee and they pulled him away."

Chapter 6

WHEN THE first French explorers invaded the northwest, about the year 1615, the Wyandot Indians occupied the territory between Georgian Bay and the Muskoka Lakes in Ontario. These Frenchmen named the tribe Huron because of the manner in which they wore their hair.

At this period the Hurons were at war with the Iroquois, and the two tribes kept up a bitter fight until in 1649, when the Hurons suffered a decisive defeat. They then abandoned their villages and sought other hunting grounds. They travelled south and settled in Ohio along the south and west shores of Lake Erie. The present site of Zanesfield, named from Isaac Zane, marks the spot where the largest tribe of Hurons once lived.

In a grove of maples on the banks of a swift little river named Mad River, the Hurons built their lodges and their wigwams. The stately elk and graceful deer abounded in this fertile valley, and countless herds of bison browsed upon the uplands.

There for many years the Hurons lived a peaceful and contented life. The long war cry was not heard. They were at peace with the neighboring tribes. Tarhe, the Huron chief, attained great influence with the Delawares. He became a friend of Logan, the Mingo chief.

With the invasion of the valley of the Ohio by the whites, with the march into the wilderness of that wild-turkey breed of heroes of which Boone, Kenton, the Zanes, and the Wetzels were the first, the Indian's nature gradually changed until he became a fierce and relentless foe.

The Hurons had sided with the French in Pontiac's war, and in the Revolution they aided the British. They allied themselves with the Mingoes, Delawares and Shawnees and made a fierce war on the Virginian pioneers. Some powerful influence must have engendered this implacable hatred in these tribes, particularly in the Mingo and the Wyandot.

The war between the Indians and the settlers along the Pennsylvania and West Virginia borders was known as "Dunmore's War." The Hurons, Mingoes, and Delawares living in the "hunter's paradise" west of the Ohio River, seeing their land sold by the Iroquois and the occupation of their possessions by a daring band of white men naturally were filled with fierce anger and hate. But remembering the past bloody war and British punishment they slowly moved backward toward the setting sun and kept the peace. In 1774 a canoe filled with friendly Wyandots was attacked by white men below Yellow Creek and the Indians were killed. Later the same year a party of men under Colonel Cresop made an unprovoked and dastardly massacre of the family and relatives of Logan. This attack reflected the deepest dishonor upon all the white men concerned, and was the principal cause of the long and bloody war which followed. The settlers on the border sent messengers to Governor Dunmore at Williamsburg for immediate relief parties. Knowing well that the Indians would not allow this massacre to go unavenged the frontiersmen erected forts and blockhouses.

Logan, the famous Mingo chief, had been a noted friend of the white men. After the murder of his people he made ceaseless war upon them. He incited the wrath of the Hurons and the Delawares. He went on the warpath, and when his lust for vengeance had been satisfied he sent the following remarkable address to Lord Dunmore:

"I appeal to any white man to say if ever he entered Logan's cabin and he gave him not meat; if ever he came cold and naked and he clothed him not. During the course of the last long and bloody war Logan remained idle in his cabin, an advocate of peace. Such was my love for the whites that my countrymen pointed as they passed and said: 'Logan is the friend of the white man.' I had even thought to have lived with you but for the injuries of one man, Colonel Cresop, who, last spring, in cold blood and unprovoked, murdered all the relatives of Logan, not even sparing my women and children. There runs not a drop of my blood in the veins of any living creature. This called upon me for vengeance. I have sought it; I have killed many; I have glutted my vengeance. For my country I will rejoice at the beams of peace. But do not harbor a thought that mine is the joy of fear. Logan never felt fear; he would not turn upon his heel to save his life. Who is there to mourn for Logan? Not one." The war between the Indians and the pioneers was waged for years. The settlers pushed farther and farther into the wilderness. The Indians, who at first sought only to save their farms and their stock, now fought for revenge. That is why every ambitious pioneer who went out upon those borders carried his life in his hands; why there was always the danger of being shot or tomahawked from behind every tree; why wife and children were constantly in fear of the terrible enemy.

To creep unawares upon a foe and strike him in the dark was Indian warfare; to an Indian it was not dishonorable; it was not cowardly. He was taught to hide in the long grass like a snake, to shoot from coverts, to worm his way stealthily through the dense woods and to ambush the paleface's trail. Horrible cruelties, such as torturing white prisoners and burning them at the stake were never heard of before the war made upon the Indians by the whites.

Comparatively little is known of the real character of the Indian of that time. We ourselves sit before our warm fires and talk of the deeds of the redman. We while away an hour by reading Pontiac's siege of Detroit, of the battle of Braddock's fields, and of Custer's last charge. We lay the book down with a fervent expression of thankfulness that the day of the horrible redman is past. Because little has been written on the subject, no thought is given to the long years of deceit and treachery practiced upon Pontiac; we are ignorant of the causes which led to the slaughter of Braddock's army; and we know little of the life of bitterness suffered by Sitting Bull.

Many intelligent white men, who were acquainted with the true life of the Indian before he was harassed and driven to desperation by the pioneers, said that he had been cruelly wronged. Many white men in those days loved the Indian life so well that they left the settlements and lived with the Indians. Boone, who knew the Indian nature, said the honesty and the simplicity of the Indian were remarkable. Kenton said he had been happy among the Indians. Col. Zane had many Indian friends. Isaac Zane, who lived most of his life with the Wyandots, said the American redman had been wrongfully judged a bloodthirsty savage, an ignorant, thieving wretch, capable of not one virtue. He said the free picturesque life of the Indians would have appealed to any white man; that it had a wonderful charm; and that before the war with the whites the Indians were kind to their prisoners, and sought only to make Indians of them. He told tales of how easily white boys become Indianized, so attached to the wild life and freedom of the redmen that it was impossible to get the captives to return to civilized life. The boys had

been permitted to grow wild with the Indian lads; to
fish and shoot and swim with them; to play the Indian
games—to live idle, joyous lives. He said these white
boys had been ransomed and taken from captivity and
returned to their homes and, although a close watch
was kept on them, they contrived to escape and return
to the Indians, and that while they were back among
civilized people it was difficult to keep the boys
dressed. In summer time it was useless to attempt it.
The strongest hemp-linen shirts, made with the strongest collar and wristband, would directly be torn off
and the little rascals found swimming in the river or
rolling on the sand.

If we may believe what these men have said—and
there seems no good reason why we may not—the
Indian was very different from the impression given of
him. There can be little doubt that the redman once
lived a noble and blameless life; that he was simple,
honest and brave; that he had a regard for honor and a
respect for a promise far exceeding that of most white
men. Think of the beautiful poetry and legends left by
these silent men; men who were a part of the woods;
men whose music was the sighing of the wind, the
rustling of the leaf, the murmur of the brook; men
whose simple joys were the chase of the stag, and the
light in the dark eye of a maiden.

If we wish to find the highest type of the American
Indian we must look for him before he was driven west
by the land-seeking pioneer and before he was degrad-
ed by the rum-selling French trader.

The French claimed all the land watered by the
Mississippi River and its tributaries. The French Canadian was a restless, roaming adventurer and he found
his vocation in the fur-trade. This fur-trade engendered
a strange class of men—bush-rangers they were called
—whose work was to paddle the canoe along the lakes
and streams and exchange their cheap rum for the

valuable furs of the Indians. To these men the Indians of the west owe their degradation. These bush-rangers or *coureurs-des-bois*, perverted the Indians and sank into barbarism with them.

The few travellers there in those days were often surprised to find in the wigwams of the Indians men who acknowledged the blood of France, yet who had lost all semblance to the white man. They lived in their tepee with their Indian squaws and lolled on their blankets while the squaws cooked their venison and did all the work. They let their hair grow long and wore feathers in it; they painted their faces hideously with ochre and vermilion.

These were the worthless traders and adventurers who, from the year 1748 to 1783, encroached on the hunting grounds of the Indians and explored the wilderness, seeking out the remote tribes and trading the villainous rum for the rare pelts. In 1784 the French authorities, realizing that these vagrants were demoralizing the Indians, warned them to get off the soil. Finding this course ineffectual they arrested those that could be apprehended and sent them to Canada. But it was too late; the harm had been done; the poor, ignorant savage had tasted of the terrible "fire-water," as he called the rum, and his ruin was inevitable.

It was a singular fact that almost every Indian who had once tasted strong drink, was unable to resist the desire for more. When a trader came to one of the Indian hamlets the braves purchased a keg of rum and then they held a council to see who was to get drunk and who was to keep sober. It was necessary to have some sober Indians in camp, otherwise the drunken braves would kill one another. The weapons would have to be concealed. When the Indians had finished one keg of rum they would buy another, and so on until not a beaverskin was left. Then the trader would move on. When the Indians sobered up they would be much dejected, for invariably they would find that some had been wounded, and often several had been killed.

Logan, using all his eloquence, travelled from village to village visiting the different tribes and making speeches. He urged the Indians to shun the dreaded "fire-water." He exclaimed against the whites for introducing liquor to the Indians and thus debasing them. At the same time Logan admitted his own fondness for rum. This intelligent and noble Indian was murdered in a drunken fight shortly after sending his address to Lord Dunmore.

Thus it was that the poor Indians had no chance to avert their downfall; the steadily increasing tide of land-stealing settlers rolling westward, and the insidious, debasing, soul-destroying liquor were the noble redman's doom.

* * * * * * * * *

Isaac Zane dropped back not altogether unhappily into his old place in the wigwam in the hunting parties, and in the Indian games.

When the braves were in camp, the greater part of the day was spent in shooting and running matches, in canoe races, in wrestling, and in the game of ball. The chiefs and the older braves who had won their laurels and the maidens of the tribe looked on and applauded.

Isaac entered into all these pastimes, partly because he had a natural love for them, and partly because he wished to win the regard of the Indians. In wrestling, and in those sports which required weight and endurance, he usually suffered defeat. In a foot race, there was not a brave in the entire tribe who could keep even with him. But it was with the rifle that Isaac won his greatest distinction. The Indians never learned the finer shooting with the rifle. Some few of them could shoot well, but for the most part they were poor marksmen.

Accordingly, Isaac was always taken on the fall hunt. Every autumn there were three parties sent out to bring in the supply of meat for the winter. Because of Isaac's fine marksmanship he was always taken with the bear hunters. Bear hunting was exciting and dangerous work. Before the weather got very cold and winter actually set in the bears crawled into a hole in a tree or a cave in the rocks, where they hibernated. A favorite place for them was in hollow trees. When the Indians found a tree with the scratches of a bear on it and a hole large enough to admit the body of a bear, an Indian climbed up the tree and with a long pole tried to punch Bruin out of his den. Often this was a hazardous undertaking, for the bear would get angry on being disturbed in his winter sleep and would rush out before the Indian could reach a place of safety. At times there were even two or three bears in one den. Sometimes the bear would refuse to come out, and on these occasions, which were rare, the hunters would resort to fire. A piece of dry, rotten wood was fastened to a long pole and was set on fire. When this was pushed in on the bear he would give a sniff and a growl and come out in a hurry.

The buffalo and elk were hunted with the bow and arrow. This effective weapon did not make a noise and frighten the game. The wary Indian crawled through the high grass until within easy range and sometimes killed several buffalo or elk before the herd became alarmed. The meat was then jerked. This consisted in cutting it into thin strips and drying it in the sun. Afterwards it was hung up in the lodges. The skins were stretched on poles to dry, and when cured they served as robes, clothing and wigwam-coverings.

The Indians were fond of honey and maple sugar. The finding of a hive of bees, or a good run of maple syrup was an occasion for general rejoicing. They found the honey in hollow trees, and they obtained the maple sugar in two ways. When the sap came up in the maple trees a hole was bored in the trees about a foot from the ground and a small tube, usually made from a piece of alder, was inserted in the hole. Through this the sap was carried into a vessel which was placed under the tree. This sap was boiled down in kettles. If the Indians had no kettles they made the frost take the place of heat in preparing the sugar. They used shallow vessels made of bark, and these were filled with water and the maple sap. It was left to freeze over night and in the morning the ice was broken and thrown away. The sugar did not freeze. When this process had been repeated several times the residue was very good maple sugar.

Isaac did more than his share toward the work of provisioning the village for the winter. But he enjoyed it. He was particularly fond of fishing by moonlight. Early November was the best season for this sport, and the Indians caught large numbers of fish. They placed a torch in the bow of a canoe and paddled noiselessly over the stream. In the clear water a bright light would so attract and fascinate the fish that they would lie motionless near the bottom of the shallow stream.

One cold night Isaac was in the bow of the canoe. Seeing a large fish he whispered to the Indians with him to exercise caution. His guides paddled noiselessly through the water. Isaac stood up and raised the spear, ready to strike. In another second Isaac had cast the iron, but in his eagerness he overbalanced himself and plunged head first into the icy current, making a great splash and spoiling any further fishing. Incidents like this were a source of infinite amusement to the Indians.

Before the autumn evenings grew too cold the Indians held their courting dances. All unmarried maidens and braves in the village were expected to take part in these dances. In the bright light of huge fires, and watched by the chiefs, the old men, the squaws, and the children, the maidens and the braves, arrayed in their gaudiest apparel, marched into the circle. They formed two lines a few paces apart. Each held in the right hand a dry gourd which contained pebbles. Advancing toward one another they sang the courting song, keeping time to the tune with the rattling of the pebbles. When they met in the center the braves bent forward and whispered a word to the maidens. At a certain point in the song, which was indicated by a louder note, the maidens would change positions, and this was continued until every brave had whispered to every maiden, when the dance ended.

Isaac took part in all these pleasures; he entered into every phase of the Indian's life; he hunted, worked, played, danced, and sang with faithfulness. But when the long, dreary winter days came with their ice-laden breezes, enforcing idleness on the Indians, he became restless. Sometimes for days he would be morose and gloomy, keeping beside his own tent and not mingling with the Indians. At such times Myeerah did not question him.

Even in his happier hours his diversions were not many. He never tired of watching and studying the Indian children. When he had an opportunity without being observed, which was seldom, he amused himself with the papooses. The Indian baby was strapped to a flat piece of wood and covered with a broad flap of buckskin. The squaws hung these primitive baby carriages up on the pole of a tepee, on a branch of a tree, or threw them round anywhere. Isaac never heard a papoose cry. He often pulled down the flap of buckskin and looked at the solemn little fellow, who would stare up at him with big, wondering eyes.

Isaac's most intimate friend was a six-year-old Indian boy, whom he called Captain Jack. He was the son of Thundercloud, the war-chief of the Hurons. Jack made a brave picture in his buckskin hunting suit and his war bonnet. Already he could stick tenaciously on the back of a racing mustang, and with his little bow he could place arrow after arrow in the center of the target. Knowing Captain Jack would some day be a mighty chief, Isaac taught him to speak English. He endeavored to make Jack love him, so that when the lad should grow to be a man he would remember his white brother and show mercy to the prisoners who fell into his power.

Another of Isaac's favorites was a half-breed Ottawa Indian, a distant relative of Tarhe's. The Indian was very old; no one knew how old; his face was seamed and scarred and wrinkled. Bent and shrunken was his form. He slept most of the time, but at long intervals he would brighten up and tell of his prowess when a warrior.

One of his favorite stories was of the part he had taken in the events of that fatal and memorable July 2, 1755, when Gen. Braddock and his English army were massacred by the French and Indians near Fort Duquesne.

The old chief told how Beaujeu with his Frenchmen and his five hundred Indians ambushed Braddock's army, surrounded the soldiers, fired from the ravines, the trees, the long grass, poured a pitiless hail of bullets on the bewildered British soldiers, who, unaccustomed to this deadly and unseen foe, huddled under the trees like herds of frightened sheep, and were shot down with hardly an effort to defend themselves.

The old chief related that fifteen years after that battle he went to the Kanawha settlement to see the Big Chief, Gen. George Washington, who was traveling on the Kanawha. He told Gen. Washington how he had fought in the battle of Braddock's Fields; how he had shot and killed Gen. Braddock; how he had fired repeatedly at Washington, and had killed two horses under him, and how at last he came to the conclusion that Washington was protected by the Great Spirit who destined him for a great future.

Myeerah was the Indian name for a rare and beautiful bird—the white crane—commonly called by the Indians, Walk-in-the-Water. It had been the name of Tarhe's mother and grandmother. The present Myeerah was the daughter of a French woman, who had been taken captive at a very early age, adopted into the Huron tribe, and married to Tarhe. The only child of this union was Myeerah. She grew to be a beautiful woman and was known in Detroit and the Canadian forts as Tarhe's white daughter. The old chief often visited the towns along the lake shore, and so proud was he of Myeerah that he always had her accompany him. White men travelled far to look at the Indian beauty. Many French soldiers wooed her in vain. Once, while Tarhe was in Detroit, a noted French family tried in every way to get possession of Myeerah.

The head of this family believed he saw in Myeerah the child of his long lost daughter. Tarhe hurried away from the city and never returned to the white settlement.

Myeerah was only five years old at the time of the capture of the Zane brothers and it was at this early age that she formed the attachment for Isaac Zane which clung to her all her life. She was seven when the men came from Detroit to ransom the brothers, and she showed such grief when she learned that Isaac was to be returned to his people that Tarhe refused to accept any ransom for Isaac. As Myeerah grew older her childish fancy for the white boy deepened into an intense love.

But while this love rendered her inexorable to Isaac on the question of giving him his freedom, it undoubtedly saved his life as well as the lives of other white prisoners, on more than one occasion.

To the white captives who fell into the hands of the Hurons, she was kind and merciful; many of the wounded she had tended with her own hands, and many poor wretches she had saved from the gauntlet and the stake. When her efforts to persuade her father to save any one were unavailing she would retire in sorrow to her lodge and remain there.

Her infatuation for the White Eagle, the Huron name for Isaac, was an old story; it was known to all the tribes and had long ceased to be questioned. At first some of the Delawares and the Shawnee braves, who had failed to win Myeerah's love, had openly scorned her for her love for the pale face. The Wyandot warriors to a man worshipped her; they would have marched straight into the jaws of death at her command; they resented the insults which had been cast on their princess, and they had wiped them out in blood: now none dared taunt her.

In the spring following Isaac's recapture a very serious accident befell him. He had become expert in the Indian game of ball, which is a game resembling the Canadian lacrosse, and from which, in fact, it had been adopted. Goals were placed at both ends of a level plain. Each party of Indians chose a goal which they endeavored to defend and at the same time would try to carry the ball over their opponent's line.

A well contested game of Indian ball presented a scene of wonderful effort and excitement. Hundreds of strong and supple braves could be seen running over the plain, darting this way and that, or struggling in a yelling, kicking, fighting mass, all in a mad scramble to get the ball.

As Isaac had his share of the Zane swiftness of foot, at times his really remarkable fleetness enabled him to get control of the ball. In front of the band of yelling

savages he would carry it down the field, and evading
the guards at the goal would throw it between the
posts. This was a feat of which any brave could be
proud.

During one of these games Red Fox, a Wyandot
brave, who had long been hopelessly in love with Myeerah, and who cordially hated Isaac, used this opportunity for revenge. Red Fox, who was a swift runner,
had vied with Isaac for the honors, but being defeated
in the end, he had yielded to his jealous frenzy and had
struck Isaac a terrible blow on the head with his bat.

It happened to be a glancing blow or Isaac's life
would have been ended then and there. As it was he
had a deep gash in his head. The Indians carried him to
his lodge and the medicine men of the tribe were
summoned.

When Isaac recovered consciousness he asked for
Myeerah and entreated her not to punish Red Fox. He
knew that such a course would only increase his difficulties, and, on the other hand, if he saved the life
of the Indian who had struck him in such a cowardly
manner such an act would appeal favorably to the
Indians. His entreaties had no effect on Myeerah, who
was furious, and who said that if Red Fox, who had
escaped, ever returned he would pay for his unprovoked assault with his life, even if she had to kill him
herself. Isaac knew that Myeerah would keep her word.
He dreaded every morning that the old squaw who
prepared his meals would bring him the news that his
assailant had been slain. Red Fox was a popular brave,
and there were many Indians who believed the blow he
had struck Isaac was not intentional. Isaac worried
needlessly, however, for Red Fox never came back, and
nothing could be learned as to his whereabouts.

It was during his convalescence that Isaac learned
really to love the Indian maiden. She showed such
distress in the first days after his injury, and such

happiness when he was out of danger and on the road to recovery that Isaac wondered at her. She attended him with anxious solicitude; when she bathed and bandaged his wound her every touch was a tender caress; she sat by him for hours; her low voice made soft melody as she sang the Huron love songs. The moments were sweet to Isaac when in the gathering twilight she leaned her head on his shoulder while they listened to the evening carol of the whip-poor-will. Days passed and at length Isaac was entirely well. One day when the air was laden with the warm breath of summer Myeerah and Isaac walked by the river.

"You are sad again," said Myeerah.

"I am homesick. I want to see my people. Myeerah, you have named me rightly. The Eagle can never be happy unless he is free."

"The Eagle can be happy with his mate. And what life could be freer than a Huron's? I hope always that you will grow content."

"It has been a long time now, Myeerah, since I have spoken with you of my freedom. Will you ever free me? Or must I take again those awful chances of escape? I cannot always live here in this way. Some day I shall be killed while trying to get away, and then, if you truly love me, you will never forgive yourself."

"Does not Myeerah truly love you?" she asked, gazing straight into his eyes, her own misty and sad.

"I do not doubt that, but I think sometimes that it is not the right kind of love. It is too savage. No man should be made a prisoner for no other reason than that he is loved by a woman. I have tried to teach you many things; the language of my people, their ways and thoughts, but I have failed to civilize you. I cannot make you understand that it is unwomanly—do not turn away. I am not indifferent. I have learned to care for you. Your beauty and tenderness have made anything else impossible."

"Myeerah is proud of her beauty, if it pleases the Eagle. Her beauty and her love are his. Yet the Eagle's words make Myeerah sad. She cannot tell what she feels. The pale face's words flow swiftly and smoothly like rippling waters, but Myeerah's heart is full and her lips are dumb."

Myeerah and Isaac stopped under a spreading elm tree the branches of which drooped over and shaded the river. The action of the high water had worn away the earth round the roots of the old elm, leaving them bare and dry when the stream was low. As though Nature had been jealous in the interest of lovers, she had twisted and curled the roots into a curiously shaped bench just above the water, which was secluded enough to escape all eyes except those of the beaver and the muskrat. The bank above was carpeted with fresh, dewy grass; blue bells and violets hid modestly under their dark green leaves; delicate ferns, like wonderful fairy lace, lifted their dainty heads to sway in the summer breeze. In this quiet nook the lovers passed many hours.

"Then, if my White Chief has learned to care for me, he must not try to escape," whispered Myeerah, tenderly, as she crept into Isaac's arms and laid her head on his breast. "I love you. I love you. What will become of Myeerah if you leave her? Could she ever be happy? Could she ever forget? No, no, I will keep my captive."

"I cannot persuade you to let me go?"

"If I free you I will come and lie here," cried Myeerah, pointing to the dark pool.

"Then come with me to my home and live there."

"Go with you to the village of the pale faces, where Myeerah would be scorned, pointed at as your captor, laughed at and pitied? No! No!"

"But you would not be," said Isaac, eagerly. "You would be my wife. My sister and people will love you.

Come, Myeerah, save me from this bondage; come
home with me and I will make you happy."

"It can never be," she said, sadly, after a long pause.
"How would we ever reach the fort by the big river?
Tarhe loves his daughter and will not give her up. If
we tried to get away the braves would overtake us and
then even Myeerah could not save your life. You
would be killed. I dare not try. No, no, Myeerah loves
too well for that."

"You might make the attempt," said Isaac, turning
away in bitter disappointment. "If you loved me you
could not see me suffer."

"Never say that again," cried Myeerah, pain and
scorn in her dark eyes. "Can an Indian Princess who
has the blood of great chiefs in her veins prove her love
in any way that she has not? Some day you will know
that you wrong me. I am Tarhe's daughter. A Huron
does not lie."

They slowly wended their way back to the camp,
both miserable at heart; Isaac longing to see his home
and friends, and yet with tenderness in his heart for the
Indian maiden who would not free him; Myeerah with
pity and love for him, and a fear that her long cher-
ished dream could never be realized.

One dark, stormy night, when the rain beat down in
torrents and the swollen river raged almost to its banks,
Isaac slipped out of his lodge unobserved and under
cover of the pitchy darkness he got safely between the
lines of tepees to the river. He had just the opportunity
for which he had been praying. He plunged into the
water and floating down with the swift current he soon
got out of sight of the flickering camp fires. Half a mile
below he left the water and ran along the bank until he
came to a large tree, a landmark he remembered, when
he turned abruptly to the east and struck out through
the dense woods. He travelled due east all that night
and the next day without resting, and with nothing to

eat except a small piece of jerked buffalo meat which he had taken the precaution to hide in his hunting shirt. He rested part of the second night and next morning pushed on toward the east. He had expected to reach the Ohio that day, but he did not and he noticed that the ground seemed to be gradually rising. He did not come across any swampy lands or saw grass or vegetation characteristic of the lowlands. He stopped and tried to get his bearings. The country was unknown to him, but he believed he knew the general lay of the ridges and the water-courses.

The fourth day found Isaac hopelessly lost in the woods. He was famished, having eaten but a few herbs and berries in the last two days; his buckskin garments were torn in tatters; his moccasins were worn out and his feet lacerated by the sharp thorns.

Darkness was fast approaching when he first realized that he was lost. He waited hopefully for the appearance of the north star—that most faithful of hunter's guides—but the sky clouded over and no stars appeared. Tired out and hopeless he dragged his weary body into a dense laurel thicket and lay down to wait for dawn. The dismal hoot of an owl nearby, the stealthy steps of some soft-footed animal prowling round the thicket, and the mournful sough of the wind in the tree-tops kept him awake for hours, but at last he fell asleep.

Chapter 7

THE CHILLING rains of November and December's flurry of snow had passed and mid-winter with its icy blasts had set in. The Black Forest had changed autumn's gay crimson and yellow to the sombre hue of winter and now looked indescribably dreary. An ice gorge had formed in the bend of the river at the head of the island and from bank to bank logs, driftwood, broken ice and giant floes were packed and jammed so tightly as to resist the action of the mighty current. This natural bridge would remain solid until spring had loosened the frozen grip of old winter. The hills surrounding Fort Henry were white with snow. The huge drifts were on a level with Col. Zane's fence and in some places the top rail had disappeared. The pine trees in the yard were weighted down and drooped helplessly with their white burden.

On this frosty January morning the only signs of life round the settlement were a man and a dog walking up Wheeling hill. The man carried a rifle, an axe, and several steel traps. His snow-shoes sank into the drifts as he labored up the steep hill. All at once he stopped. The big black dog had put his nose high in the air and had sniffed at the cold wind.

"Well, Tige, old fellow, what is it?" said Jonathan Zane, for this was he.

The dog answered with a low whine. Jonathan looked up and down the creek valley and along the hillside, but he saw no living thing. Snow, snow everywhere, its white monotony relieved here and there by a black tree trunk. Tige sniffed again and then growled. Turning his ear to the breeze Jonathan heard faint yelps from far over the hilltop. He dropped his axe and the traps and ran the remaining short distance up the hill. When he reached the summit the clear baying of hunting wolves was borne to his ears.

The hill sloped gradually on the other side, ending in a white, unbroken plain which extended to the edge of the laurel thicket a quarter of a mile distant. Jonathan could not see the wolves, but he heard distinctly their peculiar, broken howls. They were in pursuit of something, whether quadruped or man he could not decide. Another moment and he was no longer in doubt, for a deer dashed out of the thicket. Jonathan saw that it was a buck and that he was well nigh exhausted; his head swung low from side to side; he sank slowly to his knees, and showed every indication of distress.

The next instant the baying of the wolves, which had ceased for a moment, sounded close at hand. The buck staggered to his feet; he turned this way and that. When he saw the man and the dog he started toward them without a moment's hesitation.

At a warning word from Jonathan the dog sank on the snow. Jonathan stepped behind a tree, which, however, was not large enough to screen his body. He thought the buck would pass close by him and he determined to shoot at the most favorable moment.

The buck, however, showed no intention of passing by; in his abject terror he saw in the man and the dog foes less terrible than those which were yelping on his trail. He came on in a lame uneven trot, making straight for the tree. When he reached the tree he crouched, or rather fell, on the ground within a yard of Jonathan and his dog. He quivered and twitched; his nostrils flared; at every pant drops of blood flecked the snow; his great dark eyes had a strained and awful look, almost human in its agony.

Another yelp from the thicket and Jonathan looked up in time to see five timber wolves, gaunt, hungry looking beasts, burst from the bushes. With their noses close to the snow they followed the trail. When they came to the spot where the deer had fallen a chorus of angry, thirsty howls filled the air.

"Well, if this doesn't beat me! I thought I knew a little about deer," said Jonathan. "Tige, we will save this buck from those gray devils if it costs a leg. Steady now, old fellow, wait."

When the wolves were within fifty yards of the tree and coming swiftly Jonathan threw his rifle forward and yelled with all the power of his strong lungs:

"Hi! Hi! Hi! Take 'em, Tige!"

In trying to stop quickly on the slippery snowcrust the wolves fell all over themselves. One dropped dead and another fell wounded at the report of Jonathan's rifle. The others turned tail and loped swiftly off into the thicket. Tige made short work of the wounded one.

"Old White Tail, if you were the last buck in the valley, I would not harm you," said Jonathan, looking at the panting deer. "You need have no farther fear of that pack of cowards."

So saying Jonathan called to Tige and wended his way down the hill toward the settlement.

An hour afterward he was sitting in Col. Zane's comfortable cabin, where all was warmth and cheerfulness. Blazing hickory logs roared and crackled in the stone fireplace.

"Hello, Jack, where did you come from?" said Col. Zane, who had just come in. "Haven't seen you since we were snowed up. Come over to see about the horses? If I were you I would not undertake that trip to Fort Pitt until the weather breaks. You could go in the sled, of course, but if you care anything for my advice you will stay home. This weather will hold on for some time. Let Lord Dunmore wait."

"I guess we are in for some stiff weather."

"Haven't a doubt of it. I told Bessie last fall we might expect a hard winter. Everything indicated it. Look at the thick corn-husks. The hulls of the nuts from the shellbark here in the yard were larger and tougher than I ever saw them. Last October Tige killed a racoon that had the wooliest kind of a fur. I could have given you a dozen signs of a hard winter. We shall still have a month or six weeks of it. In a week will be ground-hog day and you had better wait and decide after that."

"I tell you, Eb, I get tired chopping wood and hanging round the house."

"Aha! another moody spell," said Col. Zane, glancing kindly at his brother. "Jack, if you were married you would outgrow those 'blue-devils.' I used to have them. It runs in the family to be moody. I have known our father to take his gun and go into the woods and stay there until he had fought out the spell. I have done that myself, but since I married Bessie I have had no return of the old feeling. Get married, Jack, and then you will settle down and work. You will not have time to roam around alone in the woods."

"I prefer the spells, as you call them, any day," answered Jonathan, with a short laugh. "A man with my disposition has no right to get married. This weather is trying, for it keeps me indoors. I cannot hunt because we do not need the meat. And even if I did want to hunt I should not have to go out of sight of the fort. There were three deer in front of the barn this morning. They were nearly starved. They ran off a little at sight of me, but in a few moments came back for the hay I pitched out of the loft. This afternoon Tige and I saved a big buck from a pack of wolves. The buck came right up to me. I could have touched him. This storm is sending the deer down from the hills."

"You are right. It is too bad. Severe weather like this will kill more deer than an army could. Have you been doing anything with your traps?"

"Yes, I have thirty traps out."

"If you are going, tell Sam to fetch down another load of fodder before he unhitches."

"Eb, I have no patience with your brothers," said Col. Zane's wife to him after he had closed the door. "They are all alike; forever wanting to be on the go. If it isn't Indians it is something else. The very idea of going up the river in this weather. If Jonathan doesn't care for himself he should think of the horses."

"My dear, I was just as wild and discontented as Jack before I met you," remarked Col. Zane. "You may not think so, but a home and pretty little woman will do wonders for any man. My brothers have nothing to keep them steady."

"Perhaps. I do not believe that Jonathan ever will get married. Silas may; he certainly has been keeping company long enough with Mary Bennet. You are the only Zane who has conquered that adventurous spirit and the desire to be always roaming the woods in search of something to kill. Your old boy, Noah, is growing up like all the Zanes. He fights with all the children in the settlement. I cannot break him of it. He is not a bully, for I have never known him to do anything mean or cruel. It is just sheer love of fighting."

"Ha! Ha! I fear you will not break him of that," answered Col. Zane. "It is a good joke to say he gets it all from the Zanes. How about the McCollochs? What have you to say of your father and the Major and John McColloch? They are not anything if not the fighting kind. It's the best trait the youngster could have, out here on the border. He'll need it all. Don't worry about him. Where is Betty?"

"I told her to take the children out for a sled ride. Betty needs exercise. She stays indoors too much, and of late she looks pale."

"What! Betty not looking well! She was never ill in her life. I have noticed no change in her."

"No, I daresay you have not. You men can't see anything. But I can, and I tell you, Betty is very different from the girl she used to be. Most of the time she sits and gazes out of her window. She used to be so bright, and when she was not romping with the children she busied herself with her needle. Yesterday as I entered her room she hurriedly picked up a book, and, I think, intentionally hid her face behind it. I saw she had been crying."

"Come to think of it, I believe I have missed Betty," said Col. Zane, gravely. "She seems more quiet. Is she unhappy? When did you first see this change?"

"I think it was a little while after Mr. Clarke left here last fall."

"Clarke! What has he to do with Betty? What are you driving at?" exclaimed the Colonel, stopping in front of his wife. His face had paled slightly. "I had forgotten Clarke. Bess, you can't mean——"

"Now, Eb, do not get that look on your face. You always frighten me," answered his wife, as she quietly placed her hand on his arm. "I do not mean anything much, certainly nothing against Mr. Clarke. He was a true gentleman. I really liked him."

"So did I," interrupted the Colonel.

"I believe Betty cared for Mr. Clarke. She was always different with him. He has gone away and has forgotten her. That is strange to us, because we cannot imagine any one indifferent to our beautiful Betty. Nevertheless, no matter how attractive a woman may be men sometimes love and ride away. I hear the children coming now. Do not let Betty see that we have been talking about her. She is as quick as a steel trap."

A peal of childish laughter came from without. The door opened and Betty ran in, followed by the sturdy, rosy-cheeked youngsters. All three were white with snow.

"We have had great fun," said Betty. "We went over the bank once and tumbled off the sled into the snow. Then we had a snow-balling contest, and the boys compelled me to strike my colors and fly for the house."

Col. Zane looked closely at his sister. Her cheeks were glowing with health; her eyes were sparkling with pleasure. Failing to observe any indication of the change in Betty of which his wife had spoken, he concluded that women were better qualified to judge their own sex than were men. He had to confess to himself that the only change he could see in his sister was that she grew prettier every day of her life.

"Oh, papa. I hit Sam right in the head with a big snow-ball, and I made Betty run into the house, and I slid down the hill all by myself. Sam was afraid," said Noah to his father.

"Noah, if Sammy saw the danger in sliding down the hill he was braver than you. Now both of you run to Annie and have these wet things taken off."

"I must go get on dry clothes myself," said Betty. "I am nearly frozen. It is growing colder. I saw Jack come in. Is he going to Fort Pitt?"

"No. He has decided to wait until good weather. I met Mr. Miller over at the garrison this afternoon and he wants you to go on the sled-ride tonight. There is to be a dance down at Watkins' place. All the young people are going. It is a long ride, but I guess it will be perfectly safe. Silas and Wetzel are going. Dress yourself warmly and go with them. You have never seen old Grandma Watkins."

"I shall be pleased to go," said Betty.

Betty's room was very cozy, considering that it was in a pioneer's cabin. It had two windows, the larger of which opened on the side toward the river. The walls had been smoothly plastered and covered with white birch-bark. They were adorned with a few pictures and Indian ornaments. A bright homespun carpet covered the floor. A small bookcase stood in the corner. The other furniture consisted of two chairs, a small table, a bureau with a mirror, and a large wardrobe. It was in this last that Betty kept the gowns which she had brought from Philadelphia, and which were the wonder of all the girls in the village.

"I wonder why Eb looked so closely at me," mused Betty, as she slipped on her little moccasins. "Usually he is not anxious to have me go so far from the fort; and now he seemed to think I would enjoy this dance tonight. I wonder what Bessie has been telling him."

Betty threw some wood on the smouldering fire in the little stone grate and sat down to think. Like every one who has a humiliating secret, Betty was eternally suspicious and feared the very walls would guess it. Swift as light came the thought that her brother and his wife had suspected her secret and had been talking about her, perhaps pitying her. With this thought came the fear that if she had betrayed herself to the Colonel's wife she might have done so to others. The consciousness that this might well be true and that even now the girls might be talking and laughing at her caused her exceeding shame and bitterness.

Many weeks had passed since that last night that Betty and Alfred Clarke had been together.

In due time Col. Zane's men returned and Betty learned from Jonathan that Alfred had left them at Ft. Pitt, saying he was going south to his old home. At first she had expected some word from Alfred, a letter, or if not that, surely an apology for his conduct on that last evening they had been together. But Jonathan brought her no word, and after hoping against hope and wearing away the long days looking for a letter that never came, she ceased to hope and plunged into despair.

The last few months had changed her life; changed it as only constant thinking, and suffering that must be hidden from the world, can change the life of a young girl. She had been so intent on her own thoughts, so deep in her dreams that she had taken no heed of other people. She did not know that those who loved her were always thinking of her welfare and would naturally see even a slight change in her. With a sudden shock of surprise and pain she realized that today for the first time in a month she had played with the boys. Sammy had asked her why she did not laugh any more. Now she understood the mad antics of Tige that morning; Madcap's whinney of delight; the chattering of the squirrels, and Cæsar's pranks in the snow. She had neglected her pets. She had neglected her work, her friends, the boys' lessons, and her brother. For what? What would her girl friends say? That she was pining for a lover who had forgotten her. They would say that and it would be true. She did think of him constantly.

With bitter pain she recalled the first days of the acquaintance which now seemed so long past; how much she had disliked Alfred; how angry she had been with him and how contemptuously she had spurned his first proffer of friendship; how, little by little, her pride had been subdued; then the struggle with her heart. And, at last, after he had gone, came the realization that the moments spent with him had been the sweetest of her life. She thought of him as she used to see him stand before her; so good to look at; so strong and masterful, and yet so gentle.

"Oh, I cannot bear it," whispered Betty with a half sob, giving up to a rush of tender feeling. "I love him. I love him, and I cannot forget him. Oh, I am so ashamed."

Betty bowed her head on her knees. Her slight form quivered a while and then grew still. When a half hour later she raised her head her face was pale and cold. It bore the look of a girl who had suddenly become a woman; a woman who saw the battle of life before her and who was ready to fight. Stern resolve gleamed from her flashing eyes; there was no faltering in those set lips.

Betty was a Zane and the Zanes came of a fighting race. Their blood had ever been hot and passionate; the blood of men quick to love and quick to hate. It had flowed in the veins of daring, reckless men who had fought and died for their country; men who had won their sweethearts with the sword; men who had had unconquerable spirits. It was this fighting instinct that now rose in Betty; it gave her strength and pride to defend her secret; the resolve to fight against the longing in her heart.

"I will forget him! I will tear him out of my heart!" she exclaimed passionately. "He never deserved my love. He did not care. I was a little fool to let him amuse himself with me. He went away and forgot. I hate him."

At length Betty subdued her excitement, and when she went down to supper a few minutes later she tried to maintain a cheerful composure of manner and to chat with her old-time vivacity.

"Bessie, I am sure you have exaggerated things," remarked Col. Zane after Betty had gone upstairs to dress for the dance. "Perhaps it is only that Betty grows a little tired of this howling wilderness. Small wonder if she does. You know she has always been used to comfort and many young people, places to go and all that. This is her first winter on the frontier. She'll come round all right."

"Have it your way, Ebenezer," answered his wife with a look of amused contempt on her face. "I am sure I hope you are right. By the way what do you think of this Ralfe Miller? He has been much with Betty of late."

"I do not know the fellow, Bessie. He seems agreeable. He is a good-looking young man. Why do you ask?"

"The Major told me that Miller had a bad name at Pitt, and that he had been a friend of Simon Girty before Girty became a renegade."

"Humph! I'll have to speak to Sam. As for knowing Girty, there is nothing terrible in that. All the women seem to think that Simon is the very prince of devils. I have know all the Girtys for years. Simon was not a bad fellow before he went over to the Indians. It is his brother James who has committed most of those deeds which have made the name of Girty so infamous."

"I don't like Miller," continued Mrs. Zane in a hesitating way. "I must admit that I have no sensible reason for my dislike. He is pleasant and agreeable, yes, but behind it there is a certain intensity. That man has something on his mind."

"If he is in love with Betty, as you seem to think, he has enough on his mind. I'll vouch for that," said Col. Zane. "Betty is inclined to be a couquette. If she liked Clarke pretty well, it may be a lesson to her."

"I wish she were married and settled down. It may have been no great harm for Betty to have had many admirers while in Philadelphia, but out here on the border it will never do. These men will not have it. There will be trouble come of Betty's coquettishness."

"Why, Bessie, she is only a child. What would you have her do? Marry the first man who asked her?"

"The clod-hoppers are coming," said Mrs. Zane as the jingling of sleigh bells broke the stillness.

Col. Zane sprang up and opened the door. A broad

stream of light flashed from the room and lighted up the road. Three powerful teams stood before the door. They were hitched to sleds, or clod-hoppers, which were nothing more than wagon-beds fastened on wooden runners. A chorus of merry shouts greeted Col. Zane as he appeared in the doorway.

"All right! all right! Here she is," he cried, as Betty ran down the steps.

The Colonel bundled her in a buffalo robe in a corner of the foremost sled. At her feet he placed a buckskin bag containing a hot stone Mrs. Zane thoughtfully had provided.

"All ready here. Let them go," called the Colonel. "You will have clear weather. Coming back look well to the traces and keep a watch for the wolves."

The long whips cracked, the bells jingled, the impatient horses plunged forward and away they went over the glistening snow. The night was clear and cold; countless stars blinked in the black vault overhead; the pale moon cast its wintry light down on a white and frozen world. As the runners glided swiftly and smoothly onward showers of dry snow like fine powder flew from under the horses' hoofs and soon whitened the black-robed figures in the sleds. The way led down the hill past the Fort, over the creek bridge and along the road that skirted the Black Forest. The ride was long; it led up and down hills, and through a lengthy stretch of gloomy forest. Sometimes the drivers walked the horses up a steep climb and again raced them along a level bottom. Making a turn in the road they saw a bright light in the distance which marked their destination. In five minutes the horses dashed into a wide clearing. An immense log fire burned in front of a two-story structure. Streams of light poured from the small windows; the squeaking of fiddles, the shuffling of many feet, and gay laughter came through the open door.

The steaming horses were unhitched, covered carefully with robes and led into sheltered places, while the merry party disappeared into the house.

The occasion was the celebration of the birthday of old Dan Watkins' daughter. Dan was one of the oldest settlers along the river; in fact, he had located his farm several years after Col. Zane had founded the settlement. He was noted for his open-handed dealing and kindness of heart. He had loaned many a head of cattle which had never been returned, and many a sack of flour had left his mill unpaid for in grain. He was a good shot, he would lay a tree on the ground as quickly as any man who ever swung an axe, and he could drink more whiskey than any man in the valley.

Dan stood at the door with a smile of welcome upon his rugged features and a handshake and a pleasant word for everyone. His daughter Susan greeted the men with a little curtsy and kissed the girls upon the cheek. Susan was not pretty, though she was strong and healthy; her laughing blue eyes assured a sunny disposition, and she numbered her suitors by the score.

The young people lost no time. Soon the floor was covered with their whirling forms.

In one corner of the room sat a little dried-up old woman with white hair and bright dark eyes. This was Grandma Watkins. She was very old, so old that no one knew her age, but she was still vigorous enough to do her day's work with more pleasure than many a younger woman. Just now she was talking to Wetzel, who leaned upon his inseparable rifle and listened to her chatter. The hunter liked the old lady and would often stop at her cabin while on his way to the settlement and leave at her door a fat turkey or a haunch of venison.

"Lew Wetzel, I am ashamed of you," Grandmother Watkins was saying. "Put that gun in the corner and get out there and dance. Enjoy yourself. You are only a boy yet."

"I'd better look on, mother," answered the hunter.

"Pshaw! You can hop and skip around like any of them and laugh too if you want. I hope that pretty sister of Eb Zane has caught your fancy."

"She is not for the like of me," he said gently. "I haven't the gifts."

"Don't talk about gifts. Not to an old woman who has lived three times and more your age," she said impatiently. "It is not gifts a woman wants out here in the West. If she does 'twill do her no good. She needs a strong arm to build cabins, a quick eye with a rifle, and a fearless heart. What border-women want are houses and children. They must bring up men, men to drive the redskins back, men to till the soil, or else what is the good of our suffering here."

"You are right," said Wetzel thoughtfully. "But I'd hate to see a flower like Betty Zane in a rude hunter's cabin."

"I have known the Zanes for forty year' and I never saw one yet that was afraid of work. And you might win her if you would give up running mad after Indians. I'll allow no woman would put up with that. You have killed many Indians. You ought to be satisfied."

"Fightin' redskins is somethin' I can't help," said the hunter, slowly shaking his head. "If I got married the fever would come on and I'd leave home. No, I'm no good for a woman. Fightin' is all I'm good for."

"Why not fight for her, then? Don't let one of these boys walk off with her. Look at her. She likes fun and admiration. I believe you do care for her. Why not try to win her?"

"Who is that tall man with her?" continued the old lady as Wetzel did not answer. "There, they have gone into the other room. Who is he?"

"His name is Miller."

"Lewis, I don't like him. I have been watching him all evening. I'm a contrary old woman, I know, but I have seen a good many men in my time, and his face is not honest. He is in love with her. Does she care for him?"

"No, Betty doesn't care for Miller. She's just full of life and fun."

"You may be mistaken. All the Zanes are fire and brimstone and this girl is a Zane clear through. Go and fetch her to me, Lewis. I'll tell you if there's a chance for you."

"Dear mother, perhaps there's a wife in Heaven for me. There's none on earth," said the hunter, a sad smile flitting over his calm face.

Ralfe Miller, whose actions had occasioned the remarks of the old lady, would have been conspicuous in any assembly of men. There was something in his dark face that compelled interest and yet left the observer in doubt. His square chin, deep-set eyes and firm mouth denoted a strong and indomitable will. He looked a man whom it would be dangerous to cross.

Little was known of Miller's history. He hailed from Ft. Pitt, where he had a reputation as a good soldier, but a man of morose and quarrelsome disposition. It was whispered that he drank, and that he had been friendly with the renegades McKee, Elliott, and Girty. He had passed the fall and winter at Ft. Henry, serving on garrison duty. Since he had made the acquaintance of Betty he had shown her all the attention possible.

On this night a close observer would have seen that Miller was laboring under some strong feeling. A half-subdued fire gleamed from his dark eyes. A peculiar nervous twitching of his nostrils betrayed a poorly suppressed excitement.

All evening he followed Betty like a shadow. Her kindness may have encouraged him. She danced often with him and showed a certain preference for his society. Alice and Lydia were puzzled by Betty's manner. As they were intimate friends they believed they knew something of her likes and dislikes. Had not Betty told them she did not care for Mr. Miller? What was the meaning of the arch glances she bestowed upon him, if she did not care for him? To be sure, it was nothing wonderful for Betty to smile,—she was always prodigal of her smiles—but she had never been known to encourage any man. The truth was that Betty had put her new resolution into effect; to be as merry and charming as any fancy-free maiden could possibly be, and the farthest removed from a young lady pining for an absent and indifferent sweetheart. To her sorrow Betty played her part too well.

Except to Wetzel, whose keen eyes little escaped, there was no significance in Miller's hilarity one moment and sudden thoughtfulness the next. And if there had been, it would have excited no comment. Most of the young men had sampled some of old Dane's best rye and their flushed faces and unusual spirits did not result altogether from the exercise of the dance.

After one of the reels Miller led Betty, with whom he had been dancing, into one of the side rooms. Round the dimly lighted room were benches upon which were seated some of the dancers. Betty was uneasy in mind and now wished that she had remained at home. They had exchanged several commonplace remarks when the music struck up and Betty rose quickly to her feet.

"See, the others have gone. Let us return," she said.

"Wait," said Miller hurriedly. "Do not go just yet. I wish to speak to you. I have asked you many times if you will marry me. Now I ask you again."

"Mr. Miller, I thanked you and begged you not to cause us both pain by again referring to that subject," answered Betty with dignity. "If you will persist in bringing it up we cannot be friends any longer."

"Wait, please wait. I have told you that I will not take 'No' for an answer. I love you with all my heart and soul and I cannot give you up."

His voice was low and hoarse and thrilled with a strong man's passion. Betty looked up into his face and tears of compassion filled her eyes. Her heart softened to this man, and her conscience gave her a little twinge of remorse. Could she not have averted all this? No doubt she had been much to blame, and this thought made her voice very low and sweet as she answered him.

"I like you as a friend, Mr. Miller, but we can never be more than friends. I am very sorry for you, and angry with myself that I did not try to help you instead of making it worse. Please do not speak of this again. Come, let us join the others."

They were quite alone in the room. As Betty finished speaking and started for the door Miller intercepted her. She recoiled in alarm from his white face.

"No, you don't go yet. I won't give you up so easily. No woman can play fast and loose with me. Do you understand? What have you meant all this winter? You encouraged me. You know you did," he cried passionately.

"I thought you were a gentleman. I have really taken the trouble to defend you against persons who evidently were not misled as to your real nature. I will not listen to you," said Betty coldly. She turned away from him, all her softened feeling changed to scorn.

"You *shall* listen to me," he whispered as he grasped her wrist and pulled her backward. All the man's brutal passion had been aroused. The fierce border blood boiled within his heart. Unmasked he showed himself in his true colors—a frontier desperado. His eyes gleamed dark and lurid beneath his bent brows and a short, desperate laugh passed his lips.

"I will make you love me, my proud beauty. I shall have you yet, one way or another."

"Let me go. How dare you touch me!" cried Betty, the hot blood coloring her face. She struck him a stinging blow with her free hand and struggled with all her might to free herself; but she was powerless in his iron grasp. Closer he drew her.

"If it costs me my life I will kiss you for that blow," he muttered hoarsely.

"Oh, you coward! you ruffian! Release me or I will scream."

She had opened her lips to call for help when she saw a dark figure cross the threshold. She recognized the tall form of Wetzel. The hunter stood still in the doorway for a second and then with the swiftness of light he sprang forward. The single straightening of his arm sent Miller backward over a bench to the floor with a crashing sound. Miller rose with some difficulty and stood with one hand to his head.

"Lew, don't draw your knife," cried Betty as she saw Wetzel's hand go inside his hunting shirt. She had thrown herself in front of him as Miller got to his feet. With both little hands she clung to the brawny arm of the hunter, but she could not stay it. Wetzel's hand slipped to his belt.

"For God's sake, Lew, do not kill him," implored Betty, gazing horror-stricken at the glittering eyes of the hunter. "You have punished him enough. He only tried to kiss me. I was partly to blame. Put your knife away. Do not shed blood. For my sake, Lew, for my sake!"

When Betty found that she could not hold Wetzel's arm she threw her arms round his neck and clung to him with all her young strength. No doubt her action averted a tragedy. If Miller had been inclined to draw a weapon then he might have had a good opportunity to use it. He had the reputation of being quick with his knife, and many of his past fights testified that he was not a coward. But he made no effort to attack Wetzel. It was certain that he measured with his eye the distance to the door. Wetzel was not like other men. Irrespective of his wonderful strength and agility there

was something about the Indian hunter that terrified all
men. Miller shrank before those eyes. He knew that
never in all his life of adventure had he been as near
death as at that moment. There was nothing between
him and eternity but the delicate arms of this frail girl.
At a slight wave of the hunter's hand towards the door
he turned and passed out.

"Oh, how dreadful!" cried Betty, dropping upon a
bench with a sob of relief. "I am glad you came when
you did even though you frightened me more than he
did. Promise me that you will not do Miller any further
harm. If you had fought it would all have been on my
account; one or both of you might have been killed.
Don't look at me so. I do not care for him. I never did.
Now that I know him I despise him. He lost his senses
and tried to kiss me. I could have killed him myself."

Wetzel did not answer. Betty had been holding his
hand in both her own while she spoke impulsively.

"I understand how difficult it is for you to overlook
an insult to me," she continued earnestly. "But I ask it
of you. You are my best friend, almost my brother,
and I promise you that if he ever speaks a word to me
again that is not what it should be I will tell you."

"I reckon I'll let him go, considerin' how set on it
you are."

"But remember, Lew, that he is revengeful and you
must be on the lookout," said Betty gravely as she
recalled the malignant gleam in Miller's eyes.

"He's dangerous only like a moccasin snake that
hides in the grass."

"Am I all right? Do I looked mussed or—or excited
—or anything?" asked Betty.

Lewis smiled as she turned round for his benefit.
Her hair was a little awry and the lace at her neck dis-
arranged. The natural bloom had not quite returned to
her cheeks. With a look in his eyes that would have
mystified Betty for many a day had she but seen it he

ran his gaze over the dainty figure. Then reassuring her
that she looked as well as ever, he led her into the
dance-room.

"So this is Betty Zane. Dear child, kiss me," said
Grandmother Watkins when Wetzel had brought Betty
up to her. "Now, let me get a good look at you. Well,
well, you are a true Zane. Black hair and eyes; all fire
and pride. Child, I knew your father and mother long
before you were born. Your father was a fine man but
a proud one. And how do you like the frontier? Are
you enjoying yourself?"

"Oh, yes, indeed," said Betty, smiling brightly at the
old lady.

"Well, dearie, have a good time while you can. Life
is hard in a pioneer's cabin. You will not always have
the Colonel to look after you. They tell me you have
been to some grand school in Philadelphia. Learning is
very well, but it will not help you in the cabin of one of
these rough men."

"There is a great need of education in all the pioneers' homes. I have persuaded brother Eb to have a
schoolteacher at the Fort next spring."

"First teach the boys to plow and the girls to make
Johnnycake. How much you favor your brother Isaac.
He used to come and see me often. So must you in
summertime. Poor lad, I suppose he is dead by this
time. I have seen so many brave and good lads go.
There now, I did not mean to make you sad," and the
old lady patted Betty's hand and sighed.

"He often spoke of you and said that I must come
with him to see you. Now he is gone," said Betty.

"Yes, he is gone, Betty, but you must not be sad
while you are so young. Wait until you are old like I
am. How long have you known Lew Wetzel?"

"All my life. He used to carry me in his arms when I
was a baby. Of course I do not remember that, but as
far back as I can go in memory I can see Lew. Oh, the

many times hē has saved me from disaster! But why do you ask?"

"I think Lew Wetzel cares more for you than for all the world. He is as silent as an Indian, but I am an old woman and I can read men's hearts. If he could be made to give up his wandering life he would be the best man on the border."

"Oh, indeed I think you are wrong. Lew does not care for me in that way," said Betty, surprised and troubled by the old lady's vehemence.

A loud blast from a hunting-horn directed the attention of all to the platform at the upper end of the hall, where Dan Watkins stood. The fiddlers ceased playing, the dancers stopped, and all looked expectantly. The scene was simple, strong, and earnest. The light in the eyes of these maidens shone like the light from the pine cones on the walls. It beamed soft and warm. These fearless sons of the wilderness, these sturdy sons of progress, standing there clasping the hands of their partners and with faces glowing with happiness, forgetful of all save the enjoyment of the moment, were ready to go out on the morrow and battle unto the death for the homes and the lives of their loved ones.

"Friends," said Dan when the hum of voices had ceased, "I never thought as how I'd have to get up here and make a speech tonight or I might have taken to the woods. Howsomever, mother and Susan says as it's gettin' late it's about time we had some supper. Somewhere in the big cake is hid a gold ring. If one of the girls gets it she can keep it as a gift from Susan, and should one of the boys find it he may make a present to his best girl. And in the bargain he gets to kiss Susan. She made some objection about this and said that part of the game didn't go, but I reckon the lucky young man will decide that for hisself. And now to the festal board."

Ample justice was done to the turkey, the venison,

and the bear meat. Grandmother Watkins' delicious apple and pumpkin pies, for which she was renowned, disappeared as by magic. Likewise the cakes and the sweet cider and the apple butter vanished.

When the big cake had been cut and divided among the guests, Wetzel discovered the gold ring within his share. He presented the ring to Betty, and gave his privilege of kissing Susan to George Reynolds, with the remark: "George, I calkilate Susan would like it better if you do the kissin' part." Now it was known to all that George had long been an ardent admirer of Susan's, and it was suspected that she was not indifferent to him. Nevertheless, she protested that it was not fair. George acted like a man who had the opportunity of his life. Amid uproarious laughter he ran Susan all over the room, and when he caught her he pulled her hands away from her blushing face and bestowed a right hearty kiss on her cheek. To everyone's surprise and to Wetzel's discomfiture, Susan walked up to him and saying that as he had taken such an easy way out of it she intended to punish him by kissing him. And so she did. Poor Lewis' face looked the picture of dismay. Probably he had never been kissed before in his life.

Happy hours speed away on the wings of the wind. The feasting over, the good-byes were spoken, the girls were wrapped in the warm robes, for it was now intensely cold, and soon the horses, eager to start on the long homeward journey, were pulling hard on their bits. On the party's return trip there was an absence of the hilarity which had prevailed on their coming. The bells were taken off before the sleds left the blockhouse, and the traces and the harness examined and tightened with the caution of men who were apprehensive of danger and who would take no chances.

In winter time the foes most feared by the settlers were the timber wolves. Thousands of these savage beasts infested the wild forest regions which bounded the lonely roads, and their wonderful power of scent and swift and tireless pursuit made a long night ride a thing to be dreaded. While the horses moved swiftly danger from wolves was not imminent; but carelessness or some mishap to a trace or a wheel had been the cause of more than one tragedy.

Therefore it was not remarkable that the drivers of our party breathed a sigh of relief when the top of the last steep hill had been reached. The girls were quiet, and tired out and cold they pressed close to one another; the men were silent and watchful.

When they were half way home and had just reached the outskirts of the Black Forest the keen ear of Wetzel caught the cry of a wolf. It came from the south and sounded so faint that Wetzel believed at first that he had been mistaken. A few moments passed in which the hunter turned his ear to the south. He had about made up his mind that he had only imagined he had heard something when the unmistakable yelp of a wolf came down on the wind. Then another, this time clear and distinct, caused the driver to turn and whisper to Wetzel. The hunter spoke in a low tone and the driver whipped up his horses. From out the depths of the dark woods along which they were riding came a long and mournful howl. It was a wolf answering the call of his mate. This time the horses heard it, for they threw back their ears and increased their speed. The girls heard it, for they shrank closer to the men.

There is that which is frightful in the cry of a wolf. When one is safe in camp before a roaring fire the short, sharp bark of a wolf is startling, and the long howl will make one shudder. It is so lonely and dismal. It makes no difference whether it be given while the wolf is sitting on his haunches near some cabin waiting for the remains of the settler's dinner, or while he is in full chase after his prey—the cry is equally wild, savage and bloodcurdling.

Betty had never heard it and though she was brave, when the howl from the forest had its answer in another howl from the creek thicket, she slipped her little mittened hand under Wetzel's arm and looked up at him with frightened eyes.

In half an hour the full chorus of yelps, barks and howls swelled hideously on the air, and the ever increasing pack of wolves could be seen scarcely a hundred yards behind the sleds. The patter of their swiftly flying feet on the snow could be distinctly heard. The slender, dark forms came nearer and nearer every moment. Presently the wolves had approached close enough for the occupants of the sleds to see their shining eyes looking like little balls of green fire. A gaunt beast bolder than the others and evidently the leader of the pack, bounded forward until he was only a few yards from the last sled. At every jump he opened his great jaws and uttered a quick bark as if to embolden his followers.

Almost simultaneously with the red flame that burst from Wetzel's rifle came a sharp yelp of agony from the leader. He rolled over and over. Instantly followed a horrible mingling of snarls and barks, and snapping of jaws as the band fought over the body of their luckless comrade.

This short delay gave the advantage to the horses. When the wolves again appeared they were a long way behind. The distance to the fort was now short and the horses were urged to their utmost. The wolves kept up the chase until they reached the creek bridge and the mill. Then they slowed up, the howling became desultory, and finally the dark forms disappeared in the thickets.

Chapter 8

WINTER DRAGGED by uneventfully for Betty. Unlike the other pioneer girls, who were kept busy all the time with their mending, and linsey weaving, and household duties, Betty had nothing to divert her but her embroidery and her reading. These she found very tiresome. Her maid was devoted to her and never left a thing undone. Annie was old Sam's daughter, and she had waited on Betty since she had been a baby. The cleaning or mending or darning—anything in the shape of work that would have helped pass away the monotonous hours for Betty, was always done before she could lift her hand.

During the day she passed hours in her little room and most of them were dreamed away by her window. Lydia and Alice came over sometimes and whiled away the tedious moments with their bright chatter and merry laughter, their castle-building, and their romancing on heroes and love and marriage as girls always will until the end of time. They had not forgotten Mr. Clarke, but as Betty had rebuked them with a dignity which forbade any further teasing on that score, they had transferred their fun-making to the use of Mr. Miller's name.

Fearing her brothers' wrath Betty had not told them of the scene with Miller at the dance. She had learned enough of rough border justice to dread the consequence of such a disclosure. She permitted Miller to come to the house, although she never saw him alone. Miller had accepted this favor gratefully. He said that on the night of the dance he had been a little the worse for Dan Watkins' strong liquor, and that, together with his bitter disappointment, made him act in the mad way which had so grievously offended her. He exerted himself to win her forgiveness. Betty was always tenderhearted, and though she did not trust him, she said they might still be friends, but that that depended on his respect for her forbearance. Miller had promised he would never refer to the old subject and he had kept his word.

Indeed Betty welcomed any diversion for the long winter evenings. Occasionally some of the young people visited her, and they sang and danced, roasted apples, popped chestnuts, and played games. Often Wetzel and Major McColloch came in after supper. Betty would come down and sing for them, and afterward would coax Indian lore and woodcraft from Wetzel, or she would play checkers with the Major. If she succeeded in winning from him, which in truth was not often, she teased him unmercifully. When Col. Zane and the Major had settled down to their series of games, from which nothing short of Indians could have diverted them, Betty sat by Wetzel. The silent man of the woods, an appellation the hunter had earned by his reticence, talked for Betty as he would for no one else.

One night while Col. Zane, his wife and Betty were entertaining Capt. Boggs and Major McColloch and several of Betty's girl friends, after the usual music and singing, storytelling became the order of the evening. Little Noah told of the time he had climbed the apple tree in the yard after a raccoon and got severely bitten.

"One day," said Noah, "I heard Tige barking out in the orchard and I ran out there and saw a funny little fur ball up in the tree with a black tail and white rings around it. It looked like a pretty cat with a sharp nose. Every time Tige barked the little animal showed his teeth and swelled up his back. I wanted him for a pet. I got Sam to give me a sack and I climbed the tree and the nearer I got to him the farther he backed down the limb. I followed him and put out the sack to put it over his head and he bit me. I fell from the limb, but he fell too and Tige killed him and Sam stuffed him for me."

"Noah, you are quite a valiant hunter," said Betty. "Now, Jonathan, remember that you promised to tell me of your meeting with Daniel Boone."

"It was over on the Muskingong near the mouth of the Sandusky. I was hunting in the open woods along the bank when I saw an Indian. He saw me at the same time and we both treed. There we stood a long time each afraid to change position. Finally I began to get tired and resorted to an old ruse. I put my coon-skin cap on my ramrod and cautiously poked it from behind the tree, expecting every second to hear the whistle of the redskin's bullet. Instead I heard a jolly voice yell: 'Hey, young feller, you'll have to try something better'n that.' I looked and saw a white man standing out in the open and shaking all over with laughter. I went up to him and found him to be a big strong fellow with an honest, merry face. He said: 'I'm Boone.' I was considerably taken aback, especially when I saw he knew I was a white man all the time. We camped and hunted along the river a week and at the Falls of the Muskingong he struck out for his Kentucky home."

"Here is Wetzel," said Col. Zane, who had risen and gone to the door. "Now, Betty, try and get Lew to tell us something."

"Come, Lewis, here is a seat by me," said Betty. "We have been pleasantly passing the time. We have had bear stories, snake stories, ghost stories—all kinds of tales. Will you tell us one?"

"Lewis, did you ever have a chance to kill a hostile Indian and not take it?" asked Col. Zane.

"Never but once," answered Lewis.

"Tell us about it. I imagine it will be interesting."

"Well, I ain't good at tellin' things," began Lewis. "I reckon I've seen some strange sights. I kin tell you about the only redskin I ever let off. Three years ago I was takin' a fall hunt over on the Big Sandy, and I run into a party of Shawnees. I plugged a chief and started to run. There was some good runners and I couldn't shake 'em in the open country. Comin' to the Ohio I jumped in and swum across, keepin' my rifle and powder dry by holdin' 'em up. I hid in some bulrushes and waited. Pretty soon along comes three Injuns, and when they saw where I had taken to the water they stopped and held a short pow-wow. Then they all took to the water. This was what I was waitin' for. When they got nearly acrosst I shot the first redskin, and loadin' quick I got a bullet into the others. The last Injun did not sink. I watched him go floatin' down stream expectin' every minute to see him go under as he was hurt so bad he could hardly keep his head above water. He floated down a long ways and the current carried him to a pile of driftwood which had lodged against a little island. I saw the Injun crawl up on the drift. I went down stream and by keepin' the island between me and him I got out to where he was. I pulled my tomahawk and went around the head of the island and found the redskin leanin' against a big log. He was a young brave and a fine lookin' strong feller. He was tryin' to stop the blood from my bullet-hole in his side. When he saw me he tried to get up, but he was too weak. He smiled, pointed to the wound and said: 'Deathwind not heap times bad shot.' Then he bowed his head and waited for the tomahawk. Well, I picked him up and carried him ashore and made a shack by a spring. I staid there with him. When he got well enough to stand a few days' travel I got him across the river and givin' him a hunk of deer meat I told him to go, and if I ever saw him again I'd make a better shot.

"A year afterwards I trailed two Shawnees into Wingenund's camp and got surrounded and captured. The Delaware chief is my great enemy. They beat me, shot salt into my legs, made me run the gauntlet, tied me on the back of a wild mustang. Then they got ready to burn me at the stake. That night they painted my face black and held the usual death dances. Some of the braves got drunk and worked themselves into a frenzy. I allowed I'd never see daylight. I seen that one of the braves left to guard me was the young feller I had wounded the year before. He never took no notice of me. In the gray of the early mornin' when all were asleep and the other watch dozin' I felt cold steel between my wrists and my buckskin thongs dropped off. Then my feet were cut loose. I looked round and in the dim light I seen my young brave. He handed me my own rifle, knife and tomahawk, put his finger on his lips and with a bright smile, as 'if to say he was square with me, he pointed to the east. I was out of sight in a minute."

"How noble of him!" exclaimed Betty, her eyes all aglow. "He paid his debt to you, perhaps at the price of his life."

"I have never known an Indian to forget a promise, or a kind action, or an injury," observed Col. Zane.

"Are the Indians half as bad as they are called?" asked Betty. "I have heard as many stories of their nobility as of their cruelty."

"The Indians consider that they have been robbed and driven from their homes. What we think hideously inhuman is war to them," answered Col. Zane.

"When I came here from Fort Pitt I expected to see and fight Indians every day," said Capt. Boggs. "I have been here at Wheeling for nearly two years and have never seen a hostile Indian. There have been some Indians in the vicinity during that time, but not one has shown himself to me. I'm not up to Indian tricks, I know, but I think the last siege must have been enough for them. I don't believe we shall have any more trouble from them."

"Captain," called out Col. Zane, banging his hand on the table. "I'll bet you my best horse to a keg of gunpowder that you see enough Indians before you are a year older to make you wish you had never seen or heard of the western border."

"And I'll go you the same bet," said Major McColoch.

"You see, Captain, you must understand a little of the nature of the Indian," continued Col. Zane. "We have had proof that the Delawares and the Shawnees have been preparing for an expedition for months. We shall have another siege some day and to my thinking it will be a longer and harder one than the last. What say you, Wetzel?"

"I ain't sayin' much, but I don't calkilate on goin' on any long hunts this summer," answered the hunter.

"And do you think Tarhe, Wingenund, Pipe, Cornplanter, and all those chiefs will unite their forces and attack us?" asked Betty of Wetzel.

"Cornplanter won't. He has been paid for most of his land and he ain't so bitter. Tarhe is not likely to bother us. But Pipe and Wingenund and Red Fox— they all want blood."

"Have you seen these chiefs?" said Betty.

"Yes, I know 'em all and they all know me," answered the hunter. "I've watched over many a trail waitin' for one of 'em. If I can ever get a shot at any of 'em I'll give up Injuns and go farmin'. Good night, Betty."

"What a strange man is Wetzel," mused Betty, after the visitors had gone. "Do you know, Eb, he is not at

all like any one else. I have seen the girls shudder at the
mention of his name and I have heard them say they
could not look in his eyes. He does not affect me that
way. It is not often I can get him to talk, but sometimes
he tells me beautiful things about the woods; how he
lives in the wilderness, his home under the great trees;
how every leaf on the trees and every blade of grass has
its joy for him as well as its knowledge; how he curls
up in his little bark shack and is lulled to sleep by the
sighing of the wind through the pine tops. He told me
he has often watched the stars for hours at a time. I
know there is a waterfall back in the Black Forest
somewhere that Lewis goes to, simply to sit and watch
the water tumble over the precipice."

"Wetzel is a wonderful character, even to those who
know him only as an Indian slayer and a man who
wants no other occupation. Some day he will go off on
one of these long jaunts and will never return. That is
certain. The day is fast approaching when a man like
Wetzel will be of no use in life. Now, he is a necessity.
Like Tige he can smell Indians. Betty, I believe Lewis
tells you so much and is so kind and gentle toward you
because he cares for you."

"Of course Lew likes me. I know he does and I want
him to," said Betty. "But he does not care as you seem
to think. Grandmother Watkins said the same. I am
sure both of you are wrong."

"Did Dan's mother tell you that? Well, she's pretty
shrewd. It's quite likely, Betty, quite likely. It seems to
me you were not so quick witted as you used to be."

"Why so?" asked Betty, quickly.

"Well, you used to be different somehow," said her
brother, as he patted her hand.

"Do you mean I am more thoughtful?"

"Yes, and sometimes you seem sad."

"I have tried to be brave and—and happy," said
Betty, her voice trembling slightly.

"Yes, yes, I know you have, Betty. You have done wonderfully well here in this dead place. But tell me, don't be angry, don't you think too much of some one?"

"You have no right to ask me that," said Betty, flushing and turning away toward the stairway.

"Well, well, child, don't mind me. I did not mean anything. There, good night, Betty."

Long after she had gone up-stairs Col. Zane sat by his fireside. From time to time he sighed. He thought of the old Virginia home and of the smile of his mother. It seemed only a few short years since he had promised her that he would take care of the baby sister. How had he kept that promise made when Betty was a little thing bouncing on his knee? It seemed only yesterday. How swift the flight of time! Already Betty was a woman; her sweet, gay girlhood had passed; already a shadow had fallen on her face, the shadow of a secret sorrow.

*　　*　　*　　*　　*　　*　　*

March with its blustering winds had departed, and now April's showers and sunshine were gladdening the hearts of the settlers. Patches of green freshened the slopes of the hills; the lilac bushes showed tiny leaves, and the maple-buds were bursting. Yesterday a blue-bird—surest harbinger of spring—had alighted on the fence-post and had sung his plaintive song. A few more days and the blossoms were out mingling their pink and white with the green; the red-bud, the hawthorne, and the dog-wood were in bloom, checkering the hillsides.

"Bessie, spring is here," said Col. Zane, as he stood in the doorway. "The air is fresh, the sun shines warm, the birds are singing; it makes me feel good."

"Yes, it is pleasant to have spring with us again," answered his wife. "I think, though, that in winter I am happier. In summer I am always worried. I am afraid for the children to be out of my sight, and when you are away on a hunt I am distraught until you are home safe."

"Well, if the redskins let us alone this summer it will be something new," he said, laughing. "By the way, Bess, some new people came to the fort last night. They rafted down from the Monongahela settlements. Some of the women suffered considerably. I intend to offer them the cabin on the hill until they can cut the timber and run up a house. Sam said the cabin roof leaked and the chimney smoked, but with a little work I think they can be made more comfortable there than at the block-house."

"It is the only vacant cabin in the settlement. I can accommodate the women folks here."

"Well, we'll see about it. I don't want you and Betty inconvenienced. I'll send Sam up to the cabin and have him fix things up a bit and make it more habitable."

The door opened, admitting Col. Zane's elder boy. The lad's face was dirty, his nose was all bloody, and a big bruise showed over his right eye.

"For land's sake!" exclaimed his mother. "Look at the boy. Noah, come here. What have you been doing?"

Noah crept close to his mother and grasping her apron with both hands hid his face. Mrs. Zane turned the boy around and wiped his discolored features with a wet towel. She gave him a little shake and said: "Noah, have you been fighting again?"

"Let him go and I'll tell you about it," said the Colonel, and when the youngster had disappeared he continued: "Right after breakfast Noah went with me down to the mill. I noticed several children playing in front of Reihart's blacksmith shop. I went in, leaving Noah outside. I got the plow-share which I had left with Reihart to be repaired. He came to the door with me and all at once he said: 'Look at the kids.' I looked and saw Noah walk up to a boy and say something to him. The lad was a stranger, and I have no doubt belongs to these new people I told you about. He was bigger than Noah. At first the older boy appeared very friendly and evidently wanted to join the others in their game. I guess Noah did not approve of this, for after he had looked the stranger over he hauled away and punched the lad soundly. To make it short the strange boy gave Noah the worst beating he ever got in his life. I told Noah to come straight to you and confess."

"Well, did you ever!" ejaculated Mrs. Zane. "Noah is a bad boy. And you stood and watched him fight. You are laughing about it now. Ebenezer Zane, I would not put it beneath you to set Noah to fighting. I know you used to make the little niggers fight. Anyway, it serves Noah right and I hope it will be a lesson to him."

"I'll make you a bet, Bessie," said the Colonel, with another laugh. "I'll bet you that unless we lock him up, Noah will fight that boy every day or every time he meets him."

"I won't bet," said Mrs. Zane, with a smile of resignation.

"Where's Betts? I haven't seen her this morning. I am going over to Short Creek tomorrow or next day, and think I'll take her with me. You know I am to get a commission to lay out several settlements along the river, and I want to get some work finished at Short Creek this spring. Mrs. Raymer will be delighted to have Betty. Shall I take her?"

"By all means. A visit there will brighten her up and do her good."

"Well, what on earth have you been doing?" cried the Colonel. His remark had been called forth by a charming vision that had entered by the open door. Betty—for it was she—wore a little red cap set jauntily on her black hair. Her linsey dress was crumpled and covered with hayseed.

"I've been in the hay-mow," said Betty, waving a small basket. "For a week that old black hen has circumvented me, but at last I have conquered. I found the nest in the farthest corner under the hay."

"How did you get up in the loft?" inquired Mrs. Zane.

"Bessie, I climbed up the ladder of course. I acknowledge being unusually light-hearted and happy this morning, but I have not as yet grown wings. Sam said I could not climb up that straight ladder, but I found it easy enough."

"You should not climb up into the loft," said Mrs. Zane, in a severe tone. "Only last fall Hugh Bennet's little boy slid off the hay down into one of the stalls and the horse kicked him nearly to death."

"Oh, fiddlesticks, Bessie, I am not a baby," said Betty, with vehemence. "There is not a horse in the barn but would stand on his hind legs before he would step on me, let alone kick me."

"I don't know, Betty, but I think that black horse Mr. Clarke left here would kick any one," remarked the Colonel.

"Oh, no, he would not hurt me."

"Betty, we have had pleasant weather for about three days," said the Colonel, gravely. "In that time you have let out that crazy bear of yours to turn everything topsy-turvy. Only yesterday I got my hands in the paint you have put on your canoe. If you had asked my advice I would have told you that painting your canoe should not have been done for a month yet. Silas told me you fell down the creek hill; Sam said you tried to drive his team over the bluff, and so on. We are happy to see you get back your old time spirits, but could you not be a little more careful? Your versatility is bewildering. We do not know what to look for next. I fully expect to see you brought to the house some day maimed for life, or all that beautiful black hair gone to decorate some Huron's lodge."

"I tell you I am perfectly delighted that the weather is again so I can go out. I am tired to death of staying indoors. This morning I could have cried for very joy. Bessie will soon be lecturing me about Madcap. I must not ride farther than the fort. Well, I don't care. I intend to ride all over."

"Betty, I do not wish you to think I am lecturing you," said the Colonel's wife. "But you are as wild as a March hare, and some one must tell you things. Now listen. My brother, the Major, told me that Simon Girty, the renegade, had been heard to say that he had seen Eb Zane's little sister and that if he ever got his hands on her he would make a squaw of her. I am not teasing you. I am telling you the truth. Girty saw you when you were at Fort Pitt two years ago. Now what would you do if he caught you on one of your lonely rides and carried you off to his wigwam? He has done things like that before. James Girty carried off one of the Johnson girls. Her brothers tried to rescue her and lost their lives. It is a common trick of the Indians."

"What would I do if Mr. Simon Girty tried to make a squaw of me?" exclaimed Betty, her eyes flashing fire. "Why, I'd kill him!"

"I believe it, Betts, on my word I do," spoke up the Colonel. "But let us hope you may never see Girty. All I ask is that you be careful. I am going over to Short Creek tomorrow. Will you go with me? I know Mrs. Raymer will be pleased to see you."

"Oh, Eb, that will be delightful!"

Very well, get ready and we shall start early in the morning."

Two weeks later Betty returned from Short Creek and seemed to have profited much by her short visit. Col. Zane remarked with satisfaction to his wife that Betty had regained all her former cheerfulness.

The morning after Betty's return was a perfect spring morning—the first in that month of May-days. The sun shone bright and warm; the mayflowers blossomed; the trailing arbutus scented the air; everywhere the grass and the leaves looked fresh and green; swallows flitted in and out of the barn door; the blue-birds twittered; a meadow-lark caroled forth his pure melody, and the busy hum of bees came from the fragrant apple-blossoms.

"Mis' Betty, Madcap 'pears powerfo' skittenish," said old Sam, when he had led the pony to where Betty stood on the hitching block. "Whoa, dar, you rascal."

Betty laughed as she leaped lightly into the saddle, and soon she was flying over the old familiar road, down across the creek bridge, past the old grist-mill, around the fort and then out on the river bluff. The Indian pony was fiery and mettlesome. He pranced and side-stepped, galloped and trotted by turns. He seemed as glad to get out again into the warm sunshine as was Betty herself. He tore down the road a mile at his best speed. Coming back Betty pulled him into a walk. Presently her musings were interrupted by a sharp switch in the face from a twig of a tree. She stopped the pony and broke off the offending branch. As she looked around the recollection of what had happened to her in that very spot flashed into her mind. It was here that she had been stopped by the man who had passed almost as swiftly out of her life as he had crossed her path that memorable afternoon. She fell to musing on the old perplexing question. After all could there not have been some mistake? Perhaps she might have mis-judged him? And then the old spirit, which resented her thinking of him in that softened mood, rose and fought the old battle over again. But as often happened the mood conquered, and Betty permitted herself to sink for the moment into the sad thoughts which returned

like a mournful strain of music once sung by beloved
voices, now forever silent.

She could not resist the desire to ride down to the old
sycamore. The pony turned into the bridle-path that led
down the bluff and the sure-footed beast picked his way
carefully over the roots and stones. Betty's heart beat
quicker when she saw the noble tree under whose
spreading branches she had spent the happiest day of
her life. The old monarch of the forest was not one
whit changed by the wild winds of winter. The dew
sparkled on the nearly full grown leaves; the little
sycamore balls were already as large as marbles.

Betty drew rein at the top of the bank and looked
absently at the tree and into the foam covered pool
beneath. At that moment her eyes saw nothing physi-
cal. They held the faraway light of the dreamer, the
look that sees so much of the past and nothing of the
present.

Presently her reflections were broken by the actions
of the pony. Madcap had thrown up her head, laid
back her ears, and commenced to paw the ground with
her forefeet. Betty looked round to see the cause of
Madcap's excitement. What was that! She saw a tall
figure clad in brown leaning against the stone. She saw
a long fishing-rod. What was there so familiar in the
poise of that figure? Madcap dislodged a stone from the
path and it went rattling down the rocky slope and fell
with a splash into the water. The man heard it, turned
and faced the hillside. Betty recognized Alfred Clarke.
For a moment she believed she must be dreaming. She
had had many dreams of the old sycamore. She looked
again. Yes, it was he. Pale, worn, and older he undoubtedly looked, but the features were surely those of
Alfred Clarke. Her heart gave a great bound and then
seemed to stop beating while a very agony of joy surged
over her and made her faint. So he still lived. That was

her first thought, glad and joyous, and then memory returning, her face went white as with clenched teeth she wheeled Madcap and struck her with the switch. Once on the level bluff she urged her toward the house at a furious pace.

Col. Zane had just stepped out of the barn door and his face took on an expression of amazement when he saw the pony come tearing up the road, Betty's hair flying in the wind and with a face as white as if she were pursued by a thousand yelling Indians.

"Say, Betts, what the deuce is wrong?" cried the Colonel, when Betty reached the fence.

"Why did you not tell me that man was here again?" she demanded in intense excitement.

"That man! What man?" asked Col. Zane, considerably taken back by this angry apparition.

"Mr. Clarke, of course. Just as if you did not know. I suppose you thought it a fine opportunity for one of your jokes."

"Oh, Clarke. Well, the fact is I just found it out myself. Haven't I been away as well as you. I certainly cannot imagine how any man could create such evident excitement in your mind. Poor Clarke, what has he done now?"

"You might have told me. Somebody could have told me and saved me from making a fool of myself," retorted Betty, who was plainly on the verge of tears. "I rode down to the old sycamore tree and he saw me in, of all the places in the world, the one place where I would not want him to see me."

"Huh!" said the Colonel, who often gave vent to the Indian exclamation. "Is that all? I thought something had happened."

"All! Is it not enough? I would rather have died. He is a man and he will think I followed him down there, that I was thinking of—that—Oh!" cried Betty, passionately, and then she strode into the house, slammed the door, and left the Colonel, lost in wonder.

"Humph! These women beat me. I can't make them out, and the older I grow the worse I get," he said, as he led the pony into the stable.

Betty ran up-stairs to her room, her head in a whirl. Stronger than the surprise of Alfred's unexpected appearance in Fort Henry and stronger than the mortification in having been discovered going to a spot she should have been too proud to remember was the bitter sweet consciousness that his mere presence had thrilled her through and through. It hurt her and made her hate herself in that moment. She hid her face in shame at the thought that she could not help being glad to see the man who had only trifled with her, the man who had considered the acquaintance of so little consequence that he had never taken the trouble to write her a line or send her a message. She wrung her trembling hands. She endeavored to still that throbbing heart and to conquer that sweet vague feeling which had crept over her and made her weak. The tears began to come and with a sob she threw herself on the bed and buried her head in the pillow.

An hour after, when Betty had quieted herself and had seated herself by the window a light knock sounded on the door and Col. Zane entered. He hesitated and came in rather timidly, for Betty was not to be taken liberties with, and seeing her by the window he crossed the room and sat down by her side.

Betty did not remember her father or her mother. Long ago when she was a child she had gone to her brother, laid her head on his shoulder and told him all her troubles. The desire grew strong within her now. There was comfort in the strong clasp of his hand. She was not proof against it, and her dark head fell on his shoulder.

* * * * * * *

Alfred Clarke had indeed made his reappearance in Fort Henry. The preceding October when he left the settlement to go on the expedition up the Monongahela River his intention had been to return to the fort as soon as he had finished his work, but what he did do was only another illustration of that fatality which affects everything. Man hopefully makes his plans and an inexorable destiny works out what it has in store for him.

The men of the expedition returned to Fort Henry in due time, but Alfred had been unable to accompany them. He had sustained a painful injury and had been compelled to go to Fort Pitt for medical assistance. While there he had received word that his mother was lying very ill at his old home in Southern Virginia and if he wished to see her alive he must not delay in reaching her bedside. He left Fort Pitt at once and went to his home, where he remained until his mother's death. She had been the only tie that bound him to the old home, and now that she was gone he determined to leave the scene of his boyhood forever.

Alfred was the rightful heir to all of the property, but an unjust and selfish stepfather stood between him and any contentment he might have found there. He decided he would be a soldier of fortune. He loved the daring life of a ranger, and preferred to take his chances with the hardy settlers on the border rather than live the idle life of a gentleman farmer. He declared his intention to his stepfather, who ill-concealed his satisfaction at the turn affairs had taken. Then Alfred packed his belongings, secured his mother's jewels, and with one sad, backward glance rode away from the stately old mansion.

It was Sunday morning and Clarke had been two days in Fort Henry. From his little room in the block-house he surveyed the well-remembered scene. The rolling hills, the broad river, the green forests seemed like old friends.

"Here I am again," he mused. "What a fool a man can be. I have left a fine old plantation, slaves, horses, a country noted for its pretty women—for what? Here there can be nothing for me but Indians, hard work, privation, and trouble. Yet I could not get here quickly enough. Pshaw! What use to speak of the possibilities of a new country. I cannot deceive myself. It is *she*. I would walk a thousand miles and starve myself for months just for one glimpse of her sweet face. Knowing this what care I for all the rest. How strange she should ride down to the old sycamore tree yesterday at the moment I was there and thinking of her. Evidently she had just returned from her visit. I wonder if she ever cared. I wonder if she ever thinks of me. Shall I accept that incident as a happy augury? Well, I am here to find out and find out I will. Aha! there goes the church bell."

Laughing a little at his eagerness he brushed his coat, put on his cap and went down stairs. The settlers with their families were going into the meeting house. As Alfred started up the steps he met Lydia Boggs.

"Why, Mr. Clarke, I heard you had returned," she said, smiling pleasantly and extending her hand. "Welcome to the fort. I am very glad to see you."

While they were chatting her father and Col. Zane came up and both greeted the young man warmly.

"Well, well, back on the frontier," said the Colonel, in his hearty way. "Glad to see you at the fort again. I tell you, Clarke, I have taken a fancy to that black horse you left me last fall. I did not know what to think when Jonathan brought back my horse. To tell you the truth I always looked for you to come back. What have you been doing all winter?"

"I have been at home. My mother was ill all winter and she died in April."

"My lad, that's bad news. I am sorry," said Col. Zane, putting his hand kindly on the young man's shoulder. "I was wondering what gave you that older and graver look. It's hard, lad, but it's the way of life."

"I have come back to get my old place with you, Col. Zane, if you will give it to me."

"I will, and can promise you more in the future. I am going to open a road through to Maysville, Kentucky, and start several new settlements along the river. I will need young men, and am more than glad you have returned."

"Thank you, Col. Zane. That is more than I could have hoped for."

Alfred caught sight of a trim figure in a gray linsey gown coming down the road. There were several young people approaching, but he saw only Betty. By some evil chance Betty walked with Ralfe Miller, and for some mysterious reason, which women always keep to themselves, she smiled and looked up into his face at a time of all times she should not have done so. Alfred's heart turned to lead.

When the young people reached the steps the eyes of the rivals met for one brief second, but that was long enough for them to understand each other. They did not speak. Lydia hesitated and looked toward Betty.

"Betty, here is——" began Col. Zane, but Betty passed them with flaming cheeks and with not so much as a glance at Alfred. It was an awkward moment for him.

"Let us go in," he said composedly, and they all filed into the church.

As long as he lived Alfred Clarke never forgot that hour. His pride kept him chained in his seat. Outwardly he maintained his composure, but inwardly his brain seemed throbbing, whirling, bursting.

What an idiot he had been! He understood now why his letter had never been answered. Betty loved Miller, a man who hated him, a man who would leave no stone unturned to destroy even a little liking which she might have felt for him. Once again Miller had crossed his path and worsted him. With a sudden sickening sense of despair he realized that all his fond hopes had been but dreams, a fool's dreams. The dream of that moment when he would give her his mother's jewels, the dream of that charming face uplifted to his, the dream of the little cottage to which he would hurry after his day's work and find her waiting at the gate,—these dreams must be dispelled forever. He could barely wait until the end of the service. He wanted to be alone; to fight it out with himself; to crush out of his heart that fair image. At length the hour ended and he got out before the congregation and hurried to his room.

Betty had company all that afternoon and it was late in the day when Col. Zane ascended the stairs and entered her room to find her alone.

"Betty, I wish to know why you ignored Mr. Clarke this morning?" said Col. Zane, looking down on his sister. There was a gleam in his eye and an expression about his mouth seldom seen in the Colonel's features.

"I do not know that it concerns any one but myself," answered Betty quickly, as her head went higher and her eyes flashed with a gleam not unlike that in her brother's.

"I beg your pardon. I do not agree with you," replied Col. Zane. "It does concern others. You cannot do things like that in this little place where every one knows all about you and expect it to pass unnoticed. Martin's wife saw you cut Clarke and you know what a gossip she is. Already every one is talking about you and Clarke."

"To that I am indifferent."

"But I care. I won't have people talking about you,"

replied the Colonel, who began to lose patience. Usually he had the best temper imaginable. "Last fall you allowed Clarke to pay you a good deal of attention and apparently you were on good terms when he went away. Now that he has returned you won't even speak to him. You let this fellow Miller run after you. In my estimation Miller is not to be compared to Clarke, and judging from the warm greetings I saw Clarke receive this morning, there are a number of folk who agree with me. Not that I am praising Clarke. I simply say this because to Bessie, to Jack, to everyone, your act is incomprehensible. People are calling you a flirt and saying that they would prefer some country manners."

"I have not allowed Mr. Miller to run after me, as you are pleased to term it," retorted Betty with indignation. "I do not like him. I never see him any more unless you or Bessie or some one else is present. You know that. I cannot prevent him from walking to church with me."

"No, I suppose not, but are you entirely innocent of those sweet glances which you gave him this morning?"

"I did not," cried Betty with an angry flush. "I won't be called a flirt by you or by anyone else. The moment I am civil to some man all these old maids and old women say I am flirting. It is outrageous."

"Now, Betty, don't get excited. We are getting from the question. Why are you not civil to Clarke?" asked Col. Zane. She did not answer and after a moment he continued. "If there is anything about Clarke that I do not know and that I should know I want you to tell me. Personally I like the fellow. I am not saying that to make you think you ought to like him because I do. You might not care for him at all, but that would be no good reason for your actions. Betty, in these frontier settlements a man is soon known for his real worth. Every one at the Fort liked Clarke. The youngsters adored him. Bessie liked him very much. You know he and Isaac became good friends. I think he acted like a man today. I saw the look Miller gave him. I don't like this fellow Miller, anyway. Now, I am taking the trouble to tell you my side of the argument. It is not a question of your liking Clarke—that is none of my affair. It is simply that either he is not the man we all think him or you are acting in a way unbecoming a Zane. I do not purpose to have this state of affairs continue. Now, enough of this beating about the bush."

Betty had seen the Colonel angry more than once, but never with her. It was quite certain she had angered him and she forgot her own resentment. Her heart had warmed with her brother's praise of Clarke. Then as she remembered the past she felt a scorn for her weakness and such a revulsion of feeling that she cried out passionately:

"He is a trifler. He never cared for me. He insulted me."

Col. Zane reached for his hat, got up without saying another word and went down stairs.

Betty had not intended to say quite what she had and instantly regretted her hasty words. She called to the Colonel, but he did not answer her, nor return.

"Betty, what in the world could you have said to my husband?" said Mrs. Zane as she entered the room. She was breathless from running up the stairs and her comely face wore a look of concern. "He was as white as that sheet and he stalked off toward the Fort without a word to me."

"I simply told him Mr. Clarke had insulted me," answered Betty calmly.

"Great Heavens! Betty, what have you done?" exclaimed Mrs. Zane. "You don't know Eb when he is angry. He is a big fool over you, anyway. He is liable to kill Clarke."

Betty's blood was up now and she said that would not be a matter of much importance.

"When did he insult you?" asked the elder woman, yielding to her natural curiosity.

"It was last October."

"Pooh! It took you a long time to tell it. I don't believe it amounted to much. Mr. Clarke did not appear to be the sort of a man to insult anyone. All the girls were crazy about him last year. If he was not all right they would not have been."

"I do not care if they were. The girls can have him and welcome. I don't want him. I never did. I am tired of hearing everyone eulogize him. I hate him. Do you hear? I hate him! And I wish you would go away and leave me alone."

"Well, Betty, all I will say is that you are a remarkable young woman," answered Mrs. Zane, who saw plainly that Betty's violent outburst was a prelude to a storm of weeping. "I don't believe a word you have said. I don't believe you hate him. There!"

Col. Zane walked straight to the Fort, entered the blockhouse and knocked on the door of Clarke's room. A voice bade him come in. He shoved open the door and went into the room. Clarke had evidently just returned from a tramp in the hills, for his garments were covered with burrs and his boots were dusty. He looked tired, but his face was calm.

"Why, Col. Zane! Have a seat. What can I do for you?"

"I have come to ask you to explain a remark of my sister's."

"Very well, I am at your service," answered Alfred slowly, lighting his pipe, after which he looked straight into Col. Zane's face.

"My sister informs me that you insulted her last fall before you left the Fort. I am sure you are neither a liar nor a coward, and I expect you to answer as a man."

"Col. Zane, I am not a liar, and I hope I am not a coward," said Alfred coolly. He took a long pull on his pipe and blew a puff of white smoke toward the ceiling.

"I believe you, but I must have an explanation. There is something wrong somewhere. I saw Betty pass you without speaking this morning. I did not like it and I took her to task about it. She then said you had insulted her. Betty is prone to exaggerate, especially when angry, but she never told me a lie in her life. Ever since you pulled Isaac out of the river I have taken an interest in you. That's why I'd like to avoid any trouble. But this thing has gone far enough. Now be sensible, swallow your pride and let me hear your side of the story."

Alfred had turned pale at his visitor's first words. There was no mistaking Col. Zane's manner. Alfred well knew that the Colonel, if he found Betty had really been insulted, would call him out and kill him. Col. Zane spoke quietly, even kindly, but there was an undercurrent of intense feeling in his voice, a certain deadly intent which boded ill to anyone who might cross him at that moment. Alfred's first impulse was a reckless desire to tell Col. Zane he had nothing to explain and that he stood ready to give any satisfaction in his power. But he wisely thought better of this. It struck him that this would not be fair, for no matter what the girl had done the Colonel had always been his friend. So Alfred pulled himself together and resolved to make a clean breast of the whole affair.

"Col. Zane, I do not feel that I owe your sister anything, and what I am going to tell you is simply because you have always been my friend, and I do not want you to have any wrong ideas about me. I'll tell you the truth and you can be the judge as to whether or not I insulted your sister. I fell in love with her, almost at first sight. The night after the Indians recaptured your brother, Betty and I stood out in the moonlight and she looked so bewitching and I felt so sorry for her and so carried away by my love for her that I yielded to a momentary impulse and kissed her. I simply could not help it. There is no excuse for me. She struck me across the face and ran into the house. I had intended that night to tell her of my love and place my fate in her hands, but, of course, the unfortunate occurrence made that impossible. As I was to leave at dawn next day, I remained up all night, thinking what I ought to do. Finally I decided to write. I wrote her a letter, telling her all and begging her to become my wife. I gave the letter to your slave, Sam, and told him it was a matter of life and death, and not to lose the letter nor fail to give it to Betty. I have had no answer to that letter. Today she coldly ignored me. That is my story, Col. Zane."

"Well, I don't believe she got the letter," said Col. Zane. "She has not acted like a young lady who has had the privilege of saying 'yes' or 'no' to you. And Sam never had any use for you. He disliked you from the first, and never failed to say something against you."

"I'll kill that d—n nigger if he did not deliver that letter," said Clarke, jumping up in his excitement. "I never thought of that. Good Heaven! What could she have thought of me? She would think I had gone away without a word. If she knew I really loved her she could not think so terribly of me."

"There is more to be expalined, but I am satisfied with your side of it," said Col. Zane. "Now I'll go to Sam and see what has become of that letter. I am glad I am justified in thinking of you as I have. I imagine this thing has hurt you and I don't wonder at it. Maybe we can untangle the problem yet. My advice would be— but never mind that now. Anyway, I'm your friend in this matter. I'll let you know the result of my talk with Sam."

"I thought that young fellow was a gentleman," mused Col. Zane as he crossed the green square and started up the hill toward the cabins. He found the old negro seated on his doorstep.

"Sam, what did you do with a letter Mr. Clarke gave you last October and instructed you to deliver to Betty?"

"I dun recollec' no lettah, sah," replied Sam.

"Now, Sam, don't lie about it. Clarke has just told me that he gave you the letter. What did you do with it?"

"Massa Zane, I ain dun seen no lettah," answered the old darkey, taking a dingy pipe from his mouth and rolling his eyes at his master.

"If you lie again I will punish you," said Col. Zane sternly. "You are getting old, Sam, and I would not like to whip you, but I will if you do not find that letter."

Sam grumbled, and shuffled inside the cabin. Col. Zane heard him rummaging around. Presently he came back to the door and handed a very badly soiled paper to the Colonel.

"What possessed you to do this, Sam? You have always been honest. Your act has caused great misunderstanding and it might have led to worse."

"He's one of dem no good Southern white trash; he's good fer nuttin'," said Sam. "I saw yo' sistah, Mis' Betty, wif him, and I seen she was gittin' fond of him, and I says I ain't gwinter have Mis' Betty runnin' off wif him. And I'se never gibbin de lettah to her."

That was all the explanation Sam would vouchsafe, and Col. Zane, knowing it would be useless to say more to the well-meaning but ignorant and superstitious old negro, turned and wended his way back to the house. He looked at the paper and saw that it was addressed to Elizabeth Zane, and that the ink was faded until the letters were scarcely visible.

"What have you there?" asked his wife, who had watched him go up the hill to the negro's cabin. She breathed a sigh of relief when she saw that her husband's face had recovered its usual placid expression.

"It is a little letter for that young fire-brand up stairs, and I believe it will clear up the mystery. Clarke gave it to Sam last fall and Sam never gave it to Betty."

"I hope with all my heart it may settle Betty. She worries me to death with her love affairs."

Col. Zane went up stairs and found the young lady exactly as he had left her. She gave an impatient toss of her head as he entered.

"Well, Madam, I have here something that may excite even your interest," he said cheerily.

"What?" asked Betty with a start. She flushed crimson when she saw the letter and at first refused to take it from her brother. She was at a loss to understand his cheerful demeanor. He had been anything but pleasant a few moments since.

"Here, take it. It is a letter from Mr. Clarke which you should have received last fall. That last morning he gave this letter to Sam to deliver to you, and the crazy old nigger kept it. However, it is too late to talk of that, only it does seem a great pity. I feel sorry for both of you. Clarke never will forgive you, even if you want him to, which I am sure you do not. I don't know exactly what is in this letter, but I know it will make you ashamed to think you did not trust him."

With this parting reproof the Colonel walked out, leaving Betty completely bewildered. The words "too late," "never forgive," and "a great pity" rang through her head. What did he mean? She tore the letter open with trembling hands and holding it up to the now fast-waning light, she read:

"Dear Betty:

"If you had waited only a moment longer I know you would not have been so angry with me. The words

I wanted so much to say choked me and I could not speak them. I love you. I have loved you from the very first moment, that blessed moment when I looked up over your pony's head to see the sweetest face the sun ever shone on. I'll be the happiest man on earth if you will say you care a little for me and promise to be my wife.

"It was wrong to kiss you and I beg your forgiveness. Could you but see your face as I saw it last night in the moonlight, I would not need to plead: you would know that the impulse which swayed me was irresistible. In that kiss I gave you my hope, my love, my life, my all. Let it plead for me.

"I expect to return from Ft. Pitt in about six or eight weeks, but I cannot wait until then for your answer.

"With hope I sign myself,

"Yours until death,

"ALFRED."

Betty read the letter through. The page blurred before her eyes: a sensation of oppression and giddiness made her reach out helplessly with both hands. Then she slipped forward and fell on the floor. For the first time in all her young life Betty had fainted. Col. Zane found her lying pale and quiet under the window.

Chapter 9

GYANTWAIA, OR, as he was more commonly called, Cornplanter, was originally a Seneca chief, but when the five war tribes consolidated, forming the historical "Five Nations," he became their leader. An old historian said of this renowned chieftain: "Tradition says that the blood of a famous white man coursed through the veins of Cornplanter. The tribe he led was originally ruled by an Indian queen of singular power and beauty. She was born to govern her people by the force of her character. Many a great chief importuned her to become his wife, but she preferred to cling to her power and dignity. When this white man, then a very young man, came to the Ohio valley the queen fell in love with him, and Cornplanter was their son."

Cornplanter lived to a great age. He was a wise counsellor, a great leader, and he died when he was one hundred years old, having had more conceded to him by the white men than any other chieftain. General Washington wrote of him: "The merits of Cornplanter and his friendship for the United States are well known and shall not be forgotten."

But Cornplanter had not always been a friend to the palefaces. During Dunmore's war and for years after, he was one of the most vindictive of the savage leaders against the invading pioneers.

It was during this period of Cornplanter's activity

against the whites that Isaac Zane had the misfortune to fall into the great chief's power.

We remember Isaac last when, lost in the woods, weak from hunger and exposure, he had crawled into a thicket and had gone to sleep. He was awakened by a dog licking his face. He heard Indian voices. He got up and ran as fast as he could, but exhausted as he was he proved no match for his pursuers. They came up with him and seeing that he was unable to defend himself they grasped him by the arms and led him down a well-worn bridle-path.

"D——n poor run. No good legs," said one of his captors, and at this the other two Indians laughed. Then they whooped and yelled, at which signal other Indians joined them. Isaac saw that they were leading him into a large encampment. He asked the big savage who led him what camp it was, and learned that he had fallen into the hands of Cornplanter.

While being marched through the large Indian village Isaac saw unmistakable indications of war. There was a busy hum on all sides; the squaws were preparing large quantities of buffalo meat, cutting it in long, thin strips, and were parching corn in stone vessels. The braves were cleaning rifles, sharpening tomahawks, and mixing war paints. All these things Isacc knew to be preparations for long marches and for battle. That night he heard speech after speech in the lodge next to the one in which he lay, but they were in an unknown tongue. Later he heard the yelling of the Indians and the dull thud of their feet as they stamped on the ground. He heard the ring of the tomahawks as they were struck into hard wood. The Indians were dancing the war-dance round the war-post. This continued with some little intermission all the four days that Isaac lay in the lodge rapidly recovering his strength. The fifth day a man came into the lodge. He was tall and powerful, his hair fell over his shoulders and he wore the scanty buckskin dress of the Indian. But Isaac knew at once he was a white man, perhaps one of the many French traders who passed through the Indian village.

"Your name is Zane," said the man in English, looking sharply at Isaac.

"That is my name. Who are you?" asked Isaac in great surprise.

"I am Girty. I've never seen you, but I knew Col. Zane and Jonathan well. I've seen your sister; you all favor one another."

"Are you Simon Girty?"

"Yes."

"I have heard of your influence with the Indians. Can you do anything to get me out of this?"

"How did you happen to git over here? You are not many miles from Wingenund's Camp," said Girty, giving Isaac another sharp look from his small black eyes.

"Girty, I assure you I am not a spy. I escaped from the Wyandot village on Mad River and after traveling three days lost my way. I went to sleep in a thicket and when I awoke an Indian dog had found me. I heard voices and saw three Indians. I got up and ran, but they easily caught me."

"I know about you. Old Tarhe has a daughter who kept you from bein' ransomed."

"Yes, and I wish I were back there. I don't like the look of things."

"You are right, Zane. You got ketched at a bad time. The Indians are mad. I suppose you don't know that Col. Crawford massacred a lot of Indians a few days ago. It'll go hard with any white man that gits captured. I'm afraid I can't do nothin' for you."

A few words concerning Simon Girty, the White Savage. He had two brothers, James and George, who had been desperadoes before they were adopted by the Delawares, and who eventually became fierce and relentless savages. Simon had been captured at the same time as his brothers, but he did not at once fall under the influence of the unsettled, free-and-easy life of the Indians. It is probably that while in captivity he acquired the power of commanding the Indians' interest and learned the secret of ruling them—two capabilities few white men ever possessed. It is certain that he, like the noted French-Canadian Joucaire, delighted to sit round the camp fires and to go into the council-lodge and talk to the assembled Indians.

At the outbreak of the revolution Girty was a commissioned officer of militia at Ft. Pitt. He deserted from the Fort, taking with him the Tories McKee and Elliott, and twelve soldiers, and these traitors spread as much terror among the Delaware Indians as they did among the whites. The Delawares had been one of the few peacefully disposed tribes. In order to get them to join their forces with Governor Hamilton, the British commander, Girty declared that Gen. Washington had been killed, that Congress had been dispersed, and that the British were winning all the battles.

Girty spoke most of the Indian languages, and Hamilton employed him to go among the different Indian tribes and incite them to greater hatred of the pioneers. This proved to be just the life that suited him. He soon rose to have a great and bad influence on all the tribes. He became noted for his assisting the Indians in marauds, for his midnight forays, for his scalpings, and his efforts to capture white women, and for his devilish cunning and cruelty.

For many years Girty was the Deathshead of the frontier. The mention of his name alone created terror in any household; in every pioneer's cabin it made the children cry out in fear and paled the cheeks of the stoutest-hearted wife.

It is difficult to conceive of a white man's being such a fiend in human guise. The only explanation that can be given is that renegades rage against the cause of their own blood with the fury of insanity rather than with the malignity of a naturally ferocious temper. In justice to Simon Girty it must be said that facts not known until his death showed he was not so cruel and base as believed; that some deeds of kindness were attributed to him; that he risked his life to save Kenton from the stake, and that many of the terrible crimes laid at his door were really committed by his savage brothers.

Isaac Zane suffered no annoyance at the hands of Cornplanter's braves until the seventh day of his imprisonment. He saw no one except the squaw who brought him corn and meat. On that day two savages came for him and led him into the immense council-lodge of the Five Nations. Cornplanter sat between his right-hand chiefs, Big Tree and Half Town, and surrounded by the other chiefs of the tribes. An aged Indian stood in the center of the lodge and addressed the others. The listening savages sat immovable, their faces as cold and stern as stone masks. Apparently they did not heed the entrance of the prisoner.

"Zane, they're havin' a council," whispered a voice in Isaac's ear. Isaac turned and recognized Girty. "I want to prepare you for the worst."

"Is there, then, no hope for me?" asked Isaac.

"I'm afraid not," continued the renegade, speaking in a low whisper. "They wouldn't let me speak at the council. I told Cornplanter that killin' you might bring the Hurons down on him, but he wouldn't listen. Yesterday, in the camp of the Delawares, I saw Col. Crawford burnt at the stake. He was a friend of mine at Pitt, and I didn't dare to say one word to the frenzied Indians. I had to watch the torture. Pipe and Wingenund, both old friends of Crawford, stood by and watched him walk round the stake on the red-hot coals five hours."

Isaac shuddered at the words of the renegade, but did not answer. He had felt from the first that his case was hopeless, and that no opportunity for escape could possibly present itself in such a large encampment. He set his teeth hard and resolved to show the red devils how a white man could die.

Several speeches were made by different chiefs and then an impressive oration by Big Tree. At the conclusion of the speeches, which were in an unknown tongue to Isaac, Cornplanter handed a war-club to Half Town. This chief got up, walked to the end of the circle, and there brought the club down on the ground with a resounding thud. Then he passed the club to Big Tree. In a solemn and dignified manner every chief duplicated Half Town's performance with the club.

Isaac watched the ceremony as if fascinated. He had seen a war-club used in the councils of the Hurons and knew that striking it on the ground signified war and death.

"White man, you are a killer of Indians," said Cornplanter in good English. "When the sun shines again you die."

A brave came forward and painted Isaac's face black. This Isaac knew to indicate that death awaited him on the morrow. On his way back to his prison-lodge he saw that a war-dance was in progress.

A hundred braves with tomahawks, knives, and mallets in their hands were circling round a post and keeping time to the low music of a muffled drum. Close together, with heads bowed, they marched. At certain moments, which they led up to with a dancing on rigid legs and a stamping with their feet, they wheeled, and uttering hideous yells, started to march in the other direction. When this had been repeated three times a brave stepped from the line, advanced, and struck his knife or tomahawk into the post. Then with a loud voice he proclaimed his past exploits and great deeds in war. The other Indians greeted this with loud yells of applause and a flourishing of weapons. Then the whole ceremony was gone through again.

That afternoon many of the Indians visited Isaac in his lodge and shook their fists at him and pointed their knives at him. They hissed and groaned at him. Their vindictive faces expressed the malignant joy they felt at the expectation of putting him to the torture.

When night came Isaac's guards laced up the lodge-door and shut him from the sight of the maddened Indians. The darkness that gradually enveloped him was a relief. By and by all was silent except for the occasional yell of a drunken savage. To Isaac it sounded like a long, rolling death-cry echoing throughout the encampment and murdering his sleep. Its horrible meaning made him shiver and his flesh creep. At length even that yell ceased. The watch-dogs quieted down and the perfect stillness which ensued could almost be felt. Through Isaac's mind ran over and over again the same words. His last night to live! His last night to live! He forced himself to think of other things. He lay there in the darkness of his tent, but he was far away in thought, far away in the past with his mother and brothers before they had come to this bloodthirsty country. His thoughts wandered to the days of his boyhood when he used to drive the cows to the pasture on the hillside, and in his dreamy, disordered fancy he was once more letting down the bars of the gate. Then he was wading in the brook and whacking the green frogs with his stick. Old playmates' faces, forgotten for years, were there looking at him from the dark wall of his wigwam. There was Andrew's face; the faces of his other brothers; the laughing face of his sister; the serene face of his mother. As he lay there with the shadow of death over him sweet was the thought that soon he would be reunited with that mother. The images faded slowly away, swallowed up in the gloom. Suddenly a vision appeared to him. A radiant white light illumined

the lodge and shone full on the beautiful face of the
Indian maiden who had loved him so well. Myeerah's
dark eyes were bright with an undying love and her lips
smiled hope.

A rude kick dispelled Isaac's dreams. A brawny
savage pulled him to his feet and pushed him outside of
the lodge.

It was early morning. The sun had just cleared the
low hills in the east and its red beams crimsoned the
edges of the clouds of fog which hung over the river
like a great white curtain. Though the air was warm,
Isaac shivered a little as the breeze blew softly against
his cheek. He took one long look toward the rising sun,
toward that east he had hoped to see, and then resolutely turned his face away forever.

Early though it was the Indians were astir and their
whooping rang throughout the valley. Down the main
street of the village the guards led the prisoner, followed by a screaming mob of squaws and young braves
and children who threw sticks and stones at the hated
Long Knife.

Soon the inhabitants of the camp congregated on the
green oval in the midst of the lodges. When the prisoner appeared they formed in two long lines facing each
other, and several feet apart. Isaac was to run the
gauntlet—one of the severest of Indian tortures. With
the exception of Cornplanter and several of his chiefs,
every Indian in the village was in line. Little Indian
boys hardly large enough to sling a stone; maidens and
squaws with switches or spears; athletic young braves
with flashing tomahawks; grim, matured warriors
swinging knotted war clubs,—all were there in line,
yelling and brandishing their weapons in a manner
frightful to behold.

The word was given, and stripped to the waist, Isaac
bounded forward fleet as a deer. He knew the Indian
way of running the gauntlet. The head of that long lane

contained the warriors and older braves and it was here that the great danger lay. Between these lines he sped like a flash, dodging this way and that, running close in under the raised weapons, taking what blows he could on his uplifted arms, knocking this warrior over and doubling that one up with a lightning blow in the stomach, never slacking his speed for one stride, so that it was extremely difficult for the Indians to strike him effectually. Once past that formidable array, Isaac's gauntlet was run, for the squaws and children scattered screaming before the sweep of his powerful arms.

The old chiefs grunted their approval. There was a bruise on Isaac's forehead and a few drops of blood mingled with the beads of perspiration. Several lumps and scratches showed on his bare shoulders and arms, but he had escaped any serious injury. This was a feat almost without a parallel in gauntlet running.

When he had been tied with wet buckskin thongs to the post in the center of the oval, the youths, the younger braves, and the squaws began circling round him, yelling like so many demons. The old squaws thrust sharpened sticks, which had been soaked in salt water, into his flesh. The maidens struck him with willows which left red welts on his white shoulders. The braves buried the blades of their tomahawks in the post as near as possible to his head without actually hitting him.

Isaac knew the Indian nature well. To command the respect of the savages was the only way to lessen his torture. He knew that a cry for mercy would only increase his sufferings and not hasten his death,—indeed it would prolong both. He had resolved to die without a moan. He had determined to show absolute indifference to his torture, which was the only way to appeal to the savage nature, and if anything could, make the Indians show mercy. Or, if he could taunt them into killing him at once he would be spared all the terrible agony which they were in the habit of inflicting on their victims.

One handsome young brave twirled a glittering tomahawk which he threw from a distance of ten, fifteen, and twenty feet and every time the sharp blade of the hatchet sank deep into the stake within an inch of Isaac's head. With a proud and disdainful look Isaac gazed straight before him and paid no heed to his tormentor.

"Does the Indian boy think he can frighten a white warrior?" said Isaac scornfully at length. "Let him go and earn his eagle plumes. The pale face laughs at him."

The young brave understood the Huron language, for he gave a frightful yell and cast his tomahawk again, this time shaving a lock of hair from Isaac's head.

This was what Isaac had prayed for. He hoped that one of these glittering hatchets would be propelled less skilfully than its predecessors and would kill him instantly. But the enraged brave had no other opportunity to cast his weapon, for the Indians jeered at him and pushed him from the line.

Other braves tried their proficiency in the art of throwing knives and tomahawks, but their efforts called forth only words of derision from Isaac. They left the weapons sticking in the post until round Isaac's head and shoulders there was scarcely room for another.

"The White Eagle is tired of boys," cried Isaac to a chief standing near. "What has he done that he be made the plaything of children? Let him die the death of a chief."

The maidens had long since desisted in their efforts to torment the prisoner. Even the hardened old squaws had withdrawn. The prisoner's proud, handsome face, his upright bearing, his scorn for his enemies, his indifference to the cuts and bruises, and red welts upon his clear white skin had won their hearts.

Not so with the braves. Seeing that the pale face scorned all efforts to make him flinch, the young brave turned to Big Tree. At a command from this chief the Indians stopped their maneuvering round the post and formed a large circle. In another moment a tall warrior appeared carrying an armful of fagots.

In spite of his iron nerve Isaac shuddered with horror. He had anticipated running the gauntlet, having his nails pulled out, powder and salt shot into his flesh, being scalped alive, and a host of other Indian tortures, but as he had killed no members of this tribe he had not thought of being burned alive. God, it was too horrible!

The Indians were now quiet. Their songs and dances would break out soon enough. They piled fagot after fagot around Isaac's feet. The Indian warrior knelt on the ground; the steel clicked on the flint; a little shower of sparks dropped on the pieces of punk and then—a tiny flame shot up, and a slender little column of blue smoke floated on the air.

Isaac shut his teeth hard and prayed with all his soul for a speedy death.

Simon Girty came hurriedly through the lines of waiting, watching Indians. He had obtained permission to speak to the man of his own color.

"Zane, you made a brave stand. Any other time but this it might have saved you. If you want I'll get word to your people." And then bending and placing his mouth close to Isaac's ear, he whispered, "I did all I could for you, but it must have been too late."

"Try and tell them at Ft. Henry," Isaac said simply.

There was a little cracking of dried wood and then a narrow tongue of red flame darted up from the pile of fagots and licked at the buckskin fringe on the prisoner's leggins. At this supreme moment when the attention of all centered on that motionless figure lashed to the stake, and when only the low chanting of the death-song broke the stillness, a long, piercing yell rang out on the quiet morning air. So strong, so sudden, so startling was the break in that almost perfect calm that for a moment afterward there was a silence as of death. All eyes turned to the ridge of rising ground whence that sound had come. Now came the unmistakable thunder of horses' hoofs pounding furiously on the rocky ground. A moment of paralyzed inaction ensued. The Indians stood bewildered, petrified. Then on that ridge of rising ground stood, silhouetted against the blue sky, a great black horse with arching neck and flying mane. Astride him sat a plumed warrior, who waved his rifle high in the air. Again that shrill screeching yell came floating to the ears of the astonished Indians.

The prisoner had seen that horse and rider before; he had heard that long yell; his heart bounded with hope. The Indians knew that yell; it was the terrible war-cry of the Hurons.

A horse followed closely after the leader, and then another appeared on the crest of the hill. Then came two abreast, and then four abreast, and now the hill was black with plunging horses. They galloped swiftly down the slope and into the narrow street of the village. When the black horse entered the oval the train of racing horses extended to the top of the ridge. The plumes of the riders streamed gracefully on the breeze; their feathers shone; their weapons glittered in the bright sunlight.

Never was there more complete surprise. In the early morning the Hurons had crept up to within a rifle shot of the encampment, and at an opportune moment when all the scouts and runners were round the torture-stake, they had reached the hillside from which they rode into the village before the inhabitants knew what had happened. Not an Indian raised a weapon. There were screams from the women and children, a shouted command from Big Tree, and then all stood still and waited.

Thundercloud, the war chief of the Wyandots, pulled his black stallion back on his haunches not twenty feet from the prisoner at the stake. His band of painted devils closed in behind him. Full two hundred strong were they and all picked warriors tried and true. They were naked to the waist. Across their brawny chests ran a broad bar of flaming red paint; hideous designs in black and white covered their faces. Every head had been clean-shaven except where the scalp lock bristled like a porcupine's quills. Each warrior carried a plumed spear, a tomahawk, and a rifle. The shining heads, with the little tightly-tied tufts of hair, were enough to show that they were on the war-path.

From the back of one of the foremost horses a slender figure dropped and darted toward the prisoner at the stake. Surely that wildly flying hair proved this was not a warrior. Swift as a flash of light this figure reached the stake; the blazing fagots scattered right and left; a naked blade gleamed; the thongs fell from the prisoner's wrists; and the front ranks of the Hurons opened and closed on the freed man. The deliverer turned to the gaping Indians, disclosing to their gaze the pale and beautiful face of Myeerah, the Wyandot Princess.

"Summon your chief," she commanded.

The tall form of the Seneca chief moved from among the warriors and with slow and measured tread approached the maiden. His bearing fitted the leader of five nations of Indians. It was of one who knew that he was the wisest of chiefs, the hero of a hundred battles. Who dared beard him in his den? Who dared defy the greatest power in all Indian tribes? When he stood

before the maiden he folded his arms and waited for
her to speak.

"Myeerah claims the White Eagle," she said.

Cornplanter did not answer at once. He had never
seen Myeerah, though he had heard many stories of her
loveliness. Now he was face to face with the Indian
Princess whose fame had been the theme of many an
Indian romance, and whose beauty had been sung of in
many an Indian song. The beautiful girl stood erect and
fearless. Her disordered garments, torn and bedraggled
and stained from the long ride, ill-concealed the grace
of her form. Her hair rippled from the uncovered head
and fell in dusky splendor over her shoulders; her dark
eyes shone with a stern and steady fire; her bosom
swelled with each deep breath. She was the daughter of
great chiefs; she looked the embodiment of savage love.

"The Huron squaw is brave," said Cornplanter. "By
what right does she come to free my captive?"

"He is an adopted Wyandot."

"Why does the paleface hide like a fox near the
camp of Cornplanter?"

"He ran away. He lost the trail to the Fort on the
river."

"Cornplanter takes prisoners to kill; not to free."

"If you will not give him up Myeerah will take
him," she answered, pointing to the long line of
mounted warriors. "And should harm befall Tarhe's
daughter it will be avenged."

Cornplanter looked at Thundercloud. Well he knew
that chief's prowess in the field. He ran his eyes over
the silent, watching Hurons, and then back to the sombre face of their leader. Thundercloud sat rigid upon
his stallion; his head held high; every muscle tense and
strong for instant action. He was ready and eager for
the fray. He, and every one of his warriors, would fight
like a thousand tigers for their Princess—the pride of
the proud race of Wyandots. Cornplanter saw this and

he felt that on the eve of important marches he dared not sacrifice one of his braves for any reason, much less a worthless pale face; and yet to let the prisoner go galled the haughty spirit of the Seneca chief.

"The Long Knife is not worth the life of one of my dogs," he said, with scorn in his deep voice. "If Cornplanter willed he could drive the Hurons before him like leaves before the storm. Let Myeerah take the pale face back to her wigwam and there feed him and make a squaw of him. When he stings like a snake in the grass remember the chief's words. Cornplanter turns on his heel from the Huron maiden who forgets her blood."

* * * * * * *

When the sun reached its zenith it shone down upon a long line of mounted Indians riding single file along the narrow trail and like a huge serpent winding through the forest and over the plain.

They were Wyandot Indians, and Isaac Zane rode among them. Freed from the terrible fate which had menaced him, and knowing that he was once more on his way to the Huron encampment, he had accepted his destiny and quarreled no more with fate. He was thankful beyond all words for his rescue from the stake.

Coming to a clear, rapid stream, the warriors dismounted and rested while their horses drank thirstily of the cool water. An Indian touched Isaac on the arm and silently pointed toward the huge maple tree under which Thundercloud and Myeerah were sitting. Isaac turned his horse and rode the short distance intervening. When he got near he saw that Myeerah stood with one arm over the pony's neck. She raised eyes that were weary and sad, which yet held a lofty and noble resolve.

"White Eagle, this stream leads straight to the Fort on the river," she said briefly, almost coldly. "Follow it, and when the sun reaches the top of yonder hill you will be with your people. Go, you are free."

She turned her face away. Isaac's head whirled in his amazement. He could not believe his ears. He looked closely at her and saw that though her face was calm her throat swelled, and the hand which lay over the neck of her pony clenched the bridle in a fierce grasp. Isaac glanced at Thundercloud and the other Indians near by. They sat unconcerned with the invariable unreadable expression.

"Myeerah, what do you mean?" asked Isaac.

"The words of Cornplanter cut deep into the heart of Myeerah," she answered bitterly. "They were true. The Eagle does not care for Myeerah. She shall no longer keep him in a cage. He is free to fly away."

"The Eagle does not want his freedom. I love you, Myeerah. You have saved me and I am yours. If you will go home with me and marry me there as my people are married I will go back to the Wyandot village."

Myeerah's eyes softened with unutterable love. With a quick cry she was in his arms. After a few moments of forgetfulness Myeerah spoke to Thundercloud and waved her hand toward the west. The chief swung himself over his horse, shouted a single command, and rode down the bank into the water. His warriors followed him, wading their horses into the shallow creek, with never a backward look. When the last rider had disappeared in the willows the lovers turned their horses eastward.

Chapter 10

IT WAS near the close of a day in early summer. A small group of persons surrounded Col. Zane where he sat on his doorstep. From time to time he took the long Indian pipe from his mouth and blew great clouds of smoke over his head. Major McColloch and Capt. Boggs were there. Silas Zane half reclined on the grass. The Colonel's wife stood in the door-way, and Betty sat on the lower step with her head leaning against her brother's knee. They all had grave faces. Jonathan Zane had returned that day after an absence of three weeks, and was now answering the many questions with which he was plied.

"Don't ask me any more and I'll tell you the whole thing," he had just said, while wiping the perspiration from his brow. His face was worn; his beard ragged and unkempt; his appearance suggestive of extreme fatigue. "It was this way: Colonel Crawford had four hundred and eighty men under him, with Slover and me acting as guides. This was a large force of men and comprised soldiers from Pitt and the other forts and settlers from all along the river. You see, Crawford wanted to crush the Shawnees at one blow. When we reached the Sandusky River, which we did after an arduous march, not one Indian did we see. You know Crawford expected to surprise the Shawnee camp, and when he found it deserted he didn't know what to do. Sloven and I both advised an immediate retreat. Crawford would not listen to us. I tried to explain to him that ever since the Guadenhutten massacre keen-eyed Indian scouts had been watching the border. The news of the present expedition had been carried by fleet runners to the different Indian tribes and they were working like hives of angry bees. The deserted Shawnee village meant to me that the alarm had been sounded in the towns of the Shawnees and the Delawares; perhaps also in the Wyandot towns to the north. Colonel Crawford was obdurate and insisted on resuming the march into the Indian country. The next day we met the Indians coming directly toward us. It was the combined force of the Delaware chiefs, Pipe and Wingenund. The battle had hardly commenced when the redskins were reinforced by four hundred warriors under Shanshota, the Huron chief. The enemy skulked behind trees and rocks, hid in ravines, and crawled through the long grass. They could be picked off only by Indian hunters, of whom Crawford had but few—probably fifty all told. All that day we managed to keep our position, though we lost sixty men. That night we lay down to rest by great fires which we built, to prevent night surprises.

"Early next morning we resumed the fight. I saw Simon Girty on his white horse. He was urging and cheering the Indians on to desperate fighting. Their fire became so deadly that we were forced to retreat. In the afternoon Slover, who had been out scouting, returned with the information that a mounted force was approaching, and that he believed they were the reinforcements which Col. Crawford expected. The reinforcements came up and proved to be Butler's British Rangers from Detroit. This stunned Crawford's soldiers. The fire of the enemy became hotter and hotter. Our men were falling like leaves around us. They threw aside their rifles and ran, many of them right into the hands of the savages. I believe some of the experienced bordermen escaped, but most of Crawford's force met death on the field. I hid in a hollow log. Next day when I felt that it could be done safely I crawled out. I saw scalped and mutilated bodies everywhere, but did not find Col. Crawford's body. The Indians had taken all the clothing, weapons, blankets, and everything of value. The Wyandots took a northwest trail and the Delawares and the Shawnees traveled east. I followed the latter because their trail led toward home. Three days later I stood on the high bluff above Wingenund's camp. From there I saw Col. Crawford tied to a stake and a fire started at his feet. I was not five hundred yards from the camp. I saw the war chiefs, Pipe and Wingenund; I saw Simon Girty and a British officer in uniform. The chiefs and Girty were once Crawford's friends. They stood calmly by and watched the poor victim slowly burn to death. The Indians yelled and danced round the stake; they devised every kind of hellish torture. When at last an Indian ran in and tore off the scalp of the still living man I could bear to see no more, and I turned and ran. I have been in some tough places, but this last was the worst."

"My God! it is awful—and to think that man Girty was once a white man," cried Col. Zane.

"He came very near being a dead man," said Jonathan, with grim humor. "I got a long shot at him and killed his big white horse."

"It's a pity you missed him," said Silas Zane.

"Here comes Wetzel. What will he say about the massacre?" remarked Major McColloch.

Wetzel joined the group at that moment and shook hands with Jonathan. When interrogated about the failure of Col. Crawford's expedition Wetzel said that Slover had just made his appearance at the cabin of Hugh Bennet, and that he was without clothing and almost dead from exposure.

"I'm glad Slover got out alive. He was against the

march all along. If Crawford had listened to us he would have averted this terrible affair and saved his own life. Lew, did Slover know how many men got out?" asked Jonathan.

"He said not many. The redskins killed all the prisoners exceptin' Crawford and Knight."

"I saw Col. Crawford burned at the stake. I did not see Dr. Knight. Maybe they murdered him before I reached the camp of the Delawares," said Jonathan.

"Wetzel, in your judgment, what effect will this massacre and Crawford's death have on the border?" inquired Col. Zane.

"It means another bloody year like 1777," answered Wetzel.

"We are liable to have trouble with the Indians any day. You mean that."

"There'll be war all along the river. Hamilton is hatchin' some new devil's trick with Girty. Col. Zane, I calkilate that Girty has a spy in the river settlements and knows as much about the forts and defense as you do."

"You can't mean a white spy."

"Yes, just that."

"That is a strong assertion, Lewis, but coming from you it means something. Step aside here and explain yourself," said Col. Zane, getting up and walking out to the fence.

"I don't like the looks of things," said the hunter. "A month ago I ketched this man Miller pokin' his nose round the block-house where he hadn't ought to be. And I kep watchin' him. If my suspicions is correct he's playin' some deep game. I ain't got any proof, but things looks bad."

"That's strange, Lewis," said Col. Zane soberly. "Now that you mention it I remember Jonathan said he met Miller near the Kanawha three weeks ago. That was when Crawford's expedition was on the way to the

Shawnee villages. The Colonel tried to enlist Miller, but Miller said he was in a hurry to get back to the Fort. And he hasn't come back yet."

"I ain't surprised. Now, Col. Zane, you are in command here. I'm not a soldier and for that reason I'm all the better to watch Miller. He won't suspect me. You give me authority and I'll round up his little game."

"By all means, Lewis. Go about it your own way, and report anything to me. Remember you may be mistaken and give Miller the benefit of the doubt. I don't like the fellow. He has a way of appearing and disappearing, and for no apparent reason, that makes me distrust him. But for Heaven's sake, Lew, how would he profit by betraying us?"

"I don't know. All I know is he'll bear watchin'."

"My gracious, Lew Wetzel!" exclaimed Betty as her brother and the hunter rejoined the others. "Have you come all the way over here without a gun? And you have on a new suit of buckskin."

Lewis stood a moment by Betty, gazing down at her with his slight smile. He looked exceedingly well. His face was not yet bronzed by summer suns. His long black hair, of which he was as proud as a woman could have been, and of which he took as much care as he did of his rifle, waved over his shoulders.

"Betty, this is my birthday, but that ain't the reason I've got my fine feathers on. I'm goin' to try and make an impression on you," replied Lewis, smiling.

"I declare, this is very sudden. But you have succeeded. Who made the suit? And where did you get all that pretty fringe and those beautiful beads?"

"That stuff I picked up round an Injun camp. The suit I made myself."

"I think, Lewis, I must get you to help me make my new gown," said Betty, roguishly.

"Well, I must be gettin' back," said Wetzel, rising.

"Oh, don't go yet. You have not talked to me at all," said Betty petulantly. She walked to the gate with him.

"What can an Injun hunter say to amuse the belle of the border?"

"I don't want to be amused exactly. I mean I'm not used to being unnoticed, especially by you." And then in a lower tone she continued: "What did you mean about Mr. Miller? I heard his name and Eb looked worried. What did you tell him?"

"Never mind now, Betty. Maybe I'll tell you some day. It's enough for you to know the Colonel don't like Miller and that I think he is a bad man. You don't care nothin' for Miller, do you Betty?"

"Not in the least."

"Don't see him any more, Betty. Good-night, now, I must be goin' to supper."

"Lew, stop! or I shall run after you."

"And what good would your runnin' do?" said Lewis. "You'd never ketch me. Why, I could give you twenty paces start and beat you to yon tree."

"You can't. Come, try it," retorted Betty, catching hold of her skirt. She could never have allowed a challenge like that to pass.

"Ha! ha! We are in for a race. Betty, if you beat him, start or no start, you will have accomplished something never done before," said Col. Zane.

"Come, Silas, step off twenty paces and make them long ones," said Betty, who was in earnest.

"We'll make it forty paces," said Silas, as he commenced taking immense strides.

"What is Lewis looking at?" remarked Col. Zane's wife.

Wetzel, in taking his position for the race, had faced the river. Mrs. Zane had seen him start suddenly, straighten up and for a moment stand like a statue. Her exclamation drew the attention of the others to the hunter.

"Look!" he cried, waving his hand toward the river.

"I declare, Wetzel, you are always seeing something. Where shall I look? Ah, yes, there is a dark form moving along the bank. By jove! I believe it's an Indian," said Col. Zane.

Jonathan darted into the house. When he reappeared a second later he had three rifles.

"I see horses, Lew. What do you make out?" said Jonathan. "It's a bold manœuvre for Indians unless they have a strong force."

"Hostile Injuns wouldn't show themselves like that. Maybe they ain't redskins at all. We'll go down to the bluff."

"Oh, yes, let us go," cried Betty, walking down the path toward Wetzel.

Col. Zane followed her, and presently the whole party were on their way to the river. When they reached the bluff they saw two horses come down the opposite bank and enter the water. Then they seemed to fade from view. The tall trees cast a dark shadow over the water and the horses had become lost in this obscurity. Col. Zane and Jonathan walked up and down the bank seeking to find a place which afforded a clearer view of the river.

"There they come," shouted Silas.

"Yes, I see them just swimming out of the shadow," said Col. Zane. "Both horses have riders. Lewis, what can you make out?"

"It's Isaac and an Indian girl," answered Wetzel.

This startling announcement created a commotion in the little group. It was followed by a chorus of exclamations.

"Heavens! Wetzel, you have wonderful eyes. I hope to God you are right. There, I see the foremost rider waving his hand," cried Col. Zane.

"Oh, Bessie, Bessie! I believe Lew is right. Look at Tige," said Betty excitedly.

Everybody had forgotten the dog. He had come down the path with Betty and had pressed close to her. First he trembled, then whined, then with a loud bark he ran down the bank and dashed into the water.

"Hel-lo, Betts," came the cry across the water. There was no mistaking that clear voice. It was Isaac's.

Although the sun had long gone down behind the hills daylight lingered. It was bright enough for the watchers to recognize Isaac Zane. He sat high on his horse and in his hand he held the bridle of a pony that was swimming beside him. The pony bore the slender figure of a girl. She was bending forward and her hands were twisted in the pony's mane.

By this time the Colonel and Jonathan were standing in the shallow water waiting to grasp the reins and lead the horses up the steep bank. Attracted by the unusual sight of a wildly gesticulating group on the river bluff, the settlers from the Fort hurried down to the scene of action. Capt. Boggs and Alfred Clarke joined the crowd. Old Sam came running down from the barn. All were intensely excited as Col. Zane and Jonathan reached for the bridles and led the horses up the slippery incline.

"Eb, Jack, Silas, here I am alive and well," cried Isaac as he leaped from his horse. "Betty, you darling, it's Isaac. Don't stand staring as if I were a ghost."

Whereupon Betty ran to him, flung her arms around his neck and clung to him. Isaac kissed her tenderly and disengaged himself from her arms.

"You'll get all wet. Glad to see me? Well, I never had such a happy moment in my life. Betty, I have brought you some one whom you must love. This is Myeerah, your sister. She is wet and cold. Take her home and make her warm and comfortable. You must forget all the past, for Myeerah has saved me from the stake."

Betty had forgotten the other. At her brother's words

she turned and saw a slender form. Even the wet, mud-stained and ragged Indian costume failed to hide the grace of that figure. She saw a beautiful face, as white as her own, and dark eyes full of unshed tears.

"The Eagle is free," said the Indian girl in her low, musical voice.

"You have brought him home to us. Come," said Betty, taking the hand of the trembling maiden.

The settlers crowded round Isaac and greeted him warmly, while they plied him with innumerable questions. Was he free? Who was the Indian girl? Had he run off with her? Were the Indians preparing for war?

On the way to the Colonel's house Isaac told briefly of his escape from the Wyandots, of his capture by Cornplanter, and of his rescue. He also mentioned the preparations for war he had seen in Cornplanter's camp, and Girty's story of Col. Crawford's death.

"How does it come that you have the Indian girl with you?" asked Col. Zane as they left the curious settlers and entered the house.

"I am going to marry Myeerah and I brought her with me for that purpose. When we are married I will go back to the Wyandots and live with them until peace is declared."

"Humph! Will it be declared?"

"Myeerah has promised it, and I believe she can bring it about, especially if I marry her. Peace with the Hurons may help to bring about peace with the Shawnees. I shall never cease to work for that end; but even if peace cannot be secured, my duty still is to Myeerah. She saved me from a most horrible death."

"If your marriage with this Indian girl will secure the friendly offices of that grim old warrior Tarhe, it is far more than fighting will ever do. I do not want you to go back. Would we ever see you again?"

"Oh, yes, often I hope. You see, if I marry Myeerah the Hurons will allow me every liberty."

"Well, that puts a different light on the subject."

"Oh, how I wish you and Jonathan could have seen Thundercloud and his two hundred warriors ride into Cornplanter's camp. It was magnificent! The braves were all crowded near the stake where I was bound. The fire had been lighted. Suddenly the silence was shattered by an awful yell. It was Thundercloud's yell. I knew it because I had heard it before, and anyone who had once heard that yell could never forget it. In what seemed an incredibly short time Thundercloud's warriors were lined up in the middle of the camp. The surprise was so complete that, had it been necessary, they could have ridden Cornplanter's braves down, killed many, routed the others, and burned the village. Cornplanter will not get over that surprise in many a moon."

Betty had always hated the very mention of the Indian girl who had been the cause of her brother's long absence from home. But she was so happy in the knowledge of his return that she felt it was in her power to forgive much; moreover, the white, weary face of the Indian maiden touched Betty's warm heart. With her quick intuition she had divined that this was even a greater trial for Myeerah. Undoubtedly the Indian girl feared the scorn of her lover's people. She showed it in her trembling hands, in her fearful glances.

Finding that Myeerah could speak and understand English Betty became more interested in her charge every moment. She set about to make Myeerah comfortable, and while she removed the wet and stained garments she talked all the time. She told her how happy she was that Isaac was alive and well. She said Myeerah's heroism in saving him should atone for all the past, and that Isaac's family would welcome her in his home.

Gradually Myeerah's agitation subsided under Betty's sweet graciousness, and by the time Betty had dressed her in a white gown, had brushed the dark hair and added a bright ribbon to the simple toilet, Myeerah had so far forgotten her fears as to take a shy pleasure in the picture of herself in the mirror. As for Betty, she gave vent to a little cry of delight.

"Oh, you are perfectly lovely," cried Betty. "In that gown no one would know you as a Wyandot princess."

"Myeerah's mother was a white woman."

"I have heard your story, Myeerah, and it is wonderful. You must tell me all about your life with the Indians. You speak my language almost as well as I do. Who taught you?"

"Myeerah learned to talk with the White Eagle. She can speak French with the *Coureurs-des-bois.*"

"That's more than I can do, Myeerah. And I had a French teacher," said Betty, laughing.

"Hello, up there," came Isaac's voice from below.

"Come up, Isaac," called Betty.

"Is this my Indian sweetheart?" exclaimed Isaac, stopping at the door. "Betty, isn't she——"

"Yes," answered Betty, "she is simply beautiful."

"Come, Myeerah, we must go down to supper," said Isaac, taking her in his arms and kissing her. "Now you must not be afraid, nor mind being looked at."

"Everyone will be kind to you," said Betty, taking her hand. Myeerah had slipped from Isaac's arm and hesitated and hung back. "Come," continued Betty, "I will stay with you, and you need not talk if you do not wish."

Thus reassured Myeerah allowed Betty to lead her down stairs. Isaac had gone ahead and was waiting at the door.

The big room was brilliantly lighted with pine knots. Mrs. Zane was arranging the dishes on the table. Old Sam and Annie were hurrying to and fro from the kitchen. Col. Zane had just come up the cellar stairs carrying a mouldy looking cask. From its appearance it might have been a powder keg, but the merry twinkle in the Colonel's eyes showed that the cask contained something as precious, perhaps, as powder, but not quite so dangerous. It was a cask of wine over thirty years old. With Col. Zane's other effects it had stood the test of the long wagon-train journey over the Virginia mountains, and of the raft-ride down the Ohio. Col. Zane thought the feast he had arranged for Isaac would be a fitting occasion for the breaking of the cask.

Major McColloch, Capt. Boggs and Hugh Bennet had been invited. Wetzel had been persuaded to come. Betty's friends Lydia and Alice were there.

As Isaac, with an air of pride, led the two girls into the room Old Sam saw them and he exclaimed, "For de Lawd's sakes, Marsh Zane, dar's two pippins, sure can't tell 'em from one anudder."

Betty and Myeerah did resemble each other. They were of about the same size, tall and slender. Betty was rosy, bright-eyed and smiling; Myeerah was pale one moment and red the next.

"Friends, this is Myeerah, the daughter of Tarhe," said Isaac simply. "We are to be married tomorrow."

"Oh, why did you not tell me?" asked Betty in great surprise. "She said nothing about it."

"You see Myeerah has that most excellent trait in a woman—knowing when to keep silent," answered Isaac with a smile.

The door opened at this moment, admitting Will Martin and Alfred Clarke.

"Everybody is here now, Bessie, and I guess we may as well sit down to supper," said Col. Zane. "And, good friends, let me say that this is an occasion for rejoicing. It is not so much a marriage that I mean. That we might have any day if Lydia or Betty would show some of the alacrity which got a good husband for Alice. Isaac is a free man and we expect his marriage will bring about peace with a powerful tribe of Indians.

To us, and particularly to you, young people, that is a matter of great importance. The friendship of the Hurons cannot but exert an influence on other tribes. I, myself, may live to see the day that my dream shall be realized—peaceful and friendly relations with the Indians, the freedom of the soil, well-tilled farms and growing settlements, and at last, the opening of this glorious country to the world. Therefore, let us rejoice; let every one be happy; let your gayest laugh ring out, and tell your best story."

Betty had blushed painfully at the entrance of Alfred and again at the Colonel's remark. To add to her embarrassment she found herself seated opposite Alfred at the table. This was the first time he had been near her since the Sunday at the meeting-house, and the incident had a singular effect on Betty. She found herself possessed, all at once, of an unaccountable shyness, and she could not lift her eyes from her plate. But at length she managed to steal a glance at Alfred. She failed to see any signs in his beaming face of the broken spirit of which her brother had hinted. He looked very well indeed. He was eating his dinner like any other healthy man, and talking and laughing with Lydia. This developed another unaccountable feeling in Betty, but this time it was resentment. Who ever heard of a man, who was as much in love as his letter said, looking well and enjoying himself with any other than the object of his affections? He had got over it, that was all. Just then Alfred turned and gazed full into Betty's eyes. She lowered them instantly, but not so quickly that she failed to see in his a reproach.

"You are going to stay with us a while, are you not?" asked Betty of Isaac.

"No, Betts, not more than a day or so. Now, do not look so distressed. I do not go back as a prisoner. Myeerah and I can often come and visit you. But just now I want to get back and try to prevent the Delawares from urging Tarhe to war."

"Isaac, I believe you are doing the wisest thing possible," said Capt. Boggs. "And when I look at your bride-to-be I confess I do not see how you remained single so long."

"That's so, Captain," answered Isaac. "But you see, I have never been satisfied or contented in captivity. I wanted nothing but to be free."

"In other words, you were blind," remarked Alfred, smiling at Isaac.

"Yes, Alfred, I was. And I imagine had you been in my place you would have discovered the beauty and virtue of my Princess long before I did. Nevertheless, please do not favor Myeerah with so many admiring glances. She is not used to it. And that reminds me that I must expect trouble tomorrow. All you fellows will want to kiss her."

"And Betty is going to be maid of honor. She, too, will have her troubles," remarked Col. Zane.

"Think of that, Alfred," said Isaac. "A chance to kiss the two prettiest girls on the border—a chance of a lifetime."

"It is customary, is it not?" said Alfred coolly.

"Yes, it's a custom, if you can catch the girl," answered Col. Zane.

Betty's face flushed at Alfred's cool assumption. How dared he? In spite of her will she could not resist the power that compelled her to look at him. As plainly as if it were written there, she saw in his steady blue eyes the light of a memory—the memory of a kiss. And Betty dropped her head, her face burning, her heart on fire with shame, and love, and regret.

"It'll be a good chance for me, too," said Wetzel. His remark instantly turned attention to himself.

"The idea is absurd," said Isaac. "Why, Lew Wetzel, you could not be made to kiss any girl."

"I would not be backward about it," said Col. Zane.

"You have forgotten the fuss you made when the boys were kissing me," said Mrs. Zane with a fine scorn.

"My dear," said Col. Zane, in an aggrieved tone, "I did not make so much of a fuss, as you call it, until they had kissed you a great many times more than was reasonable."

"Isaac, tell us one thing more," said Capt. Boggs. "How did Myeerah learn of your capture by Cornplanter? Surely she could not have trailed you?"

"Will you tell us?" said Isaac to Myeerah.

"A bird sang it to me," answered Myeerah.

"She will never tell, that is certain," said Isaac. "And for that reason I believe Simon Girty got word to her that I was in the hands of Cornplanter. At the last moment when the Indians were lashing me to the stake Girty came to me and said he must have been too late."

"Yes, Girty might have done that," said Col. Zane. "I suppose, though he dared not interfere in behalf of poor Crawford."

"Isaac, can you get Myeerah to talk? I love to hear her speak," said Betty, in an aside.

"Myeerah, will you sing a Huron love-song?" said Isaac. "Or, if you do not wish to sing, tell a story. I want them to know how well you can speak our language."

"What shall Myeerah say?" she said, shyly.

"Tell them the legend of the Standing Stone."

"A beautiful Indian girl once dwelt in the pine forests," began Myeerah, with her eyes cast down and her hand seeking Isaac's. "Her voice was like rippling waters, her beauty like the rising sun. From near and from far came warriors to see the fair face of this maiden. She smiled on them all and they called her Smiling Moon. Now there lived on the Great Lake a

Wyandot chief. He was young and bold. No warrior was as great as Tarhe. Smiling Moon cast a spell on his heart. He came many times to woo her and make her his wife. But Smiling Moon said: 'Go, do great deeds, and come again.'

"Tarhe searched the east and the west. He brought her strange gifts from strange lands. She said: 'Go and slay my enemies.' Tarhe went forth in his war paint and killed the braves who named her Smiling Moon. He came again to her and she said: 'Run swifter than the deer, be more cunning than the beaver, dive deeper than the loon.'

"Tarhe passed once more to the island where dwelt Smiling Moon. The ice was thick, the snow was deep. Smiling Moon turned not from her warm fire as she said: 'The chief is a great warrior, but Smiling Moon is not easily won. It is cold. Change winter into summer and then Smiling Moon will love him.'

"Tarhe cried in a loud voice to the Great Spirit: 'Make me a master.'

"A voice out of the forest answered: 'Tarhe, great warrior, wise chief, waste not thy time, go back to thy wigwam.'

"Tarhe unheeding cried: 'Tarhe wins or dies. Make him a master so that he may drive the ice northward.'

"Stormed the wild tempest; thundered the rivers of ice; chill blew the north wind, the cold northwest wind, against the mild south wind; snow-spirits and hail-spirits fled before the warm raindrops; the white mountains melted, and lo! it was summer.

"On the mountain top Tarhe waited for his bride. Never wearying, ever faithful he watched many years. There he turned to stone. There he stands today, the Standing Stone of ages. And Smiling Moon, changed by the Great Spirit into the Night Wind, forever wails her lament at dusk through the forest trees, and moans over the mountain tops."

Myeerah's story elicited cheers and praises from all. She was entreated to tell another, but smilingly shook her head. Now that her shyness had worn off to some extent she took great interest in the jest and the general conversation.

Col. Zane's fine old wine flowed like water. The custom was to fill a guest's cup as soon as it was empty. Drinking much was rather encouraged than otherwise. But Col. Zane never allowed this custom to go too far in his house.

"Friends, the hour grows late," he said. "Tomorrow, after the great event, we shall have games, shooting matches, running races, and contests of all kinds. Capt. Boggs and I have arranged to give prizes, and I expect the girls can give something to lend a zest to the competition."

"Will the girls have a chance in these races?" asked Isaac. "If so, I should like to see Betty and Myeerah run."

"Betty can outrun any woman, red or white, on the border," said Wetzel. "And she could make some of the men run their level best."

"Well, perhaps we shall give her one opportunity tomorrow," observed Colonel. "She used to be good at running but it seems to me that of late she has taken to books and——"

"Oh, Eb! that is untrue," interrupted Betty.

Col. Zane laughed and patted his sister's cheek. "Never mind, Betty," and then, rising, he continued, "Now let us drink to the bride and groom-to-be. Capt. Boggs, I call on you."

"We drink to the bride's fair beauty; we drink to the groom's good luck," said Capt. Boggs, raising his cup.

"Do not forget the maid-of-honor," said Isaac.

"Yes, and the maid-of-honor. Mr. Clarke, will you say something appropriate?" asked Col. Zane.

Rising, Clarke said: "I would be glad to speak fittingly on this occasion, but I do not think I can do it justice. I believe as Col. Zane does, that this Indian Princess is the first link in that chain of peace which will some day unite the red men and the white men. Instead of the White Crane she should be called the White Dove. Gentlemen, rise and drink to her long life and happiness."

The toast was drunk. Then Clarke refilled his cup and holding it high over his head he looked at Betty.

"Gentlemen, to the maid-of-honor. Miss Zane, your health, your happiness, in this good old wine."

"I thank you," murmured Betty with downcast eyes. "I bid you all good-night. Come, Myeerah."

Once more alone with Betty, the Indian girl turned to her with eyes like twin stars.

"My sister has made me very happy," whispered Myeerah, in her soft, low voice. "Myeerah's heart is full."

"I believe you are happy, for I know you love Isaac dearly."

"Myeerah has always loved him. She will love his sister."

"And I will love you," said Betty. "I will love you because you have saved him. Ah! Myeerah, yours has been a wonderful, wonderful love."

"My sister is loved," whispered Myeerah. "Myeerah saw the look in the eyes of the great hunter. It was the sad light of the moon on the water. He loves you. And the other looked at my sister with eyes like the blue of northern skies. He, too, loves you."

"Hush!" whispered Betty, trembling and hiding her face. "Hush! Myeerah, do not speak of him."

Chapter 11

THE FOLLOWING afternoon the sun shone fair and warm; the sweet smell of the tan-bark pervaded the air; and the birds sang their gladsome songs. The scene before the grim, battle-scarred old fort was not without its picturesqueness. The low vine-covered cabins on the hillside looked more like picture houses than like real habitations of men; the mill with its burned-out roof—a reminder of the Indians—and its great wheel, now silent and still, might have been from its lonely and dilapidated appearance a hundred years old.

On a little knoll carpeted with velvety grass sat Isaac and his Indian bride. He had selected this vantage point because it afforded a fine view of the green square where the races and the matches were to take place. Admiring women stood around him and gazed at his wife. They gossiped in whispers about her white skin, her little hands, her beauty. The girls stared with wide open and wondering eyes. The youngsters ran round and round the little group; they pushed each other over, and rolled in the long grass, and screamed with delight.

It was to be a gala occasion and every man, woman and child in the settlement had assembled on the green. Col. Zane and Sam were planting a post in the center of the square. It was to be used in the shooting matches. Capt. Boggs and Major McColloch were arranging the contestants in order. Jonathan Zane, Will

Martin, Alfred Clarke—all the young men were carefully charging and priming their rifles. Betty was sitting on the black stallion which Col. Zane had generously offered as first prize. She was in the gayest of moods and had just coaxed Isaac to lift her on the tall horse, from which height she purposed watching the sports. Wetzel alone did not seem infected by the spirit of gladsomeness which pervaded. He stood apart leaning on his long rifle and taking no interest in the proceedings behind him. He was absorbed in contemplating the forest on the opposite shore of the river.

"Well, boys, I guess we are ready for the fun," called Col. Zane, cheerily. "Only one shot apiece, mind you, except in case of a tie. Now, everybody shoot his best."

The first contest was a shooting match known as "driving the nail." It was as the name indicated, nothing less than shooting at the head of a nail. In the absence of a nail—for nails were scarce—one was usually fashioned from a knife blade, or an old file, or even a piece of silver. The nail was driven lightly into the stake, the contestants shot at it from a distance as great as the eyesight permitted. To drive the nail hard and fast into the wood at one hundred yards was a feat seldom accomplished. By many hunters it was deemed more difficult than "snuffing the candle," another border pastime, which consisted of placing in the dark at any distance a lighted candle, and then putting out the flame with a single rifle ball. Many settlers, particularly those who handled the plow more than the rifle, sighted from a rest, and placed a piece of moss under the rifle-barrel to prevent its spring at the discharge.

The match began. Of the first six shooters Jonathan Zane and Alfred Clarke scored the best shots. Each placed a bullet in the half-inch circle round the nail.

"Alfred, very good, indeed," said Col. Zane. "You have made a decided improvement since the last shooting-match."

Six other settlers took their turns. All were unsuccessful in getting a shot inside the little circle. Thus a tie between Alfred and Jonathan had to be decided.

"Shoot close, Alfred," yelled Isaac. "I hope you beat him. He always won from me and then crowed over it."

Alfred's second shot went wide of the mark, and as Jonathan placed another bullet in the circle, this time nearer the center, Alfred had to acknowledge defeat.

"Here comes Miller," said Silas Zane. "Perhaps he will want a try."

Col. Zane looked round. Miller had joined the party. He carried his rifle and accoutrements, and evidently had just returned to the settlement. He nodded pleasantly to all.

"Miller, will you take a shot for the first prize, which I was about to award to Jonathan?" said Col. Zane.

"No. I am a little late, and not entitled to a shot. I will take a try for the others," answered Miller.

At the arrival of Miller on the scene Wetzel had changed his position to one nearer the crowd. The dog, Tige, trotted closely at his heels. No one heard Tige's low growl or Wetzel's stern word to silence him. Throwing his arm over Betty's pony, Wetzel apparently watched the shooters. In reality he studied intently Miller's every movement.

"I expect some good shooting for this prize," said Col. Zane, waving a beautifully embroidered buckskin bullet pouch, which was one of Betty's donations.

Jonathan having won his prize was out of the lists and could compete no more. This entitled Alfred to the first shot for second prize. He felt he would give anything he possessed to win the dainty trifle which the Colonel had waved aloft. Twice he raised his rifle in his exceeding earnestness to score a good shot and each time lowered the barrel. When finally he did shoot the bullet embedded itself in the second circle. It was a good shot, but he knew it would never win that prize.

"A little nervous, eh?" remarked Miller, with a half sneer on his swarthy face.

Several young settlers followed in succession, but their aims were poor. Then little Harry Bennet took his stand. Harry had won many prizes in former matches, and many of the pioneers considered him one of the best shots in the country.

"Only a few more after you, Harry," said Col. Zane. "You have a good chance."

"All right, Colonel. That's Betty's prize and somebody'll have to do some mighty tall shootin' to beat me," said the lad, his blue eyes flashing as he toed the mark.

Shouts and cheers of approval greeted his attempt. The bullet had passed into the wood so close to the nail that a knife blade could not have been inserted between.

Miller's turn came next. He was a fine marksman and he knew it. With the confidence born of long experience and knowledge of his weapon, he took a careful though quick aim and fired. He turned away satisfied that he would carry off the coveted prize. He had nicked the nail.

But Miller reckoned without his host. Betty had seen the result of his shot and the self-satisfied smile on his face. She watched several of the settlers make poor attempts at the nail, and then, convinced that not one of the other contestants could do so well as Miller, she slipped off the horse and ran around to where Wetzel was standing by her pony.

"Lew, I believe Miller will win my prize," she whispered, placing her hand on the hunter's arm. "He has scratched the nail, and I am sure no one except you can do better. I do not want Miller to have anything of mine."

"And, little girl, you want me to shoot fer you," said Lewis.

"Yes, Lew, please come and shoot for me."

It was said of Wetzel that he never wasted powder. He never entered into the races and shooting-matches of the settlers, yet it was well known that he was the fleetest runner and the most unerring shot on the frontier. Therefore, it was with surprise and pleasure that Col. Zane heard the hunter say he guessed he would like one shot anyway.

Miller looked on with a grim smile. He knew that, Wetzel or no Wetzel, it would take a remarkably clever shot to beat his.

"This shot's fer Betty," said Wetzel as he stepped to the mark. He fastened his keen eyes on the stake. At that distance the head of the nail looked like a tiny black speck. Wetzel took one of the locks of hair that waved over his broad shoulders and held it up in front of his eyes a moment. He thus ascertained that there was not any perceptible breeze. The long black barrel started slowly to rise—it seemed to the interested on-lookers that it would never reach a level—and when, at last, it became rigid, there was a single second in which man and rifle appeared as if carved out of stone. Then followed a burst of red flame, a puff of white smoke, a clear ringing report.

Many thought the hunter had missed altogether. It seemed that the nail had not changed its position; there was no bullet hole in the white lime wash that had been smeared round the nail. But on close inspection the nail was found to have been driven to its head in the wood.

"A wonderful shot!" exclaimed Col. Zane. "Lewis, I don't remember having seen the like more than once or twice in my life."

Wetzel made no answer. He moved away to his former position and commenced to reload his rifle.

Betty came running up to him, holding in her hand the prize bullet pouch.

"Oh, Lew, if I dared I would kiss you. It pleases me more for you to have won my prize than if any one else had won it. And it was the finest, straightest shot ever made.

"Betty, it's a little fancy for redskins, but it'll be a keep sake," answered Lewis, his eyes reflecting the bright smile on her face.

Friendly rivalry in feats that called for strength, speed and daring was the diversion of the youth of that period, and the pioneers conducted this good-natured but spirited sport strictly on its merits. Each contestant strove his utmost to outdo his opponent. It was hardly to be expected that Alfred would carry off any of the laurels. Used as he had been to comparative idleness he was no match for the hardy lads who had been brought up and trained to a life of action, wherein a ten mile walk behind a plow, or a cord of wood chopped in a day, were trifles. Alfred lost in the foot-race and the sack-race, but by dint of exerting himself to the limit of his strength, he did manage to take one fall out of the best wrestler. He was content to stop here, and, throwing himself on the grass, endeavored to recover his breath. He felt happier today than for some time past. Twice during the afternoon he had met Betty's eyes and the look he encountered there made his heart stir with a strange feeling of fear and hope. While he was ruminating on what had happened between Betty and himself he allowed his eyes to wander from one person to another. When his gaze alighted on Wetzel it became riveted there. The hunter's attitude struck him as singular. Wetzel had his face half turned toward the boys romping near him and he leaned carelessly against a white oak tree. But a close observer would have seen, as Alfred did, that there was a certain alertness in that rigid and motionless figure. Wetzel's eyes were fixed on the western end of the island. Almost involuntarily Alfred's eyes sought the same direction. The western end of the island ran out into a long low point covered with briars, rushes and saw-grass. As Alfred directed his gaze along the water line of this point he distinctly saw a dark form flit from one bush to another. He was positive he had not been mistaken. He got up slowly and unconcernedly, and strolled over to Wetzel.

"Wetzel, I saw an object just now," he said in a low tone. "It was moving behind those bushes at the head of the island. I am not sure whether it was an animal or an Indian."

"Injuns. Go back and be natur'l like. Don't say nothin' and watch Miller," whispered Wetzel.

Much perturbed by the developments of the last few moments, and wondering what was going to happen, Alfred turned away. He had scarcely reached the others when he heard Betty's voice raised in indignant protest.

"I tell you I did swim my pony across the river," cried Betty. "It was just even with that point and the river was higher than it is now."

"You probably overestimated your feat," said Miller, with his disagreeable, doubtful smile. "I have seen the river so low that it could be waded, and then it would be a very easy matter to cross. But now your pony could not swim half the distance."

"I'll show you," answered Betty, her black eyes flashing. She put her foot in the stirrup and leaped on Madcap.

"Now, Betty, don't try that foolish ride again," implored Mrs. Zane. "What do you care whether strangers believe it or not? Eb, make her come back."

Col. Zane only laughed and made no attempt to detain Betty. He rather indulged her caprices.

"Stop her!" cried Clarke.

"Betty, where are you goin'?" said Wetzel, grabbing

at Madcap's bridle. But Betty was too quick for him.
She avoided the hunter, and with a saucy laugh she
wheeled the fiery little pony and urged her over the
bank. Almost before any one could divine her purpose
she had Madcap in the water up to her knees.

"Betty, stop!" cried Wetzel.

She paid no attention to his call. In another moment
the pony would be off the shoal and swimming.

"Stop! Turn back, Betty, or I'll shoot the pony,"
shouted Wetzel, and this time there was a ring of
deadly earnestness in his voice. With the words he had
cocked and thrown forward the long rifle.

Betty heard, and in alarm she turned her pony. She
looked up with great surprise and concern, for she
knew Wetzel was not one to trifle.

"For God's sake!" exclaimed Colonel Zane, looking
in amazement at the hunter's face, which was now
white and stern.

"Why, Lew, you do not mean you would shoot
Madcap?" said Betty, reproachfully, as she reached the
shore.

All present in that watching crowd were silent,
awaiting the hunter's answer. They felt that mysterious
power which portends the revelation of strange events.
Col. Zane and Jonathan knew the instant they saw
Wetzel that something extraordinary was coming. His
face had grown cold and gray; his lips were tightly
compressed; his eyes dilated and shone with a peculiar
lustre.

"Where were you headin' your pony?" asked Wetzel.

"I wanted to reach that point where the water is
shallow," answered Betty.

"That's what I thought. Well, Betty, hostile Injuns
are hidin' and waitin' fer you in them high rushes right
where you were makin' fer," said Wetzel. Then he
shouldered his rifle and walked rapidly away.

"Oh, he cannot be serious!" cried Betty. "Oh, how foolish I am."

"Get back up from the river, everybody," commanded Col. Zane.

"Col. Zane," said Clarke, walking beside the Colonel up the bank, "I saw Wetzel watching the island in a manner that I thought odd, under the circumstances, and I watched too. Presently I saw a dark form dart behind a bush. I went over and told Wetzel, and he said there were Indians on the island."

"This is most d——n strange," said Col. Zane, frowning heavily. "Wetzel's suspicions, Miller turns up, teases Betty attempting that foolhardy trick, and then—— Indians! It may be a coincidence, but it looks bad."

"Col. Zane, don't you think Wetzel may be mistaken?" said Miller, coming up. "I came over from the other side this morning and I did not see any Indian sign. Probably Wetzel has caused needless excitement."

"It does not follow that because you came from over the river there are no Indians there," answered Col. Zane, sharply. "Do you presume to criticise Wetzel's judgment?"

"I saw an Indian!" cried Clarke, facing Miller with blazing eyes. "And if you say I did not, you lie! What is more, I believe you know more than any one else about it. I watched you. I saw you were uneasy and that you looked across the river from time to time. Perhaps you had better explain to Col. Zane the reason you taunted his sister into attempting that ride."

With a snarl more like that of a tiger than of a human being, Miller sprang at Clarke. His face was dark with malignant hatred, as he reached for and drew an ugly knife. There were cries of fright from the children and screams from the women. Alfred stepped aside with the wonderful quickness of the trained boxer and shot out his right arm. His fist caught Miller a hard blow on the head, knocking him down and sending the knife flying in the air.

It had all happened so quickly that everyone was as if paralyzed. The settlers stood still and watched Miller rise slowly to his feet.

"Give me my knife!" he cried hoarsely. The knife had fallen at the feet of Major McColloch, who had concealed it with his foot.

"Let this end right here," ordered Col. Zane. "Clarke, you have made a very strong statement. Have you anything to substantiate your words?"

"I think I have," said Clarke. He was standing erect, his face white and his eyes like blue steel. "I knew him at Ft. Pitt. He was a liar and a drunkard there. He was a friend of the Indians and of the British. What he was there he must be here. It was Wetzel who told me to watch him. Wetzel and I both think he knew the Indians were on the island."

"Col. Zane, it is false," said Miller, huskily. "He is trying to put you against me. He hates me because your sister—"

"You cur!" cried Clarke, striking at Miller. Col. Zane struck up the infuriated young man's arm.

"Give us knives, or anything," panted Clarke.

"Yes, let us fight it out now," said Miller.

"Capt. Boggs, take Clarke to the block-house. Make him stay there if you have to lock him up," commanded Col. Zane. "Miller, as for you, I cannot condemn you without proof. If I knew positively that there were Indians on the island and that you were aware of it, you would be a dead man in less time than it takes to say it. I will give you the benefit of the doubt and twenty-four hours to leave the Fort."

The villagers dispersed and went to their homes. They were inclined to take Clarke's side. Miller had become disliked. His drinking habits and his arrogant and bold manner had slowly undermined the friendships he had made during the early part of his stay at Ft. Henry; while Clarke's good humor and willingness to help any one, his gentleness with the children, and his several acts of heroism had strengthened their regard.

"Jonathan, this looks like some of Girty's work. I wish I knew the truth," said Col. Zane, as he, his brothers and Betty and Myeerah entered the house. "Confound it! We can't have even one afternoon of enjoyment. I must see Lewis. I cannot be sure of Clarke. He is evidently bitter against Miller. That would have been a terrible fight. Those fellows have had trouble before, and I am afraid we have not seen the last of their quarrel."

"If they meet again—but how can you keep them apart?" said Silas. "If Miller leaves the Fort without killing Clarke he'll hide around in the woods and wait for a chance to shoot him."

"Not with Wetzel here," answered Col. Zane. "Betty, do you see what your——" he began, turning to his sister, but when he saw her white and miserable face he said no more.

"Don't mind, Betts. It wasn't any fault of yours," said Isaac, putting his arm tenderly round the trembling girl. "I for another believe Clarke was right when he said Miller knew there were Indians over the river. It looks like a plot to abduct you. Have no fear for Alfred. He can take care of himself. He showed that pretty well."

An hour later Clarke had finished his supper and was sitting by his window smoking his pipe. His anger had cooled somewhat and his reflections were not of the pleasantest kind. He regretted that he lowered himself so far as to fight with a man little better than an outlaw. Still there was a grim satisfaction in the thought of the blow he had given Miller. He remembered he had asked for a knife and that his enemy and he be permitted to fight to the death. After all to have ended, then and there, the feud between them would have been the better course; for he well knew Miller's desperate character, that he had killed more than one white man, and that now a fair fight might not be possible. Well, he thought, what did it matter? He was not going to worry himself. He did not care much, one way or another. He had no home; he could not make one without the woman he loved. He was a Soldier of Fortune; he was at the mercy of Fate, and he would drift along and let what came be welcome. A soft footfall on the stairs and a knock on the door interrupted his thoughts.

"Come in," he said.

The door opened and Wetzel strode into the room.

"I come over to say somethin' to you," said the hunter, taking the chair by the window and placing his rifle over his knee.

"I will be pleased to listen or talk, as you desire," said Alfred.

"I don't mind tellin' you that the punch you give Miller was what he deserved. If he and Girty didn't hatch up that trick to ketch Betty, I don't know nothin'. But we can't prove nothin' on him yet. Mebbe he knew about the redskins; mebbe he didn't. Personally, I think he did. But I can't kill a white man because I think somethin'. I'd have to know fer sure. What I want to say is to put you on your guard against the baddest man on the river."

"I am aware of that," answered Alfred. "I knew his record at Ft. Pitt. What would you have me do?"

"Keep close till he's gone."

"That would be cowardly."

"No, it wouldn't. He'd shoot you from behind some tree or cabin."

"Well, I'm much obliged to you for your kind advice, but for all that I won't stay in the house," said

Alfred, beginning to wonder at the hunter's earnest manner.

"You're in love with Betty, ain't you?"

The question came with Wetzel's usual bluntness and it staggered Alfred. He could not be angry, and he did not know what to say. The hunter went on:

"You needn't say so, because I know it. And I know she loves you and that's why I want you to look out fer Miller."

"My God! man, you're crazy," said Alfred, laughing scornfully. "She cares nothing for me."

"That's your great failin', young feller. You fly off'en the handle too easy. And so does Betty. You both care fer each other and are unhappy about it. Now, you don't know Betty, and she keeps misunderstandin' you."

"For Heaven's sake! Wetzel, if you know anything tell me. Love her? Why, the words are weak! I love her so well that an hour ago I would have welcomed death at Miller's hands only to fall and die at her feet defending her. Your words set me on fire. What right have you to say that? How do you know?"

The hunter leaned forward and put his hand on Alfred's shoulder. On his pale face was that sublime light which comes to great souls when they give up a life long secret, or when they sacrifice what is best beloved. His broad chest heaved: his deep voice trembled.

"Listen. I'm not a man fer words, and it's hard to tell. Betty loves you. I've carried her in my arms when she was a baby. I've made her toys and played with her when she was a little girl. I know all her moods. I can read her like I do the moss, and the leaves, and the bark of the forest. I've loved her all my life. That's why I know she loves you. I can feel it. Her happiness is the only dear thing left on earth fer me. And that's why I'm your friend."

In the silence that followed his words the door opened and closed and he was gone.

* * * * * * *

Betty awoke with a start. She was wide awake in a second. The moonbeams came through the leaves of the maple tree near her window and cast fantastic shadows on the wall of her room. Betty lay quiet, watching the fairy-like figures on the wall and listening intently. What had awakened her? The night was still; the crow of a cock in the distance proclaimed that the hour of dawn was near at hand. She waited for Tige's bark under her window, or Sam's voice, or the kicking and trampling of horses in the barn—sounds that usually broke her slumbers in the morning. But no such noises were forthcoming. Suddenly she heard a light, quick tap, tap, and then a rattling in the corner. It was like no sound but that made by a pebble striking the floor, bounding and rolling across the room. There it was again. Some one was tossing stones in at her window. She slipped out of bed, ran, and leaned on the window-sill and looked out. The moon was going down behind the hill, but there was light enough for her to distinguish objects. She saw a dark figure crouching by the fence.

"Who is it?" said Betty, a little frightened, but more curious.

"Sh-h-h, it's Miller," came the answer, spoken in a low voice.

The bent form straightened and stood erect. It stepped forward under Betty's window. The light was dim, but Betty recognized the dark face of Miller. He carried a rifle in his hand and a pack on his shoulder.

"Go away, or I'll call my brother. I will not listen to you," said Betty, making a move to leave the window.

"Sh-h-h, not so loud," said Miller, in a quick, hoarse whisper. "You'd better listen. I am going across the border to join Girty. He is going to bring the Indians and the British here to burn the settlement. If you will go away with me I'll save the lives of your brothers and their families. I have aided Girty and I have influence with him. If you won't go you'll be taken captive and you'll see all your friends and relatives scalped and burned. Quick, your answer."

"Never, traitor! Monster! I'd be burned at the stake before I'd go a step with you!" cried Betty.

"Then remember that you've crossed a desperate man. If you escape the massacre you will beg on your knees to me. This settlement is doomed. Now, go to your white-faced lover. You'll find him cold. Ha! Ha! Ha!" and with a taunting laugh he leaped the fence and disappeared in the gloom.

Betty sank to the floor stunned, horrified. She shuddered at the malignity expressed in Miller's words. How had she ever been deceived in him? He was in league with Girty. At heart he was a savage, a renegade. Betty went over his words, one by one.

"Your white-faced lover. You will find him cold," whispered Betty. "What did he mean?"

Then came the thought. Miller had murdered Clarke. Betty gave one agonized quiver, as if a knife had been thrust into her side, and then her paralyzed limbs recovered the power of action. She flew out into the passage-way and pounded on her brother's door.

"Eb! Eb! Get up! Quickly, for God's sake!" she cried. A smothered exclamation, a woman's quick voice, the heavy thud of feet striking the floor followed Betty's alarm. Then the door opened.

"Hello, Betts, what's up?" said Col. Zane, in his rapid voice.

At the same moment the door at the end of the hall opened and Isaac came out.

"Eb, Betty, I heard voices out doors and in the house. What's the row?"

"Oh, Isaac! Oh, Eb! Something terrible has happened!" cried Betty, breathlessly.

"Then it is no time to get excited," said the Colonel, calmly. He placed his arm round Betty and drew her into the room. "Isaac, get down the rifles. Now, Betty, time is precious. Tell me quickly, briefly."

"I was awakened by a stone rolling on the floor. I ran to the window and saw a man by the fence. He came under my window and I saw it was Miller. He said he was going to join Girty. He said if I would go with him he would save the lives of all my relatives. If I would not they would all be killed, massacred, burned alive, and I would be taken away as his captive. I told him I'd rather die before I'd go with him. Then he said we were all doomed, and that my white-faced lover was already cold. With that he gave a laugh which made my flesh creep and ran off toward the river. Oh! he has murdered Mr. Clarke."

"Hell! What a fiend!" cried Col. Zane, hurriedly getting into his clothes. "Betts, you had a gun in there. Why didn't you shoot him? Why didn't I pay more attention to Wetzel's advice?"

"You should have allowed Clarke to kill him yesterday," said Isaac. "Like as not he'll have Girty here with a lot of howling devils. What's to be done?"

"I'll send Wetzel after him and that'll soon wind up his ball of yarn," answered Col. Zane.

"Please—go—and find—if Mr. Clarke——"

"Yes, Betty, I'll go at once. You must not lose courage, Betty. It's quite probable that Miller has killed Alfred and that there's worse to follow."

"I'll come, Eb, as soon as I have told Myeerah. She is scared half to death," said Isaac, starting for the door.

"All right, only hurry," said Col. Zane, grabbing his

rifle. Without wasting more words, and lacing up his hunting shirt as he went he ran out of the room.

The first rays of dawn came streaking in at the window. The chill gray light brought no cheer with its herald of the birth of another day. For what might the morning sun disclose? It might shine on a long line of painted Indians. The fresh breeze from over the river might bring the long warwhoop of the savage.

No wonder Noah and his brother, awakened by the voice of their father, sat up in their little bed and looked about with frightened eyes. No wonder Mrs. Zane's face blanched. How many times she had seen her husband grasp his rifle and run out to meet danger!

"Bessie," said Betty. "If it's true I will not be able to bear it. It's all my fault."

"Nonsense! You heard Eb say Miller and Clarke had quarreled before. They hated each other before they ever saw you."

A door banged, quick footsteps sounded on the stairs, and Isaac came rushing into the room. Betty, deathly pale, stood with her hands pressed to her bosom, and looked at Isaac with a question in her eyes that her tongue could not speak.

"Betty, Alfred's badly hurt, but he's alive. I can tell you no more now," said Isaac. "Bessie, bring your needle, silk linen, liniment—everything you need for a bad knife wound, and come quickly."

Betty's haggard face changed as if some warm light had been reflected on it; her lips moved, and with a sob of thankfulness she fled to her room.

Two hours later, while Annie was serving breakfast to Betty and Myeerah, Col. Zane strode into the room.

"Well, one has to eat whatever happens," he said, his clouded face brightening somewhat. "Betty, there's been bad work, bad work. When I got to Clarke's room I found him lying on the bed with a knife sticking in him. As it is we are doubtful about pulling him through."

"May I see him?" whispered Betty, with pale lips.

"If the worst comes to the worst I'll take you over. But it would do no good now and would surely unnerve you. He still has a fighting chance."

"Did they fight, or was Mr. Clarke stabbed in his sleep?"

"Miller climbed into Clarke's window and knifed him in the dark. As I came over I met Wetzel and told him I wanted him to trail Miller and find if there is any truth in his threat about Girty and the Indians. Sam just now found Tige tied fast in the fence corner back of the barn. That explains the mystery of Miller's getting so near the house. You know he always took pains to make friends with Tige. The poor dog was helpless; his legs were tied and his jaws bound fast. Oh, Miller is as cunning as an Indian! He has had this all planned out, and he has had more than one arrow to his bow. But, if I mistake not he has shot his last one."

"Miller must be safe from pursuit by this time," said Betty.

"Safe for the present, yes," answered Col. Zane, "but while Jonathan and Wetzel live I would not give a snap of my fingers for Miller's chances. Hello, I hear some one talking. I sent for Jack and the Major."

The Colonel threw open the door. Wetzel, Major McColloch, Jonathan and Silas Zane were approaching. They were all heavily armed. Wetzel was equipped for a long chase. Double leggins were laced round his legs. A buck-skin knapsack was strapped to his shoulders.

"Major, I want you and Jonathan to watch the river," said Col. Zane. "Silas, you are to go to the mouth of Yellow Creek and reconnoiter. We are in for a seige. It may be twenty-four hours and it may be ten days. In the meantime I will get the Fort in shape to meet the attack. Lewis, you have your orders. Have you anything to suggest?"

"I'll take the dog," answered Wetzel. "He'll save time for me. I'll stick to Miller's trail and find Girty's forces. I've believed all along that Miller was helpin' Girty, and I'm thinkin' that where Miller goes there I'll find Girty and his redskins. If it's night when I get back I'll give the call of the hoot-owl three times, quick, so Jack and the Major will know I want to get back acrost the river."

"All right, Lewis, we'll be expecting you any time," said Col. Zane.

"Betty, I'm goin' now and I want to tell you somethin'," said Wetzel, as Betty appeared in the door. "Come as far as the end of the path with me."

"I'm sorry you must go. But Tige seems delighted," said Betty, walking beside Wetzel, while the dog ran on before.

"Betty, I wanted to tell you to stay close like to the house, fer this feller Miller has been layin' traps fer you, and the Injuns is on the war-path. Don't ride your pony, and stay home now."

"Indeed, I shall never again do anything as foolish as I did yesterday. I have learned my lesson. And Oh! Lew, I am so grateful to you for saving me. When will you return to the Fort?"

"Mebbe never, Betty."

"Oh, no. Don't say that. I know all this Indian talk will blow over, as it always does, and you will come back and everything will be all right again."

"I hope it'll be as you say, Betty, but there's no tellin', there's no tellin'."

"You are going to see if the Indians are making preparations to besiege the Fort?"

"Yes, I am goin' fer that. And if I happen to find Miller on my way I'll give him Betty's regards."

Betty shivered at his covert meaning. Long ago in a

moment of playfulness, Betty had scratched her name on the hunter's rifle. Ever after that Wetzel called his fatal weapon by her name.

"If you were going simply to avenge me I would not let you go. That wretch will get his just due some day, never fear for that."

"Betty, 'taint likely he'll get away from me, and if he does there's Jonathan. This mornin' when we trailed Miller down to the river bank Jonathan points acrost the river and says: 'You or me,' and I says: 'Me,' so it's all settled.

"Will Mr. Clarke live?" said Betty, in an altered tone, asking the question which was uppermost in her mind.

"I think so, I hope so. He's a husky young chap and the cut wasn't bad. He lost so much blood. That's why he's so weak. If he gets well he'll have somethin' to tell you."

"Lew, what do you mean?" demanded Betty, quickly.

"Me and him had a long talk last night and——"

"You did not go to him and talk of me, did you?" said Betty, reproachfully.

They had now reached the end of the path. Wetzel stopped and dropped the butt of his rifle on the ground. Tige looked on and wagged his tail. Presently the hunter spoke.

"Yes, we talked about you."

"Oh! Lewis. What did—could you have said?" faltered Betty.

"You think I hadn't ought to speak to him of you?"

"I do not see why you should. Of course you are my good friend, but he—it is not like you to speak of me."

"Fer once I don't agree with you. I knew how it was with him so I told him. I knew how it was with you so I told him, and I know how it is with me, so I told him that too."

"With you?" whispered Betty.

"Yes, with me. That kind of gives me a right, don't it, considerin' it's all fer your happiness?"

"With you?" echoed Betty in a low tone. She was beginning to realize that she had not known this man. She looked up at him. His eyes were misty with an unutterable sadness.

"Oh, no! No! Lew. Say it is not true," she cried, piteously. All in a moment Betty's burdens became too heavy for her. She wrung her little hands. Her brother's kindly advice, Bessie's warnings, and old Grandmother Watkins' words came back to her. For the first time she believed what they said—that Wetzel loved her. All at once the scales fell from her eyes and she saw this man as he really was. All the thousand and one things he had done for her, his simple teaching, his thoughtfulness, his faithfulness, and his watchful protection—all came crowding on her as debts that she could never pay. For now what could she give this man to whom she owed more than her life? Nothing. It was too late. Her love could have reclaimed him, could have put an end to that solitary wandering, and have made him a good, happy man.

"Yes, Betty, it's time to tell it. I've loved you always," he said softly.

She covered her face and sobbed. Wetzel put his arm round her and drew her to him until the dark head rested on his shoulder. Thus they stood a moment.

"Don't cry, little one," he said, tenderly. "Don't grieve fer me. My love fer you has been the only good in my life. It's been happiness to love you. Don't think of me. I can see you and Alfred in a happy home, surrounded by bright-eyed children. There'll be a brave lad named fer me, and when I come, if I ever do, I'll tell him stories, and learn him the secrets of the woods, and how to shoot, and things I know so well."

"I am so wretched—so miserable. To think I have

been so—so blind, and I have teased you—and—it might have been—only now it's too late," said Betty, between her sobs.

"Yes, I know, and it's better so. This man you love rings true. He has learnin' and edication. I have nothin' but muscle and a quick eye. And that'll serve you and Alfred when you are in danger. I'm goin' now. Stand here till I'm out of sight."

"Kiss me goodbye," whispered Betty.

The hunter bent his head and kissed her on the brow. Then he turned and with a rapid step went along the bluff toward the west. When he reached the laurel bushes which fringed the edge of the forest he looked back. He saw the slender gray clad figure standing motionless in the narrow path. He waved his hand and then turned and plunged into the forest. The dog looked back, raised his head and gave a long, mournful howl. Then, he too disappeared.

A mile west of the settlement Wetzel abandoned the forest and picked his way down the steep bluff to the river. Here he prepared to swim to the western shore. He took off his buckskin garments, spread them out on the ground, placed his knapsack in the middle, and rolling all into a small bundle tied it round his rifle. Grasping the rifle just above the hammer he waded into the water up to his waist and then, turning easily on his back he held the rifle straight up, allowing the butt to rest on his breast. This left his right arm unhampered. With a powerful back-arm stroke he rapidly swam the river, which was deep and narrow at this point. In a quarter of an hour he was once more in his dry suit.

He was now two miles below the island, where yesterday the Indians had been concealed, and where this morning Miller had crossed. Wetzel knew Miller expected to be trailed, and that he would use every art and cunning of woodcraft to elude his pursuers, or to lead them into a death-trap. Wetzel believed Miller had joined the Indians, who had undoubtedly been waiting for him, or for a signal from him, and that he would use them to ambush the trail.

Therefore Wetzel decided he would try to strike Miller's tracks far west of the river. He risked a great deal in attempting this because it was possible he might fail to find any trace of the spy. But Wetzel wasted not one second. His course was chosen. With all possible speed, which meant with him walking only when he could not run, he traveled northwest. If Miller had taken the direction Wetzel suspected, the trails of the two men would cross about ten miles from the Ohio. But the hunter had not traversed more than a mile of the forest when the dog put his nose high in the air and growled. Wetzel slowed down into a walk and moved cautiously onward, peering through the green aisles of the woods. A few rods farther on Tige uttered another growl and put his nose to the ground. He found a trail. On examination Wetzel discovered in the moss two moccasin tracks. Two Indians had passed that point that morning. They were going northwest directly toward the camp of Wingenund. Wetzel stuck close to the trail all that day and an hour before dusk he heard the sharp crack of a rifle. A moment afterward a doe came crashing through the thicket to Wetzel's right and bounding across a little brook she disappeared.

A tree with a bushy, leafy top had been uprooted by a storm and had fallen across the stream at this point. Wetzel crawled among the branches. The dog followed and lay down beside him. Before darkness set in Wetzel saw that the clear water of the brook had been roiled; therefore, he concluded that somewhere upstream Indians had waded into the brook. Probably they had killed a deer and were getting their evening meal.

Hours passed. Twilight deepened into darkness. One by one the stars appeared; then the crescent moon rose over the wooded hill in the west, and the hunter never moved. With his head leaning against the log he sat quiet and patient. At midnight he whispered to the dog, and crawling from his hiding place glided stealthily up the stream. Far ahead from the dark depths of the forest peeped the flickering light of a camp-fire. Wetzel consumed a half hour in approaching within one hundred feet of this light. Then he got down on his hands and knees and crawled behind a tree on top of the little ridge which had obstructed a view of the camp scene.

From this vantage point Wetzel saw a clear space surrounded by pines and hemlocks. In the center of this glade a fire burned briskly. Two Indians lay wrapped in their blankets, sound asleep. Wetzel pressed the dog close to the ground, laid aside his rifle, drew his tomahawk, and lying flat on his breast commenced to work his way, inch by inch, toward the sleeping savages. The tall ferns trembled as the hunter wormed his way among them, but there was no sound, not a snapping of a twig nor a rustling of a leaf. The nightwind sighed softly through the pines; it blew the bright sparks from the burning logs, and fanned the embers into a red glow; it swept caressingly over the sleeping savages, but it could not warn them that another wind, the Wind-of-Death, was near at hand.

A quarter of an hour elapsed. Nearer and nearer; slowly but surely drew the hunter. With what wonderful patience and self-control did this cold-blooded Nemesis approach his victims! Probably any other Indian slayer would have fired his rifle and then rushed to combat with a knife or a tomahawk. Not so Wetzel. He scorned to use powder. He crept forward like a snake gliding upon its prey. He slid one hand in front of him and pressed it down on the moss, at first gently, then firmly, and when he had secured to good hold he slowly dragged his body forward the length of his arm. At last his dark form rose and stood over the unconscious

Indians, like a minister of Doom. The tomahawk flashed once, twice in the firelight, and the Indians, without a moan, and with a convulsive quivering and straightening of their bodies, passed from the tired sleep of nature to the eternal sleep of death.

Foregoing his usual custom of taking the scalps, Wetzel hurriedly left the glade. He had found that the Indians were Shawnees and he had expected they were Delawares. He knew Miller's red comrades belonged to the latter tribe. The presence of Shawnees so near the settlement confirmed his belief that a concerted movement was to be made on the whites in the near future. He would not have been surprised to find the woods full of redskins. He spent the remainder of that night close under the side of a log with the dog curled up beside him.

Next morning Wetzel ran across the trail of a white man and six Indians. He tracked them all that day and half of the night before he again rested. By noon of the following day he came in sight of the cliff from which Jonathan Zane had watched the sufferings of Col. Crawford. Wetzel now made his favorite move, a wide detour, and came up on the other side of the encampment.

From the top of the bluff he saw down into the village of the Delawares. The valley was alive with Indians; they were working like beaver; some with weapons, some painting themselves, and others dancing war-dances. Packs were being strapped on the backs of ponies. Everywhere was the hurry and bustle of the preparation for war. The dancing and the singing were kept up half the night.

At daybreak Wetzel was at his post. A little after sunrise he heard a long yell which he believed announced the arrival of an important party. And so it turned out. Amid shrill yelling and whooping, the like of which Wetzel had never before heard, Simon Girty rode into

Wingenund's camp at the head of one hundred Shawnee warriors and two hundred British Rangers from Detroit. Wetzel recoiled when he saw the red uniforms of the Britishers and their bayonets. Including Pipe's and Wingenund's braves the total force which was going to march against the Fort exceeded six hundred. An impotent frenzy possessed Wetzel as he watched the orderly marching of the Rangers and the proud bearing of the Indian warriors. Miller had spoken the truth. Ft. Henry was doomed.

"Tige, there's one of them struttin' turkey cocks as won't see the Ohio," said Wetzel to the dog.

Hurriedly slipping from round his neck the bullet-pouch that Betty had given him, he shook out a bullet and with the point of his knife he scratched deep in the soft lead the letter W. Then he cut the bullet half through. This done he detached the pouch from the cord and running the cord through the cut in the bullet he bit the lead. He tied the string round the neck of the dog and pointing eastward he said: "Home."

The intelligent animal understood perfectly. His duty was to get that warning home. His clear brown eyes as much as said: "I will not fail." He wagged his tail, licked the hunter's hand, bounded away and disappeared.

Wetzel rested easier in mind. He knew the dog would stop for nothing, and that he stood a far better chance of reaching the Fort in safety than did he himself.

With a lurid light in his eyes Wetzel now turned to the Indians. He would never leave that spot without sending a leaden messenger into the heart of someone in that camp. Glancing on all sides he at length selected a place where it was possible he might approach near enough to the camp to get a shot. He carefully studied the lay of the ground, the trees, rocks, bushes, grass,— everything that could help screen him from the keen eye of savage scouts. When he had marked his course he commenced his perilous descent. In an hour he had reached the bottom of the cliff. Dropping flat on the ground, he once more started his snail-like crawl. A stretch of swampy ground, luxuriant with rushes and saw-grass, made a part of the way easy for him, though it led through mud, and slime, and stagnant water. Frogs and turtles warming their backs in the sunshine scampered in alarm from their logs. Lizards blinked at him. Moccasin snakes darted wicked forked tongues at him and then glided out of reach of his tomahawk. The frogs had stopped their deep bass notes. A swamp-blackbird rose in fright from her nest in the saw-grass, and twittering plaintively fluttered round and round over the pond. The flight of the bird worried Wetzel. Such little things as these might attract the attention of some Indian scout. But he hoped that in the excitement of the war preparations these unusual disturbances would escape notice. At last he gained the other side of the swamp. At the end of the cornfield before him was the clump of laurel which he had marked from the cliff as his objective point. The Indian corn was now about five feet high. Wetzel passed through this field unseen. He reached the laurel bushes, where he dropped to the ground and lay quiet a few minutes. On the dash which he would soon make to the forest he needed all his breath and all his fleetness. He looked to the right to see how far the woods was from where he lay. Not more than one hundred feet. He was safe. Once in the dark shade of those trees, and with his foes behind him, he could defy the whole race of Delawares. He looked to his rifle, freshened the powder in the pan, carefully adjusted the flint, and then rose quietly to his feet.

Wetzel's keen gaze, as he swept it from left to right, took in every detail of the camp. He was almost in the village. A tepee stood not twenty feet from his hiding-place. He could have tossed a stone in the midst of squaws, and braves, and chiefs. The main body of Indians was in the center of the camp. The British were lined up further on. Both Indians and soldiers were resting on their arms and waiting. Suddenly Wetzel started and his heart leaped. Under a maple tree not one hundred and fifty yards distant stood four men in earnest consultation. One was an Indian. Wetzel recognized the fierce, stern face, the haughty, erect figure. He knew that long, trailing war-bonnet. It could have adorned the head of but one chief—Wingenund, the sachem of the Delawares. A British officer, girdled and epauletted, stood next to Wingenund. Simon Girty, the renegade, and Miller, the traitor, completed the group.

Wetzel sank to his knees. The perspiration poured from his face. The mighty hunter trembled, but it was from eagerness. Was not Girty, the white savage, the bane of the poor settlers, within range of a weapon that never failed? Was not the murderous chieftain, who had once whipped and tortured him, who had burned Crawford alive, there in plain sight? Wetzel revelled a moment in fiendish glee. He passed his hands tenderly over the long barrel of his rifle. In that moment as never before he gloried in his power—a power which enabled him to put a bullet in the eye of a squirrel at the distance these men were from him. But only for an instant did the hunter yield to this feeling. He knew too well the value of time and opportunity.

He rose again to his feet and peered out from under the shading laurel branches. As he did so the dark face of Miller turned full toward him. A tremor, like the intense thrill of a tiger when he is about to spring, ran over Wetzel's frame. In his mad gladness at being within rifle-shot of his great Indian foe, Wetzel had forgotten the man he had trailed for two days. He had forgotten Miller. He had only one shot—and Betty was to be avenged. He gritted his teeth. The Delaware chief was as safe as though he were a thousand miles away.

This opportunity for which Wetzel had waited so many years, and the successful issue of which would have gone so far toward the fulfillment of a life's purpose, was worse than useless. A great temptation assailed the hunter.

Wetzel's face was white when he raised the rifle; his dark eye, gleaming vengefully, ran along the barrel. The little bead on the front sight first covered the British officer, and then the broad breast of Girty. It moved reluctantly and searched out the heart of Wingenund, where it lingered for a fleeting instant. At last it rested upon the swarthy face of Miller.

"Fer Betty," muttered the hunter, between his clenched teeth as he pressed the trigger.

The spiteful report awoke a thousand echoes. When the shot broke the stillness Miller was talking and gesticulating. His hand dropped inertly; he stood upright for a second, his head slowly bowing and his body swaying perceptibly. Then he plunged forward like a log, his face striking the sand. He never moved again. He was dead even before he struck the ground.

Blank silence followed this tragic denouement. Wingenund, a cruel and relentless Indian, but never a traitor, pointed to the small bloody hole in the middle of Miller's forehead, and then nodded his head solemnly. The wondering Indians stood aghast. Then with loud yells the braves ran to the cornfield; they searched the laurel bushes. But they only discovered several moccasin prints in the sand, and a puff of white smoke wafting away upon the summer breeze.

Chapter 12

ALFRED CLARKE lay between life and death. Miller's knife-thrust, although it had made a deep and dangerous wound, had not pierced any vital part; the amount of blood lost made Alfred's condition precarious. Indeed, he would not have lived through that first day but for a wonderful vitality. Col. Zane's wife, to whom had been consigned the delicate task of dressing the wound, shook her head when she first saw the direction of the cut. She found on a closer examination that the knife-blade had been deflected by a rib, and had just missed the lungs. The wound was bathed, sewed up, and bandaged, and the greatest precaution taken to prevent the sufferer from loosening the linen. Every day when Mrs. Zane returned from the bedside of the young man she would be met at the door by Betty, who, in that time of suspense, had lost her bloom, and whose pale face showed the effects of sleepless nights.

"Betty, would you mind going over to the Fort and relieving Mrs. Martin an hour or two?" said Mrs. Zane one day as she came home, looking worn and weary. "We are both tired to death, and Nell Metzar was unable to come. Clarke is unconscious, and will not know you, besides he is sleeping now."

Betty hurried over to Capt. Bogg's cabin, next the block-house, where Alfred lay, and with a palpitating heart and a trepidation wholly out of keeping with the brave front she managed to assume, she knocked gently on the door.

"Ah, Betty, 'tis you, bless your heart," said a matronly little woman who opened the door. "Come right in. He is sleeping now, poor fellow, and it's the first real sleep he has had. He has been raving crazy forty-eight hours."

"Mrs. Martin, what shall I do?" whispered Betty.

"Oh, just watch him, my dear," answered the elder woman. "If you need me send one of the lads up to the house for me. I shall return as soon as I can. Keep the flies away—they are bothersome—and bathe his head every little while. If he wakes and tries to sit up, as he does sometimes, hold him back. He is as weak as a cat. If he raves, soothe him by talking to him. I must go now, dearie."

Betty was left alone in the little room. Though she had taken a seat near the bed where Alfred lay, she had not dared to look at him. Presently conquering her emotion, Betty turned her gaze on the bed. Alfred was lying easily on his back, and notwithstanding the warmth of the day he was covered with a quilt. The light from the window shone on his face. How deathly white it was! There was not a vestige of color in it; the brow looked like chiseled marble; dark shadows underlined the eyes, and the whole face was expressive of weariness and pain.

There are times when a woman's love is all motherliness. All at once this man seemed to Betty like a helpless child. She felt her heart go out to the poor sufferer with a feeling before unknown. She forgot her pride and her fears and her disappointments. She remembered only that this strong man lay there at death's door because he had resented an insult to her. The past with all its bitterness rolled away and was lost, and in its place welled up a tide of forgiveness strong and sweet and hopeful. Her love, like a fire that had been choked and smothered, smouldering but never extinct, and which blazes up with the first breeze, warmed and quickened to life with the touch of her hand on his forehead.

An hour passed. Betty was now at her ease and happier than she had been for months. Her patient continued to sleep peacefully and dreamlessly. With a feeling of womanly curiosity Betty looked around the room. Over the rude mantelpiece were hung a sword, a brace of pistols, and two pictures. These last interested Betty very much. They were portraits; one of them was a likeness of a sweet-faced woman who Betty instinctively knew was his mother. Her eyes lingered tenderly on that face, so like the one lying on the pillow. The other portrait was of a beautiful girl whose dark, magnetic eyes challenged Betty. Was this his sister or—someone else? She could not restrain a jealous twinge, and she felt annoyed to find herself comparing that face with her own. She looked no longer at that portrait, but recommenced her survey of the room. Upon the door hung a broad-brimmed hat with eagle plumes stuck in the band. A pair of high-topped riding-boots, a saddle, and a bridle lay on the floor in the corner. The table was covered with Indian pipes, tobacco pouches, spurs, silk stocks, and other articles.

Suddenly Betty felt that some one was watching her. She turned timidly toward the bed and became much frightened when she encountered the intense gaze from a pair of steel-blue eyes. She almost fell from the chair; but presently she recollected that Alfred had been unconscious for days, and that he would not know who was watching by his bedside.

"Mother, is that you?" asked Alfred, in a weak, low voice.

"Yes, I'm here," answered Betty, remembering the old woman's words about soothing the sufferer.

"But I thought you were ill."

"I was, but I am better now, and it is you who are ill."

"My head hurts so."

"Let me bathe it for you."

"How long have I been home?"

Betty bathed and cooled his heated brow. He caught and held her hands, looking wonderingly at her the while.

"Mother, somehow I thought you had died. I must have dreamed it. I am very happy; but tell me, did a message come for me today?"

Betty shook her head, for she could not speak. She saw he was living in the past, and he was praying for the letter which she would gladly have written had she but known.

"No message, and it is now so long."

"It will come tomorrow," whispered Betty.

"Now, mother, that is what you always say," said the invalid, as he began to toss his head wearily to and fro. "Will she never tell me? It is not like her to keep me in suspense. She was the sweetest, truest, loveliest girl in all the world. When I get well, mother, I am going to find out if she loves me."

"I am sure she does. I know she loves you," answered Betty softly.

"It is very good of you to say that," he went on in his rambling talk. "Some day I'll bring her to you and we'll make her a queen here in the old home. I'll be a better son now and not run away from home again. I've given the dear old mother many a heartache, but that's all past now. The wanderer has come home. Kiss me good-night, mother."

Betty looked down with tear-blurred eyes on the haggard face. Unconsciously she had been running her fingers through the fair hair that lay so damp over his brow. Her pity and tenderness had carried her far beyond herself, and at the last words she bent her head and kissed him on the lips.

"Who are you? You are not my mother. She is dead," he cried, starting up wildly, and looking at her with brilliant eyes.

Betty dropped the fan and rose quickly to her feet. What had she done? A terrible thought had flashed into her mind. Suppose he were not delirious, and had been deceiving her. Oh! for a hiding-place, or that the floor would swallow her. Oh! if some one would only come.

Footsteps sounded on the stairs and Betty ran to the door. To her great relief Mrs. Martin was coming up.

"You can run home now, there's a dear," said the old lady. "We have several watchers for tonight. It will not be long now when he will commence to mend, or else he will die. Poor boy, please God that he gets well. Has he been good? Did he call for any particular young lady? Never fear, Betty, I'll keep the secret. He'll never know you were here unless you tell him yourself."

Meanwhile the days had been busy ones for Col. Zane. In anticipation of an attack from the Indians, the settlers had been fortifying their refuge and making the block-house as nearly impregnable as possible. Everything that was movable and was of value they put inside the stockade fence, out of reach of the destructive redskins. All the horses and cattle were driven into the inclosure. Wagon-loads of hay, grain and food were stored away in the block-house.

Never before had there been such excitement on the frontier. Runners from Ft. Pitt, Short Creek, and other settlements confirmed the rumor that all the towns along the Ohio were preparing for war. Not since the outbreak of the Revolution had there been so much confusion and alarm among the pioneers. To be sure, those on the very verge of the frontier, as at Ft. Henry, had heretofore little to fear from the British. During most of this time there had been comparative peace on the western border, excepting those occasional murders, raids, and massacres perpetrated by the different Indian tribes, and instigated no doubt by Girty and the British at Detroit. Now all kinds of rumors were afloat: Washington was defeated; a close alliance between England and the confederated western tribes had been formed; Girty had British power and wealth back of him. These and many more alarming reports travelled from settlement to settlement.

The death of Col. Crawford had been a terrible shock to the whole country. On the border spread an universal gloom, and the low, sullen mutterings of revengeful wrath. Crawford had been so prominent a man, so popular, and, except in his last and fatal expedition, such an efficient leader that his sudden taking off was almost a national calamity. In fact no one felt it more keenly than did Washington himself, for Crawford was his esteemed friend.

Col. Zane believed Ft. Henry had been marked by the British and the Indians. The last runner from Ft. Pitt had informed him that the description of Miller tallied with that of one of the ten men who had deserted from Ft. Pitt in 1778 with the tories Girty, McKee, and Elliott. Col. Zane was now satisfied that Miller was an agent of Girty and therefore of the British. So since all the weaknesses of the Fort, the number of the garrison, and the favorable conditions for a siege were known to Girty, there was nothing left for Col. Zane and his men but to make a brave stand.

Jonathan Zane and Major McColloch watched the river. Wetzel had disappeared as if the earth had swallowed him. Some pioneers said he would never return. But Col. Zane believed Wetzel would walk into the Fort, as he had done many times in the last ten years, with full information concerning the doings of the Indians. However, the days passed and nothing happened. Their work completed, the settlers waited for the first sign of an enemy. But as none came, gradually their fears were dispelled and they began to think the alarm had been a false one.

All this time Alfred Clarke was recovering his health and strength. The day came when he was able to leave his bed and sit by the window. How glad it made him feel to look out on the green woods and the broad, winding river; how sweet to his ears were the songs of the birds; how soothing was the drowsy hum of the bees in the fragrant honeysuckle by his window. His hold on life had been slight and life was good. He smiled in pitying derision as he remembered his recklessness. He had not been in love with life. In his gloomy moods he had often thought life was hardly worth the living. What sickly sentiment! He had been on the brink of the grave, but he had been snatched back from the dark river of Death. It needed but this to show him the joy of breathing, the glory of loving, the sweetness of living. He resolved that for him there would be no more drifting, no more purposelessness. If what Wetzel had told him was true, if he really had not loved in vain, then his cup of happiness was overflowing. Like a far-off and almost forgotten strain of music some memory struggled to take definite shape in his mind; but it was so hazy, so vague, so impalpable, that he could remember nothing clearly.

Isaac Zane and his Indian bride called on Alfred that afternoon.

"Alfred, I can't tell you how glad I am to see you up again," said Isaac, earnestly, as he wrung Alfred's hand. "Say, but it was a tight squeeze! It has been a bad time for you."

Nothing could have been more pleasing than Myeerah's shy yet eloquent greeting. She gave Alfred her little hand and said in her figurative style of speaking, "Myeerah is happy for you and for others. You are strong like the West Wind that never dies."

"Myeerah and I are going this afternoon, and we came over to say good-bye to you. We intend riding down the river fifteen miles and then crossing, to avoid running into any band of Indians."

"And how does Myeerah like the settlement by this time?"

"Oh, she is getting on famously. Betty and she have fallen in love with each other. It is amusing to hear Betty try to talk in the Wyandot tongue, and to see Myeerah's consternation when Betty gives her a lesson in deportment."

"I rather fancy it would be interesting, too. Are you not going back to the Wyandots at a dangerous time?"

"As to that I can't say. I believe, though, it is better that I get back to Tarhe's camp before we have any trouble with the Indians. I am anxious to get there before Girty or some of his agents."

"Well, if you must go, good luck to you, and may we meet again."

"It will not be long, I am sure. And, old man," he continued, with a bright smile, "when Myeerah and I come again to Ft. Henry we expect to find all well with you. Cheer up, and good-bye."

All the preparations had been made for the departure of Isaac and Myeerah to their far-off Indian home. They were to ride the Indian ponies on which they had arrived at the Fort. Col. Zane had given Isaac one of his pack horses. This animal carried blankets, clothing, and food which insured comparative comfort in the long ride through the wilderness.

"We will follow the old trail until we reach the hickory swale," Isaac was saying to the Colonel, "and then we will turn off and make for the river. Once across the Ohio we can make the trip in two days."

"I think you'll make it all right," said Col. Zane.

"Even if I do meet Indians I shall have no fear, for I

have a protector here," answered Isaac as he led My-eerah's pony up to the step.

"Good-bye, Myeerah; he is yours, but do not forget he is dear to us," said Betty, embracing and kissing the Indian girl.

"My sister does not know Myeerah. The White Eagle will return."

"Good-bye, Betts, don't cry. I shall come home again. And when I do I hope I shall be in time to celebrate another event, this time with you as the heroine. Good-bye. Good-bye."

The ponies cantered down the road. At the bend Isaac and Myeerah turned and waved their hands until the foliage of the trees hid them from view.

"Well, these things happen naturally enough. I suppose they must be. But I should much have preferred Isaac staying here. Hello! What the deuce is that? By Lord! It's Tige!"

The exclamation following Col. Zane's remarks had been called forth by Betty's dog. He came limping painfully up the road from the direction of the river. When he saw Col. Zane he whined and crawled to the Colonel's feet. The dog was wet and covered with burrs, and his beautiful glossy coat which had been Betty's pride, was dripping with blood.

"Silas, Jonathan, come here," cried Col. Zane. "Here's Tige, back without Wetzel, and the poor dog has been shot almost to pieces. What does it mean?"

"Indians," said Jonathan, coming out of the house with Silas, and Mrs. Zane and Betty, who had heard the Colonel's call.

"He has come a long way. Look at his feet. They are torn and bruised," continued Jonathan. "And he has been near Wingenund's camp. You see that red clay on his paws. There is no red clay that I know of round here, and there are miles of it this side of the Delaware camp."

"What is the matter with Tige?" asked Betty.

"He is done for. Shot through, poor fellow. How did he ever reach home?" said Silas.

"Oh, I hope not! Dear old Tige," said Betty as she knelt and tenderly placed the head of the dog in her lap. "Why, what is this? I never put that there. Eb, Jack, look here. There is a string around his neck," and Betty pointed excitedly to a thin cord which was almost concealed in the thick curly hair.

"Good gracious! Eb, look! It is the string off the prize bullet pouch I made, and that Wetzel won on Isaac's wedding-day. It is a message from Lew," said Betty.

"Well, by Heavens! This is strange. So it is. I remember that string. Cut it off, Jack," said Col. Zane.

When Jonathan had cut the string and held it up they all saw the lead bullet. Col. Zane examined it and showed them what had been rudely scratched on it.

"A letter W. Does that mean Wetzel?" asked the Colonel.

"It means war. It's a warning from Wetzel—not the slightest doubt of that," said Jonathan. "Wetzel sends this because he knows we are to be attacked, and because there must have been great doubt of his getting back to tell us. And Tige has been shot on his way home."

This called the attention to the dog, which had been momentarily forgotten. His head rolled from Betty's knee; a quiver shook his frame; he struggled to rise to his feet, but his strength was too far spent; he crawled close to Betty's feet; his eyes looked up at her with almost human affection; then they closed, and he lay still. Tige was dead.

"It is all over, Betty. Tige will romp no more. He will never be forgotten, for he was faithful to the end. Jonathan, tell the Major of Wetzel's warning, and both of you go back to your posts on the river. Silas, send Capt. Boggs to me."

An hour after the death of Tige the settlers were waiting for the ring of the meeting-house bell to summon them to the Fort.

Supper at Col. Zane's that night was not the occasion of good-humored jest and pleasant conversation. Mrs. Zane's face wore a distressed and troubled look; Betty was pale and quiet; even the Colonel was gloomy; and the children, missing the usual cheerfulness of the evening meal, shrank close to their mother.

Darkness slowly settled down; and with it came a feeling of relief, at least for the night, for the Indians rarely attacked the settlements after dark. Capt. Boggs came over and he and Col. Zane conversed in low tones.

"The first thing in the morning I want you to ride over to Short Creek for reinforcements. I'll send the Major also and by a different route. I expect to hear tonight from Wetzel. Twelve times has he crossed that threshold with the information which made an Indian surprise impossible. And I feel sure he will come again."

"What was that?" said Betty, who was sitting on the doorstep.

"Sh-h!" whispered Col. Zane, holding up his finger.

The night was warm and still. In the perfect quiet which followed the Colonel's whispered exclamation the listeners heard the beating of their hearts. Then from the river bank came the cry of an owl; low but clear it came floating to their ears, its melancholy note thrilling them. Faint and far off in the direction of the island sounded the answer.

"I knew it. I told you. We shall know all presently," said Col. Zane. "The first call was Jonathan's, and it was answered."

The moments dragged away. The children had fallen

asleep on the bearskin rug. Mrs. Zane and Betty had heard the Colonel's voice, and sat with white faces, waiting, waiting for they knew not what.

A familiar, light-moccasined tread sounded on the path, a tall figure loomed up from the darkness; it came up the path, passed up the steps, and crossed the threshold.

"Wetzel!" exclaimed Col. Zane and Capt. Boggs. It was indeed the hunter. How startling was his appearance! The buckskin hunting coat and leggins were wet, torn and bespattered with mud; the water ran and dripped from him to form little muddy pools on the floor; only his rifle and powder horn were dry. His face was ghastly white except where a bullet wound appeared on his temple, from which the blood had oozed down over his cheek. An unearthly light gleamed from his eyes. In that moment Wetzel was an appalling sight.

"Col. Zane, I'd been here days before, but I run into some Shawnees, and they gave me a hard chase. I have to report that Girty, with four hundred Injuns and two hundred Britishers, are on the way to Ft. Henry."

"My God!" exclaimed Col. Zane. Strong man as he was the hunter's words had unnerved him.

The loud and clear tone of the church-bell rang out on the still night air. Only once it sounded, but it reverberated among the hills, and its single deep-toned ring was like a knell. The listeners almost expected to hear it followed by the fearful war-cry, that cry which betokened for many desolation and death.

Chapter 13

MORNING FOUND the settlers, with the exception of
Col. Zane, his brother Jonathan, the negro Sam, and
Martin Wetzel, all within the Fort. Col. Zane had
determined, long before, that in the event of another
siege, he would use his house as an outpost. Twice it
had been destroyed by fire at the hands of the Indians.
Therefore, surrounding himself by these men, who were
all expert marksmen, Col. Zane resolved to protect his
property and at the same time render valuable aid to
the Fort.

Early that morning a pirogue loaded with cannon
balls, from Ft. Pitt and bound for Louisville, had arrived and Captain Sullivan, with his crew of three men,
had demanded admittance. In the absence of Capt.
Boggs and Major McColloch, both of whom had been
dispatched for reinforcements, Col. Zane had placed his
brother Silas in command of the Fort. Sullivan informed Silas that he and his men had been fired on by
Indians and that they sought the protection of the Fort.
The services of himself and men, which he volunteered,
were gratefully accepted.

All told, the little force in the block-house did not
exceed forty-two, and that counting the boys and the
women who could handle rifles. The few preparations
had been completed and now the settlers were awaiting
the appearance of the enemy. Few words were spoken.
The children were secured where they would be out of

the way of flying bullets. They were huddled together silent and frightened; pale-faced but resolute women passed up and down the length of the block-house; some carried buckets of water and baskets of food; others were tearing bandages; grim-faced men peered from the portholes; all were listening for the war-cry.

They had not long to wait. Before noon the well-known whoop came from the wooded shore of the river, and it was soon followed by the appearance of hundreds of Indians. The river, which was low, at once became a scene of great animation. From a placid, smoothly flowing stream it was turned into a muddy, splashing, turbulent torrent. The mounted warriors urged their steeds down the bank and into the water; the unmounted improvised rafts and placed their weapons and ammunition upon them; then they swam and pushed, kicked and yelled their way across; other Indians swam, holding the bridles of the pack-horses. A detachment of British soldiers followed the Indians. In an hour the entire army appeared on the river bluff not three hundred yards from the Fort. They were in no hurry to begin the attack. Especially did the Indians seem to enjoy the lull before the storm, and as they stalked to and fro in plain sight of the garrison, or stood in groups watching the Fort, they were seen in all their hideous war-paint and formidable battle-array. They were exultant. Their plumes and eagle feathers waved proudly in the morning breeze. Now and then the long, peculiarly broken yell of the Shawnees rang out clear and strong. The soldiers were drawn off to one side and well out of range of the settlers' guns. Their red coats and flashing bayonets were new to most of the little band of men in the block-house.

"Ho, the Fort!"

It was a strong, authoritative voice and came from a man mounted on a black horse.

"Well, Girty, what is it?" shouted Silas Zane.

"We demand unconditional surrender," was the answer.

"You will never get it," replied Silas.

"Take more time to think it over. You see we have a force here large enough to take the Fort in an hour."

"That remains to be seen," shouted some one through a porthole.

. An hour passed. The soldiers and the Indians lounged around on the grass and walked to and fro on the bluff. At intervals a taunting Indian yell, horrible in its suggestiveness, came floating on the air. When the hour was up three mounted men rode out in advance of the waiting Indians. One was clad in buckskin, another in the uniform of a British officer, and the third was an Indian chief whose powerful form was naked except for his buckskin belt and leggins.

"Will you surrender?" came in the harsh and arrogant voice of the renegade.

"Never! Go back to your squaws!" yelled Sullivan.

"I am Capt. Pratt of the Queen's Rangers. If you surrender I will give you the best protection King George affords," shouted the officer.

"To hell with King George! Go back to your hair-buying Hamilton and tell him the whole British army could not make us surrender," roared Hugh Bennet.

"If you do not give up, the Fort will be attacked and burned. Your men will be massacred and your women given to the Indians," said Girty.

"You will never take a man, woman or child alive," yelled Silas. "We remember Crawford, you white traitor, and we are not going to give up to be butchered. Come on with your red-jackets and your red-devils. We are ready."

"We have captured and killed the messenger you sent out, and now all hope of succor must be abandoned. Your doom is sealed."

"What kind of a man was he?" shouted Sullivan.

"A fine, active young fellow," answered the outlaw.

"That's a lie," snapped Sullivan, "he was an old, gray-haired man."

As the officer and the outlaw chief turned, apparently to consult their companion, a small puff of white smoke shot forth from one of the portholes of the block-house. It was followed by the ringing report of a rifle. The Indian chief clutched wildly at his breast, fell forward on his horse, and after vainly trying to keep his seat, slipped to the ground. He raised himself once, then fell backward and lay still. Full two hundred yards was not proof against Wetzel's deadly small-bore, and Red Fox, the foremost war chieftain of the Shawnees, lay dead, a victim to the hunter's vengeance. It was characteristic of Wetzel that he picked the chief, for he could have shot either the British officer or the renegade. They retreated out of range, leaving the body of the chief where it had fallen, while the horse, giving a frightened snort, galloped toward the woods. Wetzel's yell coming quickly after his shot, excited the Indians to a very frenzy, and they started on a run for the Fort, discharging their rifles and screeching like so many demons.

In the cloud of smoke which at once enveloped the scene the Indians spread out and surrounded the Fort. A tremendous rush by a large party of Indians was made for the gate of the Fort. They attacked it fiercely with their tomahawks, and a log which they used as a battering-ram. But the stout gate withstood their united efforts, and the galling fire from the portholes soon forced them to fall back and seek cover behind the trees and the rocks. From these points of vantage they kept up an uninterrupted fire.

The soldiers had made a dash at the stockade-fence, yelling derision at the small French cannon which was mounted on top of the block-house. They thought it a "dummy" because they had learned that in the 1777 siege the garrison had no real cannon, but had tried to utilize a wooden one. They yelled and hooted and mocked at this piece and dared the garrison to fire it. Sullivan, who was in charge of the cannon, bided his time. When the soldiers were massed closely together and making another rush for the stockade-fence Sullivan turned loose the little "bulldog," spreading consternation and destruction in the British ranks.

"Stand back! Stand back!" Capt. Pratt was heard to yell. "By God! there's no wood about that gun."

After this the besiegers withdrew for a breathing spell. At this early stage of the seige the Indians were seen to board Sullivan's pirogue, and it was soon discovered they were carrying the cannon balls from the boat to the top of the bluff. In their simple minds they had conceived a happy thought. They procured a white-oak log probably a foot in diameter, split it through the middle and hollowed out the inside with their tomahawks. Then with iron chains and bars, which they took from Riehart's blacksmith shop, they bound and securely fastened the sides together. They dragged the improvised cannon nearer to the Fort, placed it on two logs and weighted it down with stones. A heavy charge of powder and ball was then rammed into the wooden gun. The soldiers, though much interested in the manoeuvre, moved back to a safe distance, while many of the Indians crowded round the new weapon. The torch was applied; there was a red flash—boom! The hillside was shaken by the tremendous explosion, and when the smoke lifted from the scene the naked forms of the Indians could be seen writhing in agony on the ground. Not a vestige of the wooden gun remained. The iron chains had proved terrible death-dealing missiles to the Indians near the gun. The Indians now took to their natural methods of warfare. They hid in the long grass, in the deserted cabins, behind the trees and up in the branches. Not an Indian was visible, but the rain of bullets pattered steadily against the block-house. Every bush and every tree spouted little puffs of white smoke, and the leaden messengers of Death whistled through the air.

After another unsuccessful effort to destroy a section of the stockade-fence the soldiers had retired. Their red jackets made them a conspicuous mark for the sharp-eyed settlers. Capt. Pratt had been shot through the thigh. He suffered great pain, and was deeply chagrined by the surprising and formidable defense of the garrison which he had been led to believe would fall an easy prey to the King's soldiers. He had lost one-third of his men. Those who were left refused to run straight in the face of certain death. They had not been drilled to fight an unseen enemy. Capt. Pratt was compelled to order a retreat to the river bluff, where he conferred with Girty.

Inside the block-house was great activity, but no confusion. That little band of fighters might have been drilled for a king's bodyguard. Kneeling before each porthole on the river side of the Fort was a man who would fight while there was breath left in him. He did not discharge his weapon aimlessly as the Indians did, but waited until he saw the outline of an Indian form, or a red coat, or a puff of white smoke; then he would thrust the rifle-barrel forward, take a quick aim and fire. By the side of every man stood a heroic woman whose face was blanched, but who spoke never a word as she put the muzzle of the hot rifle into a bucket of water, cooled the barrel, wiped it dry and passed it back to the man beside her.

Silas Zane had been wounded at the first fire. A glancing ball had struck him on the head, inflicting a painful scalp wound. It was now being dressed by Col. Zane's wife, whose skilled fingers were already tired with the washing and the bandaging of the injuries received by the defenders. In all that horrible din of battle; the shrill yells of the savages, the hoarse shouts of the settlers, the boom of the cannon overhead, the cracking of rifles and the whistling of bullets; in all that din of appalling noise, and amid the stifling smoke, the smell of burned powder, the sickening sight of the desperately wounded and the already dead, the Colonel's brave wife had never faltered. She was here and there; binding the wounds, helping Lydia and Betty mould bullets, encouraging the men, and by her example, enabling those women to whom border war was new to bear up under the awful strain.

Sullivan, who had been on top of the block-house, came down the ladder almost without touching it. Blood was running down his bare arm and dripping from the ends of his fingers.

"Zane, Martin has been shot," he said hoarsely. "The same Indian who shot away these fingers did it. The bullets seem to come from some elevation. Send some scout up there and find out where that damned Indian is hiding."

"Martin shot? God, his poor wife! Is he dead?" said Silas.

"Not yet. Bennet is bringing him down. Here, I want this hand tied up, so that my gun won't be so slippery."

Wetzel was seen stalking from one porthole to another.

His fearful yell sounded above all the others. He seemed to bear a charmed life, for not a bullet had so much as scratched him. Silas communicated to him what Sullivan had said. The hunter mounted the ladder and went up on the roof. Soon he reappeared, descended into the room and ran into the west end of the block-house. He kneeled before a porthole through which he pushed the long black barrel of his rifle. Silas and Sullivan followed him and looked in the direction indicated by his weapon. It pointed toward the bushy top of a tall poplar tree which stood on the hill west of the Fort. Presently a little cloud of white smoke issued from the leafy branches, and it was no sooner seen than Wetzel's rifle was discharged. There was a great commotion among the leaves, the branches swayed and thrashed, and then a dark body plunged downward to strike on the rocky slope of the bluff and roll swiftly out of sight. The hunter's unnatural yell pealed out.

"Great God! The man's crazy," cried Sullivan, staring at Wetzel's demon-like face.

"No, no. It's his way," answered Silas.

At that moment the huge frame of Bennet filled up the opening in the roof and started down the ladder. In one arm he carried the limp body down and beckoned to Mrs. Zane. Those watching saw that the young man was Will Martin, and that he was still alive. But it was evident that he had not long to live. His face had a leaden hue and his eyes were bright and glassy. Alice, his wife, flung herself on her knees beside him and tenderly raised the drooping head. No words could express the agony in her face as she raised it to Mrs. Zane. In it was a mute appeal, an unutterable prayer for hope. Mrs. Zane turned sorrowfully to her task. There was no need of her skill here. Alfred Clark, who had been ordered to take Martin's place on top of the block-house, paused a moment in silent sympathy. When he saw that little hole in the bared chest, from which the blood welled up in an awful stream, he shuddered and passed on. Betty looked up from her work and then turned away sick and faint. Her mute lips moved as if in prayer.

Alice was left alone with her dying husband. She tenderly supported his head on her bosom, leaned her face against his and kissed the cold, numb lips. She murmured into his already deaf ear the old tender names. He knew her, for he made a feeble effort to pass his arm round her neck. A smile illumined his face. Then death claimed him. With wild, distended eyes and with hands pressed tightly to her temples Alice rose slowly to her feet.

"Oh, God! Oh, God!" she cried.

Her prayer was answered. In a momentary lull in the battle was heard the deadly hiss of a bullet as it sped through one of the portholes. It ended with a slight sickening spat as the lead struck the flesh. Then Alice, without a cry, fell on the husband's breast. Silas Zane found her lying dead with the body of her husband clasped closely in her arms. He threw a blanket over them and went on his wearying round of the bastions.

* * * * * * *

The besiegers had been greatly harassed and hampered by the continual fire from Col. Zane's house. It was exceedingly difficult for the Indians, and impossible for the British, to approach near enough to the Colonel's house to get an effective shot. Col. Zane and his men had the advantage of being on higher ground. Also they had four rifles to a man, and they used every spare moment for reloading. Thus they were enabled to pour a deadly fire into the ranks of the enemy, and to give the impression of being much stronger in force than they really were.

About dusk the firing ceased and the Indians repaired to the river bluff. Shortly afterward their campfires were extinguished and all became dark and quiet. Two hours passed. Fortunately the clouds, which had at first obscured the moon, cleared away somewhat, and enough light was shed on the scene to enable the watchers to discern objects near by.

Col. Zane had just called together his men for a conference. He suspected some cunning deviltry on part of the Indians.

"Sam, take what stuff to eat you can lay your hands

on and go up to the loft. Keep a sharp lookout and report anything to Jonathan or me," said the Colonel.

All afternoon Jonathan Zane had loaded and fired his rifles in sullen and dogged determination. He had burst one rifle and disabled another. The other men were fine marksmen, but it was undoubtedly Jonathan's unerring aim that made the house so unapproachable. He used an extremely heavy, large bore rifle. In the hands of a man strong enough to stand its fierce recoil it was a veritable cannon. The Indians had soon learned to respect the range of that rifle, and they gave the cabin a wide berth.

But now that darkness had enveloped the valley the advantage lay with the savages. Col. Zane glanced apprehensively at the blackened face of his brother.

"Do you think the Fort can hold out?" he asked in a husky voice. He was a bold man, but he thought now of his wife and children.

"I don't know," answered Jonathan. "I saw that big Shawnee chief today. His name is Fire. He is well named. He is a fiend. Girty has a picked band."

"The Fort has held out surprisingly well against such combined and fierce attacks. The Indians are desperate. You can easily see that in the way in which they almost threw their lives away. The green square is covered with dead Indians."

"If help does not come in twenty-four hours not one man will escape alive. Even Wetzel could not break through that line of Indians. But if we can hold the Indians off a day longer they will get tired and discouraged. Girty will not be able to hold them much longer. The British don't count. It's not their kind of war. They can't shoot, and so far as I can see they haven't done much damage."

"To your posts, men, and every man think of the women and children in the block-house."

For a long time, which seemed hours to the waiting

and watching settlers, not a sound could be heard, nor any sign of the enemy seen. Thin clouds had again drifted over the moon, allowing only a pale, wan light to shine down on the valley. Time dragged on and the clouds grew thicker and denser until the moon and the stars were totally obscured. Still no sign or sound of the savages.

"What was that?" suddenly whispered Col. Zane.

"It was a low whistle from Sam. We'd better go up," said Jonathan.

They went up the stairs to the second floor from which they ascended to the loft by means of a ladder. The loft was as black as pitch. In that Egyptian darkness it was no use to look for anything, so they crawled on their hands and knees over the piles of hides and leather which lay on the floor. When they reached the small window they made out the form of the negro.

"What is it, Sam?" whispered Jonathan.

"Look, see thar, Massa Zane," came the answer in a hoarse whisper from the negro and at the same time he pointed down toward the ground.

Col. Zane put his head alongside Jonathan's and all three men peered out into the darkness.

"Jack, can you see anything?" said Col. Zane.

"No, but wait a minute until the moon throws a light."

A breeze had sprung up. The clouds were passing rapidly over the moon, and at long intervals a rift between the clouds let enough light through to brighten the square for an instant.

"Now, Massa Zane, that!" exclaimed the slave.

"I can't see a thing. Can you, Jack?"

"I am not sure yet. I can see something, but whether it is a log or not I don't know."

Just then there was a faint light like the brightening of a firefly, or like the blowing of a tiny spark from a stick of burning wood. Jonathan uttered a low curse.

"D——n 'em! At their old tricks with fire. I thought all this quiet meant something. The grass out there is full of Indians, and they are carrying lighted arrows under them so as to cover the light. But we'll fool the red devils this time."

"I can see 'em, Massa Zane."

"Sh-h-h! no more talk," whispered Col. Zane.

The men waited with cocked rifles. Another spark rose seemingly out of the earth. This time it was nearer the house. No sooner had its feeble light disappeared than the report of the negro's rifle awoke the sleeping echoes. It was succeeded by a yell which seemed to come from under the window. Several dark forms rose so suddenly that they appeared to spring out of the ground. Then came the peculiar twang of Indian bows. There were showers of sparks and little streaks of fire with long tails like comets winged their parabolic flight toward the cabin. Falling short they hissed and sputtered in the grass. Jonathan's rifle spoke and one of the fleeing forms tumbled to the earth. A series of long yells from all around the Fort greeted this last shot, but not an Indian fired a rifle.

Fire-tipped arrows were now shot at the block-house, but not one took effect, although a few struck the stockade-fence. Col. Zane had taken the precaution to have the high grass and the clusters of goldenrod cut down all round the Fort. The wisdom of this course now became evident, for the wily savages could not crawl near enough to send their fiery arrows on the roof of the block-house. This attempt failing, the Indians drew back to hatch up some other plot to burn the Fort.

"Look!" suddenly exclaimed Jonathan.

Far down the road, perhaps five hundred yards from the Fort, a point of light had appeared. At first it was still, and then it took an odd jerky motion, to this side and to that, up and down like a jack-o-lantern.

"What the hell?" muttered Col. Zane, sorely puzzled. "Jack, by all that's strange it's getting bigger."

Sure enough the spark of fire, or whatever it was, grew larger and larger. Col. Zane thought it might be a light carried by a man on horseback. But if this were true where was the clatter of the horse's hoofs? On that rocky bluff no horse could run noiselessly. It could not be a horse. Fascinated and troubled by this new mystery which seemed to presage evil to them the watchers waited with that patience known only to those accustomed to danger. They knew that whatever it was, it was some satanic stratagem of the savages, and that it would come all too soon.

The light was now zigzagging back and forth across the road, and approaching the Fort with marvelous rapidity. Now its motion was like the wide swinging of a lighted lantern on a dark night. A moment more of breathless suspense and the lithe form of an Indian brave could be seen behind the light. He was running with almost incredible swiftness down the road in the direction of the Fort. Passing at full speed within seventy-five yards of the stockade-fence the Indian shot his arrow. Like a fiery serpent flying through the air the missile sped onward in its graceful flight, going clear over the block-house, and striking with a spiteful thud the roof of one of the cabins beyond. Unhurt by the volley that was fired at him, the daring brave passed swiftly out of sight.

Deeds like this were dear to the hearts of the savages. They were deeds which made a warrior of a brave, and for which honor any Indian would risk his life over and over again. The exultant yells which greeted this performance proclaimed its success.

The breeze had already fanned the smouldering arrow into a blaze and the dry roof of the cabin had caught fire and was burning fiercely.

"That infernal redskin is going to do that again," ejaculated Jonathan.

It was indeed true. That same small bright light could be seen coming down the road gathering headway with every second. No doubt the same Indian, emboldened by his success, and maddened with that thirst for glory so often fatal to his kind, was again making the effort to fire the block-house.

The eyes of Col. Zane and his companions were fastened on the light as it came nearer and nearer with its changing motion. The burning cabin brightened the square before the Fort. The slender, shadowy figure of the Indian could be plainly seen emerging from the gloom. So swiftly did he run that he seemed to have wings. Now he was in the full glare of the light. What a magnificent nerve, what a terrible assurance there was in his action! It seemed to paralyze all. The red arrow emitted a shower of sparks as it was discharged. This time it winged its way straight and true and imbedded itself in the roof of the block-house.

Almost at the same instant a solitary rifle shot rang out and the daring warrior plunged headlong, sliding face downward in the dust of the road, while from the Fort came that demoniac yell now grown so familiar.

"Wetzel's compliments," muttered Jonathan. "But the mischief is done. Look at that damned burning arrow. If it doesn't blow out the Fort will go."

The arrow was visible, but it seemed a mere spark. It alternately paled and glowed. One moment it almost went out, and the next it gleamed brightly. To the men, compelled to look on and powerless to prevent the burning of the now apparently doomed block-house, that spark was like the eye of Hell.

"Ho, the Fort," yelled Col. Zane with all the power of his strong lungs. "Ho, Silas, the roof is on fire!"

Pandemonium had now broken out among the Indians. They could be plainly seen in the red glare thrown by the burning cabin. It had been a very dry season, the rough shingles were like tinder, and the inflammable material burst quickly into great flames, lighting up the valley as far as the edge of the forest. It was an awe-inspiring and a horrible spectacle. Columns of yellow and black smoke rolled heavenward; every object seemed dyed a deep crimson; the trees assumed fantastic shapes; the river veiled itself under a red glow. Above the roaring and crackling of the flames rose the inhuman yelling of the savages. Like demons of the inferno they ran to and fro, their naked painted bodies shining in the glare. One group of savages formed a circle and danced hands-around a stump as gayly as a band of school-girls at a May party. They wrestled with and hugged one another; they hopped, skipped and jumped, and in every possible way manifested their fiendish joy.

The British took no part in this revelry. To their credit it must be said they kept in the background as though ashamed of this horrible fire-war on people of their own blood.

"Why don't they fire the cannon?" impatiently said Col. Zane. "Why don't they do something?"

"Perhaps it is disabled, or maybe they are short of ammunition," suggested Jonathan.

"The block-house will burn down before our eyes. Look! The hell-hounds have set fire to the fence. I see men running and throwing water."

"I see something on the roof of the block-house," cried Jonathan. "There, down towards the east end of the roof, and in the shadow of the chimney. And as I'm a living sinner it's a man crawling towards that blazing arrow. The Indians have not discovered him yet. He is still in the shadow. But they'll see him. God! What a nervy thing to do in the face of all those redskins. It is almost certain death."

"Yes, and they see him," said the Colonel.

With shrill yells the Indians bounded forward and aimed and fired their rifles at the crouching figure of the man. Some hid behind the logs they had rolled toward the Fort; others boldly faced the steady fire now pouring from the portholes. The savages saw in the movement of that man an attempt to defeat their long-cherished hope of burning the Fort. Seeing he was discovered, the man did not hesitate, nor did he lose a second. Swiftly he jumped and ran toward the end of the roof where the burning arrow, now surrounded by blazing shingles, was sticking in the roof. How he ever ran along that slanting roof and with a pail in his hand was incomprehensible. In moments like that men become superhuman. It all happened in an instant. He reached the arrow, kicked it over the wall, and then dashed the bucket of water on the blazing shingles. In that single instant, wherein his tall form was outlined against the bright light behind him, he presented the fairest kind of a mark for the Indians. Scores of rifles were levelled and discharged at him. The bullets pattered like hail on the roof of the block-house, but apparently none found their mark, for the man ran back and disappeared.

"It was Clarke!" exclaimed Col. Zane. "No one but Clarke has such light hair. Wasn't that a plucky thing?"

"It has saved the block-house for to-night," answered Jonathan. "See, the Indians are falling back. They can't stand in the face of that shooting. Hurrah! Look at them fall! It could not have happened better. The light from the cabin will prevent any more close attacks for an hour and daylight is near."

Chapter 14

THE SUN rose red. Its ruddy rays peeped over the eastern hills, kissed the tree-tops, glinted along the stony bluffs, and chased away the gloom of night from the valley. Its warm gleams penetrated the portholes of the Fort and cast long bright shadows on the walls; but it brought little cheer to the sleepless and almost exhausted defenders. It brought to many of the settlers the familiar old sailor's maxim: "Redness 'a the morning, sailor's warning." Rising in its crimson glory the sun flooded the valley, dyeing the river, the leaves, the grass, the stones, tingeing everything with that awful color which stained the stairs, the benches, the floor, even the portholes of the block-house.

Historians call this the time that tried men's souls. If it tried the men, think what it must have been to those grand, heroic women. Though they had helped the men load and fire nearly forty-eight hours; though they had worked without a moment's rest and were now ready to succumb to exhaustion; though the long room was full of stifling smoke and the sickening odor of burned wood and powder, and though the row of silent, covered bodies had steadily lengthened, the thought of giving up never occurred to the women. Death there would be sweet compared to what it would be at the hands of the redmen.

At sunrise Silas Zane, bare-chested, his face dark and fierce, strode into the bastion which was connected

278

with the block-house. It was a small shedlike room, and with portholes opening to the river and the forest. This bastion had seen the severest fighting. Five men had been killed here. As Silas entered four haggard and powder-begrimed men, who were kneeling before the portholes, looked up at him. A dead man lay in one corner.

"Smith's dead. That makes fifteen," said Silas. "Fifteen out of forty-two, that leaves twenty-seven. We must hold out. Men, don't expose yourselves recklessly. How goes it at the south bastion?"

"All right. There's been firin' over there all night," answered one of the men. "I guess it's been kinder warm over that way. But I ain't heard any shootin' for some time."

"Young Bennet is over there, and if the men needed anything they would send him for it," answered Silas. "I'll send some food and water. Anything else?"

"Powder. We're nigh out of powder," replied the man addressed. "And we might jes as well make ready fer a high old time. The red devils hain't been quiet all this last hour fer nothin'."

Silas passed along the narrow hallway which led from the bastion into the main room of the block-house. As he turned the corner at the head of the stairway he encountered a boy who was dragging himself up the steps.

"Hello! Who's this? Why, Harry!" exclaimed Silas, grasping the boy and drawing him into the room. Once in the light Silas saw that the lad was so weak he could hardly stand. He was covered with blood. It dripped from a bandage wound tightly about his arm; it oozed through a hole in his hunting shirt, and it flowed from a wound over his temple. The shadow of death was already stealing over the pallid face, but from the grey eyes shone an indomitable spirit, a spirit which nothing but death could quench.

"Quick!" the lad panted. "Send men to the south wall. The redskins are breakin' in where the water from the spring runs under the fence."

"Where are Metzar and the other men?"

"Dead! Killed last night. I've been there alone all night. I kept on shootin'. Then I gets plugged here under the chin. Knowin' it's all up with me I deserted my post when I heard the Injuns choppin' on the fence where it was on fire last night. But I only—run—because—they're gettin' in."

"Wetzel, Bennet, Clarke!" yelled Silas, as he laid the boy on the bench.

Almost as Silas spoke the tall form of the hunter confronted him. Clarke and the other men were almost as prompt.

"Wetzel, run to the south wall. The Indians are cutting a hole through the fence."

Wetzel turned, grabbed his rifle and an axe and was gone like a flash.

"Sullivan, you handle the men here. Bessie, do what you can for this brave lad. Come, Bennet, Clark, we must follow Wetzel," commanded Silas.

Mrs. Zane hastened to the side of the fainting lad. She washed away the blood from the wound over his temple. She saw that a bullet had glanced on the bone and that the wound was not deep or dangerous. She unlaced the hunting shirt at the neck and pulled the flaps apart. There on the right breast, on a line with the apex of the lung, was a horrible gaping wound. A murderous British slug had passed through the lad. From the hole at every heart-beat poured the dark, crimson life-tide. Mrs. Zane turned her white face away for a second; then she folded a small piece of linen, pressed it tightly over the wound, and wrapped a towel round the lad's breast.

"Don't waste time on me. It's all over," he whispered. "Will you call Betty here a minute?"

Betty came, white-faced and horror-stricken. For forty hours she had been living in a maze of terror. Her movements had almost become mechanical. She had almost ceased to hear and feel. But the light in the eyes of this dying boy brought her back to the horrible reality of the present.

"Oh, Harry! Harry! Harry!" was all Betty could whisper.

"I'm goin', Betty. And I wanted—you to say a little prayer for me—and say good-bye to me," he panted.

Betty knelt by the bench and tried to pray.

"I hated to run, Betty, but I waited and waited and nobody came, and the Injuns was gettin' in. They'll find dead Injuns in piles out there. I was shootin' fer you, Betty, and every time I aimed I thought of you."

The lad rambled on, his voice growing weaker and weaker and finally ceasing. The hand which had clasped Betty's so closely loosened its hold. His eyes closed. Betty thought he was dead, but no! he still breathed. Suddenly his eyes opened. The shadow of pain was gone. In its place shone a beautiful radiance.

"Betty, I've cared a lot for you—and I'm dyin'—happy because I've fought fer you—and somethin' tells me—you'll—be saved. Good-bye." A smile transformed his face and his gray eyes gazed steadily into hers. Then his head fell back. With a sigh his brave spirit fled.

Hugh Bennet looked once at the pale face of his son, then he ran down the stairs after Silas and Clarke. When the three men emerged from behind Capt. Boggs' cabin, which was adjacent to the block-house, and which hid the south wall from their view, they were two hundred feet from Wetzel. They heard the heavy thump of a log being rammed against the fence; then a splitting and splintering of one of the six-inch oak planks. Another and another smashing blow and the lower half of one of the planks fell inwards, leaving an aperture large enough to admit an Indian. The men dashed forward to the assistance of Wetzel, who stood by the hole with upraised axe. At the same moment a shot rang out. Bennet stumbled and fell head-long. An Indian had shot through the hole in the fence. Silas and Alfred sheered off toward the fence, out of line. When within twenty yards of Wetzel they saw a swarthy-faced and athletic savage squeeze through the narrow crevice. He had not straightened up before the axe, wielded by the giant hunter, descended on his head, cracking his skull as if it were an eggshell. The savage sank to the earth without even a moan. Another savage, naked and powerful, slipped in. He had to stoop to get through. He raised himself, and seeing Wetzel, he tried to dodge the lightning sweep of the axe. It missed his head, at which it had been aimed, but struck just over the shoulders, and buried itself in flesh and bone. The Indian uttered an agonizing yell which ended in a choking, gurgling sound as the blood spurted from his throat. Wetzel pulled the weapon from the body of his victim, and with the same motion he swung it around. This time the blunt end met the next Indian's head with a thud like that made by the butcher when he strikes the bullock to the ground. The Indian's rifle dropped, his tomahawk flew into the air, while his body rolled down the little embankment into the spring. Another and another Indian met the same fate. Then two Indians endeavored to get through the aperture. The awful axe swung by those steel arms, dispatched both of them in the twinkling of an eye. Their bodies stuck in the hole.

Silas and Alfred stood riveted to the spot. Just then Wetzel in all his horrible glory was a sight to freeze the marrow of any man. He had cast aside his hunting shirt in that run to the fence and was now stripped to the waist. He was covered with blood. The muscles of his broad back and his brawny arms swelled and rippled under the brown skin. At every swing of the gory ax he let out a yell the like of which had never before been heard by the white men. It was the hunter's mad yell of revenge. In his thirst for vengeance he had forgotten that he was defending the Fort with its women and its children; he was fighting because he loved to kill.

Silas Zane heard the increasing clamor outside and knew that hundreds of Indians were being drawn to the spot. Something must be done at once. He looked around and his eyes fell on a pile of white-oak logs that had been hauled inside the Fort. They had been placed there by Col. Zane, with wise forethought. Silas grabbed Clarke and pulled him toward the pile of logs, at the same time communicating his plan. Together they carried a log to the fence and dropped it in front of the hole. Wetzel immediately stepped on it and took a vicious swing at an Indian who was trying to poke his rifle sideways through the hole. This Indian had discharged his weapon twice. While Wetzel held the Indians at bay, Silas and Clarke piled the logs one upon another, until the hole was closed. This effectually fortified and barricaded the weak place in the stockade fence. The settlers in the bastions were now pouring such a hot fire into the ranks of the savages that they were compelled to retreat out of range.

While Wetzel washed the blood from his arms and his shoulders Silas and Alfred hurried back to where Bennet had fallen. They expected to find him dead, and were overjoyed to see the big settler calmly sitting by the brook binding up a wound in his shoulder.

"It's nothin' much. Jest a scratch, but it tumbled me over," he said. "I was comin' to help you. That was the wust Injun scrap I ever saw. Why didn't you keep on lettin' 'em come in? The red varmints would 'a kept on comin' and Wetzel was good fer the whole tribe. All you'd had to do was to drag the dead Injuns aside and give him elbow room."

Wetzel joined them at this moment, and they hurried back to the block-house. The firing had ceased on the bluff. They met Sullivan at the steps of the Fort. He was evidently coming in search of them.

"Zane, the Indians and the Britishers are getting ready for a more determined and persistent effort than any that has yet been made," said Sullivan.

"How so?" asked Silas.

"They have got hammers from the blacksmith's shop, and they boarded my boat and found a keg of nails. Now they are making a number of ladders. If they make a rush all at once and place ladders against the fence we'll have the Fort full of Indians in ten minutes. They can't stand in the face of a cannon charge. We *must* use the cannon."

"Clarke, go into Capt. Boggs' cabin and fetch out two kegs of powder," said Silas.

The young man turned in the direction of the cabin, while Silas and the others ascended the stairs.

"The firing seems to be all on the south side," said Silas, "and is not so heavy as it was."

"Yes, as I said, the Indians on the river front are busy with their new plans," answered Sullivan.

"Why does not Clarke return?" said Silas, after waiting a few moments at the door of the long room. "We have no time to lose. I want to divide one keg of that powder among the men."

Clark appeared at the moment. He was breathing heavily as though he had run up the stairs, or was laboring under a powerful emotion. His face was gray.

"I could not find any powder!" he exclaimed. "I searched every nook and corner in Capt. Boggs' house. There is no powder there."

A brief silence ensued. Everyone in the block-house heard the young man's voice. No one moved. They all seemed waiting for someone to speak. Finally Silas Zane burst out:

"Not find it? You surely could not have looked well. Capt. Boggs himself told me there were three kegs of powder in the storeroom. I will go and find it myself."

Alfred did not answer, but sat down on a bench, with an odd numb feeling round his heart. He knew what was coming. He had been in the Captain's house and had seen those kegs of powder. He knew exactly where they had been. Now they were not on the accustomed shelf, nor at any other place in the storeroom. While he sat there waiting for the awful truth to dawn on the garrison, his eyes roved from one end of the room to the other. At last they found what they were seeking. A young woman knelt before a charcoal fire which she was blowing with a bellows. It was Betty. Her face was pale and weary, her hair dishevelled, her shapely arms blackened with charcoal, but notwithstanding she looked calm, resolute, self-contained. Lydia was kneeling by her side holding a bullet-mould on a block of wood. Betty lifted the ladle from the red coals and poured the hot metal with a steady hand and an admirable precision. Too much or too little lead would make an imperfect ball. The little missile had to be just so for those soft-metal, smooth-bore rifles. Then Lydia dipped the mould in a bucket of water, removed it and knocked it on the floor. A small, shiny lead bullet rolled out. She rubbed it with a greasy rag and then dropped it in a jar. For nearly forty hours, without sleep or rest, almost without food, those brave girls had been at their post.

Silas Zane came running into the room. His face was ghastly, even his lips were white and drawn.

"Sullivan, in God's name, what can we do? The powder is gone!" he cried in a strident voice.

"Gone?" repeated several voices.

"Gone?" echoed Sullivan. "Where?"

"God knows. I found where the kegs stood a few

days ago. There were marks in the dust. They have been moved."

"Perhaps Boggs put them here somewhere," said Sullivan. "We will look."

"No use. No use. We were always careful to keep the powder out of here on account of fire. The kegs are gone, gone."

"Miller stole them," said Wetzel in his calm voice.

"What difference does that make now?" burst out Silas, turning passionately on the hunter, whose quiet voice in that moment seemed so unfeeling. "They're gone!"

In the silence which ensued after these words the men looked at each other with slowly whitening faces. There was no need of words. Their eyes told one another what was coming. The fate which had overtaken so many border forts was to be theirs. They were lost! And every man thought not of himself, cared not for himself, but for those innocent children, those brave young girls and heroic women.

A man can die. He is glorious when he calmly accepts death; but when he fights like a tiger, when he stands at bay his back to the wall, a broken weapon in his hand, bloody, defiant, game to the end, then he is sublime. Then he wrings respect from the souls of even his bitterest foes. Then he is avenged even in his death.

But what can women do in times of war? They help, they cheer, they inspire, and if their cause is lost they must accept death or worse. Few women have the courage for self-destruction. "To the victor belong the spoils," and women have ever been the spoils of war.

No wonder Silas Zane and his men weakened in that moment. With only a few charges for their rifles and none for the cannon how could they hope to hold out against the savages? Alone they could have drawn their tomahawks and have made a dash through the lines of

Indians, but with the women and the children that was impossible.

"Wetzel, what can we do? For God's sake, advise us!" said Silas hoarsely. "We cannot hold the Fort without powder. We cannot leave the women here. We had better tomahawk every woman in the block-house than let her fall into the hands of Girty."

"Send some one fer powder," answered Wetzel.

"Do you think it possible," said Silas quickly, a ray of hope lighting up his haggard features. "There's plenty of powder in Eb's cabin. Whom shall we send? Who will volunteer?"

Three men stepped forward, and others made a movement.

"They'd plug a man full of lead afore he'd get ten foot from the gate," said Wetzel. "I'd go myself, but it wouldn't do no good. Send a boy, and one as can run like a streak."

"There are no lads big enough to carry a keg of powder. Harry Bennet might go," said Silas. "How is he, Bessie?"

"He is dead," answered Mrs. Zane.

Wetzel made a motion with his hands and turned away. A short, intense silence followed this indication of hopelessness from him. The women understood, for some of them covered their faces, while others sobbed.

"I will go."

It was Betty's voice, and it rang clear and vibrant throughout the room. The miserable women raised their drooping heads, thrilled by that fresh young voice. The men looked stupefied. Clarke seemed turned to stone. Wetzel came quickly toward her.

"Impossible!" said Sullivan.

Silas Zane shook his head as if the idea were absurd.

"Let me go, brother, let me go?" pleaded Betty as she placed her little hands softly, caressingly on her brother's bare arm. "I know it is only a forlorn chance, but still it is a chance. Let me take it. I would rather die that way than remain here and wait for death."

"Silas, it ain't a bad plan," broke in Wetzel. "Betty can run like a deer. And bein' a woman they may let her get to the cabin without shootin'."

Silas stood with arms folded across his broad chest. As he gazed at his sister great tears coursed down his dark cheeks and splashed on the hands which so tenderly clasped his own. Betty stood before him transformed; all signs of weariness had vanished; her eyes shone with a fateful resolve; her white and eager face was surpassingly beautiful with its light of hope, of prayer, of heroism.

"Let me go, brother. You know I can run, and oh! I will fly today. Every moment is precious. Who knows? Perhaps Capt. Boggs is already near at hand with help. You cannot *spare* a man. Let me go."

"Betty, Heaven bless and save you, you shall go," said Silas.

"No! No! Do not let her go!" cried Clarke, throwing himself before them. He was trembling, his eyes were wild, and he had the appearance of a man suddenly gone mad.

"She shall not go," he cried.

"What authority have you here?" demanded Silas Zane, sternly. "What right have you to speak?"

"None, unless it is that I love her and I will go for her," answered Alfred desperately.

"Stand back!" cried Wetzel, placing his powerful hand on Clarke's breast and pushing him backward. "If you love her you don't want to have her wait here for them red devils," and he waved his hand toward the river. "If she gets back she'll save the Fort. If she fails she'll at least escape Girty."

Betty gazed into the hunter's eyes and then into Alfred's. She understood both men. One was sending her out to her death because he knew it would be a thousand times more merciful than the fate which awaited her at the hands of the Indians. The other had not the strength to watch her go to her death. He had offered himself rather than see her take such fearful chances.

"I know. If it were possible you would both save me," said Betty, simply. "Now you can do nothing but pray that God may spare my life long enough to reach the gate. Silas, I am ready."

Downstairs a little group of white-faced men were standing before the gateway. Silas Zane had withdrawn the iron bar. Sullivan stood ready to swing in the ponderous gate. Wetzel was speaking with a clearness and a rapidity which were wonderful under the circumstances.

"When we let you out you'll have a clear path. Run, but not very fast. Save your speed. Tell the Colonel to empty a keg of powder in a table cloth. Throw it over your shoulder and start back. Run like you was racin' with me, and keep on comin' if you do get hit. Now go!"

The huge gate creaked and swung in. Betty ran out, looking straight before her. She had covered half the distance between the Fort and the Colonel's house when long taunting yells filled the air.

"Squaw! Waugh! Squaw! Waugh!" yelled the Indians in contempt.

Not a shot did they fire. The yells ran all along the river front, showing that hundreds of Indians had seen the slight figure running up the gentle slope toward the cabin.

Betty obeyed Wetzel's instructions to the letter. She ran easily and not at all hurriedly, and was as cool as if there had not been an Indian within miles.

Col. Zane had seen the gate open and Betty come forth. When she bounded up the steps he flung open the door and she ran into his arms.

"Betts, for God's sake! What's this?" he cried.

"We are out of powder. Empty a keg of powder into a table cloth. Quick! I've not a second to lose," she answered, at the same time slipping off her outer skirt. She wanted nothing to hinder that run for the block-house.

Jonathan Zane heard Betty's first words and disappeared into the magazine-room. He came out with a keg in his arms. With one blow of an axe he smashed in the top of the keg. In a twinkling a long black stream of the precious stuff was piling up in a little hill in the center of the table. Then the corners of the table cloth were caught up, turned and twisted, and the bag of powder was thrown over Betty's shoulder.

"Brave girl, so help me God, you are going to do it!" cried Col. Zane, throwing open the door. "I know you can. Run as you never ran in all your life."

Like an arrow sprung from a bow Betty flashed past the Colonel and out on the green. Scarcely ten of the long hundred yards had been covered by her flying feet when a roar of angry shouts and yells warned Betty that the keen-eyed savages saw the bag of powder and now knew they had been deceived by a girl. The crackling of rifles began at a point on the bluff nearest Col. Zane's house, and extended in a half circle to the eastern end of the clearing. The leaden messengers of Death whistled past Betty. They sped before her and behind her, scattering pebbles in her path, striking up the dust, and ploughing little furrows in the ground. A quarter of the distance covered! Betty had passed the top of the knoll now and she was going down the gentle slope like the wind. None but a fine marksman could have hit that small, flitting figure. The yelling and screeching had become deafening. The reports of the rifles blended in a roar. Yet above it all Betty heard Wetzel's stentorian yell. It lent wings to her feet. Half the distance covered! A hot, stinging pain shot through

Betty's arm, but she heeded it not. The bullets were raining about her. They sang over her head; hissed close to her ears, and cut the grass in front of her; they pattered like hail on the stockade-fence, but still untouched, unharmed, the slender brown figure sped toward the gate. Three-fourths of the distance covered! A tug at the flying hair, and a long, black tress cut off by a bullet, floated away on the breeze. Betty saw the big gate swing; she saw the tall figure of the hunter; she saw her brother. Only a few more yards! On! On! On! A blinding red mist obscured her sight. She lost the opening in the fence, but unheeding she rushed on. Another second and she stumbled; she felt herself grasped by eager arms; she heard the gate slam and the iron bar shoot into place; then she felt and heard no more.

Silas Zane bounded up the stairs with a doubly precious burden in his arms. A mighty cheer greeted his entrance. It aroused Alfred Clarke, who had bowed his head on the bench and had lost all sense of time and place. What were the women sobbing and crying over? To whom belonged that white face? Of course, it was the face of the girl he loved. The face of the girl who had gone to her death. And he writhed in his agony.

Then something wonderful happened. A warm, living flush swept over that pale face. The eyelids fluttered; they opened, and the dark eyes, radiant, beautiful, gazed straight into Alfred's.

Still Alfred could not believe his eyes. That pale face and the wonderful eyes belonged to the ghost of his sweetheart. They had come back to haunt him. Then he heard a voice.

"O-h! but that brown place burns!"

Alfred saw a bare and shapely arm. Its beauty was marred by a cruel red welt. He heard that same sweet voice laugh and cry together. Then he came back to life and hope. With one bound he sprang to a porthole.

"God, what a woman!" he said between his teeth, as he thrust the rifle forward.

It was indeed not a time for inaction. The Indians, realizing they had been tricked and had lost a golden opportunity, rushed at the Fort with renewed energy. They attacked from all sides and with the persistent fury of savages long disappointed in their hopes. They were received with a scathing, deadly fire. Bang! roared the cannon, and the detachment of savages dropped their ladders and fled. The little "bull dog" was turned on its swivel and directed at another rush of Indians. Bang! and the bullets, chainlinks, and bits of iron ploughed through the ranks of the enemy. The Indians never lived who could stand in the face of well-aimed cannon-shot. They fell back. The settlers, inspired, carried beyond themselves by the heroism of a girl, fought as they had never fought before. Every shot went to a redskin's heart. Impelled by the powder for which a brave girl had offered her life, guided by hands and arms of iron, and aimed by eyes as fixed and stern as Fate, every bullet shed the life-blood of a warrior.

Slowly and sullenly the red men gave way before that fire. Foot by foot they retired. Girty was seen no more. Fire, the Shawnee chief, lay dead in the road almost in the same spot where two days before his brother chief, Red Fox, had bit the dust. The British had long since retreated.

When night came the exhausted and almost famished besiegers sought rest and food.

The moon came out; clear and beautiful, as if ashamed of her traitor's part of the night before, and brightened up the valley, bathing the Fort, the river, and the forest in her silver light.

Shortly after daybreak the next morning the Indians, despairing of success, held a pow-wow. While they were grouped in plain view of the garrison, and probably conferring over the question of raising the siege, the

long, peculiar whoop of an Indian spy, who had been
sent out to watch for the approach of a relief party,
rang out. This seemed a signal for retreat. Scarcely had
the shrill cry ceased to echo in the hills when the
Indians and the British, abandoning their dead, moved
rapidly across the river.

After a short interval a mounted force was seen
galloping up the creek road. It proved to be Capt.
Boggs, Swearengen, and Williamson with seventy men.
Great was the rejoicing. Capt. Boggs had expected to
find only the ashes of the Fort. And the gallant little
garrison, although saddened by the loss of half its
original number, rejoiced that it had repulsed the united
forces of braves and British.

Chapter 15

PEACE AND quiet reigned once more at Ft. Henry.
Before the glorious autumn days had waned the settlers
had repaired the damage done to their cabins, and
many of them were now occupied with the fall plowing.
Never had the Fort experienced such busy days. Many
new faces were seen in the little meetinghouse. Pioneers
from Virginia, from Ft. Pitt, and eastward had learned
that Fort Henry had repulsed the biggest force of indians and soldiers that Governor Hamilton and his min-
ions could muster. Settlers from all points along the
river were flocking to Col. Zane's settlement. New cabins dotted the hillside; cabins and barns in all stages of
construction could be seen. The sounds of hammers,
the ringing stroke of the axe, and the crashing down of
mighty pines or poplars were heard all day long.

Col. Zane sat oftener and longer than ever before in
his favorite seat on his doorstep. On this evening he had
just returned from a hard day in the fields, and sat
down to rest a moment before going to supper. A few
days previous Isaac Zane and Myeerah had come to the
settlement. Myeerah brought a treaty of peace signed
by Tarhe and the other Wyandot chieftains. The once
implacable Huron was now ready to be friendly with
the white people. Col. Zane and his brothers signed the
treaty, and Betty, by dint of much persuasion, prevailed
on Wetzel to bury the hatchet with the Hurons. So

Myeerah's love, like the love of many other women, accomplished more than years of war and bloodshed.

The genial and happy smile never left Col. Zane's face, and as he saw the well-laden rafts coming down the river, and the air of liveliness and animation about the growing settlement, his smile broadened into one of pride and satisfaction. The prophecy that he had made twelve years before was fulfilled. His dream was realized. The wild, beautiful spot where he had once built a bark shack and camped half a year without seeing a white man was now the scene of a bustling settlement; and he believed he would live to see that settlement grow into a prosperous city. He did not think of the thousands of acres which would one day make him a wealthy man. He was a pioneer at heart; he had opened up that rich new country; he had conquered all obstacles, and that was enough to make him content.

"Papa, when shall I be big enough to fight bars and bufflers and Injuns?" asked Noah, stopping in his play and straddling his father's knee.

"My boy, did you not have Indians enough a short time ago?"

"But, papa, I did not get to see any. I heard the shooting and yelling. Sammy was afraid, but I wasn't. I wanted to look out of the little holes, but they locked us up in the dark room."

"If that boy ever grows up to be like Jonathan or Wetzel it will be the death of me," said the Colonel's wife, who had heard the lad's chatter.

"Don't worry, Bessie. When Noah grows to be a man the Indians will be gone."

Col. Zane heard the galloping of a horse and looking up saw Clarke coming down the road on his black thoroughbred. The Colonel rose and walked out to the hitching-block, where Clarke had reined in his fiery steed.

"Ah, Alfred. Been out for a ride?"

"Yes, I have been giving Roger a little exercise."

"That's a magnificent animal. I never get tired watching him move. He's the best bit of horseflesh on the river. By the way, we have not seen much of you since the siege. Of course you have been busy. Getting ready to put on the harness, eh? Well, that's what we want the young men to do. Come over and see us."

"I have been trying to come. You know how it is with me—about Betty, I mean. Col. Zane, I—I love her. That's all."

"Yes, I know, Alfred, and I don't wonder at your fears. But I have always liked you, and now I guess it's about time for me to put a spoke in your wheel of fortune. If Betty cares for you—and I have a sneaking idea she does—I will give her to you."

"I have nothing. I gave up everything when I left home."

"My lad, never mind about that," said the Colonel, laying his hand on Clarke's knee. "We don't need riches. I have so often said that we need nothing out here on the border but honest hearts and strong, willing hands. These you have. That is enough for me and for my people, and as for land, why, I have enough for an army of young men. I got my land cheap. That whole island there I bought from Cornplanter. You can have that island or any tract of land along the river. Some day I shall put you at the head of my men. It will take you years to cut that road through to Maysville. Oh, I have plenty of work for you."

"Col. Zane, I cannot thank you," answered Alfred, with emotion. "I shall try to merit your friendship and esteem. Will you please tell your sister I shall come over in the morning and beg to see her alone."

"That I will, Alfred. Goodnight."

Col. Zane strode across his threshold with a happy smile on his face. He loved to joke and tease, and never lost an opportunity.

"Things seem to be working out all right. Now for some fun with Her Highness," he said to himself.

As the Colonel surveyed the pleasant home scene he felt he had nothing more to wish for. The youngsters were playing with a shaggy little pup which had already taken Tige's place in their fickle affections. His wife was crooning a lullaby as she gently rocked the cradle to and fro. A wonderful mite of humanity peacefully slumbered in that old cradle. Annie was beginning to set the table for the evening meal. Isaac lay with a contented smile on his face, fast asleep on the couch, where, only a short time before, he had been laid bleeding and almost dead. Betty was reading to Myeerah, whose eyes were rapturously bright as she leaned her head against her sister and listened to the low voice.

"Well, Betty, what do you think?" said Col. Zane, stopping before the girls.

"What do I think?" retorted Betty. "Why, I think you are very rude to interrupt me. I am reading to Myeerah her first novel."

"I have a very important message for you."

"For me? What! From whom?"

"Guess."

Betty ran through a list of most of her acquaintances, but after each name her brother shook his head.

"Oh, well, I don't care," she finally said. The color in her cheeks had heightened noticeably.

"Very well. If you do not care, I will say nothing more," said Col. Zane.

At this juncture Annie called them to supper. Later, when Col. Zane sat on the doorstep smoking, Betty came and sat beside him with her head resting against his shoulder. The Colonel smoked on in silence. Presently the dusky head moved restlessly.

"Eb, tell me the message," whispered Betty.

"Message? What message?" asked Col. Zane. "What are you talking about?"

"Do not tease—not now. Tell me." There was an undercurrent of wistfulness in Betty's voice which touched the kindhearted brother.

"Well, today a certain young man asked me if he could relieve me of the responsibility of looking after a certain young lady."

"Oh——"

"Wait a moment. I told him I would be delighted."

"Eb, that was unkind."

"Then he asked me to tell her he was coming over tomorrow morning to fix it up with her."

"Oh, horrible!" cried Betty. "Were those the words he used?"

"Betts, to tell the honest truth, he did not say much of anything. He just said: 'I love her,' and his eyes blazed."

Betty uttered a half articulate cry and ran to her room. Her heart was throbbing. What could she do? She felt that if she looked once into her lover's eyes she would have no strength. How dared she allow herself to be so weak! Yet she knew this was the end. She could deceive him no longer. For she felt a stir in her heart, stronger than all, beyond all resistance, an exquisite agony, the sweet, blind, tumultuous exultation of the woman who loves and is loved.

* * * * * * * *

"Bess, what do you think?" said Col. Zane, going into the kitchen next morning, after he had returned from the pasture. "Clarke just came over and asked for Betty. I called her. She came down looking as sweet and cool as one of the lilies out by the spring. She said: 'Why, Mr. Clarke, you are almost a stranger. I am pleased to see you. Indeed, we are all very glad to know you have recovered from your severe burns.' She went on talking like that for all the world like a girl who didn't care a snap for him. And she knows as well as I do. Not only that, she has been actually breaking her heart over him all these months. How did she do it? Oh, you women beat me all hollow!"

"Would you expect Betty to fall into his arms?" asked the Colonel's worthy spouse, indignantly.

"Not exactly. But she was too cool, too friendly. Poor Alfred looked as if he hadn't slept. He was nervous and scared to death. When Betty ran up stairs I put a bug in Alfred's ear. He'll be all right now, if he follows my advice."

"Humph! What did Colonel Ebenezer Zane tell him?" asked Bessie, in disgust.

"Oh, not much. I simply told him not to lose his nerve; that a woman never meant 'no'; that she often says it only to be made say 'yes.' And I ended up with telling him if she got a little skittish, as thoroughbreds do sometimes, to try a strong arm. That was my way."

"Col. Zane, if my memory does not fail me, you were as humble and beseeching as the proudest girl could desire."

"I beseeching? Never!"

"I hope Alfred's wooing may go well. I like him very much. But I'm afraid. Betty has such a spirit that it is quite likely she will refuse him for no other reason than that he built his cabin before he asked her."

"Nonsense. He asked her long ago. Never fear, Bess, my sister will come back as meek as a lamb."

Meanwhile Betty and Alfred were strolling down the familiar path toward the river. The October air was fresh with a suspicion of frost. The clear notes of a hunter's horn came floating down from the hills. A flock of wild geese had alighted on the marshy ground at the end of the island where they kept up a continual honk! honk! The brown hills, the red forest, and the yellow fields were now at the height of their autumnal beauty. Soon the November north wind would thrash the trees bare, and bow the proud heads of the daisies and the goldenrod; but just now they flashed in sun, and swayed back and forth in all their glory.

"I see you limp. Are you not entirely well?" Betty was saying.

"Oh, I am getting along famously, thank you," said Alfred. "This one foot was quite severely burned and is still tender."

"You have had your share of injuries. I heard my brother say you had been wounded three times within a year."

"Four times."

"Jonathan told of the axe wound; then the wound Miller gave you, and finally the burns. These make three, do they not?"

"Yes, but you see, all three could not be compared to the one you forgot to mention."

"Let us hurry past here," said Betty, hastening to change the subject. "This is where you had the dreadful fight with Miller."

"As Miller did go to meet Girty, and as he did not return to the Fort with the renegade, we must believe he is dead. Of course, we do not know this to be actually a fact. But something makes me think so. Jonathan and Wetzel have not said anything; I can't get any satisfaction on that score from either; but I am sure neither of them would rest until Miller was dead."

"I think you are right. But we may never know. All I can tell you is that Wetzel and Jack trailed Miller to the river, and then they both came back. I was the last to see Lewis that night before he left on Miller's trail. It isn't likely I shall forget what Lewis said and how he looked. Miller was a wicked man; yes, a traitor."

"He was a bad man, and he nearly succeeded in every one of his plans. I have not the slightest doubt that had he refrained from taking part in the shooting match he would have succeeded in abducting you, in killing me, and in leading Girty here long before he was expected."

"There are many things that may never be explained, but one thing Miller did always mystifies us. How did he succeed in binding Tige?"

"To my way of thinking that was not so difficult as climbing into my room and almost killing me, or stealing the powder from Capt. Boggs' room."

"The last, at least, gave me a chance to help," said Betty, with a touch of her old roguishness.

"That was the grandest thing a woman ever did," said Alfred, in a low tone.

"Oh, no, I only ran fast."

"I would have given the world to have seen you, but I was lying on the bench wishing I were dead. I did not have strength to look out of a porthole. Oh! that horrible time! I can never forget it. I lie awake at night and hear the yelling and shooting. Then I dream of running over the burning roofs and it all comes back so vividly I can almost feel the flames and smell the burnt wood. Then I wake up and think of that awful moment when you were carried into the block-house white, and, as I thought, dead."

"But I wasn't. And I think it best for us to forget that horrible siege. It is past. It is a miracle that any one was spared. Ebenezer says we should not grieve for those who are gone; they were heroic; they saved the Fort. He says, too, that we shall never again be troubled by Indians. Therefore let us forget and be happy. I have forgotten Miller. You can afford to do the same."

"Yes, I forgive him." Then, after a long silence, Alfred continued, "Will you go down to the old sycamore?"

Down the winding path they went. Coming to a steep place in the rocky bank Alfred jumped down and then turned to help Betty. But she avoided his gaze, pretended to not see his outstretched hands, and leaped lightly down beside him. He looked at her with perplexity and anxiety in his eyes. Before he could speak she ran on ahead of him and climbed down the bank to the pool. He followed slowly, thoughtfully. The supreme moment had come. He knew it, and somehow he did not feel the confidence the Colonel had inspired in him. It had been easy for him to think of subduing this imperious young lady; but when the time came to assert his will he found he could not remember what he had intended to say, and his feelings were divided between his love for her and the horrible fear that he should lose her.

When he reached the sycamore tree he found her sitting behind it with a cluster of yellow daisies in her lap. Alfred gazed at her, conscious that all his hopes of happiness were dependent on the next few words that would issue from her smiling lips. The little brown hands, which were now rather nervously arranging the flowers, held more than his life.

"Are they not sweet?" asked Betty, giving him a fleeting glance. "We call them black-eyed Susans." Could anything be lovelier than that soft, dark brown?"

"Yes," answered Alfred, looking into her eyes.

"But—you are not looking at my daisies at all," said Betty, lowering her eyes.

"No, I am not," said Alfred. Then suddenly: "A year ago this very day we were here."

"Here? Oh, yes, I believe I do remember. It was the day we came in my canoe and had such fine fishing."

"Is that all you remember?"

"I can recollect nothing in particular. It was so long ago."

"I suppose you will say you had no idea why I wanted you to come to this spot in particular."

"I supposed you simply wanted to take a walk, and it is very pleasant here."

"Then Col. Zane did not tell you?" demanded Alfred. Receiving no reply he went on.

"Did you read my letter?"

"What letter?"

"The letter old Sam should have given you last fall. Did you read it?"

"Yes," answered Betty, faintly.

"Did your brother tell you I wanted to see you this morning?"

"Yes, he told me, and it made me very angry," said Betty, raising her head. There was a bright red spot in each cheek. "You—you seemed to think you—that I—well—I did not like it."

"I think I understand; but you are entirely wrong. I have never thought you cared for me. My wildest dreams never left me any confidence. Col. Zane and Wetzel both had some deluded notion that you cared——"

"But they had no right to say that or to think it," said Betty, passionately. She sprang to her feet, scattering the daisies over the grass. "For them to presume that I cared for you is absurd. I never gave them any reason to think so, for—for I—I don't."

"Very well, then, there is nothing more to be said," answered Alfred, in a voice that was calm and slightly cold. "I am sorry if you have been annoyed. I have been mad, of course, but I promise you that you need fear no further annoyance from me. Come, I think we should return to the house."

And he turned and walked slowly up the path. He had taken perhaps a dozen steps when she called him.

"Mr. Clarke, come back."

Alfred retraced his steps and stood before her again. Then he saw a different Betty. The haughty poise had disappeared. Her head was bowed. Her little hands were tightly pressed over a throbbing bosom.

"Well," said Alfred, after a moment.

"Why—why are you in such a hurry to go?"

"I have learned what I wanted to know. And after that I do not imagine I would be very agreeable. I am going back. Are you coming?"

"I did not mean quite—quite what I said," whispered Betty.

"Then what did you mean?" asked Alfred, in a stern voice.

"I don't know. Please don't speak so."

"Betty, forgive my harshness. Can you expect a man to feel as I do and remain calm? You know I love you. You must not trifle any longer. You must not fight any longer."

"But I can't help fighting."

"Look at me," said Alfred, taking her hands. "Let me see your eyes. I believe you care a little for me, or else you wouldn't have called me back. I love you. Can you understand that?"

"Yes, I can; and I think you should love me a great deal to make up for what you made me suffer."

"Betty, look at me."

Slowly she raised her head and lifted the downcast eyes. Those telltale traitors no longer hid her secret. With a glad cry Alfred caught her in his arms. She tried to hide her face, but he got his hand under her chin and held it firmly so that the sweet crimson lips were very near his own. Then he slowly bent his head.

Betty saw his intention, closed her eyes and whispered:

"Alfred, please don't—it's not fair—I beg of you—Oh!"

That kiss was Betty's undoing. She uttered a strange little cry. Then her dark head found a hiding place over his heart, and her slender form, which a moment before had resisted so fiercely, sank yielding into his embrace.

"Betty, do you dare tell me now that you do not care

for me?" Alfred whispered into the dusky hair which rippled over his breast.

Betty was brave even in her surrender. Her hands moved slowly upward along his arms, slipped over his shoulders, and clasped round his neck. Then she lifted a flushed and tear-stained face with tremulous lips and wonderful shining syes.

"Alfres, I do love you—with my whole heart I love you. I never knew until now."

The hours flew apace. The prolonged ringing of the dinner bell brought the lovers back to earth, and to the realization that the world held others than themselves. Slowly they climbed the familiar path, but this time as never before. They walked hand in hand. From the bluff they looked back. They wanted to make sure they were not dreaming. The water rushed over the fall more musically than ever before; the white patches of foam floated round and round the shady pool; the leaves of the sycamore rustled cheerily in the breeze. On a dead branch a woodpecker hammered industriously.

"Before we get out of sight of that dear old tree I want to make a confession," said Betty, as she stood before Alfred. She was pulling at the fringe on his hunting-coat.

"You need not make confessions to me."

"But this was dreadful; it preys on my conscience."

"Very well, I will be your judge. Your punishment shall be slight."

"One day when you were lying unconscious from your wound, Bessie sent me to watch you. I nursed you for hours, and—and—do not think badly of me—I—I kissed you."

"My darling," cried the enraptured young man.

When they at last reached the house they found Col. Zane on the doorstep.

"Where on earth have you been?" he said. "Wetzel

was here. He said he would not wait to see you. There he goes up the hill. He is behind that laurel."

They looked and presently saw the tall figure of the hunter emerge from the bushes. He stopped and leaned on his rifle. For a minute he remained motionless. Then he waved his hand and plunged into the thicket. Betty sighed and Alfred said:

"Poor Wetzel! ever restless, ever roaming."

"Hello, there!" exclaimed a gay voice. The lovers turned to see the smiling face of Isaac, and over his shoulder Myeerah's happy face beaming on them. "Alfred, you are a lucky dog. You can thank Myeerah and me for this; because if I had not taken to the river and nearly drowned myself to give you that opportunity you would not wear that happy face today. Blush away, Betts, it becomes you mightily."

"Bessie, here they are!" cried Col. Zane, in his hearty voice. "She is tamed at last. No excuses, Alfred, in to dinner you go."

Col. Zane pushed the young people up the steps before him, and stopping on the threshold while he knocked the ashes from his pipe, he smiled contentedly.

Afterword

BETTY LIVED all her life on the scene of her famous exploit. She became a happy wife and mother. When she grew to be an old lady, with her grandchildren about her knee, she delighted to tell them that when a girl she had run the gauntlet of the Indians.

Col. Zane became the friend of all redmen. He maintained a trading-post for many years, and his dealings were ever kind and honorable. After the country got settled he received from time to time various marks of distinction from the State, Colonial, and National governments. His most noted achievement was completed about 1796. President Washington, desiring to open a National road from Fort Henry to Maysville, Kentucky, paid a great tribute to Col. Zane's ability by employing him to undertake the arduous task. His brother Jonathan and the Indian guide, Tomepome-hala, rendered valuable aid in blazing out the path through the wilderness. This road, famous for many years as Zane's Trace, opened the beautiful Ohio valley to the ambitious pioneer. For this service Congress granted Col. Zane the privilege of locating military warrants upon three sections of land, each a square mile in extent, which property the government eventually presented to him. Col. Zane was the founder of Wheeling, Zanesville, Martin's Ferry, and Bridgeport. He died in 1811.

Isaac Zane received from the government a patent of

ten thousand acres of land on Mad river. He established his home in the center of this tract, where he lived with the Wyandots until his death. A white settlement sprang up, prospered, and grew, and today it is the thriving city of Zanesfield.

Jonathan Zane settled down after peace was declared with the Indians, found himself a wife, and eventually became an influential citizen. However, he never lost his love for the wild woods. At times he would take down the old rifle and disappear for two or three days. He always returned cheerful and happy from these lonely hunts.

Wetzel alone did not take kindly to the march of civilization; but then he was a hunter, not a pioneer. He kept his word of peace with his old enemies, the Hurons, though he never abandoned his wandering and vengeful quests after the Delawares.

As the years passed Wetzel grew more silent and taciturn. From time to time he visited Ft. Henry, and on these visits he spent hours playing with Betty's children. But he was restless in the settlement, and his sojourns grew briefer and more infrequent as time rolled on. True to his conviction that no wife existed on earth for him, he never married. His home was the trackless wilds, where he was true to his calling—a foe to the redman.

Wonderful to relate his long, black hair never adorned the walls of an Indian's lodge, where a warrior might point with grim pride and say: "No more does the Deathwind blow over the hills and vales." We could tell of how his keen eye once again saw Wingenund over the sights of his fatal rifle, and how he was once again a prisoner in the camp of that lifelong foe, but that's another story, which, perhaps, we may tell some day.

Today the beautiful city of Wheeling rises on the banks of the Ohio, where the yells of the Indians once blanched the cheeks of pioneers. The broad, winding river rolls on as of yore; it alone remains unchanged. What were Indians and pioneers, forts and cities to it? Eons of time before human beings lived it flowed slowly toward the sea, and ages after men and their works are dust, it will roll on placidly with its eternal scheme of nature.

Upon the island still stand noble beeches, oaks, and chestnuts—trees that long ago have covered up their bullet-scars, but they could tell, had they the power to speak, many a wild thrilling tale. Beautiful parks and stately mansions grace the island; and polished equipages roll over the ground that once knew naught save the soft tread of the deer and the moccasin.

McColloch's Rock still juts boldly out over the river as steep and rugged as when the brave Major leaped to everlasting fame. Wetzel's Cave, so named to this day, remains on the side of the bluff overlooking the creek. The grapevines and wild rose-bushes still cluster round the cavern-entrance, where, long ago, the wily savage was wont to lie in wait for the settler, lured there by the false turkey-call. The boys visit the cave on Saturday afternoons and play "Injuns."

Not long since the writer spent a quiet afternoon there, listening to the musical flow of the brook, and dreaming of those who had lived and loved, fought and died by that stream one hundred and twenty years ago. The city with its long blocks of buildings, its spires and bridges, faded away, leaving the scene as it was in the days of Fort Henry—unobscured by smoke, the river undotted by puffing boats, and everywhere the green and verdant forest.

Nothing was wanting in that dream picture: Betty tearing along on her pony; the pioneer plowing in the field; the stealthy approach of the savage; Wetzel and Jonathan watching the river; the deer browsing with the cows in the pasture, and the old fort, grim and menacing on the bluff—all were there as natural as in those times which tried men's souls.

And as the writer awoke to the realities of life, that his dreams were of long ago, he was saddened by the thought that the labor of the pioneer is ended; his faithful, heroic wife's work is done. That beautiful country, which their sacrifices made ours, will ever be a monument to them.

Sad, too, is the thought that the poor Indian is unmourned. He is almost forgotten; he is in the shadow; his songs are sung; no more will he sing to his dusky bride; his deeds are done; no more will he boast of his all-conquering arm or of his speed like the Northwind; no more will his heart bound at the whistle of the stag, for he sleeps in the shade of the oaks, under the moss and the ferns.

THE END

ADVENTURE

5325. FIRST ON THE MOON   **75¢**
Hugh Walters. The U.S. rocket Columbus and the Russian rocket Lenin are hurtling toward the moon, each carrying a human passenger intent on making the first landing on its surface.

4871. Rod Serling's TWILIGHT ZONE REVISITED   **60¢**
Edited by Walter Gibson. By the Emmy Award-winning TV writer, a collection of chilling stories.
Readers will share the terror of a young army officer cursed with the ability to see the glow of death on the faces of men about to die; they will fight under Custer in the battle of the Little Big Horn and marvel at those who miraculously survived—or did they?

5354. MINDS UNLEASHED   **95¢**
Edited by Groff Conklin. The power and the possibilities of the human mind—as uncharted as deep space—are explored in this collection of science fiction stories by masters of imagination, Isaac Asimov, Robert Heinlein, Arthur C. Clarke, Murray Leinster, Poul Anderson and others expand the limits of the mind and suggest some of the dramatic potentialities of the future.

5356. PLANETS FOR SALE   **75¢**
A. E. Van Vogt and E. Mayne Hull. In this future world, space travel is a commonplace and business tycoons scramble for advantage on far-flung planets. The action is in the Ridge Stars, a pioneer galaxy as yet uncontrolled by anyone, and the attempts of billionaire Arthur Blord to seize control

5313. GREAT STORIES OF SPACE TRAVEL   **60¢**
Groff Conklin. Who knows what strange things will confront those brave Earthlings in the years to come who dare to invade the far reaches of outer space . . . and beyond?
In these stories, a group of science fiction's greatest writers (Isaac Asimov, Ray Bradbury, A. E. Van Vogt, and others) speculate on the nature those dangers.

5306. ATTACK FROM ATLANTIS   **75¢**
Lester del Rey. Here is a suspense-filled tale of underwater adventure written by one of America's most honored science fiction writers. In this intriguing tale, Lester del Rey writes of an outcast race that has migrated into the sea and of a young boy who tries to escape from "the city of no return."

5344. VOYAGERS IN TIME   **95¢**
Edited by Robert Silverberg. A collection of twelve science fiction stories about time travel by such authors as H. G. Wells, Lester del Rey, Poul Anderson and others. Exciting, challenging accounts of voyages back and forward in time—their complexities and hazardous consequences.

4709. MYSTERY OF SATELLITE 7   **50¢**
Charles Coombs. When Argus 7 mysteriously explodes at an altitude of 42 miles, talk of sabotage runs loud. And suddenly three young people are catapulted from their role of privileged observers to land square in the center of the satellite mystery.

5359. THE WEAPON MAKERS   **75¢**
A. E. Van Vogt. One of the all-time great science fiction novels by one of the great masters. A psychological suspense novel about a man whose secret is that he is immortal and whose goal is to save the world when the weapon makers forget that they are sworn to preserve peace and attempt to take over the entire universe.

CLASSICS

4867.   THE JUNGLE BOOK   50¢
Rudyard Kipling. Saved from the snatching jaws of Shere Khan, Mowgli is raised by Mother Wolf as one of her own cubs. The full original text.

5322.   PENROD   75¢
Booth Tarkington. This is the only inexpensive edition of the classic which has delighted and inspired mischief-lovers for years. The story of Penrod Schofield is the story of all high-spirited American boys. Stirring up fun for himself and his friends, and trouble for his enemies and elders, Penrod does all the things that boys have always done, but somehow they turn out funnier.

4755.   DADDY-LONG-LEGS   60¢
Jean Webster. A girl grows to young womanhood in an orphanage, and is sent to college by an unknown benefactor. This gay, tender, whimsical record of Judy's correspondence with her mysterious guardian has enchanted readers of all ages since it was first published. It has been translated into eighteen languages, and filmed twice, most recently with Leslie Caron and Fred Astaire playing the leading roles.

5341.   DEAR ENEMY   75¢
Joan Webster. This sequel to *Daddy-Long-Legs* follows in the same engaging tradition of delighted romance. It's all here, the timeless appeal, humor and youthful wisdom that endeared Jean Webster's first youngster to millions of readers and to her now famous Daddy-Long-Legs.

4761.   A LANTERN IN HER HAND   60¢
Bess Streeter Aldrich. Abbie Deal, brought up in a log cabin in Iowa, took the covered wagon trail to Nebraska as a young bride. In a rude shelter on the prairie she raised her family and stood beside her husband through all the heartbreaking struggles of the pioneer days—and became part of an epic.

5304.   ANNE OF GREEN GABLES   75¢
Lucy M. Montgomery. The only unabridged reprint available. Redheaded, dreamy Anne, the orphan who brings happiness and love into the lives of her foster parents, is one of the most beloved heroines in all literature. Millions of girls throughout the world have taken her to their hearts.

4795.   PETER PAN   60¢
James M. Barrie. The only inexpensive paperback version of this delightful fantasy—the classic story of Peter and Wendy and the amazing adventures that befall them in Never-Never-Land.

4763.   REBECCA OF SUNNYBROOK FARM   75¢
Kate Douglas Wiggin. Living with her maiden aunts would doubtless be "the making of Rebecca" everybody thought, so the little girl with the enormous eyes and most remarkable talent for mischief was shipped to a house where children were supposed to be seen and not heard. Yet nothing could dampen Rebecca's lively spirits, and nobody could resist her winsome charm.

4841.   WIND IN THE WILLOWS   60¢
Kenneth Grahame. If a poll were taken of the book best loved by boys and girls over the generations, the winner hands down, would most likely be this one. This enchanting book, packed with the adventures of Mole, Rat, Toad and their friends, is the kind of story that keeps children spellbound. Illustrated.